SHADOW WARRIOR

CHRISTINE FEEHAN

piatkus

PIATKUS

First published in the US in 2019 by Jove
An imprint of Penguin Random House LLC
First published in Great Britain in 2019 by Piatkus

1 3 5 7 9 10 8 6 4 2

A CIP catalogue record for this book is available from the British Library.

ISBN: 978-0-349-42319-7

Printed and bound in Great Britain by Clays Ltd, Elcograf S.p.A.

Papers used by Piatkus are from well-managed forests
and other responsible sources.

Piatkus
An imprint of
Little, Brown Book Group
Carmelite House
50 Victoria Embankment
London EC4Y 0DZ

An Hachette UK Company
www.hachette.co.uk

www.littlebrown.co.uk

New York Times bestselling author **Christine Feehan** has had over thirty novels published and has thrilled legions of fans with her seductive Dark Carpathian tales. She has received numerous honours throughout her career, including being a nominee for the Romance Writers of America RITA and receiving a Career Achievement Award from *Romantic Times*, and has been published in multiple languages.

Visit Christine Feehan online:

www.christinefeehan.com
www.facebook.com/christinefeehanauthor
@AuthorCFeehan

Praise for Christine Feehan:

'The erotic, gripping series that has defined an entire genre . . . I love everything [Christine Feehan] does'
J. R. Ward

'The queen of paranormal romance'
USA Today

'Gritty, brutal and wonderfully magical . . .
Unexpected and mesmerizing perfection'
Library Journal

'Once again, Christine Feehan brings a sizzling story of seduction and sorcery to her readers' Examiner.com

'Book after book, Feehan gives readers emotionally rich and powerful stories that are hard to forget!'
RT Book Reviews

'The amaz***ingly****mes***tale***ity***create ca***ptivating
and ***ad***

*For Katie, my beautiful niece who handles
her complicated life with grace.*

FOR MY READERS

Be sure to go to christinefeehan.com/members/ to sign up for my PRIVATE book announcement list and download the FREE ebook of *Dark Desserts*. Join my community and get firsthand news, enter the book discussions, ask your questions and chat with me. Please feel free to email me at Christine @christinefeehan.com. I would love to hear from you.

ACKNOWLEDGMENTS

As with any book, there are so many people to thank, and this one is no exception. Brian, thank you for challenging me to write faster and better. Domini, as always, your editing was invaluable. Sheila, thank you for the notes you put together for me in one place when I thought I might lose my mind because they were scattered everywhere after the computer crash! Katie, thank you for all the advice on handling major events. I had no idea how difficult that business truly is. Cheryl and Denise, what would I do without you?

CHAPTER ONE

Vittorio Ferraro stood in the shadows, his skin crawling with the need to move. Something was wrong. Not just wrong. Whatever his churning gut was about, he'd never quite felt the urgency of finding the source of the trouble as he did right then.

He'd come home from work exhausted. Work had been in Los Angeles this time. He'd been there numerous times, but this particular one had been a bloodbath. He was a shadow rider, one of the very few in existence worldwide. With that came tremendous responsibilities and absolute secrecy. He'd begun his training at the age of two and continued every day of his life since. Now, after carrying out justice in Los Angeles, he'd been more than happy to get home. His house was his sanctuary, and usually, once inside, he felt peace, not this terrible sense of impending doom.

He hadn't been able to shake the feeling, so he got dressed and followed the dark dread that strengthened as he approached the nightclub his family owned. The Ferraro

Club was in full swing, the music loud, the laughter and conversation blending with the energy of the music.

The nightclub was the most popular in Chicago and people stood in lines, sometimes for hours, on the chance of getting in. Celebrities frequented the Ferraro Club, and there was always the possibility that one might catch a glimpse of a member of the famous Ferraro family. Tonight, the place was packed.

As a rule, his family didn't make it a habit to interfere in the running of the club—they had managers who ran the place far better than any of them ever could—but they dropped in when they needed to be visible. The paparazzi always swarmed around them, giving them better alibis for their work than anything else ever could. Right now, visibility was the last thing Vittorio wanted. The sense of urgency was growing stronger, not weaker, and that meant he needed to find whatever was wrong and fix it before it was too late. That something was here. In his club. Close now.

He moved from shadow to shadow without being seen. It was a slow process and his body was already torn up from doing this very thing in Los Angeles. Still, this wasn't about work. This wasn't about bringing justice to criminals no one else could get to. This was about the knots in his gut that coiled tighter and tighter, and felt personal. Very personal. And that in itself was shocking.

Vittorio was the largest of the Ferraro men. He was tall, broad-shouldered and very fit, as all riders had to be. He was also a man who knew himself very well. Every strength. Every flaw. What he wanted in life, what he needed—both were impossible, and he'd accepted that he would never have a wife and family the way his brothers Stefano, Ricco and Giovanni had. Even Taviano had a much better chance than he would ever have. It was just this growing feeling that this portent of trouble was connected to him personally.

He was a man apart—even within his family, he stood apart. Maybe they all did. It was possible their women strengthened the connection between them in some way.

Certainly, Francesca, Stefano's wife, did. Vittorio loved her—they all did—but at the same time, it only emphasized his loneliness.

He knew it would already be nearly impossible to find a woman he could love the way he needed to love her. Finding a woman who could ride shadows was in and of itself extremely difficult, but finding one who would suit his peculiarities, that was asking far too much. He knew the odds, and they weren't in his favor.

Shadow riders were obligated to have children, so if they weren't married to a suitable woman by a certain age—one he was approaching—an arranged marriage would follow. For a man like Vittorio, that would be an utter disaster.

For a moment he stood in the shadows watching the women dancing, knowing not a single one of them would ever tolerate him as a life partner. He had to find a woman who would have the genetics to produce children capable of riding the shadows and carrying on their work. That was his obligation. He could never simply fall in love; he had to fall in love with the right person. The odds of finding that were so slim, most riders never believed it could happen.

For Vittorio, the odds were even slimmer. He didn't want a traditional partnership. He didn't have that kind of personality. He needed his woman to trust him implicitly and allow him to care for her. For every aspect of her life. Where, in the modern world, could a woman like that be found? That would be impossible as well. Two impossibilities meant it wasn't going to happen for him. He would be in a loveless, arranged marriage for the rest of his life.

He sighed and turned his attention back to that whisper of impending danger that had drawn him to the club. The floor plan had three tiers. The top tier was extremely expensive but provided the most privacy. Most of the celebrities stayed there to party. Bodyguards were prevalent, and the club's highly trained security were visible as well. The third tier wasn't a place Vittorio would expect to have any real trouble, but his every instinct pointed him in that direction.

He waited for the music to change and the light show to begin. The dancing colors cast all kinds of shadows throughout the large club, giving him plenty of choices. He selected a shadow that cut through the bar on the second-tier landing and zigzagged its way up to the highest tier where the Ferraros kept a table reserved just for family.

He stepped into a thin, dark streak and instantly his body was sucked into the tube, pulled apart and flung through tables and chairs and up two winding staircases to the top tier. Standing in the mouth of the tube, he needed a few seconds for his body to feel as if it had come back together. There was always the sick feeling that came with fast travel, with being pulled apart and put back together.

The moment Vittorio was up on the top floor, the sense of conspiracy, of danger, became overwhelming. He closed himself off from the noise and concentrated on that feeling of trouble. Of a fated doom. At the third table from the Ferraros' exclusive seating sat three men. He recognized two as enforcers for the Saldi family. Just seeing them in his club caused the knots in his gut to tighten.

No one could keep drugs out of a club, but they didn't allow sales there. The Saldis, a notorious crime family, brought drugs in and sold them from streets and alleys to the private parties of the rich. Every kind of drug anyone could possibly want, they provided. But not in a Ferraro club. It was one of the few things the Saldis knew the Ferraros would go to war with them over.

The Saldis were recognized as a branch of the largest crime family in the States. Giuseppi Saldi was the acknowledged leader and was certainly the biggest crime boss in Chicago. These particular men worked for his brother, Miceli Saldi. The big question was, why were two of Saldi's goons sitting in the Ferraro nightclub making a deal with some lowlife junkie? Clearly they were conducting business of sorts. The Saldi enforcers blended in, with their expensive suits and Rolex watches, but the man sitting across from them was, by comparison, in disheveled clothes that had seen better days.

Vittorio was going to have to review the security tapes. There were certain protocols in place. Every doorman, every bouncer and every security guard was required to be familiar with the Saldis and their employees. If they entered the nightclub, the Ferraro family was to be informed immediately. That hadn't happened.

The fact that the two Saldi enforcers sat in the VIP section on the third tier and no one had called a family member to let them know added an additional sin against the club's security measures—or the Saldis had paid off someone high enough up in the nightclub's management that they were able to sneak through. If that were the case, who else had they allowed in?

Vittorio needed to move around and listen to the conversations. The sale of drugs was always going to be a problem in clubs the world over, but the Saldis blatantly selling in the Ferraro nightclub was going to start a war no one wanted, and it didn't make sense.

Vittorio stayed in the shadows and moved as close as possible in order to hear the conversation over the pounding beat of the music. He recognized Ale Sarto and Lando Gori, Miceli Saldi's top enforcers. If either or both showed up at your door, chances were you weren't going to survive the encounter. They were dressed in suits and looked sharp and handsome, but Vittorio had seen their work. There was nothing remotely civilized or benevolent about what they did to human beings. They wouldn't be sent on some small errand. Not ever.

"She's worth every cent of the money," the stranger in disheveled clothes assured. He twitched a couple of times but kept direct eye contact.

Anyone sitting with Sarto and Gori should have been intimidated, especially a two-bit pimp who seemed to be talking about his prostitute.

Ale Sarto hitched forward. "You're pushing your luck, Haydon. Her service is for your past debts, not any new ones you incur."

Vittorio suppressed a groan of annoyance. The Saldis had stooped to an all-time low, negotiating for prostitutes in the Ferraro Club. He didn't turn away, his gut still screaming at him. Nothing really made sense about the small exchange he'd overheard. Top-level enforcers like Sarto and Gori didn't get involved in such mundane matters as acquiring another prostitute for the Saldi stables.

"I can get her to see reason and go along with you without any trouble," Haydon responded. "She'll do whatever I tell her." He poured confidence into his voice. "That's got to be worth another two hundred and fifty thousand."

Lando Gori drew back and pinned Haydon with cold, dead eyes. "You're really pushing your luck. We're taking her tonight, and this new crap you're trying to pull is going to get you killed. Take the deal wiping out your past debt for the woman's services and walk away. We don't need you. We can pick her up anytime and just cut you out of the transaction altogether."

Haydon sat back immediately and threw his hands into the air as if in surrender. "Fine. Fine. But at least talk to him about the possibility of giving me a two-hundred-and-fifty-thousand-dollar credit. I brought the deal to him."

Lando stood up, ending the conversation. "You didn't bring the deal to him, Haydon. He gave you no choice. The woman, or we break every bone in your body. Personally, I think it should be both, but he's a compassionate man."

"Where is she?" Ale Sarto demanded, standing as well.

Haydon flashed a grin, revealing dark, stained teeth. "She wasn't as cooperative as I would have liked, and I didn't think she'd sit through negotiations, so I stashed her somewhere safe."

"You're a lying asshole, Haydon. You just told us she'd do anything for you. Now she's not being cooperative. Which is it?" Lando snapped.

Vittorio stiffened. That didn't sound like the woman was privy to what these men had said. Worse, it didn't sound as if she was in any way cooperating.

"You'd better not be playing games, Haydon," Ale warned. "Let's go. I want to see her right now."

Haydon's cocky smile faded as he got to his feet as well. "You don't understand. Grace would do just about anything for me, but she can get stubborn. Sometimes she needs a little persuasion."

Lando Gori reached out and jerked Haydon close. "Stop stalling and get walking. We can be very persuasive if the situation calls for it."

Vittorio rode the shadows down the winding stairs to the main dance floor, keeping the three men in sight at all times. They were clearly headed for the nearest exit. He wove his way through the shadows, choosing to leave through a private door that spilled him into the darkest corner of the parking lot. The reserved family parking was just in front of him, empty of course, because he'd ridden the shadows there, not wanting anyone to know he was around.

The three men he followed were halfway across the parking lot to his left. They stopped beside an old, beat-up Honda. Haydon reached down and unlatched the trunk.

Vittorio's breath hissed out between his teeth. He wasn't a man to get angry. It wasn't in his nature. Ordinarily, he was the peacemaker, the solution-finder. He watched as Haydon jumped back. A small ball of whirling fury exploded out of the truck, hitting the man directly in the chest.

The overhead light was out, something not tolerated in any of the Ferraro parking garages or lots, so the figures were no more than darker silhouettes as he neared them.

"What is wrong with you, Haydon? Get your hands off me."

The woman shoved at the man, but he caught both her wrists and yanked hard. "Stop, Grace. Just listen for a minute. I'm in trouble."

"You're *always* in trouble. *Always*, Haydon. I told you

the last time if you kept gambling you were on your own. I can't take out any more loans. I can't work any more hours. You messed up, you're going to have to fix it yourself."

Vittorio's breath left his lungs in a long rush of shock. Something tight in his chest loosened. Someplace vulnerable. Someplace guarded and protected. He pressed his hand tightly over the spot, feeling as if that voice had been a key, fitting perfectly into the lock and turning it before he had a chance to react—and he had lightning-fast reflexes.

"I'm done with you. With your gambling and debts. I'm out of it, Haydon. I mean it. You've had more chances than anyone in life should expect to have." Grace threw her hands into the air and turned away from him.

She was small. Vittorio would have been surprised if she was much more than five feet or five one. She had a figure, full breasts and a very nice ass on her. He appreciated that. He could see why these men would be interested in her. Her skin was very pale, and her hair was a true red. She had it pulled back in a long ponytail. There was something about that thick length of hair that got to him. The woman, as small as she was, standing valiantly in the face of the threat the Saldi enforcers presented, sent heat rushing through his veins.

Lando blocked her exit, stepping directly in front of her, a solid mass of muscle. "You're going to have to come with us. The car is right over there." He pointed to a town car with tinted windows.

She shook her head. "I'm not going anywhere with you. I have nothing to do with his debts. Nothing at all."

"You're his sister. Family pays debts."

"I'm *not* his sister," Grace denied, sending a furious look at Haydon. "We were raised in the same foster home. That's our connection. Whatever he's into, he's in it alone."

"Really?" Ale whipped out a gun, pressing it against Haydon's temple. "You want me to kill him right now? That's the second option."

"Gracie." Haydon squeaked her name.

Vittorio could see Haydon wasn't worried in the least. He didn't believe Ale would kill him. Vittorio knew better.

Grace froze when she saw the gun, turning slowly toward Ale. "What are you doing? Are you crazy?" She whispered it. "Put that away."

Lando grinned at Ale. "I think she's beginning to get the picture. Your friend Haydon made a deal. You pay his debts for him. You're going to come work for us. A close friend of our boss wants you as his companion for a few weeks. Maybe longer. You make him happy and the debt goes away. It's that simple."

Grace's gaze flicked to Haydon. "You *sold* me into prostitution? For your debts?"

Lando's fingers settled around Grace's arm. "Get in the car."

"I'm not a prostitute." She stubbornly refused to walk.

"I don't give a damn what you are. The boss says bring you to him, you go to him," Lando said. His fingers tightened like a vise and he yanked her toward the car.

Vittorio rode the shadow that would bring him straight to Ale Sarto. He wrenched the gun from Sarto's hand and flung it away from them, so that it skittered across the parking lot, coming to rest under a BMW some distance away. He slammed his elbow into Ale's jaw, breaking it, and swept his legs out from under him, stomping on his ribs to keep him down.

He leapt for the shadow, let it sweep him straight to Lando, and was on him so fast, Lando hadn't had time to react to seeing his partner put on the ground. Vittorio wrenched Grace from Lando's grip and thrust her behind him, out of harm's way, as he attacked. Vittorio, always the one to seek solutions verbally, had no middle gear. Either he was talking logically, or he was acting, and when he went into action, he made every blow count.

He wasn't trying to kill Lando Gori, but he wanted him down and out. Every punch, every kick, every single blow was a punishment. Vittorio was strong, and he trained every single day, as did the other riders. They trained against one another, and that meant speed and strength as well as technique. They all studied anatomy so they knew exactly where to strike to do the most damage. He broke bones when he hit or kicked, and Lando was on the ground, trying to reach inside his jacket for his weapon within seconds.

Grace tried to call out a warning, but Vittorio was already on it, kicking the gun from his hand.

"You'd better stop while you can, Lando," Vittorio cautioned, using his soothing voice. He could calm with that voice and he did so now. "You know the Ferraro Club is off-limits. You were out of line, and you don't put your hands on a woman on our property ever. You got your ass handed to you and you deserved it."

Grace cried out. "Haydon, don't. He helped us."

Vittorio spun around to see the woman in motion, racing to get between him and Haydon. The gun from under the BMW was in his hand and he was aiming at Vittorio. Not at either of the Saldi enforcers, but at Vittorio. The bullet slammed Grace back into Vittorio and he caught her, turning so his body protected her against another shot.

Haydon threw the gun and ran. Vittorio dropped down on one knee, taking Grace to the asphalt. She was fully awake and looking at him. She had green eyes, the color of jewels, although shock was wearing off and excruciating pain settling in.

"Don't move. Just let me handle this." He gave the command without thinking, already mass texting his family and calling for an ambulance. "I'm going to take a look at the wound. Keep looking at me. At my face." He could already see the bullet had done damage. His worst fear was that it had severed an artery and she would bleed out before help could get there.

She swallowed hard. Her lashes fluttered, but she was definitely courageous. Tears swam. He leaned closer, keeping his hand over the wound.

"This isn't anything we can't deal with. I'm Vittorio Ferraro. You are?"

Her lips trembled. She opened her mouth twice to try to form words. He would have told her to stay quiet, but he was a little terrified of her losing consciousness. "Grace. Grace Murphy."

"An ambulance is on its way. I'm going to tell them you're my fiancée, just to make things easier in the ER. We'll get faster results that way. Let me take over for you and get this done."

Vittorio stared down into her eyes, willing her to stay alert, to stay alive. He needed her to live, more than he needed to breathe. Very gently he pushed the hair spilling into her eyes from her face, his thumb as soothing as his voice.

"Just stay with me, kitten. I'll get you through this." She was writhing, her feet pushing up on the asphalt, trying to get away from the pain. Every movement only made it worse.

"You have to stay still, Grace. You can do that. I know it's hard, but look at me. I'm right here with you. You can do it because I'm asking you to. Just stay still. Don't let your body move."

Every nerve ending had to be screaming at her. There were broken bones. His hand pressing on the wound couldn't be helping. In the distance he heard the scream of the siren, but the ambulance wasn't coming fast enough.

Her gaze jumped to his and stayed there. She swallowed hard, but he could see her make a brave attempt to stop the fight her body was making to run. He smiled at her. "That's my girl. Keep breathing for me. They're on their way."

His oldest brother, Stefano, emerged from the shadows first, took in the scene with a quick look and then was on the other side of Grace, leaning down with his Ferraro smile and that way he had with women.

"This is Grace," Vittorio said. "My fiancée." That should tell his brother everything, and it did. Stefano glanced at him sharply and then down at the woman lying on the ground, trying desperately not to move in spite of the agonizing pain because Vittorio had asked her not to.

"What the hell are the Saldis doing here? The cops will be here any moment."

Ricco and Taviano converged from two different locations in the parking lot. Both scanned their brother first to ensure Vittorio was free from wounds and then took in the entire scene.

"They do this?" Ricco demanded.

Vittorio shook his head. "His gun." He nodded toward Ale Sarto. "It's over there. Her foster brother, Haydon—don't know his last name yet—tried to sell her for his gambling debts. Had her in the trunk of his car. They were going to take her, too. Haydon tried to shoot me after I dealt with Ale and Lando. She stepped between us. Her last name is Murphy. She was raised in a foster home with this Haydon. Check the trunk of the Honda for her purse. Get this information to Rosina immediately. As her fiancé I will be expected to know everything about her."

Taviano was already up, on his phone and hurrying to the Honda where he recovered Grace's purse. Vittorio kept his eyes locked with Grace's. Shudders went through her body. Tears tracked down her face. Several times she started to move, but the moment he murmured softly to her, she fought back the urge.

"That's my girl. Stay with me. You're doing great. They're here."

She looked desperate. He felt that way. He wasn't about to be separated from her. "No matter what, I'll be with you," he promised. He glanced at his brother. Stefano made things happen, even impossible things.

His oldest brother was on the phone to Giuseppi Saldi and the conversation wasn't pleasant. Stefano was pissed as all hell and the cold, clipped way he was talking to Giuseppi let the man know there were going to be repercussions.

"Two of your men are here in my parking lot. My brother's fiancée has been shot with one of their guns and the cops are crawling all over my club. What the fuck, Giuseppi? You making a move on my family?"

There was silence. Vittorio continued to murmur to Grace as the ambulance screamed into the parking lot.

"Some asshole threw her into the trunk of his car, her foster brother or something, and these two clowns were going to take her as payment for his gambling debts. Since when has that been going on? Just letting you know, they're both going to the hospital and then to jail, and if I see them on the fucking street, they're dead. You get me, Giuseppi? You come at my family, we're coming back at you and yours. And we'll come back hard."

Stefano ended the call and strode back to Grace and Vittorio. The EMTs were already running IV lines to Grace. Stefano was back on the phone, calling their surgeon, demanding he get his team ready and be waiting for Grace when they brought her in. Then he was diverting the police, while Taviano and Ricco kept a loose barrier between Vittorio and anyone coming into the parking lot. Bodyguards showed up. Three carloads, led by Emilio and Enzo Gallo. They were out and taking charge of the entire lot.

Two detectives arrived, and Stefano beckoned them through the security line. Art Maverick and Jason Bradshaw had investigated the Ferraro family on more than one occasion. Vittorio, like the rest of his family, considered them fair and decent men. They weren't egotistical, and they always remained polite, even when frustrated. The family tried to cooperate with them as best they could. When the Ferraros had evidence involving a crime that they could pass on, they always saw to it that the evidence ended up with Maverick and Bradshaw.

"Who beat the shit out of Gori and Sarto?" Art Maverick asked. There was a trace of amusement in his voice that he tried his best to hide. EMTs were working on both men.

"Vittorio," Stefano said immediately. "He came out into

the parking lot to see Grace's foster brother dragging her out of the trunk of the Honda." He indicated the car with the open trunk. "Apparently, Haydon was going to sell her to the two morons in exchange for his gambling debt. In other words, sell her into prostitution."

Art and Jason exchanged a long look of smoldering anger. "Are you certain about that?" Jason asked.

"Vittorio overheard them, and Grace can verify if she lives through this."

"Who shot her?" Art directed the question at Vittorio.

Vittorio was on his feet following the gurney to the ambulance, grateful for the information coming so fast to his phone. "Haydon Phillips, her foster brother. Ale put a gun to Haydon's head to scare Grace into complying. I knocked it away, beat the crap out of him and then went after Lando because he had his hands on Grace. While I had him down, Haydon picked up the gun and went to shoot me, and she took the bullet." He pushed past the detective and slid into the ambulance. No one tried to stop him.

As the door was being closed he spotted his sister, Emmanuelle, running across the parking lot toward the ambulance. Then the door was slammed shut and the ambulance was moving fast through the streets of Chicago toward the hospital. His phone was blowing up with information regarding his woman. He didn't glance down, not yet. Her eyes were locked with his again and he wasn't about to let her down.

"I'm with you, baby," he said softly. "The OR is set up and our surgeon is standing by. He's the best and his team are miracle workers. You're going to be fine."

She tried to form words, but he leaned in close, staying out of the EMTs' way in the tight quarters. "Don't talk, Grace. Save your strength. I've got this. All you have to do is stay alive for me. I'll take care of everything else. Will you do that for me? Just stay alive."

Her nod was nearly imperceptible, but it was there. He was a complete stranger to her, but he knew that connection between them had started there in the parking lot, their shadows touching, coiling together, their eyes meeting. His hands buried in the blood and massive damage to her shoulder. His voice connected them. His compelling promises. He meant every word he said, and she had to feel that. It was all he could give her before she went alone into that cold operating room.

Her foster brother had betrayed her. No matter that she'd known he was a gambler and a drug addict, he still had meant something to her. That had been clear. She'd taken out loans to pay his debt. Took on extra work. He'd heard that very clearly. This was a woman who knew what it was to be loyal, and yet someone close to her would have sold her into prostitution. He wanted to rip the man in half.

The ambulance tore into the parking lot and halted at the double doors. A team waited for her, and then he was running with them toward the operating room where one of the best orthopedic surgeons the family had access to waited with his team to put her shoulder back together. Vittorio had no idea whether or not the artery had been nicked but it was possible. He'd applied pressure as best he could until the EMTs had taken over.

"You stay alive, Grace." He poured command into his voice, his gaze clinging to hers.

For a heartbeat she just stared at him, and then she nodded. Or he thought she did. The doors swung shut and he was left standing there, her blood on his hands and shirt. His heart beating too fast. He had always known he had no chance at finding a woman of his own, one who might be able to love him, to live with him, and in the blink of an eye that had turned around. Just that fast, she was being taken from him.

"Mr. Ferraro?" A nurse indicated he follow her.

"It's her blood, not mine," Vittorio explained. He wanted to be alone to look at his phone. He was going to find Haydon Phillips, the name the Ferraros' investigator, Rosina, had sent to him, and he was going to kill him. He brought justice to all kinds of criminals. The rule had been drilled into him over and over: *Never* let it be personal. This was as personal as it was going to get.

The nurse indicated a small private bathroom off a waiting room that wasn't open to the public. The Ferraro family had contributed several million dollars toward the hospital, a wing and equipment. They were kept out of the public eye when they were there. Most of the time they managed to fly under the radar of the paparazzi unless a nurse or orderly sold them out. One photo was often worth thousands of dollars.

When he came out of the private restroom, his sister, Emmanuelle, was waiting for him. She rushed to him, waited until he tore off the bloody shirt and replaced it with the one she'd brought him, and then hugged him tightly. "Vittorio. You could have been shot. Why would that horrible toad want to shoot you when you saved his life?"

He tightened his arms around her, taking comfort in her presence. "I'm okay, honey. Grace ran between us just as I was turning around. She took the bullet, not me. Phillips wanted her to pay his gambling debts and I interfered. That's the short version."

"But you can't deal with men like Sarto or Gori. Everyone knows that."

"Phillips believed Sarto wouldn't shoot him, that it was all for effect, so she'd go with Saldi's men."

"I can't believe they would do such a thing. Stefano told me what they were there for. It's disgusting."

He was grateful she didn't protest. She had crushed on Valentine Saldi, Giuseppi's adopted son, since she was sixteen years old and they'd had an on-again, off-again relationship for some time. Vittorio was certain Emmanuelle genuinely loved him, which was too bad. The relationship had been doomed from the start. Her brothers had tried to tell her, tried to protect her, but until recently, she hadn't listened to them. His heart ached for her. He could see the genuine sorrow and distress in her eyes.

"Yes, it is. They were blatant about being in the club, Emme. How they got in without any of us being told, or how Haydon slipped through, I have no idea."

"Tell me about her," Emme invited. "When did you meet her? Stefano says you're claiming her as your fiancée. Rosina is sending us information as fast as she gets it so we can answer any questions posed to us by the police or anyone else."

Vittorio rubbed his chest. He still felt her there. Deep. Her voice had opened something soft in him that had been locked away. "Tonight was the first time I ever laid eyes on her. She was . . . unexpected."

"Are you certain she's the one?" Emme whispered. "Do you just know it, Vittorio? In your soul, where you live, do you just know?"

He glanced down at her sharply, his gaze moving over her face. He nodded slowly because she deserved an answer, especially when tears swam in her eyes and the family of the man she loved was involved in kidnapping and forcing a woman into prostitution.

"She's the one. I never thought it would be possible. I'd just been thinking that, looking around the club at all the women, knowing there wasn't one out there that would suit me . . . and maybe there isn't. Maybe she's a rider and she would be good for someone other than me. I'm not so . . . lovable."

"Don't say that." Emme's defense of him was fierce. "Don't ever say that, Vittorio, because it isn't true."

"I love you, honey," Vittorio said. He pulled away from her and looked at the woman waiting so patiently for him to give her details about his fiancée. "I claimed her, but she doesn't have a clue who I am. If she knows about the Ferraros . . ."

"Everyone knows about our family or they've been living off planet," Emmanuelle quipped. "She knows. She might not care, but she knows."

"I'm no bargain, Emme. I need things from a woman

most men don't. She stood up to those men." He found himself smiling at the memory of her flying out of the trunk of the car, straight at Haydon. "That red hair of hers is natural."

"Good for her."

"Yeah. Good for her." He'd loved that she'd fought back, that she was no pushover. That wasn't what he wanted in a woman, but maybe it was what he needed.

Hell, he didn't know. Right now, all he felt was sick inside, his guts twisted into vicious knots. He'd done his best to keep her alive, his hands in that mess that had been her shoulder, trying to stem the tidal wave of blood.

"She's going to live, Vittorio," Emmanuelle assured. "She has to, if she's yours. Shadow riders fight. She may not know she's capable of riding, but that strength is in her. She'll pull through and she'll need lots of help after."

He was good with that. "I'm going to have to fill out paperwork for her. Rosina has sent me all kinds of information, so most of it will be easy enough." He rubbed her cheek with his thumb. "What about you, honey? This has to hurt."

Emmanuelle didn't pretend she didn't know what he was talking about. "I broke things off with Val a few weeks ago. I think about him every minute of every day, but I have discipline. I heard him say—I *heard* him, with my own ears—say that his father had ordered him to seduce me. He told another woman that. A woman he was clearly going to bed with."

Vittorio wrapped his arm around her again, drawing her under his shoulder, wanting to take the hurt from her. "I'm sorry, Emme. Really, really sorry."

"It was better to find out now before I made an even bigger fool of myself than I've already made." She paused for a moment. "I would have given up riding the shadows for him. I would have given up everything I am for him and he's not worth it."

"No, he's not." Vittorio wanted to shake the man until every bone in his body turned to powder, but he refrained from saying so. Emme would have been more upset if she thought he threatened Val with bodily harm. He didn't want to give her any excuse to champion Valentino Saldi.

"Val was *my* 'the one.' The lesson here is, we can get it wrong. Make certain this woman suits you, Vittorio. If she doesn't, don't go there. Don't let yourself fall too hard. It's a long road back and every step is painful."

Vittorio wanted to wrap his sister in a cocoon. She didn't deserve what Val had put her through. She'd broken it off with him many times and he always managed to get her to come back to him—until recently.

"Rosina is searching for everything she can find on Haydon Phillips." Emmanuelle changed the subject. "Stefano called a meeting at his home at breakfast. Hopefully, your girl will be out of surgery by then and you can join us."

"I told her I'd be there when she woke up."

"Ask the surgeon when that will be," Emme prompted. "That way we can have the meeting, prepare a battle plan and then you can get back here. You have to know, for the Saldis to come to our club, something is up."

She was right about that. "The footage needs reviewing. Someone let them in. They allowed them onto the third tier. They had to have paid for that, or they couldn't have gotten up there, unless someone we trust snuck them in."

"In which case, we know where all the drugs are coming from," Emmanuelle said.

He nodded. "We can access the recordings from our phones if need be. The managers know we don't as a rule, so if they can wipe out the recordings, we might get lucky and they overlooked that."

"But they won't for long. With Grace getting shot, the two Saldi employees getting arrested and all of us involved, they're going to be doing damage control. I'll get on that right now." Emme pulled away from him, going toward the door. "Try to make the meeting, Vittorio. It won't do either of you any good to be sitting by her side when she's out of surgery and unconscious. In any case, if we're going to war with a major crime family, we have to be prepared."

It was a huge concession for Emmanuelle to acknowledge that Valentino's family were criminals.

"I'll be there if at all possible," he promised. The meeting was going to be very painful for his sister and he wanted to be there for her. He wouldn't leave if Grace was awake, but if not, he was determined to be there for Emme.

CHAPTER TWO

Vittorio rode the private elevator that took him to the penthouse suite in the Ferraro. The chain of hotels the family owned were renowned for their opulence and meticulous attention to every comfort and detail. Most were frequented by celebrities and politicians. Actors and actresses, singers and bands, the wealthiest of the wealthy. The hotel catered to them, pampered them and gave them every luxury.

Stefano Ferraro lived in the penthouse suite, with his wife, Francesca. Francesca had been the woman to provide hope for the entire Ferraro family, and that included their New York, San Francisco and Los Angeles cousins. Until Stefano found Francesca, none of them had believed they would find a woman capable of bearing shadow riders who would be a perfect match. That she and Stefano had fallen so deeply in love with each other was icing on the cake. Stefano was the leader of the Chicago Ferraros, but Francesca was the heart of them.

The elevator opened directly into Stefano's foyer. The

place was elegant, always had been, but when Stefano had lived there alone, it had been cold. Now, it was warm and welcoming and smelled like heaven. That was Francesca. She could make a cave a home. Breakfast at Stefano's wasn't hotel food, never mind that they had five-star chefs. Francesca insisted on cooking and usually his youngest brother, Taviano, helped her in the kitchen. There was something special about their concoctions, most likely the love they put into them.

"Hey, you," Francesca greeted, leaning into him so he could brush a kiss along her cheek. "How's Grace doing?"

Vittorio noted, with some alarm, that she looked tired. "She was in surgery most of the night. Doc says she lost a lot of blood. It's going to take some time to heal all the smashed bones, but he says everything looks good. Told me to get some sleep and come back around noon. They want to keep her out as long as possible because the pain is going to be barely manageable."

He gave the report to his family because they'd all ceased their boisterous conversations to hear what he had to say.

"Breakfast is ready," Taviano said. "We were just waiting for you."

There was no reprimand, but Vittorio didn't want Francesca to think he'd held them up for no reason. "The doc had a lot to say about her care and I needed to hear it." He made his way to the large table, already set with white china rimmed in gold.

Each of them tended to choose the same seat when they ate at Stefano's, which was often. They hadn't been allowed to attend schools as other children had. They'd trained together. They'd studied with tutors and had been expected to learn multiple languages and excel in everything required of them, particularly when it came to mastering weapons and turning their bodies into weapons.

Their family had to be protected at all times. Once, a

hundred years earlier, the Saldis had attempted to wipe out the Ferraro family.

That didn't allow for friendships outside the family. What they did was done in complete secrecy and would always have to be. No one outside the family knew what they were capable of doing. There were other shadow riders in the world, but very few. They policed themselves and were extremely careful at all times.

Every rider had personal bodyguards whether they wanted them or not. It was a fact of life they'd learned to live with. Most people thought they were a crime family, just as the Saldis were. They were investigated often, but had never been indicted for a crime. They couldn't have close friends outside the family. They had to portray a lavish, extravagant lifestyle to the public, to further their images as playboys with far too much money.

They played polo. They raced cars and gambled. Those unmarried had a different woman on their arm at night at charity events and clubs. They flew from one country to another, seemingly just to party. On the other hand, they had many legitimate businesses, including international banks and their hotels.

"Did anyone review the security tapes?" Vittorio asked as he took several homemade pastries from the basket being passed around.

"Mariko and I did," Ricco said, indicating his wife. "Someone definitely messed with them, but I sent them to Rigina to see what she could recover. She's working on it now."

They employed only family when it came to the shadow riders. Rigina and Rosina Greco were Ferraro cousins and investigators. Both women were geniuses when it came to anything to do with computers or electronic equipment.

"I spoke with Giuseppi twice," Stefano said. He took a sip of his latte. "He swears they aren't running any operations out of our club. He spoke to his brother Miceli, and

Miceli claims he has no idea why Sarto or Gori would have been at the club. He also claims complete ignorance of the fact that his two very loyal soldiers were involved in anything as heinous as human trafficking, prostitution and kidnapping. Neither knew the connection between Grace and our family, which is probably the only true statement made."

"Leonardo Saldi was head of the family for years," Giovanni explained to bring Francesca, Mariko and Sasha, Giovanni's new bride, up to speed. "He had three sons: Giuseppi, Miceli and his youngest son, Fons. When Leonardo died, the oldest, Giuseppi, took over as head of the Saldi family. They have the entire East Coast locked down as their territory and they rule with an iron and very bloody fist." He speared sausage onto his plate.

Ricco took over. "When Valentino, the now heir apparent, was eight, there was a car bombing. It killed his father, Fons, and mother, leaving him an orphan. Giuseppi and his wife, Greta, had always been in Val's life. Supposedly, they adored him and were the favorite aunt and uncle. Greta has never had children, and there isn't even a whisper of Giuseppi cheating on her. They took Val in and later adopted him legally. He was around ten when they made it legal."

Giovanni took over the explanation. "Miceli had one son, Dario, out of wedlock. He never married his mother, but Dario came to live with him when he was fifteen, after she died. Miceli has two sons with his current wife, Tommaso and Angelo. Because Giuseppi adopted Val legally, Val, who would have stood in line behind Miceli and his three sons, was now the official heir to the Saldi throne."

Vittorio slid his hand under the table and covered Emme's hand. She was pressing her palm hard into her thigh. He felt her tremble and he waited until she looked up at him before he smiled at her. "We don't have the first clue what's going on, and as with any investigation, we don't make a move until we know for certain." He kept his voice soothing. Gentle. He pitched his tones to be comforting and even peaceful.

Emmanuelle visibly relaxed. "I can tell you that Giuseppi treats Val as his own son and clearly loves Greta. She has stage four pancreatic cancer and Giuseppi isn't leaving her side."

Stefano raised his head alertly, his dark eyes pinning his sister. Vittorio shook his head and immediately intervened. "Thanks, Emme. We'll have Rosina see what she can dig up on Greta's health and where she stands right now. It's possible Giuseppi really isn't in the know about what's going on in his territory."

"That would be a first," Taviano said. "Nicoletta was assaulted in the flower shop by Saldi scum. I took care of it, but the bastard actually put his hands on her. And Val's bodyguard, Dario, you know, Miceli's oldest son, has twice called Nicoletta, just in case anyone's interested in that bit of information."

Nicoletta was a young woman they'd rescued when she was a teen. She lived with Amo and Lucia Fausti as their foster daughter and she'd recently turned eighteen. That made things difficult for the riders as they watched over her. She was one of them, that rare woman who could produce the type of child who was capable of riding shadows and dispensing justice.

Emmanuelle stiffened. "Are you kidding me? When did that happen? Why didn't you tell me?"

Taviano halted in the act of lifting a scone to his mouth. "What's wrong, Emme?" She had their complete attention.

"The Saldi family has definitely told their younger men to attempt to seduce the women in our family, me included. If they're going after Nicoletta, I need to talk to her. She'll listen to me. Taviano, you didn't go by her house and lay down the law, did you?"

"You mean to tell her to stay the hell away from the

Saldis? Damn right, I did. I told her if I caught her with one of them, I'd break his fucking neck."

All four women at the table groaned in unison. Taviano glared at them. "What? I would. She had to have heard the truth of that. I'm not kidding around with her anymore. I'm done with her bullshit parties. She's so damned wild I can't even see straight thinking about it."

Stefano shook his head. "You're such a hothead, Taviano. You handle that girl all wrong. If you tell her not to do something, what do you think she's going to do? You're smarter than that. Think with your brain instead of your dick."

Vittorio laughed softly, leading the others who followed suit. Even Taviano had to smile and shrug, conceding his older brother was probably right.

"I'll talk to her," Emmanuelle said when the laughter died down. "Don't worry, she won't go near Dario or any other Saldi."

"The last thing we need is to have Nicoletta kidnapped and used in human trafficking," Taviano said, exasperation warring with annoyance in his voice. "And believe me, it could happen to her. Just about everything else has. Did anyone think to put a tracker on her when she comes to classes?"

"Don't you dare." Francesca's gasp of shock had everyone's immediate attention. "Taviano, I mean it. That's just wrong."

"Nothing's wrong when you're dealing with unruly women," Taviano stated, nudging Vittorio's foot under the table.

Vittorio tried not to smile while Taviano struggled to hide a smirk. Stirring up the women in their family was a little like poking a nest of vipers, but always fun.

Francesca glared at the youngest Ferraro brother. Mariko put down her fork, her exotic almond-shaped hazel eyes narrowing as she leaned toward him. Ricco laughed and put a restraining hand on her shoulder.

Sasha, Giovanni's wife, wadded up her napkin and threw

it with deadly accuracy. "You're lucky that isn't a rope." She was referring to the art of Shibari that both Ricco and Mariko practiced.

Taviano picked the napkin out of the air, laughing at the reaction he got. "So easy, the three of you. Look at Emmanuelle. She's just sitting there."

"Plotting revenge," she said sweetly and took a sip of her latte.

The smirk left Taviano's face. "Emme, you know I was damn well kidding."

"And watch your language," Francesca said. "You're not talking that way around the baby." She leaned toward Stefano.

Instantly he put his hand on the little bump showing at her belly. "We're going to do it this time," he said. "Francesca is resting, just as the doctor wants. We walk several times a day, but only for a few minutes. The rest of the time, she has to have her feet up."

Taviano sat up straighter. "What were you doing helping to make breakfast? Stefano, that's not resting. She shouldn't be in the kitchen."

"I love the kitchen," Francesca said. "I'm not on bed rest. Just light stuff."

"The doc comes out to see her three times a week," Stefano said. "I agreed to abide by his rules. He said she wasn't on bed rest, so . . ." He shrugged.

Giovanni nudged Sasha with his shoulder and then grinned at her. "He can be bribed, Stefano, you ever think of that?"

Sasha kicked him under the table. "Try doing that, and I'll get Emme to help me plot revenge. She's already working up a plan to carry out against Taviano. It wouldn't take much to include you."

Another round of laughter went up. When it faded, Stefano turned his attention to Vittorio. "Tell us whatever you've got."

Vittorio knew Rosina had copied Stefano on everything. As head of the family he was privy to anything that affected any or all family members. His word was law. He listened to the others, but in the end, it was up to him to make decisions. They were used to Stefano as head of the household. It had been Stefano providing any positive attention they'd had as young children.

"Her name is Grace Murphy. She's twenty-three. Was raised in the foster care system. She was one of the lucky ones at first. The family she was with wanted to keep her, but an accident took the father, and the mother turned to alcohol. The adoption fell through and Grace was moved to a series of homes."

He kept his voice even. Calm. That was his way. He didn't react to things, not even when examining his woman's past and the things she'd been through as a child.

"When she was thirteen she landed in the same home with Haydon Phillips. That particular home was run by a very abusive couple, Owen and Becca Mueller. They had one biological son, Dwayne. They did everything from beatings to withholding food. Haydon took the brunt of the punishments and has the scars to prove it, although there are photographs of Grace's body showing burn marks on her."

Emme put her hand on Vittorio's arm. He was still inside, refusing to allow any negative energy to emerge. Vittorio practiced discipline at all times. This was one of those times when he needed to stay very calm. Deep inside, the volcano that could emerge was at a boiling point. Rosina had sent the photographs they'd used to convict the couple before moving both Grace and Haydon, but it was far too late by the time the investigation had been taken seriously and horrendous things had continued to happen.

"Neighbors had complained. It had taken months before anyone acted. Four visits from the police. Another six from a social worker. The investigation came to a screeching halt when Dwayne was tortured and murdered, his body found several miles away from the home in a ditch along the highway. The investigation turned into a murder investigation, with Owen as prime suspect, but he was cleared."

"Were they at least removed?" Sasha asked.

Vittorio shook his head. "It was almost as if all the allegations brought against the couple just disappeared. Maybe the social worker felt sorry for them or had too much work. In any case, they were left there another four months and one night, Owen got drunk. That was a common occurrence, according to the neighbors. His wife locked him out of the house, another common occurrence. He went to sleep in the garage and decided to work on his car. It fell on him and crushed his lower extremities. He lay on the cement with the car on top of him all night before Becca discovered him the next morning. He's in a wheelchair and can't function very well."

"Sometimes justice can be found in strange ways," Taviano said, and held up his glass of fresh-squeezed orange juice.

The others followed suit, Sasha with a little obvious reluctance. She wasn't used to their ways. Vittorio noticed Giovanni put his arm around her, lean close and whisper something that had his wife smiling. Vittorio liked that his brother was always aware when Sasha was uncomfortable with anything.

"Grace was in that home four years before an actual investigation was conducted and the couple were arrested and charged." His hands fisted so hard his knuckles cracked. "Four years of fucking hell before the couple was finally arrested. The husband was given a suspended sentence due to his injuries from the accident and the wife was given two years, but never served time. She has since applied for a foster care license numerous times and been turned down, but Rosina found they run an unlicensed daycare."

"Are you fucking kidding me?" Ricco asked. "That's insane."

"Where are they?" Giovanni asked.

"Upstate New York," Vittorio said with some satisfaction. "Our territory. We can turn over the investigation to the cousins there. See what turns up. No way have they stopped what they were doing, not with that kind of slap on the wrist."

Stefano nodded. "It's already done. The New York branch of the family is on it."

"That's so terrible, Vittorio," Francesca said. "I can't go see her in the hospital, but when you can, please bring her here."

"Dr. Arnold explained they wanted her kept in intensive care for a long stay with round-the-clock nurses," Stefano said gently, "but we'll bring her here as soon as they tell us it's okay to do so."

"She's in our private suite, eyes on her all the time. An artery had to be repaired and the shoulder is in pieces. If you see the damage done, the bone was shattered. Dr. Arnold doesn't want to move her. The first few days he'll keep her as sedated as he can. Then, once they bring her around, they don't want any movement until those bones begin to heal. She has enough plates and pins everywhere, trying to hold her together. She's going to have a long rehab, honey," Vittorio explained to Francesca, "but I'll definitely bring her to you when I can. In the meantime, I have to convince her I'm the one for her."

"There's no doubt she'll think you're amazing," Emme said staunchly.

The other women nodded their heads. "She'll be so lucky to have you," Mariko said.

Sasha remained silent, but her eyes met Vittorio's and he could see the knowledge there. She saw inside him. She knew what kind of man he was. What he needed and would insist on. His woman had to be very courageous—and very trusting. You didn't get the latter trait living in the kind of home Grace had lived in and then being betrayed by the one person you probably thought of as family. He had a long road ahead of him to win his lady.

"What else do you have on her?" Giovanni asked.

"She works for an event planner, a woman by the name of Katie Branscomb."

All four women nodded their heads. "Katie owns KB Events and is the number-one event planner here in that industry," Emme said. "Everyone we know uses her."

"Grace is her personal assistant and according to Katie, she's the force behind the real planning. She makes things happen. They're very popular with customers because Grace always gets the customer exactly what they want."

"Why would the Saldis think they could kidnap a woman with a reputation like that?" Taviano asked. "Her boss would come looking for her. She had customers that have all the money in the world at their disposal. Those customers would most likely help Katie Branscomb find her absent assistant."

"Do you think they were after her specifically, or that's who Phillips had to offer for his gambling debts?"

"It sounded more like it was very specific and they were going to take her regardless of what either of them said. Phillips was too far gone to read them accurately. They were going to kill him the moment they had her in the car," Vittorio said with absolute certainty. He'd spent his life reading others. He knew Sarto and Gori were there to kill Haydon Phillips. "Miceli never sends those two out without a reason. I'm afraid that reason is Grace."

"She stands out," Stefano said. "Even with blood all over her, and her face as white as a sheet, you could still see the beauty there. Someone noticed her. Maybe Miceli, but if not him, maybe someone he owed a favor to. If Grace was that favor, is she still?"

Good question. Vittorio had to consider that even with Sarto and Gori in the hospital, but in police custody, Grace might still be in danger.

"If she disappeared, the last person to see her would have been Haydon, and he would have been dead. No one would have a clue she was taken by the Saldis," Emme said.

Vittorio knew what it cost her to state that. He dropped his hand to the nape of her neck and massaged gently to ease the tension out of her. He couldn't give her back her heart, but he could let her know he stood solidly with her.

"I know Grace is the one for me, even though I didn't connect with her shadow first. The lights in the parking lot had been deliberately broken, most likely by Sarto and Gori. Or Phillips. The camera footage will tell us when Rigina recovers what we need."

"We have a remote backup that feed goes to," Stefano pointed out. "What about that?"

"Rigina has access to it, even though the original was wiped," Ricco said. "Fortunately, no one but our family knows about the backup. When she finds the right footage, whoever is selling us out to the Saldis won't know we've discovered what they're doing, and we might have a way to use them."

"Maybe," Vittorio said, his voice mild. "But whoever it is was aiding human trafficking, and the woman he helped them take was mine. That makes this very personal." He ignored the way Stefano's head came up, his gaze suddenly sharp and assessing. Vittorio doggedly continued, "The fact that they can wipe the security feed and slip Saldis into the club along with a junkie—it has to be someone high up in management we trust."

"We're going to handle this, Vittorio," Stefano assured. "When it was Francesca's life in danger, or Mariko's, or Sasha's, for that matter, we took care of the problem ourselves. We'll find out who's behind this without jumping to conclusions." His gaze touched Emme's face just for a moment. "We aren't going to make any mistakes with this one."

Emme's fingers tightened around Vittorio's. He knew she loved Val Saldi and that wasn't going away anytime soon—even though she knew his family were criminals. When the Ferraros loved, they did it wholly, and they did it once. This exact scenario had always been the thing they'd feared the most for Emme—that the two families would end up in a war.

"Who was on last night, managing the club?" Ricco asked.

"Martin Shanks," Stefano said. "He's been with us as a manager for six years, worked an additional four in the club. Rosina is looking into his financials. Shanks went home around midnight very ill. There were witnesses to him being extremely sick. His assistant, Timothy Vane, took over for him. Vane had been working for the club about three years when he was promoted to assistant manager. That was two years ago. So, he's been in the club for a good five years. These are not new employees. They're paid extremely well, receive bonuses and have been with our family for a lot of years, so they receive profit sharing as well."

"Who was at the door?" Emme asked.

"Clay Pierson. He's been one of our bouncers for ten years," Stefano said. "Emilio and Enzo trained him. Again, he's long-time employed, makes good money and receives profit sharing."

"I saw Peter Franks," Vittorio said. "He's hard to miss. He was on last night as well. Not working the door, but inside."

"I don't know who that is," Francesca said.

Sasha and Mariko both indicated they didn't know him, either.

"Franks works security. Essentially, he's a bouncer. He works the door when he's scheduled, but like Clay Pierson, he trained under Emilio and Enzo," Stefano provided.

Vittorio handed his coffee cup to Taviano, who had risen, and pointed toward the kitchen where the espresso machine was. He needed to hear everything being said, but he wanted to be at the hospital. He'd promised Grace he would be there when she woke up, and he was determined to make that happen.

He was going on forty-eight hours without sleep and he needed to crash soon. Giovanni, Sasha, Taviano and Ricco had gone to Los Angeles in their private jet. He'd taken the shadows to the airport, secretly entering the plane right under the noses of the paparazzi. Once in Los Angeles, his brothers and sister-in-law headed to the nearest nightclub with their LA cousins to party the night away. Being out in the open like that, getting photographed dancing and drinking, gave their cousins alibis just in case anyone ever suspected them of wrongdoing. No one had any idea that Vittorio was in Los Angeles. As far as they knew, he was still at home in Chicago, nowhere near the city in California.

"What about the waitress or bartender?" Sasha asked. She had worked at the club as a top-tier waitress.

Giovanni shook his head. "If someone is on the two top tiers, they were already vetted. We've never given that kind of responsibility to a bartender or waitress."

"Only management and security have that level of authority," Vittorio said. He rubbed his chest again. His muscles ached, right over his heart. "Still, one would think they would have questioned it. I'm going to have to get back to Grace soon. I don't want her to wake up without me being there." He took the latte Taviano handed to him, grateful for the caffeine when he felt like he was running on empty.

Stefano nodded his understanding. "Let's get back to Grace. She's the main concern right now."

Vittorio nodded. "Rosina has dug up quite a bit on her. I don't know how she escaped our notice until now. Because she worked for Katie Branscomb, she was in our circles. We didn't have her on our radar, but she was on someone's. That person is either part of or connected to the Saldi family, and Miceli or Giuseppi owe him."

"Is she safe in the hospital?" Francesca asked. "I'd rather she be in one of our homes and the doctor come to her."

"He'll come to her, baby," Stefano said. "Just right now, they don't want to move her."

"I've got bodyguards on her," Vittorio assured. "And I'll be with her most of the time. I'm planning on taking her home with me when they let her out of the hospital. She wouldn't get any care at her apartment and with me, she'll have everything she needs for rehabilitation."

Stefano sent him a quick grin. "Nice move, brother. Get in good while she's down."

Francesca rolled her eyes. "You're so bad, Stefano, although, in this case I have to agree, it's good to bring Grace home with you, Vittorio. From what Stefano said, it doesn't sound like she'd have anyone to look after her."

"Does that answer the question of whether or not you think it's over for her? Or do you think someone is going to make another try for her?" Mariko asked. "Do you really think the Saldi family would start a war with us over her?"

Vittorio shrugged and sipped the hot latte to give himself time to choose his words carefully. He detested hurting Emme, and any mention of a war between the families was going to break her heart. "If Grace was the specific target, and it sounded like she was, then yes, I think she's still in danger. We just don't know where that danger is going to come from, and like Stefano says, we'll handle this carefully. The right way. Although, having said that, I want to hunt Haydon down and find out what he has to say before—" He broke off and shrugged again.

Stefano glanced at him sharply but didn't say anything.

Ricco put down his latte and looked straight into Vittorio's eyes. "I think it's safe to say, we're all feeling the same way, Vittorio. Not just because she's your woman, but because she's *a* woman. She could have been anyone. Had you not gone to the club, we wouldn't have known they were using it to conduct their business."

"They were definitely thumbing their noses at us," Taviano agreed.

"Maybe," Stefano said. "But we all agree we don't do anything stupid. We treat this the way we would any job." His gaze touched Vittorio's, making his point. "We investigate, and we call in our cousins from New York to dispense justice. The cops are all over this one. We're going to have to have alibis at all times and make certain we can publicly account for every minute of the day. When dead bodies start turning up, we don't want to be in any way associated with them. Since this started at our club with Vittorio's fiancée, the best-kept secret of all time, we will be scrutinized."

Vittorio knew Stefano was right, but it didn't sit well with him to have Grace in danger while he did nothing about it. He knew that would be impossible for him. His brothers knew it as well. Only Sasha and Francesca, the two non-riders, would believe what Stefano was saying, and were assured by his statement that no one there would do anything rash—like find Haydon and kill him. Vittorio was hoping his own intentions weren't stamped on his forehead for the world to see—because he was definitely going after that asshole and taking him out permanently.

Maybe he should feel some sympathy for Haydon, because for Grace to love him so much, he must have been a decent human being at one time, but Vittorio didn't. Grace had gone through the same things Haydon had, although from what Rigina had uncovered so far, Haydon had tried to protect Grace and taken the brunt of the abuse. Still, from everything the investigators had found in the short time they'd had, she remained a decent, hardworking, honorable human being. One who gave way too much love and loyalty to a douchebag who deserved neither.

"We're going to be scrutinized by the press," Ricco said. "No one has caught a glimpse of Vittorio with Grace. Were they at any event at the same time? We need to start building a plausible story for them."

Emme nodded. "I'm on that already. Rigina has helped me, sending all the charity events Vittorio went to in the past year and a half." She looked up at him. "You attended thirteen large and well-publicized events as well as three smaller ones. Four were for brain traumas, six for cancer research, three for women's shelters and the three smaller ones were to raise money for rescues for animals. Eloisa put on most of the bigger events."

"Animals?" Giovanni said. "When did you do that, Vittorio?"

Vittorio flipped him off.

Sasha looked up at her husband. "Giovanni, are you giving your brother a hard time when you just this morning told me about the horse rescue—"

Giovanni wrapped his hand around his wife's mouth, laughing, his eyes dancing. "Not the time, woman. What are you thinking?"

Vittorio found himself laughing along with his brothers and the women seated at the breakfast table. That was how they were together. Discussing business one minute, and then erupting into laughter together the next. He wanted that for Grace. According to everything Rosina was sending to him, she'd never had a family—well, except that loser Haydon. Vittorio could, at least, provide that for her. He had no idea if it would be enough to balance out living with him.

That thought took his smile immediately. He was lonely. He wanted his own family. A wife. Children. Someone to come home to. Someone to care for, to take care of. He needed a purpose. His lifestyle had no balance. He needed someone to become his center, to anchor him. He recognized and owned every flaw he had. He worked to be a better man every day. He found, over time, it was getting more and more difficult to sustain who he was when he had no one of his own. No one to share his life with and to make him realize there was purpose to his work.

"Was Grace at any of the events, Emme?" Stefano asked.

Emmanuelle nodded. "KB Events put on nine of the fund-raisers he attended. Katie Branscomb's reputation is impeccable. Everyone tries for her first, and she's so busy, you have to book her over a year in advance. Grace worked behind the scenes at all nine, including the dinners. According to Katie, she couldn't do what she does without Grace."

Grace had been at *nine* events over the last year and half and he hadn't seen her? Why hadn't his sixth sense kicked in until last night? His radar should have gone off. At the very least, his shadow should have connected with hers. When there was a group, sometimes it was difficult to sort them out, but the sexual jolt was so strong when his shadow connected with Grace's there was no way he wouldn't have noticed.

"We can build off that," Taviano said. "You met her at one of the events and you fell for her on the spot. She was leery—after all, you have a bad reputation as a playboy, bro, so you courted the old-fashioned way out of the spotlight."

Francesca laughed. "What is old-fashioned, Taviano? Taking a woman out on a date without jumping her?"

"Jumping her?" Stefano echoed. He brought Francesca's hand to his mouth and sucked on her fingers for a long moment. "You can't say things like that, baby. It puts ideas in my head."

"As if you don't have those ideas twenty-four seven," Francesca accused, laughing, leaning toward him.

"I do," Stefano admitted. "Vittorio showed so much more restraint than I ever could have. He's a saint."

Again, his brothers and sisters laughed. The sound made Vittorio's heart a little lighter. He knew he had a long way to go with Grace, but once he was set on a task, once he made up his mind, he was relentless. He wanted Grace, he wanted to give her all the things she'd never had, and buffer her from the worst the world had to offer. He was tough and knew there was little anyone could do to hurt him, other than those in his family. He didn't want Grace to have to be like he was. She could be soft and sensitive. He'd provide the armor for her.

"I am a saint to sit here listening to this crap when I could be sitting with her," Vittorio proclaimed, sitting back in his chair. "Was she seeing anyone?" If she had been, Rosina hadn't sent him evidence or a name of a man who might be after her because she turned him down.

"Not that Rosina could find," Emme said. "If she was, it was kept very quiet."

"What about her relationship with Haydon Phillips?" Taviano asked.

Vittorio's gut tightened. "What about it? They were in a foster home together. She clearly tried to get him off drugs and to quit gambling."

"She paid his gambling debts twice, Vittorio," Taviano pointed out. "It's possible they had more of a relationship than being thrown together in a home."

Vittorio shook his head. He knew absolutely the two of them hadn't had an intimate relationship. "No way. It wasn't there."

"He locked her in the trunk of a car," Ricco said. "He took that woman, ambushed her somehow—she didn't just climb in for him—and he drove her to the club with the intention of selling her into slavery to pay his debts."

"He kept saying he deserved a two-hundred-and-fifty-thousand-dollar credit," Vittorio said. "Who in the Saldi family loans money?" He shook his head. "Let's narrow that down to Miceli's crew. Ale Sarto and Lando Gori work for Miceli. I doubt that Giuseppi would have used either of them to deliver messages or even to pick up a potential prostitute for them."

"I'm shocked Miceli used them to deliver his message," Ricco said.

"No way was Phillips going to live through that," Vittorio said. "They were there to kill him. If they wanted money from him, they wouldn't have sent Sarto and Gori. They wanted him dead because they cared more about getting Grace than they did the money."

"So, whoever loaned the money would have had to sign

off on that," Stefano concluded. "That narrows things down, doesn't it?"

There was a moment of silence. "Let's get Rosina on it," Stefano added.

"Someone who loans out large amounts of money, not penny-ante crap," Vittorio said. "It has to be someone Miceli is indebted to, owes a favor, something of that nature."

Stefano was already texting his cousin. "She'll find them, Vittorio. You know she's never missed yet."

"Who runs the girls?" Emme asked. "That's another lead right there. High-end, it sounds like. They aren't going to trade that kind of debt and put someone like Grace into a stable. She's special and they know it."

"That would be Marco Simoncini," Ricco said. "He runs all kinds of girls from street-level to very high escort girls. If you want to party, you call Marco."

"How would you know that?" Mariko asked very softly. Her large eyes were fixed on her husband's face.

"Yes, Ricco, how did you know that?" Giovanni asked.

Ricco threw a buttery pastry at his brother, who caught it before it hit him in the head. "Everyone knows Marco runs the girls for Miceli."

"I didn't know," Mariko said. She turned to Sasha. "Did you?"

"No, I wasn't informed. What about you, Francesca? Did you know?"

"No, but I'm betting Stefano knew."

"That's because almost everyone knows," Stefano said, leaning in to steal the laughter from his wife with his kiss.

"Did you know, Emme?" Mariko persisted.

"I'm afraid I did," Emmanuelle admitted, her lips twitching. "Marco is very loud about his girls. More, he tried to recruit me once. Ricco, Stefano and Vittorio paid him a visit. He quit harassing me. I didn't need them to bail me out, but they insisted it would raise too many questions to have a girl beat up one of the Saldis." She gave a little sniff.

"You could have done it, too," Vittorio said, pride in his voice. He brushed a kiss on top of her head. "Marco's ego would have insisted he try to retaliate. We would have gone to war."

Emmanuelle shook her head. "Val would have taken care of it." The moment the words left her mouth, she pressed two fingers over her lips as if she could have stopped them.

"Has anyone heard from Eloisa?" Vittorio asked, turning the attention away from his younger sister. His mother was notorious for her cold, cutting remarks. She had made things so uncomfortable for Francesca that Stefano had forbidden her to come to his home. "Does she know Francesca is pregnant?"

"No." Stefano's voice was clipped. "Francesca has to be as stress-free as possible, and we all know anytime Eloisa comes around, stress levels go through the roof. She's still banned. I fear, since she can't come at Francesca, she's going to lose her mind when she hears you're engaged to Grace Murphy—a girl raised in foster homes."

Vittorio sighed. "I should tell her face-to-face, but I need to get back to the hospital."

"You're wiped, Vittorio," Stefano said. "You need to sleep. In any case, the news has probably leaked."

"I'll tell Eloisa," Emmanuelle volunteered. "You go see your fiancée and as soon as you give the word, I'll come to meet her. We all need to look as if we've been around her quite often, so others believe you've been dating her. Others meaning the Saldis."

That was so like Emme. Vittorio squeezed her hand. "Keep me informed, whatever any of you or Rosina and Rigina uncover. The cops are going to want to keep after us, so make certain you're seen and have alibis just in case Phillips or Gori and Sarto end up dead."

Stefano gave him another one of his sharp looks but refrained from speaking. Vittorio sent him his cool smile, the one that meant he had everything under control. He'd been thrown finding Grace existed, but being with his family had settled him. His family would hopefully find Haydon before the Saldis did. They needed him alive to tell them who wanted Grace. No one was taking her from Vittorio, and Stefano and every one of his brothers and Emmanuelle knew that was a fact.

CHAPTER THREE

It was just her luck to be in the worst possible circumstances when she met the hottest man in the entire world. Grace Murphy wished the earth would just open up and swallow her, hospital bed and all. The Ferraro family certainly had a strong sense of responsibility when it came to someone getting shot in their parking lot. Even that was embarrassing, having her own foster brother try to sell her into prostitution to pay his gambling debts.

She was like everyone else, following the life of the Ferraros in magazines bought at the grocery store or flipped through at the beauty parlor. She'd always been drawn to Vittorio, finding herself reading every single thing about him. Now, here he was in person, sprawled out in a chair, more beautiful than the photographs could capture, as big as life. Bigger even, the reality of him taking up an enormous amount of space, his wide shoulders and long legs keeping her attention riveted on him.

She groaned aloud and covered her red face with one hand. He'd been there every single day. Right there. In that chair. Pacing around the room. Talking on his cell. It didn't matter what he was doing, he saw to her every need. He noticed before she did that her pain level was rising, and he took care of it. He didn't like the food they were serving her, and she was given catered, very nutritious meals for breakfast, lunch and dinner. She hadn't been able to feed herself those first few days and he had been the one to sit on the edge of her bed and feed her.

The first week after she'd been shot and operated on, there'd been so much pain she could barely breathe, and she hadn't been able to fully comprehend who he was. Mostly, she'd slept and thought she was dreaming. One of the nurses had referred to him as her fiancé and she had been confused. She'd started to correct her, but then looked beyond her to see Vittorio Ferraro hovering behind the woman.

Their eyes had locked. Had she known that eyes like his existed in real life? She'd been captivated. Spellbound. Unable to think. Those eyes had turned her brain to mush. Her heart had leapt to her throat. Grace had felt as if he was willing her not to speak, not to contradict what the nurse was saying—and she hadn't. Then the morphine had kicked in and the pain had gone enough for her to drift off.

"Grace?"

His voice. It was beautiful. Low. Soothing, yet at the same time, there was absolute command, as if he ruled the world and knew it. She'd heard that voice in the parking lot, stopping everyone, giving him the chance to act, to save her from the two men Haydon was selling her to for his debts.

Vittorio remained silent after just saying her name. She couldn't help but look at him, that tone compelled her to raise her gaze to his no matter how reluctant she was. It took her a few moments to gather the courage to meet those eyes. Deep blue, like the deepest, clearest sea. She felt as if she were drowning when she looked into his eyes.

She touched her tongue to her lips—the lips he'd personally applied lip balm to—and lifted her lashes. At once she had the strange sensation of falling, of tumbling into those dark depths, and there was no saving herself. Her heart beat wildly and, in her veins, there was a rush of heat that spread through her body like a wildfire.

"Tell me what's wrong."

She had no idea how he could make her want to tell him the truth, no matter that she wanted to hide it from him. She didn't want to admit that he was the problem, that he was that fantasy she went to bed with every night, and now he was there, larger than life, and way more than she could ever handle. She'd watched him at every charity event, sometimes nearly forgetting her job, which was to stay behind the scenes and make certain everything ran smoothly.

"Grace."

Again with the name. It sounded so different when he said it. She'd always thought her name plain. Old-fashioned. When Vittorio said it in that enthralling tone, she liked the way it sounded.

"I'm very confused," she admitted.

He remained silent, his gaze holding her captive. How could she not answer him more fully when he was looking at her so directly? When the deep, commanding way he said her name made her feel that if she didn't tell him the truth, he would be disappointed. The thought of disappointing him was worse than anything she could conceive of in that moment.

"I know I was shot in your parking lot, but you don't have to be here. You're a very busy man, but you're here every day and the nurses and doctors discuss everything with you rather than me. They think—" She broke off, unable to say it aloud. *Fiancé*. Just the thought of the word in association with him sent the heat sweeping through her again.

"There's no one more important to me than you, Grace," Vittorio answered.

More heat. He sounded so sincere. She couldn't talk, feeling as if she'd woken up in an alternate universe, maybe one of her dreams.

He came closer, looking taller and even more muscular as he approached the bed. His shoulders were very wide, his chest thick, and beneath that tightly stretched shirt, muscles went on forever. The paparazzi hadn't captured the true commanding presence of the man, and they'd photographed him thousands of times.

"Do you remember everything that happened to you leading up to this point?"

She nodded. "I think so. Haydon came by my house and asked me to go to the club with him. I said no. He acted cool, but then he told me I'd left my sweater in his car and asked me to walk out with him, which I did."

She shifted her gaze, afraid he would see she was misleading him—which she was. "When we reached the street, he went around to the back of the car. He was talking to me and I just followed him, thinking my sweater was in the trunk. He opened it, still talking, acting so casual. The next thing I know, he'd thrown me into the trunk and slammed it closed, trapping me." She'd been terrified, but a part of her had gone calm, thinking the reign of terror for her was finally over.

He reached for her hand as if he knew her heart was beating out of control at the memory. His thumb slid over her knuckles and then began to sweep back and forth lightly over the back of her hand. Each stroke felt like a caress and she felt her pulse flutter wildly. "Thank you for sharing that with me, Grace. I know it wasn't easy. You're safe now."

There was that strange rush of heat moving through her body she was coming to associate with him. He made her feel extraordinary just for answering his question. It was his voice when he complimented her, brushing over her nerve endings like black velvet.

Grace couldn't let him think everything was all right. She was misleading him, and that might make him think there was no danger. "I'm not. *You're* not. He aimed that gun at you, the person trying to save his life, not the two men he was trading me to. He's that far gone." She closed her mouth abruptly and pressed her lips together, feeling nearly faint.

That was more than she'd ever told anyone about Haydon, and she'd only blurted it out because he already knew her foster brother had wanted to kill him. How did she explain Haydon to a man like Vittorio? The differences between them were so wide, Vittorio couldn't possibly understand.

"What is it, *gattina bella*?" He brought her hand to his mouth and nibbled on her knuckles. All the while his blue eyes held hers. She loved his eyes. The way they commanded. Compelled. Once he locked on to her, she was totally captivated and couldn't look away. The connection was intense, sometimes to the point of being uncomfortable, but it was because looking into his eyes made her feel as if he saw everything about her. Knew everything about her, strengths and weaknesses.

She hesitated. As children, in a violent foster home, Haydon and she had protected each other. Then, it became very real self-preservation not to ever speak of him to anyone. Ever. For any reason. A little shiver went through her body. She wished the morphine would kick in and hopefully she'd just fall asleep, but they had been slowly decreasing the pain medications in an effort to get her out of the hospital. It was extremely hard to sleep when pain beat at her constantly.

"You have to trust someone, Grace."

Grace was desperate to look away from him. To close her eyes and slip back into sleep where she felt safe. She'd been in a cocoon for days and she wanted to remain there. Clarity brought reality and that was too much for her when she could barely move, barely take care of herself.

Silence filled the room and she detested that. Disappointment didn't show on his face, but she felt it. It was as if the very shadows connected them and she could feel his emotions. He was disappointed that she couldn't trust him. Or maybe he wasn't disappointed and she was projecting her own feelings about herself onto him.

"Haydon isn't like most people." She couldn't keep the tremor from her hand and she tried to pull it away from him, so he wouldn't feel her shaking.

She hated that she was appearing so weak in front of him. She had a demanding job, one she excelled at. She had no problems seeing to every detail and finding the right people to get things done, but her personal life was just the opposite. She was a complete mess, out of control, unable to find a way to fix it. Even when she'd taken a stand, that had backfired.

Vittorio's long fingers tightened around hers and his thumb stroked over the back of her hand as he pressed her palm over his heart. "Tell me why you're so afraid of this man."

No one knew she was afraid of Haydon. No one. Her boss thought they were close, like brother and sister. Most people thought the same thing. No one else had ever seen through her careful mask, not the social workers, foster parents or cops.

She shook her head, even as she tried to form the right words. There was no denying Vittorio when he looked at her that way. She didn't want to disappoint him, and he needed to know he was still in danger, probably more than ever now.

Vittorio didn't speak, allowing the silence to stretch on and on for so long she was afraid she might scream. She didn't mind silence, but the way those blue eyes moved over her face, the compulsion to tell him everything was so strong she nearly blurted the entire story out, but years of silence kept her strong.

"Haydon isn't like other people. He won't stop. You interfered with his plans and he won't allow that." Grace bit down hard on her lip to stop herself from speaking. She didn't dare. She warned Vittorio because he deserved to be warned, but that was as far as she ventured to take a risk.

His finger slid over her lips where her teeth had sunk. Exquisitely gentle. Almost nonexistent. "You thwarted him as well," he pointed out.

Her lips tingled. "Yes, I'm well aware." Her gaze slid away from his to look over his shoulder at the door. She tried not to think how Haydon was going to react, but she knew him better than anyone else did. She knew all the dark compulsions moving in his mind, swallowing him.

Vittorio's long fingers settled gently on her chin, turning her face so her gaze jumped back to his. "You're safe with me. There are bodyguards at the door and they're very experienced."

He was so incredibly beautiful. Everything about him. His face was sculpted perfectly, every angle and plane. His eyes were gorgeous. Absolutely gorgeous. Blue. But far more than blue—indigo was the color that came to mind. With his black lashes framing that blue, he took her breath away. She didn't want him to die and Haydon would be fixated on him now.

"We'll find him. The cops are looking. My people are looking. He doesn't have money and very few friends. Haydon will be found."

Grace shook her head. She had to tell him things she'd never told anyone if she wanted him to stay alive. They stared at each other for a long time.

His thumb swept across her chin. "I know this is difficult for you, Grace. You have to trust someone. You need to talk to me about this man. You're visibly trembling. You look frightened and I don't want you to be."

"I don't know you," she protested, but she knew she was stalling for time, trying to figure out a way to keep him safe without revealing the things she knew about Haydon Phillips.

"You know me," he countered.

A faint smile touched his mouth, and her heart reacted with a curious flutter.

"After all, I am your fiancé."

"Why does everyone think that?" She pounced on that.

"I told you in the parking lot when you were shot, but you probably don't remember. In order to make certain the doctors would talk to me, I had to be your fiancé. Our top

orthopedic surgeon removed the fragments of bone and repaired the damage, but you have a long road ahead of you.
They're giving you antibiotics to prevent any infection and
you'll have to be here a couple of weeks. You were in and
out for a few days so we're counting down past that first
week."

"Every time I wake up you're here." Grace had gotten
used to seeing him there, a fixture in her room, even when
the pain medication kept her sleepy. She looked for him
first thing now, that quick sweep of the room while she held
her breath. Then she saw him and the terror in her calmed.

"I don't want to be anywhere else. When you leave,
you're going to need care. I've got your room ready for you
and set up for physical therapy so when the doctor gives
you the okay, we'll have that in place."

"Room ready for me?" she echoed faintly.

He nodded, his eyes holding hers. "With me. At my
house. My sister, Emmanuelle, and my sister-in-law Mariko
can go to your apartment and get whatever things you want.
You can make a list."

She shook her head. "No. Absolutely not."

He got that look she detested. Disappointment. As if she
had somehow hurt him just by saying no to him. She had to
clarify. "You don't understand. No one can go to my apartment. It isn't safe, least of all for anyone you love or care
about. They're going to be in danger as well."

He stared down at her for what seemed an eternity, then
he shifted her casually. Easily. He simply slid his arms
under her body, lifted and moved her to the side of the bed
so he could sit on it fully. His arm slid around her hips. She
was half sitting, and there was a thin sheet and blanket over
her, but the heat of him nearly scorched her.

"We're back to Haydon, *il mia bellissima gattina*. Don't
you think it's time you told me why you're so afraid of him?
The thought that he might try to harm any member of my
family is . . . unsettling. I'll warn them, of course, but if we
all are targets, I need to know why."

"Because he's seriously ill. He isn't going to stop, and no one will ever catch him. You won't. The cops won't. He can find his way into someone's home and live in their attic and they never know he's there. He watches them. He watches me. He knows everything I say and do. If he knew I was talking to you about him—" She broke off, shuddering. "He does horrible things, and no one knows it was him."

"You know."

She nodded, wishing she could control the tremors running through her body. "I'm not really a coward, but he makes me feel like one." She didn't want Vittorio to think she was a weakling, although she was letting him take over her life. She told herself she didn't have many choices, she certainly couldn't go back to her apartment until Haydon was found—and she knew he wouldn't be. She was never going to be safe again, but then she hadn't been for years.

"I met him in one of the homes I was sent to. I'm not very big, so it was easy for other kids to push me around." She didn't know if she prefaced her story with that because she was ashamed she hadn't been able to fight back or that she wanted him to understand how grateful she'd been, at first, to Haydon.

He nodded, those dark brilliant blue eyes fixed on her. His thumb stroked tender caresses along her inner wrist, right over her pulse, soothing her. There was something innately gentle about him and that got to her. He radiated calm, his energy peaceful, surrounding her in a cocoon of tranquility. He made her feel safe, wrapped up in their world together, even though she knew neither one of them was.

"Grace, keep looking at me and breathe. Once you tell me, Haydon is my problem, not yours anymore. You've been carrying him far too long on your own."

Grace studied his face. Trusting him was huge. She didn't trust anyone, certainly not with what she knew about Haydon. A part of her wanted to protect Vittorio, but another part wanted to share the burden of her knowledge.

If she admitted the truth to herself, she also wanted to

please Vittorio, see that look on his face when those blue eyes lit up. She wanted to give him back something when he'd already given her so much by seeing her through the gunshot wound when so many others would have left her alone. If she'd been alone, she would have been vulnerable, and Haydon would have struck. She was terrified Vittorio really would try to hunt Haydon, and that would be such a mistake. He had to know the truth.

Vittorio didn't say another word, not prompting her one way or the other. He was patient, still stroking her wrist with the pad of his thumb, that movement hypnotic, his gaze spellbinding. She made up her mind and just blurted the truth right out.

"Haydon Phillips is a monster, one so terrifying and so invincible, no one will ever be able to stop him." She'd stated it out loud. Giving the actual fact to another human being was freeing. She felt as if she'd been breathing shallowly for a lifetime, but now she could take a deep breath and fill her lungs to capacity.

Vittorio, to her astonishment, leaned in and brushed a kiss on her temple. "He's not going to be able to ever hurt you again, Grace."

"Do you believe me?" she challenged. Most people looked at Haydon and saw an addict, someone weak. He was thin and looked used up. He was so much more.

"You know him better than anyone else. I've done some investigating and it appears that since that first foster home the two of you have been tied together in one form or another. So, yes, if you say the man is a monster, I'm inclined to believe that he is."

Relief swept through her. The first time she'd tried to tell the cops, they'd quietly investigated Haydon and come back stating there was no evidence whatsoever and he didn't come across in the least bit violent. After they left, she'd had to face Haydon's wrath. She'd never tried to convince anyone again.

"He terrifies you." Vittorio stated it as a fact.

"Because I know what he does, and worse, he knows I know."

Again, he waited. He didn't try to hurry her. If he felt impatient, it didn't show on his face, nor could she feel it in the energy surrounding her. She only felt as if he had woven some kind of a safe cocoon around her. That made it easier to share the things she knew about Haydon.

"When I first got to the foster home, Haydon already was there. The couple, Owen and Becca Mueller, had a son, Dwayne. He was a horrible boy and would shove our plates off the table when his parents weren't looking, although they knew it was him. Immediately we were beaten for it and forced to clean up the mess with his mother or father kicking and punching us. He would do nasty things, like pee in our beds, and that would earn us a trip to the 'punishment' room."

Vittorio's eyes turned dangerous. His energy did as well. She felt the difference in him immediately, although she couldn't see it on his face.

"Keep going, *bella*."

There was that low, compelling tone again. She was fairly certain he could hypnotize an entire roomful of people into doing anything he wanted them to do.

"I was terrified, and all three, Becca, Owen and Dwayne, hit and kicked us repeatedly. The longer I was there, the worse the beatings got. Haydon began stepping in, distracting them, when they were punishing me. He took horrible beatings, sometimes so bad he couldn't get up. I'd bring him water and food, but I had to sneak it to him. Dwayne suspected and would lie in wait for me, and he'd beat me in front of Haydon and taunt him. It was a pretty horrific life."

Vittorio nodded. "The social worker didn't check on you?"

She shook her head. "I think she was too overworked, and she thought they were good people. They appeared to be. I don't know if Haydon was born the way he is, or if they created him, but he is a planner and doesn't care if anyone ever knows he got his revenge, as long as he does get it."

The throbbing in her shoulder was increasing to straight-up agony. She glanced at the clock. It was getting close to the time she should take more painkillers, and she wasn't going to be able to wait if the radiating pain was anything to go by.

"Are you hurting?" Vittorio was reaching for her machine before she even answered him, but he didn't deliver the dose of morphine, just kept his hand there.

"I was trying to stretch out the time between taking doses. For some reason, it makes me feel drowsy and I want to stay alert." But she wasn't going to make it by more than a half an hour at the very most.

"There's no need for that," Vittorio said, his voice as gentle as always, but there was a note of absolute command in it. "There's no need for you to be alert, because I'm here to watch over you. The surgeon explained that you had to stay on top of the pain meds, Grace. He said there was no danger of you becoming addicted, and I know that's your greatest worry. The doctor knows what he's talking about. I promised him you'd follow his plan to the letter."

He gave her that faint smile, the one that turned her inside out. "You wouldn't want to make a liar out of me, would you?"

Grace shook her head and watched him release the dose that would take the pain away and have her floating away soon.

"Thank you, *gattina bella*, I appreciate that although you have a difficult time taking the pain meds, you do it anyway."

She was taking the pain medication because Vittorio had asked her to. Had it been anyone else she would have balked. "I'm going to fall asleep soon. I know some people have clarity and aren't in the least sleepy, but morphine makes me a little loopy."

"That's all right. When you sleep, you heal. Do you want me to lower the bed for you?"

A part of her wondered how Vittorio Ferraro knew how to lower a hospital bed. She had watched the Ferraros at countless events and read about them in magazines. They seemed like irresponsible playboys. She might lust after one of them, but she felt a little sorry for the women in their lives. Here she was, wishing she was one of those women.

"I don't need you to do that yet. I want you to understand about Haydon, so you can get your family to realize they're in real danger."

He nodded, once more taking possession of her hand. This time he brought it to his chest, pressing her palm over his heart. She was acutely aware of the play of his muscles beneath the thin material of his shirt. She took his nod as a go-ahead.

"A few days after Dwayne beat me, they found his body in a ditch about eight miles from the house. He was naked, and he'd been tortured. I overheard the cops talking with his parents and they said every bone in his body had been broken. He was only a few months older than Haydon, a big boy, like his father. Very husky and strong. You've seen Haydon. When he was a kid, he was very thin. He looked almost frail."

"He was never charged?"

"No. He never said a word to me. I tried not to be happy Dwayne wasn't there, but secretly, and I'm ashamed to admit it, I was. I didn't like the way he died, and the cops were always coming around investigating, but we were afraid to talk to them and they didn't come near us. At first, the beatings stopped and then one day Becca went after me in the kitchen, throwing dishes at me and saying she wished I was dead the way Dwayne was dead. I think that was the signal to her husband that it was okay to take out their frustration, grief and anger on the two of us."

She was shaking, remembering those days, going without food, being locked in small, confined spaces. She wasn't claustrophobic, and neither was Haydon, but it wasn't pleasant with no bathroom. Haydon made a tiny doorway at the floor on one side and they snuck each other food and water when they could.

Vittorio brought her knuckles to his mouth, pressing a kiss there, all the while his eyes on hers, holding her captive so she felt like she was falling into him. Instantly, she was distracted. Her stomach did a slow roll and a million butterflies took wing. She should have jerked her hand away, no one had ever done such a thing to her before. She couldn't have moved even if she wanted to, not when he was once again pressing her palm over his heart with his thumb rubbing caresses in a soothing, hypnotizing way, back and forth across the back of her hand. He had a way of compelling her to want to let him do anything to make him happy—and she liked him holding her hand. It made her feel as if they really did belong together and he would keep her safe from any harm.

"Keep going, *gattina*."

"One day Owen came home from work pretty drunk, and got into a terrible fight with his wife. I heard Becca screaming, and knew he'd hit her, and when I said I was going to check on her, Haydon wouldn't let me. We both heard Owen coming down the hall. Haydon opened the window for me, but he got us before we escaped. He beat Haydon so bad. I tried to stop him by hitting him with a chair. It was the only thing I could think to do. He dropped Haydon and started on me."

"This man deserves a hell all his own," Vittorio said in that same low tone that felt calm and peaceful. "I'm sorry you had to experience that kind of evil, Grace."

Something in Vittorio's eyes told her there was a lot more going on below the surface that she couldn't see, but he continued to give off that soothing energy she had come to associate with him.

"Owen was a bad man, but not evil. I've seen true evil. That's Haydon. Two weeks later, our foster father came home drunk again and Becca locked him out of the house because when he was drunk, he smacked her around. He'd been getting drunk more and more since Dwayne died. He went out to the garage to sleep in his car. They found him the next morning under the car. He was still alive, but the car had fallen on him, crushing his leg and groin. He'd lain there most of the night suffering."

"Not an accident?"

She shook her head. "The investigators said someone had put something in his drink at home that night just before he went out to the garage. They found a glass from the kitchen tipped over and there were remnants of a sleeping aid mixed with whiskey in it. Becca took sleeping pills and they thought she'd done it, but when they were talking, I looked at Haydon's face." Dread crept down her spine. She would never forget that look as long as she lived. "He did it, but there was no way to prove it. It would have been easy for him to sneak Becca's pills and get Owen a drink. The car was dropped hard to do the most damage."

"It's difficult to have much sympathy for Owen when he was beating two children who were in his care."

"I might not have had sympathy if he'd died outright, but he was made to suffer for hours. I'm not certain that can be called justice. Haydon didn't kill him outright, he wanted Owen to suffer. He chose a way to make it happen and he executed his plan. I had no proof, and who would I ever say anything to? Owen beat us all the time. Haydon defended me. I was scared of all of them and didn't know what to do."

Vittorio nodded. He laid her hand, palm down, on his thigh. That felt . . . intimate. The morphine had already kicked in and she could feel herself drifting. She didn't understand, when she'd been so leery with every other single person in the world, why she felt so connected to Vittorio. He was leagues out of her world.

"Becca told the social worker she couldn't take care of us any longer. She didn't suspect Haydon at first, but he sat around staring at her, and once when she lifted her hand to him, he said he hoped nothing happened to her the way it had her son and husband. She began watching us. I think she was afraid at that point, and she wanted to get rid of us. Before they took us out of the home, they finished conducting the investigation and she was arrested and charged with abuse. She was sentenced to two years with time served; unfortunately for me, another very kind foster mother who had been told we were close took us both in."

"I take it it didn't end there."

She shook her head. A wave of weariness swept over her. "I haven't slept much in the last few years, afraid if I closed my eyes, I'd wake up with Haydon standing over me. He does that often. I know it's to show me he can get into my apartment no matter how often I change the locks. Once he sent me a picture of Katie Branscomb, asleep in her room. He was in the picture, standing above Katie, a grin on his face. He hadn't threatened her with words, just let me know in his not-so-subtle way that Katie was in danger if I stopped doing what he wanted. So, I took out more loans, went into debt until I was stretched so thin there was no way to pay it all back. I told him so, and you saw the results."

Vittorio rubbed his chin with her fingertips. The shadow on his jaw was faint, but she could feel the bristles and for some reason she didn't understand, that feeling shot straight from her fingertips to her core. She'd never experienced anything like it. He was naturally sensual and didn't even seem to notice, while she, in her floaty state, was afraid she would blurt out how hot he was. How could she even notice when she was telling him about Haydon and the things she knew he'd done but couldn't prove?

"Other than seeing the smirk on his face when the detectives were investigating Owen's accident, was there anything else that tied him to it?"

"This doesn't tie him to it, but usually he slept in my bedroom, in front of the door. We'd taken to keeping the window open so we both could run if we had to. We knew Owen was going to retaliate because I'd hit him with a chair. It was the first night since that terrible beating that Haydon hadn't slept there."

"What happened when you were at the new foster home? Who were they?"

"Her name was Julie Vaughn. Her husband was Kyle. They were really good people. They gave us great rooms. Each of us had a laptop to use, and when Haydon asked for an iPod for music, they got him one. I thought they were awesome. Haydon often complained about them. He didn't like doing the chores and said they got us to be their slaves. They were light chores and reasonable. Things like picking up our own rooms and doing our laundry. He refused, and I would do his share of the work because I was afraid he was trying to get them to punish him in some way."

Vittorio slipped off the bed. "I'm going to lower the bed for you, *gattina bella*."

Grace was grateful that he noticed she was getting tired. She didn't like bringing attention to herself in any way. She made certain she could fade into the background and not be noticed. She'd discovered that if she kept to the shadows, the darkness helped to hide her. Haydon had colored her life in so many ways.

"In school, Haydon didn't want me to have other friends. I made a girlfriend the first day at our new school and he was furious when we were walking home, telling me I was a sellout and wanted to be popular, that after all he'd done for me, I was going to be like everyone else and ignore him. I defended myself, but the next day, my new friend didn't come to school. Someone had hung her cat in her doorway."

She pulled her hand away from Vittorio and pressed her fingers against her lip, choking for a moment, trying not to think she was responsible. "He was sweet to me all that day, walking me to my classes. I kept my head down and let him."

Vittorio fixed her pillows as if knowing she was uncomfortable. He pulled the cover up. "I know it must be hard for you to relive these things." His long fingers slipped into her hair, massaging her scalp. *"Mia bella ragazza, sei cosi coraggiosa,"* he murmured.

"What does that mean?"

"Only that you're very brave."

She didn't think of herself as brave. "I didn't know how to stop Haydon," she felt compelled to confess. "He was considered a nerd and a few members of the football team shoved him around one day in school. One by one, accidents happened to them. One nearly broke his neck because his skateboard broke in half on a dangerous hill he'd bragged to everyone he could skate. As it was, he had a broken femur and knee. It was the end of his playing football because the leg was so screwed up. Another one of the players had this car he loved more than anything. He'd saved for it for years, souped it up himself in his dad's garage. Then one day, after he shoved Haydon at school, the brakes went out. He totaled the car and was lucky he survived."

"Could these accidents have been coincidences?"

Grace shook her head and then winced when her shoulder reacted to the movement with a wave of pain. "The cops said he must've made a mistake when he installed new brakes, but this guy was a total gearhead. He wouldn't have made that sort of mistake. I tried to tell myself that, but I knew better."

"Do you want to stop and go to sleep? We can talk later."

His voice was so gentle, almost a caress of velvet stroking over her skin. Caring. Tender even. She'd never heard a voice quite like his. She should have known he would notice the way the color drained from her face when the pain hit. She hated moving, but she had to finish telling him about Haydon. If her foster brother managed to get to her, someone had to know and believe her. Vittorio Ferraro was a man everyone would listen to.

"I want you to hear this before I lose my courage," she said. His hand pressed hers to his thigh and once again, his thumb started that soothing rhythm that somehow relaxed the tension that was cramping her muscles.

"Haydon got mad at Kyle for insisting that he do his own chores when Julie told him I was doing all the laundry and cleaning his room. They had a beautiful lab that went missing. Kyle loved that dog. They looked for weeks for it. Someone found its remains in a park—it had been tortured."

"Grace, it's clear this man is fixated on you. Is it about money? Did he try to take your relationship to a romantic level?"

His voice remained the same, gentle and low, but something made her gaze jump to his when she'd been closing her eyes because her lids had suddenly gotten so heavy. Just his saying it aloud made her heart go crazy.

"He never so much as tried to kiss me, but he doesn't like anyone close to me at all. I don't go out with friends, not even Katie. She suspects I have a stalker, but I always act as if Haydon is my friend. I never let on that I'm afraid of him to anyone. That would be disastrous to them. He was angry with me for not getting another loan, and I'm certain whatever deal he was making with those men was temporary. He'd probably kill anyone who was with me. That would be like him."

"Are there other bodies? Others you have suspected he killed?"

She closed her eyes. "I've suspected, but I don't have proof. There's never anything to connect him. He lets time go by before he strikes. When he does retaliate, it's usually gruesome. I've read about three individuals killed in the same way Dwayne was, or at least similar enough that I suspected. One was my first landlord, who wouldn't allow me to have any visitors, Haydon included. The man disappeared three months after I moved out. They found his body in a freezer across town. It was quite awful. They said he'd been kept alive for hours."

"The three you know of that you suspect he killed, were all three connected to you in some way?"

She nodded. "One was a cop who gave me a ticket. Haydon was in the car and he was angry with me. He stomped on my foot on the gas pedal to scare me. He said he'd drive head-on into oncoming traffic. When the cop gave chase, he laughed and let up, so I could pull over. The cop gave me a lecture and said if I did something like that again, and he heard about it, he'd take me to jail. The cop died in a similar way to my ex-landlord. It wasn't here in Chicago. I'd moved to another city in order to get away from Haydon, but he followed me."

"And the third?"

She gave a little shudder that she knew he saw even though she tried not to let what she was saying affect her. "One of my neighbors at the apartment I lived in when I first moved back to Chicago. I accidentally bumped into him in the hall. He caught my arms and we both laughed. After that he'd always say hello. Really, that was it. But Haydon got angry with me because I wouldn't let him move in. The man, Howard Bennet, disappeared. People came knocking on my door asking if I'd seen him. Haydon was in the hallway, just lounging there with that smirk and I knew Howard was dead. They found the body about a month later. It was very gruesome." She didn't want to think about Haydon Phillips anymore. Not when she was about to go to sleep.

His fingers felt like magic in her hair. So soothing. She just wanted to close her eyes and give in to the drug, let it take her away. She turned her face into his arm and breathed in the intoxicating scent of his skin. It was a mixture of sexy sandalwood and vetiver, but so faint it was almost elusive, making her want to chase after the scent. The combination was masculine and powerful, very sensual to her. "You smell so good."

"Thank you, *bella*. I hope you always tell me what you like and don't like. You've been so incredibly brave today. I appreciate your trust and I do know it was difficult for you."

It had been hard to tell him. Very hard. She'd learned not to trust anyone, but more importantly, she knew not to get close to anyone. Vittorio was already in Haydon's sights. His family probably was as well, and she owed it to them to warn them.

"He's capable of being anywhere, Vittorio." Her words slurred a little and she knew she was going out. "Small spaces, attics. Locks can't keep him out. He can get in this room through the vents. He might be there now, listening to us."

CHAPTER FOUR

Have they found him?" Vittorio asked, pushing his hand through his hair. He was getting tired of hearing the same answer.

"Haydon Phillips is a cunning little weasel," Ricco said. "From everything we've gathered, that's the general consensus. He's gone to some little hole and is hiding. He knows he's being hunted, and we're not the only ones looking for him."

"Grace has weeks of therapy on that shoulder. The doc told me she's lucky she can use the arm. He didn't think she'd have the use of her hand at all, but she can move her fingers and that's a good sign. I'm taking her home with me, but we've got to find him."

"Is your house secure?"

Vittorio gave his brother a look. "You know me."

Ricco gave him a faint smile. "Does she?"

"She's getting to know me. We've been here a little over two weeks. I can get her laughing, keep her mind off the fact that she thinks Phillips is going to kill a member of my family. Half the time she's worried he's in the vents here. I know she tries to stay awake. The little bastard has kept her from sleeping for ages. The doctor said she has to sleep to heal."

He couldn't keep the edge out of his voice, no matter how hard he tried. He needed to be out there in the city hunting, and he also needed to be with Grace, but he couldn't be in two places at one time.

Ricco put a hand on his shoulder. "He's not going to be able to hide forever."

"She says he's patient, that he'll wait weeks or months before he strikes at someone."

Stefano turned toward them. He'd been staring out the window, and who knew what he'd been thinking, but Vittorio immediately gave his older brother his full attention, as did Ricco.

"We're not going to find him the way we usually find someone. He doesn't have a bank account, so no money trail. He doesn't rent or own. He doesn't have a car. He takes money from other people, he lives in the attics of homes or apartments and he steals cars when he wants a ride. He can become anonymous in a crowd. He's small enough to fit in vents and has no problems getting in and out of locked doors."

Vittorio massaged the back of his neck. Already he was becoming restless, everything in him urging him to get back to Grace. "We've got to hurry this meeting."

"She isn't alone," Stefano reminded. "She has a bodyguard in the room with her and two outside. Mariko and Emmanuelle will be there in a few minutes."

Having his sister and sister-in-law in the room with Grace helped. Both were shadow riders and every bit as capable as he was. They'd trained every day of their lives since they were two years old, just as he had, and they dispensed justice when their rotation came up. They did it with efficiency and without hesitation. Grace was in good hands, and yet he still had this restless feeling of urgency that just wouldn't go away.

"What do you think about Phillips?" Vittorio countered, not wanting to look too closely at the reason he was becoming so edgy. He was always centered. He'd trained himself to be that way. To always feel absolute calm.

Grace had spent two weeks in the hospital . . . suffering. The bullet had shattered her shoulder; fortunately the surgeon had been able to piece it back together, but she would always have problems. The injury was particularly painful. The surgeon had saved the arm, but it would be a long road to recovery and she would always have some pain. He detested that for her. She was definitely getting stronger and he needed to get her home before she had too much time to think about it. He'd been putting her boss, Katie Branscomb, off visiting her, saying to wait until he got her settled, but he was afraid Katie would insist on Grace going home with her.

"I think Phillips won't stop. Grace knows him better than anyone else and if she says he's likely to come after you and every member of our family, I think we'd better pay attention. I also think Grace is the only anchor he has in this world. He might punish her for not doing exactly what he wants, but he won't kill her. He can't afford to lose her and he's intelligent. A twisted killer, but a very intelligent one. The Saldis don't have a clue what they've unleashed," Stefano gave his opinion.

Ricco nodded. "Rigina and Rosina have been mapping a trail of murders that appear similar to the first one Grace knew about—Dwayne Mueller. They're scattered over a very wide range and two cities that we know of. The girls are working now to place Phillips in the kill zone at the time of the deaths. It's a tedious process, but they're tenacious. If he left any trace at all, they'll find it."

"LA cousins concluded the problem of Owen and Becca Mueller. A few days ago they were found in their New York home dead, both with broken necks," Stefano said.

The sense of urgency in Vittorio was growing, instead

of satisfaction or relief. The small conference room the hospital had lent them was two floors down from Grace's private suite. She would go home today, and he knew he could better protect her in his house. He wanted to get her there as fast as possible.

"We can't do anything about Phillips until he shows himself, and then we can get his trail. Anywhere he steps in a shadow, he'll leave a 'print' we can follow, but until then, let the investigators do their work. We're on alert and we've got extra guards on Grace." There was always a trail, skin cells, a scent, thermal imaging, parts left behind that the riders called prints. Sometimes those things proved helpful when tracking an individual, especially if they were fresh.

"Are you protecting our women?" Vittorio asked.

Stefano gave him a look that was meant to shrivel him. "Of course. Emme's difficult because she already despises having bodyguards. She knows it's mandatory for a rider, but extra guards just annoy the hell out of her."

"How is she doing?" Vittorio hated seeing his sister hurting.

"She's in love with Val," Stefano answered honestly. "I wish he wasn't a Saldi. It doesn't matter to me that he isn't a rider. I know Eloisa would have a fit, and so would the International Council, but the bottom line for me is Emme's happiness. If he weren't the heir apparent to the largest crime family in Chicago, I would have allowed the match. But as head of the family, I can't welcome the very thing we fight against into our home, nor do I want my sister anywhere near that business."

"Don't ride her too hard, Stefano," Vittorio cautioned. "Emme's hurting, and that makes her volatile. Right now, she's made the decision for herself. If we say anything negative to her, that could change."

Ricco nodded his head. "I've had to caution Taviano a few times. You might have a word with him."

Stefano sighed. "That's my fault. I always want to be her

parent instead of her brother. Giovanni is closest to her and he's worried, too. Even Francesca is concerned about Emmanuelle. But you're right, Vittorio. I'll be careful and remind Taviano this is a situation that calls for diplomacy, not our usual tactics."

There was a wash of relief that didn't alleviate the sense of urgency growing in Vittorio. "Has Sarto left the hospital? I heard he was being released soon. I know Gori was released last week."

"Sarto should have left more than a week ago," Ricco said, "but you broke his femur and he's been in traction and got an infection."

The three men exchanged smiles.

"I was pretty pissed," Vittorio admitted. "It helps to know exactly where to hit or kick them."

"Which is why Gori's arm was in traction for a while as well. The cops took him to jail with his arm in a cast." Ricco said. "We've been checking on both of them. Sarto has a police guard. Gori's in solitary and only their lawyer's been allowed to see either of them. Neither Miceli nor his sons have come near them. In fact, Miceli continues to deny he knows anything at all about what transpired."

"The two men claim they were at the club having a good time and when they left, you assaulted them in the parking lot, Vittorio," Stefano said.

Vittorio shrugged. "Did they think we wouldn't have cameras everywhere?"

"I think they were told by whoever is helping them in the club—and I've narrowed it down to three men and one woman—that they would erase the footage. Fortunately, we took it that night before anyone could get to it. Giovanni jumped all over that the minute he got there."

"We've got eyes on the Saldis, although both Giuseppi and Miceli claim they had nothing to do with this. Giuseppi wants a meet with us," Stefano added.

"When?" Vittorio would be going to that meeting.

"Next week. His wife is bad, and he asked for more time.

So, Wednesday at five o'clock in the hotel conference room. Val will be there. Miceli and his sons as well. We should be able to hear lies, but they won't know that," Stefano said.

"Are you certain?" Vittorio asked, keeping his voice low. It wasn't only Taviano who had a hot temper. "They're direct descendants from the Saldi line in Sicily. You know that it's said more than one of our women fell for a Saldi back then."

"Or was taken," Stefano said. "Never a rider."

"The possibility of other gifts is there, Stefano," Vittorio insisted. "I'm just saying we need to be cautious. Maybe they can hear lies."

"What about Emme?" Ricco asked. "Will she be at the meeting?"

"I wanted Emmanuelle to stand down, but she said she's a rider, a member of our family and she knows the Saldis better than any of us. I had to agree with her logic," Stefano answered.

"If they even smirk at her . . ." Ricco trailed off.

Vittorio looked at his brother and shook his head. "We've got to play this one cool. They might try to provoke us using Emmanuelle. If she can take the heat, so can we."

"Always the voice of reason," Stefano said. "Let's hope we listen to you."

"I've got to get back to Grace. I just have this bad feeling," Vittorio admitted. "Whenever my gut says something's wrong, it usually is."

Stefano's gaze narrowed. "You should have said something." He was already moving toward the door.

"I thought it was because I was away from her," Vittorio declared, uncaring what that admission said to his brothers. Both Ricco and Stefano were married to women they were very much in love with. They probably understood, but Vittorio had never expected to find Grace, let alone have a real shot at keeping her.

"Not likely," Ricco said as they strode through the hall toward the elevator. "I'm feeling a little uneasy myself."

Ignoring the stares and several cell phones snapping photographs of them, Stefano impatiently tapped his thigh as they waited for the doors to open. "I've texted Emme and Mariko as well as the bodyguards. They're on alert."

As they stepped into the elevator and the doors began to close, alarms began shrieking throughout the floor. Vittorio slammed his hand on the door, physically preventing it from closing. All three men bailed out, texting Emme and Mariko to make certain they were all right.

No alarms on this floor, Emme mass texted to them.

The nurses and doctors were running for one of the rooms.

"That's the room Sarto is staying in," Ricco said.

Stay alert, Vittorio commanded. Could be a distraction.

A nurse rushed from the room and vomited on the floor, a security guard not far behind her. Vittorio, Ricco and Stefano stopped abruptly in the doorway.

"You're contaminating the scene," Vittorio said, his voice pitched low, but carrying a firm command. "There's nothing any of you can do for them. Get out of there now. We'll need your names for the police."

Stefano was already calling for them.

Vittorio glanced up at the vent. It appeared to be in place, but that didn't mean Phillips hadn't crawled through the air-conditioning system. He could have entered the room any number of ways, as an orderly, a phlebotomist, even as a nurse or doctor. If that had been the case, the police officer would have checked his ID and then followed him into the room. Vittorio could make out the policeman. He was dead, his throat cut, but his body hadn't been hacked up the way that Ale Sarto's had been. The Saldi enforcer looked almost as if he'd been skinned alive. A cursory study showed his mouth taped shut and his eyes taped open.

Vittorio glanced at Stefano, who nodded. Immediately, he and Ricco jogged to the stairwell, leaving their older brother to secure the scene and handle the police. Once out of sight of anyone else, they chose shadows that would carry them straight up the stairs to the private wing where Grace's suite was. The shadow Vittorio chose was considered the proverbial greased lightning.

All three brothers wore their signature three-piece suit. Gray, pin-striped, made of a special material one of the many cousins had invented, the stripes allowing the rider to fade immediately into the shadows, making it more difficult for anyone to see them. More importantly, the suit would come apart with them when they were pulled apart, drawn into the tubes in the shadows.

The thinner, smaller tubes were hard on the body but delivered a rider to their destination much faster. Still, the rider was often disoriented when he arrived at the mouth of the tube. This shadow hit the floor and slid along the wall, connecting with several other shadows that were cast by the overhead lighting and objects in the halls.

Vittorio rode one shadow right to the entrance of Grace's hospital room. He waited in the mouth of the tube until his body felt his own again and then, looking around to make certain only his bodyguards would be able to see him emerge, he stepped out onto the floor.

Emilio, his cousin and head of security for the Ferraro riders, greeted him with a grim face. "I've got Enzo inside, Vittorio." He looked over Vittorio's shoulder and nodded at Ricco. "They're safe for the moment."

"Watch the vents," Ricco cautioned. "The bastard came right into the hospital and sliced Sarto to pieces. The door wasn't locked. Anyone could have walked right in, but Phillips took his time. He didn't seem to be worried he'd get caught. He's a cocky little son of a bitch."

"Don't trust any doctor, nurse, orderly or technician. He could be a chameleon for all we know, blending in with the hospital staff," Vittorio added, one hand on the door to Grace's room. He spread his fingers wide, as if he could physically touch her. He wasn't looking at Emilio, but rather he looked through the little window toward Grace.

She looked to be asleep. Emmanuelle was seated beside her, and her head was on the bed as if she, too, was napping.

Instant alarm skittered down Vittorio's spine. He slammed his palm hard on the door, swinging it open, shoving it all the way to the doorstop. Mariko was seated in a chair and she barely looked up as he burst into the room, Ricco on his heels.

"He's venting some kind of gas into the room," Vittorio said. "Get out of here, Enzo. Mariko. Both of you go now."

Ricco already had his wife up on her feet and was lifting her into his arms and running out of the room. Emilio caught up Emme and carried her out. Vittorio unhooked the bag of fluids from the stand, set it on Grace's lap and then she was cradled against him, her head lolling back against his chest as he rushed her out of the room. It was only then that he realized Drago and Demetrio Palagonia had waited for him to get his woman, in spite of the fact that they'd both been exposed to the gas, before they fell into step behind him.

He glanced behind him at them. Their faces were gray, but their hands were steady, weapons out, as they moved with Vittorio, Ricco and Emilio, all three carrying the women.

"We need oxygen," Vittorio called to the two nurses who manned the private suite around the clock. "Hurry."

The nurses came running.

"Little bastard," Vittorio muttered. He set Grace down on another bed inside one of the suites. "All of you need oxygen immediately." He glanced at the vent and then his brother.

"I'll take care of it," Emilio said. "Go. Get that fucking little weasel."

Vittorio had already covered Grace's mouth and nose with an oxygen mask. She wasn't unconscious, but definitely woozy. She kept bringing her good hand to her face and he was afraid she'd try to remove the mask. Mariko was holding her own mask as were the bodyguards, but

Emilio was helping Emme. Emmanuelle and Grace had been closest to the vent.

"Let's go," Ricco said.

Several nurses had responded to the call for help and Enzo, Drago and Demetrio were identifying them, not allowing any male nurses into the room. When Vittorio was certain everyone was safe, he and Ricco hurried back to Grace's hospital suite. Tomas and Cosimo Abatangelo followed them. The two were cousins and had both been shot a few months earlier, the same time Giovanni had been shot. Both were back to work, and Vittorio didn't like that already they would be pitting themselves against a madman.

Vittorio pulled the curtains in the room to darken it and then he snapped on lights. Immediately the shadows crawled up the wall to spill into the vent. He stepped into the nearest one and was instantly pulled apart, his body in fragments, molecules racing up the wall, pouring through the slivers of openings into the darkened maze of ducts.

The moment he was inside, still moving fast, although the light throwing shadows was lessening so his speed diminished somewhat, he saw the cylinder. Carbon monoxide. That explained why those across the large hospital room weren't as affected as Emme and Grace had been. He was certain the others would have headaches, but they hadn't gotten near the dose the two women sitting under the vent had. Haydon must have managed to shut down the alarm as well, or it would have been blaring.

Staying in the tube, so he wouldn't have to crawl on his hands and knees, Vittorio examined the shaft and the cylinder with the hose. Phillips had set it several feet inside the vent, most likely so it would slowly do its work without tipping anyone off. Vittorio was certain when he looked in the vent in the hospital room Sarto had been in, he'd find a similar canister.

There was no way Phillips was still in the ducts. He would have entered Sarto's room through the door, pretending to be a nurse or technician. The policeman had followed him in and Phillips had slit his throat. Sarto was groggy from the gas and probably hadn't cried out or tried to ring for help. Phillips had calmly gone about his business, torturing the enforcer, and then walked out. There would have been blood. Lots of it. He could have washed up in the bathroom and changed his clothes if he'd brought more. Phillips was a planner. He'd planned for every possibility.

Just to be safe, Vittorio flashed the specially prepared light they all carried to cast more shadows and followed the ducting all the way out. Phillips hadn't bothered to screw the vent closed at the other end, he'd just pushed it out, leaving it ajar, held by one screw. Vittorio went back through the vent to the room and then emerged just in front of Tomas.

"Where's your brother?" Cosimo demanded.

Ricco had entered the vent just as Vittorio did but had gone down to the second floor to make certain Phillips wasn't hiding in the vent gleefully watching the crime scene people process his gruesome kills, or worse, watching Grace and his family in the room opposite the suite.

"He's checking things out. He'll be back soon." Vittorio glanced at his watch. He'd give his brother a couple of minutes and then he'd go looking for him. It wasn't as if Phillips could spot Ricco, but they always preferred to look out for one another at all times.

Just as Vittorio was about to reenter the duct, Ricco emerged. He shook his head. "He's long gone, Vittorio. Let's get our women out of here. I'd like to see the bastard break into my house, or yours. He won't get three feet into a duct or the attic without us knowing."

Vittorio wanted to bring Grace home. She was alert now, although still on heavy pain medication. The surgeon said she'd need to be for a week or two more. She was managing, always trying to extend the time in between taking them, but Vittorio continued to coax her to do as the doctor advised.

Grace was sitting up in the hospital bed, the oxygen

mask still on her, when he walked into the room. Instantly, her gaze jumped to his face. She'd been anxious, he could see the worry, the alarm on her face. Her eyes shifted to Ricco, checking to make certain he was unhurt, and then she was fixed on Vittorio.

He sent her a reassuring smile and crossed to the bed, stopping briefly to drop a kiss on his sister's forehead. She looked up at him, still pale, shaking her head.

"I can't believe I fell for that," Emmanuelle said. "Gas. She even warned us he liked entering houses and living in attics. He travels through the pipes and ducts just like a rat. I got a headache and I'm not prone to them. That should have tipped me off." She sent a quick smile in Grace's direction. "I was enjoying getting to know your fiancée."

Grace gave a little groan as she pulled off the mask. "Stop calling me that. It's bad enough that the nurses do. They give me thumbs-up signs and make crazy faces behind Vittorio's back. They're all madly in love with him."

Vittorio leaned in and kissed her chin and then her temple before taking the mask out of her hand and replacing it on her face. "That was a scare we all could have done without. You took a few years off my life." He nudged her until she moved over, and he immediately sat next to her, taking her hand. "You are my fiancée, so of course my family will refer to you as such."

She pulled her hand away, took off the mask again, narrowing her eyes. "Ha. Ha. Ha. You're beginning to believe all the lies you've told everyone." She looked beyond him to his family members. They were all exchanging smiles. "It isn't funny. You know the press will have a field day, reporting Vittorio is engaged. His women friends are all in mourning right now, or plotting along with Haydon to do me in."

"I don't have any female friends," Vittorio denied, once more replacing her mask. "I have only you. And we'll be a lot friendlier once you're healed, so behave yourself. I'm looking forward to that."

He enjoyed seeing the color sweep into her face. He grinned at her, liking that she relaxed, and that even now, under these circumstances, she still could tease him. She didn't even pull her hand away when he took it again, this time bringing her fingers to his mouth.

"Detectives on their way up," Ricco warned in a low voice, looking down at the text on his phone. "Stefano has sent for Vinci. He's on the way."

Vittorio didn't pull his phone out to see the mass text Stefano sent them all. "Vinci is our lawyer, Grace." He kept his voice gentle, holding her gaze. "Let me talk to them, and just follow my lead. If they question you and you're uncomfortable, look to me and I'll handle it."

He hated watching the smile leave her eyes and her body grow tense. She'd withdrawn, the way she did when she felt vulnerable.

Grace nodded, and he moved to place himself squarely between her and the door. As he did, Art Maverick and Jason Bradshaw entered. The two detectives were well known to the Ferraros. They had started out certain the Ferraros were a crime family, just as the Saldis were, but now, having investigated them on more than one occasion, they weren't so certain.

Ricco greeted the two men, his body slightly in front of his wife. "I didn't expect to see you with all the business going down on the second floor. We called in the fact that someone tried to kill Grace and Emme with some kind of gas, but we're all safe. You have a crime scene down there."

Grace's hand jerked in his. Vittorio immediately turned his full attention on her. His thumb slid over the back of her hand and he pressed her palm tightly to his thigh. He hadn't had the chance to gently tell her what had happened to Ale Sarto. She was intelligent, and she knew that whatever had brought the police detectives to the second floor probably wasn't a coincidence with Haydon's strike at her.

"Grace and Emme need care," he said. "Perhaps we should take this into another room."

"We need to speak to Ms. Murphy," Art said.

Vittorio frowned. "You are aware she was shot and the surgery was . . . complicated. She's in pain and another attempt has been made on her life. She has to use oxygen in order to counteract the gas. This isn't a good time."

"Vittorio." Jason Bradshaw gave a little sigh. "We wouldn't bother her if it wasn't important. I believe you were on the second floor in a meeting with your brothers when the bodies were discovered. We were told Stefano cleared the crime scene and held everyone who had gone into the room. You and Ricco raced upstairs to make certain Ms. Murphy and your sister were okay. Clearly, they weren't. We have to do everything we can to catch this man."

"I can tell you Haydon Phillips is a serial killer and he's been killing for years. Unfortunately, there's no proof."

Art's gaze jumped to Grace's face. He looked like what he was, a shrewd, intelligent man capable of putting pieces of a puzzle together very fast. "I need to know everything you know." He directed his statement to Grace, deliberately bypassing Vittorio, who he knew to be immovable. "We have to stop him, Ms. Murphy, and I don't believe we can do that without your help."

Vittorio felt tremors running through Grace's body as she nodded. Her gaze clung almost desperately to his. Now she knew Haydon had killed someone on the second floor of the hospital. Not only had he attacked her, but also Emme, Mariko and their bodyguards. He'd done so in broad daylight. Very gently, Vittorio gathered her closer, shifting her body so he could keep her injured shoulder and arm away from everyone while he positioned himself between her and the detectives. He was the one to remove the mask for her, retaining possession of her hand.

"She'll need to use the oxygen after five minutes," Vittorio said. "I've texted her doctor to see if that will be problematic. If it is, she's back on it." He glanced at his younger sister to make certain she was continuing to use the oxygen.

Emme winked at him but kept her head turned away

from the two detectives. She didn't want to answer questions or talk to them. Both men were waiting for Vittorio to give them the okay to question Grace. Grace actually shifted closer to him. He knew she wasn't aware of it, but the tremors had increased.

"Someone murdered Ale Sarto, and the policeman guarding him. Sarto was tortured before he was killed. It was very ugly."

Grace tried to jerk her hand away, but Vittorio kept his fingers firmly around hers, pressing her palm into his thigh and stroking his thumb soothingly across her hand. He turned his head to look at her, letting her see he was with her. She wasn't going through it alone, the way she'd done all of her life. He was there to help her if she needed it, but anyone brave enough to step in front of a gun for a virtual stranger would help the police when she got the chance.

He held her gaze for as long as it took. He didn't care if the detectives were waiting. He cared about Grace and her state of mind. The police weren't going to find Haydon Phillips if the Ferraros couldn't, not that night. The detectives could wait until she was steady. He saw it in her eyes first. She had the beginnings of trust in him. He needed that from her. To gain the kind of absolute faith and trust he needed from her, he had to show in every way that he would always be there for her. That trust could never be in any way taken for granted or abused.

He nodded his head at her in approval the moment he saw her conquer the fear that had been so deeply ingrained in her by Haydon. Her restless fingers stopped digging into his thigh, but she pressed her palm harder into his muscle, a purely instinctive kind of reaction she didn't seem aware of.

"I've known Haydon Phillips for ten years and I've been terrified of him for most of that time. I believe he's a serial killer and that if anyone gets in his way, he hurts them. He's been doing it since he was a boy. I've tried to get away from him. When that didn't work, I tried to pretend to be his family in order to find proof. Neither worked. I know he lives in the attics of houses that belong to perfectly nice families, ones with children, and he watches them day and night. He's never been caught. He claims no one's ever suspected him and he's gone into their bedrooms and held knives to their throats, including the young children. He's eaten their food and made friends with the family pets. That's always risky for the animals."

"In what way?"

"He tortures and kills them and tends to leave them on the doorstep for the family to find."

"How would you know that?"

"He shows me photographs when I don't cooperate and pay his gambling debts."

Now her fingers did dig into his thigh. He kept his body pressed against hers, taking some of her weight. Grace was shaking hard enough that the detectives couldn't fail to see.

"I understand this must be difficult, Ms. Murphy," Art said, gentling his voice.

That surprised Vittorio. The detectives were fair men, but hard-driving when they were after answers. Grace did look fragile, her arm in its collar and cuff as well as the bracing and padded bandages around the shoulder itself. She had plates and pins in her shoulder. More than one nurse had said it was a miracle that the surgeon had managed to piece her back together. They were all worried that one wrong move could undo everything he'd done.

"I'm afraid for every single person in this room. He takes delight in taunting me that he can go after the people I care about. I've lived a fairly solitary existence in order to placate him. I'm concerned for Katie Branscomb. Once, when I refused to take out a loan to pay his gambling debts, he showed me a picture of her sleeping, with him standing over her."

Vittorio glanced over at Emme. She was dutifully using her oxygen mask, fading into the corner, staying quiet. Her phone was in her hand and she was busy texting, using lightning speed and one thumb so as not to draw any attention.

If Haydon liked to gamble, so much so that he was willing to use his one real connection to pay his debts, he wouldn't be able to stay away from it long. They could use that to find him.

"He's a drug user, too, right?" Ricco asked.

She shook her head. "He *looks* like a drug user when he wants to. People ignore him when he does that. Most people dismiss users and won't even look at them. He's got the look down to perfection. He will smoke pot, but not all that often. He doesn't want the smell on him. He told me that would ruin his living arrangements if someone actually smelled it in their home."

Vittorio had to admit he was shocked. He'd believed absolutely that Phillips was a meth addict. He shot his sister another quick look. She was already spreading the word to family members. If Phillips wasn't using, his addiction was gambling. Gambling and killing. He was probably just as obsessed with torturing and killing as he was with gambling.

"He passes himself off as a meth user," Jason muttered, frowning. "That's unusual. And smart. He blends in. He can be on the streets or in the shelters and make friends there. Street people don't often talk freely to law enforcement and he knows it. What about a ride?"

"He mostly walks or uses public transit. He steals cars when he wants to go a distance, but it isn't his preferred method because there's always the chance the car has been reported stolen. He usually takes them off a long-term parking lot if he's going to do it."

"How did he get you to go out to the car if you knew it was stolen?" Art asked in his deceptively mild voice.

Vinci Sanchez strode into the room. He wore the Ferraro three-piece suit, but his was a slate blue gray without the thin pinstripes. His tie was just a shade darker blue. "I'm sorry I'm late, gentlemen, but I had to find out how Grace, Emme and Mariko were doing. And what they should be doing." His shrewd dark brown eyes took in the room, resting briefly on Emme and the oxygen mask she was wearing. "Shouldn't Grace be using oxygen as well? That was my understanding."

When Grace frowned, clearly wondering who Vinci was and why he needed to know her medical condition, Vittorio squeezed her hand in warning.

"Thanks for coming, cousin," he greeted. "I know we shouldn't need a lawyer, but it's always nice to have one just to be safe."

Grace ran events that cost hundreds of thousands of dollars. She was intelligent and quick, she couldn't fail to perceive his warning. He wanted her to be very cautious in what she said to the cops. Cooperative, but cautious. He didn't want Art and Jason to consider for one moment that she was anything other than Haydon's victim.

"Grace was just telling us how Phillips lured her to his car even though she knew it was stolen," Art said helpfully.

Vinci frowned. "That sounds like a question designed to entrap my client."

"Since when did Grace Murphy become your client, Sanchez?" Jason asked.

"She's family. Every family member is my client. Grace, perhaps you should use that oxygen mask."

She shook her head. "I want to help them catch him if it's at all possible. I had refused to take out another loan. I have three already outstanding major debts and I told him that. He acted like he understood, but I knew he would do something. I tried to explain it was a matter of economics, I *couldn't* take out another loan. I was already in over my head. He told me that I'd left my sweater at a venue and he'd grabbed it. My sweater had been missing for a couple of weeks and just to freak me out, Haydon sometimes showed up at the KB events. He asked me to walk out to his car with him."

"Did it occur to you that you could be in danger?"

"I was always in danger. Always. I felt every minute of the day that I was walking a tightrope and any moment I was going to fall. Part of me just wanted it over." She looked at Vittorio and there was a plea for understanding as well as definite shame.

"*Il mia bellissima gattina.*" Vittorio kept his voice low as he turned her hand over and brought it to his mouth, so he could press a kiss into the center of her palm. "You are very brave. Very few people could have held up all those years of living in terror."

Her gaze clung to his for a moment as if drawing strength from him and he hoped she would. He wanted to be her strength. He couldn't imagine growing up knowing the boy who had protected you was a serial killer.

"I didn't see a way out. Once, a long time ago, I had told a cop I was certain Haydon had had something to do with a death. The cop all but laughed at me and implied I was jealous because he was seeing another girl. That didn't go over so well with Haydon." A shiver went through her. "I had to have proof and I never got it. He never once admitted to doing anything wrong."

She looked Art straight in the eyes. "I thought killers liked to brag. That's the way they're portrayed in the movies. He never did. He would throw out scary lines, like it would be terrible if anything happened to you, or to them or to that dog, but he never said anything that I could record or admit anything that would help me convince the police he was guilty. I wouldn't have even been able to tell them where to find him."

Vittorio could see she was just about done. The pain meds were wearing off and she was struggling a little with breathing, although he thought that was more emotional than because she'd been exposed to too much gas. They'd gotten there quickly. Phillips had started the gas and then when the alarms went off, he must have taken off and left the hospital. Vinci had twice given Vittorio the signal to stop Grace from saying anything more. His cousin wanted time to talk to her first and go through everything that she could say and caution her how to say it.

"Grace needs to rest now." He turned on the oxygen machine and fit the mask over her mouth and nose. "She's going home today."

Art's eyebrow shot up. "To her apartment?"

"Of course not. She's coming home with me," Vittorio said. "All along we were planning to move in together eventually. This just sped up the process. We knew we couldn't keep our relationship out of the tabloids forever, but we liked having privacy." Again, he curled his fingers around her wrist and brought her knuckles to his mouth, distracting the two detectives. "Dr. Arnold is adamant that she not move around too much, although later she'll need aggressive physical therapy. He wants another week before she gets active, which means it will be difficult for her to answer more questions at the police station, but you're welcome to come to my home."

"That's a good thing, Vittorio, because the killer left behind a photograph of you. He dropped it right in the middle of what was left of Ale Sarto's chest."

Grace gasped, a sound much like a hurt animal might make escaping. Vittorio stood up and when he did, Ricco did as well. Every bodyguard was already on their feet.

"That was unnecessary," Vittorio said, "and just lost you all cooperation. You can talk through Vinci. We'd like you to leave now. This conversation is over."

Art hesitated, but Vittorio refused to look away. It was a bullshit move and the detective knew it. Jason went through the door first and Art followed him, leaving him with a very distraught Grace.

CHAPTER FIVE

"This conversation is over."

Vittorio had said it decisively, in that same low tone, but it carried command, so much so that the detectives had left, and Grace didn't dare bring the subject up. His lawyer had followed the police detectives out and the next thing she knew, the surgeon, Dr. Arnold, signed her release papers and talked with Vittorio about her care. Then she was wheeled out, surrounded by the Ferraro family and bodyguards. She heard cameras flashing and people calling out as they made their way to the waiting car, but in the middle of the moving group, protected from everything, she didn't see much.

Grace looked over at Vittorio. She sat right where he'd put her, on the cool leather seat of a very expensive car and somehow, she'd just let him take her over. She knew exactly what that photograph pinned to a dead man's chest meant—it was a warning to her.

"Mr. Ferraro." She started with his name. She had to take charge of her life. Her mind still felt a little woozy, and her shoulder hurt beyond anything she'd ever felt before. The way they had immobilized her shoulder and arm made her feel awkward and clunky, almost frozen and unable to move, making it difficult to think properly. "We have to discuss what I'm going to do." She poured firmness into her tone, even though it was an effort and she would have preferred to let herself float away. "And we have to talk about Haydon and what that photograph means."

Grace forced herself to look up at him. Meeting his eyes was a mistake and she knew it the moment she looked into that deep indigo blue. Liquid heat, so that she fell in and drowned there. There was no saving herself. He smiled, his lips curving, revealing his perfect white teeth. That focus, making her feel as if she were the only woman in the entire world, was heady, especially when she looked a complete mess. For a moment her mind went blank and she could only stare at him.

Where was her sharp intellect? She relied on her brain. She could think fast and was good at details. When Vittorio was around, the only details she could remember were how his smile was so beautiful and how the sound of his voice was so gentle and yet compelling. She was going to have to take charge of her life and that meant getting her brain going from meltdown to working. She dreaded having to be in charge again. She would much prefer lying on cool sheets, closing her eyes and willing the pain in her shoulder to let up even if it was for just a few minutes.

"What is it, *bella*?"

His voice had a way of whispering over her like a caress. She wrapped herself in the sound of it and forced herself to do the right thing even though it would have been so much easier to let someone care for her.

"Haydon threatened you."

"Yes, he did." He smiled down at her. "We expected that. Maybe not this soon, but you did say he doesn't like anyone close to you. Our engagement has been big news. The uproar hasn't settled down these last two weeks, mostly because my beautiful fiancée is in the hospital. I imagine with me staying right by your side, he's not so happy."

"Please take him seriously."

"Why would you think that I don't?"

"You're smiling at me." He had a gorgeous smile and it was distracting, even in the face of trying to warn him about Haydon. What was even more distracting was the way his fingers were once again closed around hers and that thumb of his was sliding over her inner wrist, wreaking havoc with her ability to think clearly.

"It's nearly impossible to look at you and not smile, Grace."

She sighed and tried to sit up straighter although she didn't pull her hand away as she should have. The instant she did, pain sliced through her body, radiating outward from her shoulder. She gave a sharp gasp and froze.

At once his eyes darkened and every hint of his white teeth disappeared. "Didn't you hear the doctor say you couldn't make any sudden movements? He wants you as still as possible for the next week."

"I forgot." It was a lame excuse as excuses went, but it was the truth. She knew Dr. Arnold had insisted on an x-ray before she left the hospital. She had the feeling that he would have been happy to lock her up in a tiny room where she couldn't move or see the light of day for the next few weeks. Fortunately, Vittorio had insisted she go home with him.

"Here's what we're going to do for the next few days, *gattina bella*. You're going to let me take care of you while you get better and you're not going to worry about Haydon Phillips, the police or anything else."

"That sounds like you're taking over my life. I can't just let you make all the decisions for me."

"Why not? Would that be so bad?" His low, velvety voice stroked over her skin. "I've been making the decisions for the last two weeks."

That was true. Someone had to have made a lot of decisions for her. She was fairly certain she wouldn't have an arm if it hadn't been for Vittorio. Would it be so terrible to let him take over for another week while she rested? The idea was very tempting. Still, there was the matter of Haydon Phillips.

She steeled herself to do the right thing. "You know you're not really my fiancé. You don't have any responsibility to me at all. In fact, you've done more than anyone else would have done under the same circumstances, and I appreciate it more than you can possibly know. I can't let this continue no matter how much I want it to. Haydon Phillips will kill you if I stay with you."

"Grace, you aren't thinking straight. I've been with you for two weeks. I've rarely left your side. He's going to come after me anyway, whether you're with me or not. Am I right about that?"

His deep blue eyes looked directly into hers and she couldn't look away. She nodded, because it was the truth. Her heart started beating faster for no reason at all other than whenever she looked at him like this, she felt almost as if she belonged to him. For a woman who had been alone her entire life, isolated and afraid, feeling that way was shocking, frightening and exhilarating all mixed together.

"Then, *la mia ragazza molto coraggiosa*, be brave a little longer and give me your trust. My home is a fortress. He is welcome to try for me there, but he won't succeed. Let me have the privilege of taking care of you until you're well enough to take care of yourself."

"I don't want anything to happen to you." She blurted it out, terrified she was going to give in. To let the prince take her to his castle like some absurd fairy tale.

"Nothing will happen to me."

He absolutely looked invincible.

"I don't know you."

He bent his head and gently brushed a kiss across her forehead. "You know me, *gattina*, you're just conditioned to think you can't trust anyone. He did that to you. Don't let him interfere with us. You have the right to live your life, Grace. Don't let him take that away from you any more than he's already done. You're safe with me. I give you my word, and a Ferraro never goes back on his word. Keep trusting me. I swear you won't regret it."

Her wild imagination immediately interpreted his statement as him claiming her, making her his, letting her know no matter what, he would stand for her. A million butterflies had taken wing in her stomach at the touch of his lips on her skin in spite of the pain threatening to swamp her. He could do that. Make her forget, even if it was just for a few seconds. She couldn't stop the slow nod of assent. Relief swept through her and she put her head back against the seat and closed her eyes. She didn't have to think anymore.

His hand went to her scalp, his strong fingers doing a slow massage that somehow kept the throbbing pain at bay enough that she could tolerate the rest of the ride without wanting to be sick. Neither said anything more until she felt the car slow.

Opening her eyes, she saw the vehicle was going down what was obviously a thousand-foot driveway with woods on either side. She started to sit up straighter to get a better view. She'd heard of places like this one along Lake Michigan, but she'd never actually seen one of the beautiful wooded estates. The moment she moved, wrenching pain radiated from her shoulder throughout her body. Her stomach reacted with a frightening lurch and she couldn't quite suppress the sound that was torn from her throat in spite of her every effort not to cry out.

Vittorio immediately caught her body and steadied her. "You can't move around yet, Grace. Dr. Arnold was very clear that the car ride had to be smooth. No jarring you. That means when you shift positions, you have to take it very slow. Let me know ahead of time so I can help you."

She bit down on her lip and struggled not to cry. She refused to be a baby in front of him. She was exhausted and wanted to lie down. More, she wanted the pain to stop, just for a few minutes, just long enough to allow her to catch her breath.

"It looks so beautiful, Mr. . . ." She hesitated. She was unsure what to call him. "Mr. Ferraro" sounded a little formal for being engaged—even when the engagement was pure fiction.

"Vittorio," he supplied, his hand moving to the nape of her neck, massaging slowly to help ease the tension from her. "It isn't that difficult to say my name, is it, *gattina*?" Amusement spilled over from his laughing eyes to his voice. "I've been waiting to hear the way my name sounds when you say it."

She didn't understand how he could look and sound and even *smell* so sexy and still, somehow, make her feel beautiful. Desirable. How did he do that when she was such a mess?

"The property looks so beautiful, Vittorio. I wanted to see it better."

He smiled down at her and once again leaned in to brush a kiss along her temple. "Saying my name wasn't that hard, was it?"

The car had come to a halt, but she was caught in his eyes, staring up at him, feeling as if the world around her was spinning and he was the calm center. "A little," she admitted truthfully. "I feel like I know you, but the reality is . . ." Again she trailed off. The reality was he'd been her fantasy man for so long, she felt like she was caught in a bizarre dream. Between the painkillers and her overactive imagination, she was a little afraid of what she might blurt out.

His smile twisted her insides into knots of anticipation. She loved to see that smile, the way it transformed his face from rugged, dangerous, very masculine beauty to something much softer and approachable. She could pretend he was hers alone and that look was reserved for her. Still, she knew the difference between fantasy and reality and she wasn't going to be so ridiculous as to believe in something not real. In the meantime, she was going to keep pretending.

"Don't move, Grace. Let me come around and get you. I'll describe the house and property to you, if you'd like."

He slid across the seat, putting distance between them

as one of the bodyguards she recognized—Emilio— opened the door for him. She was familiar with quite a few of the Ferraro bodyguards because they accompanied each of the Ferraros to the fund-raisers KB Events put on for their clients. The names were always on the lists and their faces became familiar out of necessity.

The moment Vittorio slid across the seat to the door, she felt unsteady and alone. Once again, the pain in her shoulder and arm was overwhelming, as if somehow his mere closeness had taken some of the agony from her. She watched him go around the hood and then he was opening her door and bending in, those incredible eyes of his moving over her face, assessing how bad the pain was just from the ride to his home.

"I'm so grateful to be out of the hospital," she assured him, wanting to take some of the worry from his eyes.

"You don't have to pretend everything is all right with me, Grace."

Vittorio very gently unsnapped her seat belt. She tried not to feel like a child, wanting him to see her as a woman, not a broken thing that he had to take care of. She inhaled his scent, all that alluring woods and spice that shouted pure power and danger. Grace pressed her lips together to keep from blurting out again how good he smelled. Instead, she took another deep breath, wanting to concentrate on him and how good it felt to be cared for when she knew the lift out of the car was going to be excruciatingly painful.

"Don't tense up, *bella*. Let me do the work. Just slide your arm around my neck and I'll bring you out. We don't want your shoulder jarred at all. Doc said he stabilized it very well, but you weren't to move it yet."

"I can't believe you call him Doc." She had to say something. Anything. She didn't want to feel what was coming.

"Look at me."

He waited until she did, his arm around her back, the other arm under her legs, his face very close to hers. That close he looked . . . intimidating. Reassuring.

"Breathe, *gattina*. I'm not going to hurt you."

It was almost automatic to follow his order. She was used to trusting him when she didn't trust anyone else, and she didn't even know how she got that way. The moment he told her to breathe, to relax, her body was already doing it. Tension eased from every muscle and air filled her lungs and exited. His smile sent familiar heat swirling through her bloodstream. As a reward, she thought it was an excellent one.

He slid her out of the car as if she were the most delicate piece of porcelain there was. She was out and blinking up at the clear blue sky before she realized he'd moved her. She'd been lost in his smile. In his eyes. The shadow on his jaw, all that delicious dark stubble she was tempted to touch.

Grace hadn't thought it was possible to move from the car to the outside without jarring her shoulder, but somehow, Vittorio managed to do it. He cradled her against his chest, turning her so she could see the house. She knew her mouth dropped open and she wasn't even embarrassed.

The exterior of the structure was blue-gray stone. A New England–style two-story house with a rounded turret that gave it the feeling of a castle—at least to her. It was a sprawling mansion complete with a five-car garage.

"You live here?" Her voice came out a squeak. "Alone?" Anyone would get lost in that house.

"I do. I like privacy and peace. This house has both."

"It's massive."

"I have a staff."

"A staff?" she echoed faintly, her fingers involuntarily curling around the nape of his neck. They were moving closer to the front entrance, where a very ornate door drew the eye. The car had driven up the circular drive in front of the house to allow Vittorio to get close to the door. She could see it looming up in front of them and she suddenly had the desire to leap out of his arms and make a run for it.

"What's wrong?" He stopped moving instantly. "Grace? Talk to me."

The rounded turret was to their left and he began walking that way, taking her into a private patio space that was large enough to have not one, but two double glass doors separated by several feet. In the center of that space set into the blue-gray stone was a very large shield carved out of wood. Before she could get a good look at the shield, he took her to one of the chairs set up for an intimate conversation. He sank down onto a wide glider facing the forest.

The sounds of birds and water reached her. The wind rustled the leaves on the trees and turned them into a silvery dance. She was acutely aware she was out of her depth here, but how did she say that to someone who was being so wonderful to her?

"Grace, talk to me. Something is upsetting you. If you don't tell me what it is, I can't fix it. Look at me, *gattina*."

She both loved and detested that command. It didn't matter that he spoke in a low, gentle tone, it was definitely a demand and one she couldn't seem to resist. She also knew that once she looked into his eyes, where all that liquid blue was, she would be lost.

"If I do, you're going to get your way." She made a small attempt to save herself. She could fall hard for Vittorio Ferraro and that would shatter her heart. Probably her soul as well.

"Most likely, but is that so bad? What's the worst that can happen? You look at me and tell me what is upsetting you and I fix it. That can't possibly be so bad."

"That's what's bad, Vittorio. I don't belong here. I wouldn't know what to do in a house like this. It's intimidating."

There was a small silence and her gaze jumped to his. He studied her face with eyes that seemed to see everything, see right into her, every fear she had. "Houses are just that, Grace. A place to live. This one appealed to me and I think, if you give it a chance, you'll like it."

Was she seeing hurt in his eyes? That was the last thing she wanted. "It isn't a matter of liking it, Vittorio. It's beautiful." It wasn't the house and they both knew it. She was used to working with wealthy clients and staff.

He studied her face and she had the urge to bury it against his shoulder, but she refused to be a coward.

"Am I intimidating to you?"

Was he? She nodded slowly.

"Because of who I am? My money? This house? What is it?"

That was a good question. A fair one. She wasn't going to answer fast, he deserved better than that. It was difficult to think when her shoulder throbbed and burned, radiating pain throughout her body, but she was determined to think the questions through. Was she intimidated by his money? No. She was used to putting together fund-raisers, and men and women running in Vittorio's circles were the clients her company targeted. She catered to them, designed food, drink and themes around their particular likes and dislikes.

"Not your money." She was decisive. "I don't even think that much about it. When it does enter my head, I just dismiss it because you can't help what you have and I'm not in that category and never will be. It doesn't matter." Her world would never be about money. "I might get lost in the house, but it's beautiful."

"And intimidating. You used that word. So, it's me. You find me intimidating."

She nodded. "Doesn't everyone?"

He gave her a small smile. "Is it so bad to be a little intimidated by me?"

"I feel off-balance."

"It could be just the hardware in your shoulder."

She blinked. It took a minute to register what he'd said, and she couldn't help laughing. Real laughter. One minute she'd been afraid to go inside, and now the strange tension was gone and she was looking forward to seeing the interior, even though it honestly felt as if she was giving herself to him.

"How do you do that? You make everything okay so easily . . ." She stumbled over saying his name.

"Vittorio," he said firmly.

She made a face at him. "You're always 'Mr. Ferraro' on the guest list." It took effort not to wince when her shoulder was throbbing.

He brushed his mouth against her temple. "You're my guest this time and I refuse to call you Ms. Murphy."

The touch of his lips set her heart stuttering. "I would hope not. I much prefer Grace." Or whatever he called her in Italian. That rolled off his tongue all sexy. Like a caress.

He stood, except it was more like he flowed to his feet, not a single jarring move and with her in his arms. Lifting her with him was effortless. "Let's go in. You need to rest."

The inside of the house was every bit as breathtaking as the outside. She looked up at the cathedral ceilings and gleaming floors.

"There's a very large master bedroom suite," he informed her. "And seven bedrooms, so plenty of space for a family and guests. I'm putting you in the guest room downstairs so there won't be the necessity of climbing up and down stairs, although there is a lift."

"Of course there is," she said faintly, looking around. Wide-open spaces, a stone fireplace that was enormous but fit with the size of the house. She wanted to see the house, but she wanted to lie down and rest. The pain in her shoulder was difficult to ignore.

"Nine thousand square feet of house, plus a temperature-controlled garage. The pool is heated, of course, and the views of the lake are outstanding. I purchased the properties on either side of this one, so we have complete privacy, and the staff have homes they can live in as well."

She might have to take it back that his money didn't intimidate her. He said it all so casually, as if everyone could afford to buy multimillion-dollar properties. The problem was, she was at her limit. If he didn't get her somewhere she could lie down and take more pain meds, she was going to start vomiting all over his beautiful house.

"Vittorio." That was all she could get out before she had to clamp her lips together.

He took one look at her pale face, the sweat breaking out—so attractive—and picked up the pace, using long strides to take her down a very wide hall to a room at the end. She managed to look around as he placed her on the side of the bed.

Her bedroom was huge, glass on one wall, giving her an incredible view of the lake. She caught a glimpse of the dazzling blue as the sun danced off the surface when Vittorio lowered her to the bed. All she wanted to do was lie down, but she realized immediately she was in trouble. She looked up at him a little helplessly, her tongue touching her upper lip.

"I really need to go to the bathroom." She had no idea why it was so embarrassing to admit it. Everyone had to use a bathroom, but it wasn't a glamourous function. Admitting it to the sexiest man she'd ever met just added to her growing misery.

"I should have thought of that," he said immediately and lifted her again.

Grace slid her arm around his neck, her mind racing frantically. She was dressed in a skirt, and a top with the sleeve cut out of it. There had been nothing easy about getting into the top or skirt and she didn't want to ever have to take them off. Still, going to the bathroom wasn't going to be easy, either, and she hadn't done it yet on her own.

Vittorio set her down right in front of the toilet and she found she couldn't look at him, her face turning a particularly unattractive shade of red. He bunched her skirt in one hand and pushed it into her fist. "Stand still and wait for me to help. I don't want you to jar your shoulder. You're about done in."

"You can't help me."

He was already crouched down in front of her, his hands hooking into the waistband of her panties. His eyes met hers and once again, her stomach did a peculiar flip. "Someone has to, and I'm all you've got. I like helping you, Grace. It's a privilege. This is just part of life. You shouldn't feel embarrassed."

"It isn't very sexy," she groused before she could stop herself. If she'd had any choice at all she would have insisted on doing it herself, but she knew she'd fall on her face. She had to lie down as soon as possible and she just wanted this over.

He slid her panties down, and then stood to help her sit. "There isn't much about you that isn't sexy, *bella*, but I understand what you're saying." He walked away from her, leaving her in the room with the toilet, but with the door open. The rest of the bathroom was enormous, so much so that she was fairly certain her entire apartment could fit into it. She'd glimpsed a double sink, all gleaming marble with gold faucets.

She didn't have any choice. If she'd been thinking about it, she would have protested coming to his home, but she was just so grateful someone else had taken over and she didn't have to think too much about anything. This was a huge lesson. She tried not to cry, because she knew it had been a long, terrible day with the revelations about Haydon and the things he'd done. The fact that he was crawling around in the hospital vents, which she knew might happen, made her uneasy for Vittorio's family. If Haydon could get into the hospital, why couldn't he get into their homes?

She managed to stand unsteadily, swaying, feeling as if she might fall over at any moment, but wiping was disastrous until she figured out how to tuck her skirt under her arm while she took care of business. How did people do this when they didn't have help? If she'd gone home to her apartment, she would have been in a real mess. She needed to be grateful, not worried about her dignity.

"You ready, *il mia gattina*?"

"Yes. I just have to wash my hands. Hand. Whatever."

"You look exhausted. I'm sorry it was such a long drive. I was afraid if I took you in the helicopter it would be too jarring when it set down."

"You have a helicopter?"

"Yes, of course. I have to get places fast at times. We all have one close for transport." He lifted her and carried her through to the twin sinks, so she could wash her hand. The other was cuffed out of the way, holding her arm stable. She knew he couldn't fail to feel her body trembling. Every movement was jarring now, no matter how careful and smooth he was. She clenched her teeth together to keep from making a sound.

"Don't do that, Grace. When you're hurting, you need to tell me. I'd like you to make an effort to share what you're feeling, good or bad, with me. I'll do the same. If we're honest with each other in our communication this will work for us." He set her on the bed and went down on one knee to remove her shoes.

"I'd be the biggest whiner in the history of mankind."

"To tell me the honest truth about what you need?" His eyes met hers. "I don't think so. I think that's called communication. I'm asking you to try. For me. That's what I need from you. Honesty."

"I thought you'd have staff, a housekeeper, someone who would do this while you worked." Tiny beads of sweat formed on her forehead and trickled down her chest. She wanted to close her eyes and just go to sleep, but the pain was swamping her to the point there was a roaring in her ears and chaos beginning in her mind.

"Would you prefer them to me?"

There it was was again, that hurt in his eyes. Maybe hurt. Something. Sadness. That was it. She detested that look. He shouldn't ever feel unhappy. It was more than unhappy. Desolate, as if he was completely alone and she'd taken his last joy from him. It wasn't the truth anyway. Of course she would prefer him to help her. If it meant so much to him, who cared about her dignity? What was she thinking? That he'd find her sexy and want to spend the rest of his life with her? Now she was believing the fiancé lie.

She took a breath and shook her head. "No, Vittorio. I just hate to be a bother to you. I'm certain you have more important things to do than to carry me to the bathroom." She tried to make her statement sound a little humorous, but her voice was too strained.

"Believe me, helping you is the most important thing to me right now."

He shook a pill from a bottle and handed it to her and then held out a cool bottle of water that was already sitting on the nightstand. It had beads of condensation on it, which meant someone else was in the house. She shivered and glanced up to look at the vents piping in the air-conditioning.

"He can't get in here," Vittorio assured. "We have all sorts of alarms he wouldn't have a clue about. Just to be safe, I had my men go through every vent and add more precautions. You need to lie down. Let's get this skirt off."

Her first fleeting thought was to protest, but she was too tired, and the skirt was heavy. Everything felt heavy. She just wanted to lie down. The faster she managed to do that, the better the chances to go to sleep. She pressed her feet to the mattress and lifted her hips, so he could slide the skirt off her, leaving her in the semi-sheer stretch lace low-rise boy short underwear his sister had brought for her. She had them in every color. They were the only panties she had with her. The back rose up to show off her cheeks and there were little laces threaded through the material right at the seam of her cheeks, giving them a corset effect and showing off a lot of her bottom.

She didn't even blush. She couldn't. He had pulled back the covers to reveal ivory sheets. She slid both legs between the cool sheets and let him help her lie back. The shifting of her body from upright to prone had black edges pouring around the light so she was afraid she might actually faint. It felt like it. Dizziness swamped her and without thinking she reached for him to steady her. An anchor. She was already beginning to think of him like that.

His hand turned to catch hers, strong fingers closing over her entire hand, enveloping it, and then his thumb was there, back to sliding caresses over her skin. She concentrated on the way the movement made her feel, letting it soothe her, letting it chase away the dizziness.

"Thank you, Vittorio."

"You're very welcome, Grace. I've had an intercom installed. You just press this button." He put what appeared to be a remote onto the mattress beside her hand. "If you need me for any reason, I'll be here immediately."

She nodded, but she didn't want him to leave. Her body was already adjusting to the position, so the brutal pain was easing enough that she knew she could sleep if she wasn't so programmed to fear Haydon could find her and hurt her. She looked up again at the vents. They were up along the high ceilings and down along the floor. Everywhere. He had too many ways in. She told herself not to be a baby or a bother, but . . .

"I'm going to stay here, Grace," Vittorio assured suddenly. "I won't leave while you're asleep. He's not going to get past my guards, and he won't get past me. He can't gas us without setting off alarms, and the alarms have battery backups, so he can't disable the system. You're safe here. I'm not leaving you, *bella*, so close your eyes for me and go to sleep."

She felt the whisper of his fingers slide over her eyes, and then along her temples and back to her eyes. Vittorio made it easy to feel safe with him. She didn't fully understand why, when she hadn't allowed anyone close to her since she was a child, she trusted Vittorio Ferraro. It was a strange choice, but he made her feel safe, when no one else ever had. She let her lashes sweep down and drifted away on a sea of pain but dreaming of a man who stood in front of her, refusing to allow Haydon Phillips to terrify her anymore.

Grace woke choking in the dark, fighting, pinned down, trying to kick her way free. Her legs were tangled in the sheets. Her body was drenched in sweat, so much so that her hair was clinging to her head in a damp mess. Her heart pounded wildly, and her lungs refused to work properly. She heard sobbing and knew she was the one crying, but she was so disconnected from it that she couldn't find a way to stop.

"Grace, you're okay. I'm right here."

The voice came out of the darkness. Low. Gentle. Calm. She barely heard over the roar of her blood in her ears. Still, the sound caught at her and she clung to it like an anchor in a storm.

"Open your eyes for me, *gattina*. I'm right here with you. I'm going to put my hand on your shoulder. I want you to feel my touch, know it's me."

There was no mistaking Vittorio's voice or his touch. His voice was like velvet, wiping away every bad memory. The sound filled those places inside her that were empty and frightened, a child cowering in her room, waiting for the demon to destroy her. It seemed as if Haydon had always been there, crouched like an evil entity, ready to rip her to pieces. Vittorio had found a way to push that relentless fear she'd been conditioned to feel into the background.

His hand moved lightly on her good shoulder, and at once she felt his calm spread through the panic gripping her. She fought the sensation of choking and struggled to take a breath, to allow his quiet composure to calm her. The pads of his fingers traced down her cheeks and then brushed at the tears there.

"He's not here, Grace. I am. He can't get to you." He snapped on a low light, one that didn't hurt her eyes, but allowed her to see around the room. "I want you to look at me, *bella*. Really see me. I don't want you to have any illusions about who I am."

Her gaze darted fearfully to every corner, then to the vents before coming to rest on Vittorio's face. It was a strong face and it held masculine beauty, as if a sculptor had carved his finest work. She made herself really study his face, get past the beauty to see what was really Vittorio, the man. There was the stamp of ruthlessness. Danger. Power. He looked invincible. Implacable. So many things that could be negative. She could also see his protective streak. His caring. His sense of responsibility. Vittorio Ferraro was a man of mystery, but she was beginning to think of him as hers. She probably should have been afraid of him, but he brought her such a sense of well-being that fearing him was impossible.

"I'm going to get these sheets off of you and move you to the chair."

He had a tone that indicated he was in complete charge and could be relied on to solve any problem. She knew, because in her business, that was the role she played—problem solver—and she was very good at it. She found it was especially tempting to be able to just not think, to let him do it for her. Her mind was in chaos and she just wanted to be wrapped up in his protection, just for a little while, until she gained her strength and will to fight back.

Vittorio pulled the sheets off her, unwinding them from her legs and stripping the top sheet from the bed. He slid her off the mattress, lifting her easily so that she was cradled against his chest.

"I need a shower."

"You're fine. We'll take care of that tomorrow morning."

"You're not showering with me." She was a little shocked at herself. The image of him naked in the shower with her was . . . intriguing.

His laughter was low and carried sensual undertones that seemed to slide under her skin to wreak havoc with her nerve endings.

"As much as the thought is tempting, I'll wait until you're fully healed."

She should have laughed it off, but she found her gaze meeting his. "Are we going to shower together?"

"Yes, Grace. We will definitely be showering together."

Her heart thudded. "We're not really engaged, Vittorio."

"Yes, we *are* really engaged, but we wouldn't have to be to shower together, my little innocent. Since we are, you don't have to look so shocked."

"Why do you insist on saying we're engaged?"

"Because I intend to marry you."

"Why?"

He set her in a very comfortable chair that was right in front of the gas fireplace built into the wall. "Because the moment I saw you, I knew you were the one I'd been searching for. I've been all over the world, met all kinds of women, and I know you're right for me."

She watched him strip the bed and remake it with clean sheets. He did it with sure hands, as if he'd been doing such a thing for years when she knew he had people who must have made his beds for him from the time he was born.

"I don't know you."

"You have great instincts, Grace. What do your instincts tell you?"

"That you're very sexy and I'm very vulnerable right now."

He glanced up from changing the pillowcases. "At least you think I'm sexy. That's a start. Just give us a little time before you make up your mind."

She remained silent, afraid of saying the wrong thing, afraid to allow her brain to make any decisions, right or wrong, when she was doped up and in such a mess.

CHAPTER SIX

"Come in, Vittorio," Grace invited, swinging around to face the door at the knock. The window seat was tempting, but she refused to give in to the need to sit down. Her shoulder felt very heavy. After showering and struggling to get dressed, even with Emmanuelle's help, she was already exhausted, but determined that Vittorio wouldn't see that. Still, she was grateful for the cuff that held her wrist up to help immobilize her injured shoulder.

The moment the door opened, her stomach did a slow somersault, the way it often did when Vittorio first walked into a room. Every time, she found herself staring at his wide shoulders and defined chest. He walked like she imagined a panther might stalk prey, fluid and powerful, giving the illusion of danger, though she knew him to be gentle and kind.

He flashed his heart-stopping smile, those indigo eyes drifting over her, taking in every detail. She knew he saw everything about her, because he always knew what she wanted or needed. It didn't matter that she tried to keep from him how much just dressing wore her out; he would see it. That was both disconcerting and exhilarating.

"Good morning, *gattina*. You look better this morning. Your color is good."

"Good morning, Vittorio." She knew he preferred her to acknowledge his greeting. It was a small enough courtesy to give when he was doing so much for her. "I think cutting back even more on the pain medication helped. I feel much more alert and able to handle things." She wanted to make that clear. She didn't want to be a burden on him. She'd already taken up three weeks of his time.

"That's good. I thought you might prefer to have breakfast in the kitchen. You haven't really had time to explore, and I want you to feel at home here." He held out his hand.

Grace did her best to try to be that woman who helped run a multimillion-dollar-a-year business, but when she was around him, she liked that feeling he gave her of taking care of her. She'd never had anyone take real care of her. He focused completely on her and saw to her every need. She told herself every day that she shouldn't want that, that she was independent and could do for herself—but so far, she hadn't convinced herself.

At her job, she saw to every detail behind the scenes of every event and had absolute confidence in herself. She did the ordering and was insistent about getting exactly what their clients asked for—and on time. She'd earned a reputation as a strong, exacting businesswoman who let nothing and nobody stand in her way when it came to ensuring that KB's venues were the absolute best and worth every penny they charged.

But she wasn't that woman around Vittorio. She was wholly a woman, totally attracted, and more, glowing in his care. The fact that she liked having a man care for her shocked her. She didn't want to get used to that much attention. It was too addictive. Already, he'd ruined her for any other man. She would always compare every man she met to him—and no other would fare very well.

Vittorio stood in the doorway, his hand out to her, and watched her cross the room to him. He didn't take his gaze from her face, and his expression sent heat curling through her body to pool low. His fingers wrapped around hers, that first touch of his strong hand making her heart beat faster. The way he drew her so gently to him felt like care. He bent his head slowly to hers, always giving her time to withdraw—which she knew she should but never did.

She waited. Anticipated. His lips were sensual. Perfect. Those beautiful eyes were framed with long, thick black lashes. He was—*gorgeous* was the only adjective that came to mind. She almost went up on her toes. She had enough dignity not to, but she did lift her face to his. His mouth skimmed hers. The briefest of touches. It didn't matter that the kiss was brief, the effect on her was instantaneous.

Fireworks exploded in her veins—in her belly. Electricity short-circuited, zapping her, so every nerve ending sparked hot and wild. Liquid heat raced through her body, spreading like a wildfire. From a touch. One touch. She couldn't look at him when he lifted his head. She lowered her lashes to veil her expression. Vittorio's hand cupped her chin and lifted her face so, in spite of her intentions, her gaze jumped to his. Immediately she felt like she was drowning in all that dark, beautiful blue. There was no hiding from him. He never allowed it.

"What is it, Grace?"

Even his low voice was sexy to her. How was she going to explain that to him? She had to work to suppress a groan, feeling a little foolish. She'd saved his life and he was repaying her by taking care of her. She was falling fast, probably, if she had to be logical, because no one had ever made her feel safe or cared for. He'd done both and on top of that, he made her feel like a beautiful, desirable woman.

A million ways to deceive him rushed through her head,

but she didn't like the idea. He'd been good to her. Careful of her. Even to the point of deflecting all talk about the photograph Haydon had left behind, the way he'd done it, and what it meant. She decided on the truth no matter how embarrassing—and it was.

She forced herself to look him in the eye while she confessed. "It's just so easy to be with you. You're doing everything, giving me everything and asking nothing at all in return. It isn't right. I'm taking advantage of you and I don't like that."

He studied her face for what seemed forever and then his thumb slid over her chin. That brief caress nearly undid her resolution to tell him she had to go. It was time. If she stayed, she would never want to leave. Never. He had said their engagement was real to him, but that didn't make sense and they'd never spoken of it again. She was drowning here with him. The more she was with him, the more she wanted to be.

"Grace, I want it to be easy for you to stay with me. I like having you here and doing things for you. You're wrong about asking for nothing in return. I'm asking for quite a bit and I'll be asking for quite a bit more. I'm asking for you to put your complete trust in me. I want you to know, with every fiber of your being, that I won't let you down. Not ever. That everything I do is for you. For your health, your happiness and your well-being and your pleasure."

Heat rushed through her veins and spread like wildfire to every nerve ending in her body, igniting them. "Vittorio." Grace was floored. She had wanted to stop pain medication for this—these talks they occasionally had. She had to know what was real and what wasn't.

Vittorio Ferraro had more money than anyone could possibly imagine. He was a high-profile playboy, with expensive toys and a jet-setting lifestyle. Still, he didn't seem anything like the tabloids made him out to be. None of his family did, and she was having a difficult time putting the two completely different men together.

He was in glamorous magazines and sleazy tabloids as well as newspapers and television reports, usually with a beautiful starlet or a famous model on his arm. He was depicted as a love-them-and-leave-them type, discarding women after one or two dates, yet he'd been spending twenty-four hours a day with her for the last three weeks.

"I couldn't let Haydon just shoot you. You saved me from those terrible men, so we're really even."

He waited on her. He hadn't hired others to come in and take care of her, he was doing it himself. He wasn't like anyone she'd ever known. He was calm and sure, always confident, giving her the feeling he could handle any problem that came along—that he *would* handle any problem—with his cool efficiency.

"Do you want me to carry you or do you want to try to walk? It's a bit of a distance."

His arm had already slid around her, making her feel safe. Sometimes when she walked across the room, she felt as if she was listing to one side with the weight of the straps holding her shoulder in one place.

"I'd like to walk."

What woman wouldn't want to be carried by Vittorio? The feeling she got when she was cradled close to his chest was indescribable. When he moved, it was like floating through the air. Still, she had to be rational and start doing a few things for herself—like walking. She also wanted to check out the house and start paying attention to Vittorio—really get to know his likes and dislikes. She had the feeling that he was very particular in the things that mattered to him and she wanted to know every single thing she could about him. It was time she started giving back to him, especially if he meant what he said about a relationship between them. Sometimes she thought she might have hallucinated that conversation.

Vittorio didn't protest her decision to walk, but stayed on the side of her good shoulder, his hand resting on the small of her back. That was so like him. She loved that he always made her feel as if she wasn't alone. Just by being close he gave her the illusion of safety. She glanced down at the floor, a beautiful cherrywood in contrast to the high ceilings, glass and white walls. For the first time she realized he was barefoot.

Her breath caught in her throat. Vittorio Ferraro was barefoot. She had never seen him in anything but his three-piece suit and exquisitely polished shoes—at least she didn't think she had. Had she been too self-absorbed to notice him dressing informally in his own house? She glanced down at her own feet. She had clothes in the closet, thanks to him, but she hadn't thought about shoes. She normally wore heels to work, but at home, she was much more casual, preferring bare feet, but that was because after wearing heels all day, she couldn't stand anything on her feet.

Vittorio was wearing faded denim that looked soft and vintage, with a few real threadbare spots, as if he'd owned the jeans for a very long time. They were button up versus having a zipper and the top button was undone. They rode low on his hips and shaped the powerful columns of his thighs. She liked his casual look. His shirt was tight, stretched across his thick chest, as if every muscle was straining to break free.

She searched for something to say that made sense, so she wouldn't blurt out how much she liked his casual clothes. "I need to call my boss."

"That would be a good idea. Katie has called several times, mostly to inquire about your progress, but I could hear a sense of urgency in her voice this last time."

She liked that he didn't protest her needing to check in with her boss. She didn't want to think he was trying to take over and control her life. "I'll call her after breakfast."

She made an effort to pay attention to where they were going. The house was so big with so many doors that she was really afraid if she was left on her own, she'd get lost. Already, she could smell freshly brewed coffee.

"I missed half the rooms we passed because I was looking at your feet." If he didn't have her hand pressed to his ribs, she would have slapped it over her mouth. *So much for not blurting out ridiculous things.*

"I'm looking at yours. I think my feet are at least twice the size of yours. Maybe more." There was amusement in his voice.

His ability to find humor in things was one of the most endearing traits about him. She flashed him a smile and then regarded their feet as they walked along the gleaming floor. He was right, her foot was probably half the size of his. "How tall are you?"

"At least a foot taller than you," he pointed out.

She made a face at him. "I suppose I'll have to concede you're right about that. I can't argue facts."

"You never argue with me." Vittorio turned her hand over and pressed a kiss into the center of her palm. "I like that you don't pick a fight just for the sake of argument."

"It would be a little difficult to do that with you. You're pretty reasonable, Vittorio."

He led her into a very large kitchen. There was a small, intimate table already set with dishes and warmers. He led her straight to it and pulled back her chair for her. "There are three dining areas. This one, which is perfect for the two of us in the mornings," he told her, seating her. "The two larger dining areas have varying views. One is a bit larger than the other; in other words, if my family comes over, we use that one." He flashed a small grin at her.

His smile was warm, impossible to ignore, and did something to her insides, making her feel happy. Happiness wasn't something she was used to feeling and it shocked her a little. "You have a very large family." The women came and went very quickly in the morning, helping her to shower and dress and then they simply were gone, disappearing as if they'd never been.

"We're loud and always in one another's business," he pointed out. "But we always have one another's backs."

The way he said it, she wondered why they would need

to stand for one another—as if they had problems similar to hers. She doubted they had had a serial killer after them until she'd brought one with her.

Before she could remind him of Haydon stalking them all, he turned the conversation back to his earlier subject. "Do you really think I'm reasonable? Not every woman would think it was reasonable that I need to take care of my lady. In fact, I think most wouldn't like it, Grace."

She looked up at his face. There was a hint of worry there and that shocked her. Vittorio was the most confident man she'd ever met, and in her profession, she routinely met CEOs of powerful businesses. Such men didn't worry about what other people thought. They did what they thought best and expected everyone else to get with the program. And yet the look in Vittorio's eyes told her that, to her at least, he was vulnerable—that her good opinion mattered to him. On the heels of that realization came the immediate and compelling need to reassure him, to erase that hint of doubt.

"Vittorio, I love the way you are with me. For my business, I make decisions all day, argue with vendors and push and push to get what I want for my clients. By the time I go home, I think my brain is fried. I don't want to make another decision or think about anything until I go to work the next morning. I imagine most people are like that. You've given me this opportunity to actually relax and I appreciate it more than you will ever know. It's been a relief not to have to think too much about anything. I realize that's unrealistic and that sooner or later I have to come to some decisions and take back charge of my life, but for right now, it's been the most amazing three weeks in spite of the pain in my shoulder, so thank you."

Vittorio had opened the warmers sitting on the table and poured coffee for Grace. He straightened slowly and looked down at her upturned face. He wanted to frame her face with both hands and kiss her senseless. She had no idea what a gift she'd just given him. She was the one he'd searched for. She was the one he hadn't believed could possibly exist. She had strength, a backbone of steel, and yet she could put herself in his hands and give him what he needed in their relationship.

He couldn't help himself. He leaned down and took her mouth, one hand settling in her hair, bunching the silk into his fist. At the first touch of his lips, the first demand of his tongue, she opened for him and he tasted everything he'd ever need. He'd kissed a lot of women, more than he ever cared to admit, but he'd never felt. Not like this. Not this shocking hunger that consumed him. Not a need that would never be sated.

Her taste was unique and appealed to him on every level. She didn't have a lot of—if any—experience. He had never considered that he would ever be with an untutored woman. His demands were too intense, his passion too consuming, yet he couldn't imagine kissing anyone else ever again.

He was careful with her, keeping the kisses light when he wanted to devour her. Very reluctantly, he released her hair, and then lifted his mouth from hers. Her lashes lifted, and he was staring into her eyes. She had beautiful eyes. Large, a beautiful green, framed with thick long lashes that curled at the tips. He couldn't resist brushing a kiss across her eyes. Reluctantly releasing her, he pulled the lids all the way off the warmers.

"Why is it unrealistic?" He indicated for her to make her food choices.

She stared at him, her eyes still adorably dazed. "Unrealistic?" she echoed.

It was all he could do not to smile. "Yes, *gattina*. You said it was unrealistic not to have to think too much about everything. Why would that be unrealistic?"

She frowned and indicated the scrambled eggs and toast. He put a small portion on her plate. She hadn't eaten much, so he didn't want to overwhelm her with a large amount of food.

"I can't keep relying on you for everything, Vittorio. I'm

getting stronger and I'm going to have to start figuring things out."

He lifted the cream and she shook her head. It surprised him that she didn't take cream in her coffee. "Why not? I like you relying on me."

"It would get very old fast."

He took a healthy portion of eggs, bacon and hash browns. "No, it wouldn't. In our home, I would want you to feel as if you can rely on me. We both know you're capable of making your own decisions, but why should you have to if you prefer me to make them?"

She looked as if she might protest, but then she forked a small bit of eggs awkwardly into her mouth. Her dominant hand clearly was the one with the shattered shoulder. She chewed and swallowed before she tilted her head and looked at him. "For you, I meant. That would get old for you."

"Some men need to take care of their women. It isn't politically correct for a man to dictate in his household. I'm well aware of that, but I'm one of those men. I want my woman to know she can rely on my judgment. I want her to trust me to make the decisions." He gave her his preferences cautiously, knowing it was unpopular, but he couldn't change the way he was wired.

She gave him her frown but looked more thoughtful than condemning. He liked that about her. "Vittorio, are you looking for blind faith?"

"Of course not. That would be foolish and you're far too intelligent to be foolish. Trust has to be earned. I hope that happens between us over time. I'm well aware I'm asking for far too much in our relationship, but I still hope you'll give it thought. I've been making the decisions for the last three weeks."

"Out of necessity, and I'm really, really grateful. I wouldn't have known what to do without you . . ." She trailed off and looked down at her eggs, as if realization was dawning on her.

He watched her eat her eggs almost gingerly. It clearly

took effort to keep them from spilling off the fork and more did than not. He couldn't take watching her struggle. "I don't in any way think you can't do things for yourself or that you're inept, but I enjoy doing things for you." He took the fork from her and pulled his chair closer.

"I feel a little silly with you feeding me."

He leaned down and brushed another kiss across her lips to stop them from trembling. "Grace, I want to discuss this with you, but you're going to need an open mind. I want our engagement to be real and I want you to think of it that way. You'll need to stay here with me no matter what for a while and we can take that time to really get to know each other. You can get to know my family."

"I think you're moving too fast, Vittorio. It must have been very upsetting to have me run in front of a gun when clearly you're a very protective man."

He could tell she chose each word carefully, as if she was afraid she would upset him.

"But I think if you take a step back, you'll see that your lifestyle and mine in no way mesh. I love my job, and I'm good at it. It's the only thing that's kept me sane all these years. You've had a lifetime of travel, adrenaline and women."

He knew it would come back to the women. "I'll admit that my family has played out our lives in the tabloids—but it's all for show. I never gave who I am to any of those women. What would be the point? So they could sell what they knew to the nearest tabloid? Think about that, Grace. Think about how much damage you could do to my reputation if the things I will share with you were to be splashed all over the newspapers, headlines, media. I'm a business-man. My family owns international banks. Hotels. You name it, we've got it. I'm a very private man and I expect what we share between us to remain private."

Her gaze moved over his face, searching for something. He'd given her the truth and he hoped she saw, because he always intended to give her the truth. There were going to be stumbling blocks, but he hoped he could guide her successfully over every one. Wariness had crept into her eyes. She was getting that he didn't want a normal relationship.

"Are you opposed to trying an engagement with me?"

Her eyes dropped, but not before he saw the fear. He couldn't blame her. He was asking for a hell of a lot of trust on her part and he wasn't making it easy. She was in his home and she couldn't leave. It wasn't as if she was a prisoner, but if she left, she'd be giving Haydon Phillips access to her and she wasn't in any state to fight him off.

She visibly took a breath and he had to resist pulling her into his arms to comfort her. "The thought scares me," she admitted.

"Grace." He waited, letting the silence stretch out between them. Finally, she sighed and lifted her gaze once again to his. He smiled at her, proud of her for showing her inevitable courage. He knew, even better than she did, that she was extremely brave. "Tell me why it scares you."

The tip of her tongue touched her top lip and then her teeth bit down on her lower lip. She swallowed once. "You're everything I could ever dream about in a man, but it isn't real. Men like you aren't real. The man in the tabloids has been around for years, but this one I met only three weeks ago under extreme circumstances. You'd break my heart, and I don't think I'm strong enough to take that."

He waited patiently because he could see there was more she was reluctant to admit.

"I know that sounds ridiculous," she added hastily. "I've never had a home or a family. I've always had to work out every problem and figure out how to survive. I've always been alone. Haydon is the only person that's ever been a constant in my life and certainly not in a positive way. If I let myself fall in love with you, which would be so easy to do, and then you turned out to be that man in the tabloids, especially if I depended completely on you, I think I would be so broken there would be no fixing me."

Vittorio felt such pride in her he knew it showed on his face. She was magnificent. That had to have been so difficult to admit to him, and he knew most women would never have done it. Her admission told him she trusted him already far more than she thought she did.

"*Grazie, a mia ragazza molto coraggiosa.* You are fast becoming *mia vita.* I can't imagine what kind of courage it took to tell me the truth, and I appreciate it. I want to be able to have honest communication between us. That's the only way a relationship like we would have would work. I need to know how you feel and you have to know how I feel. I understand that you're nervous and even scared. I'm a little terrified of losing you because of who I am and what I need. I'm hoping your needs coincide with mine."

He fed her several bites of egg, watching the expressions chase across her face. When she finished the eggs, he switched back to his chair to give her some breathing room. At least she wasn't trying to run for the hills. She was actually giving the things he said real thought.

Grace took a drink of her coffee and picked up the piece of toast. "I don't like that. You being terrified of losing me because of who and what you are. You're a good man, Vittorio. No matter what, you're a good man."

"Am I? I'm a man who wants my woman to let me be dominant in our home." He deliberately used the adjective, hoping she would start making that connection.

Most people would assume his brother Ricco, because he practiced the art of shibari, would be a dominant in his home with his woman. He wasn't. Neither was Stefano, who was a natural commander. As head of the Ferraro family, he was responsible for their lives. Vittorio had been born dominant. He'd always known that was his cross to bear. His needs would make it doubly difficult to find a woman who could have shadow-riding children and would live with a man like him.

"There's nothing wrong with that, Vittorio. Nothing is wrong between two consenting adults."

He put down his fork. "Look at me." He poured authority into his voice and she looked up immediately. "Don't do that. Don't spout platitudes. I want you to understand exactly what you would be getting into if you stayed with me. It isn't like you read in stories or they portray in movies. This isn't about whips per se. But it is about bondage. This is about who I am and how we would live together in this house. This is about the way I have to live. I don't just want to be in control, Grace. I need to be. I need to take care of my woman and know that she trusts me to have her best interests at heart. I need to make the decisions, to decide what's best for us both. And I will take absolute control in the bedroom. I would expect you to trust me to take care of you there as well. For me to be happy in a relationship, Grace, you have to be happy. That's the way it works."

His heart accelerated, and he took a breath to find his center, to stay in complete control of his emotions. He didn't want to lose her, but he didn't want her to stay with him and then find she detested their lifestyle. He'd laid it all out on the line for her. What he was. What he needed. What he would expect from her.

It would be better to give her up and let another rider find happiness. The thought, the moment it came, filled him with a kind of dark aggression. He saw it as a bloodred swirling cloud in his mind that filtered through his system. He couldn't have that, not with his gifts. He knew better. He knew he had to have harmony in his home at all times. He had to have a sanctuary where, no matter the horrors he saw, the things he had to do in order to bring justice to those who would harm others, he could find his peace.

"Would it be so bad to continue your life the way it's been?"

She took another sip of coffee, clearly stalling for time while she thought things over. That was very much like her. At least she hadn't run screaming from the room or demanded he call her a cab.

"If you really want honesty, Vittorio, I don't have a clue. The idea of bondage is both a little terrifying and intriguing."

"We would work up to the things I would like to do to

you in the bedroom, building your trust in me. Not just jump right into it, but what do your instincts tell you, *gattina*?"

"I don't have a lot of experience, so I have no idea if I'd really like it, but the thought . . ." She trailed off.

He didn't need her to say more. He read her body. The heightened breathing. Her nipples pushing against her thin blouse. Her restless movements in her chair.

"This time, I won't ask you to continue because this is such a difficult conversation, but communication and honesty with yourself as well as with me will always be important. Your body likes the idea, am I correct?"

She nodded.

He waited.

Grace pressed her lips together. "Yes, Vittorio."

He smiled at her and rubbed his thumb over her knuckles. "Thank you, Grace. I know talking about these things right now isn't always easy, but it will become automatic. What about me making the decisions? Would it be so bad for me to continue the way we've been?"

"Am I drawn to you? Absolutely yes. Do I like the way you take care of me? I've never had care before and it feels amazing to have someone treat me like I'm special. When I'm with you, I feel as if you're totally focused on me. On the other hand, you've *had* to take care of me. I haven't been strong enough to care for myself. I want to continue to work. That's important to me . . ."

"*Bella*, part of having you in my care is knowing what's necessary in your life and making sure you're happy. If something is a priority to you, then obviously, it would be one to me."

Her chin lifted, and she looked him straight in the eye. "And if we disagree?"

"We communicate. Talk it out. Isn't that what most couples do? I've watched Stefano and Francesca very closely. She doesn't always give in to him. She lets things go that don't matter to her, but if she really wants something he's opposed to, she has no qualms about presenting her case to him. He knows when he has to give in."

"And if you still don't agree after we argue?" she challenged.

He sighed. "I would suggest both of us shelve the discussion, sleep on it and discuss it again. In the end, if we still couldn't find a compromise, I would expect my woman to let me make the ultimate decision. I can only give you my word that I would take everything you say or feel to heart and make my decision with your happiness and health in mind."

Grace didn't react immediately and again, he liked that trait in her. She was thoughtful, her eyes on his face. "If I can't give you these things?"

"I would understand. I never ever expected to meet a woman I wanted to spend my life with, let alone think I would ever admit to anyone what I was really like. You said you had nothing to give me in return for the things I do for you, but you can clearly see that wouldn't be the case."

"I can't be in a one-sided relationship, always taking with you always giving." She put the coffee cup down and turned her head to look out the window. "That's what it would feel like to me."

His heart reacted again, this time with a jump of hope. She hadn't rejected him or his needs yet. She was considering everything he'd said. He had thought to give her more time, let her get used to his care and then tell her about his needs, but he knew that wouldn't be fair to her—or to him. He was too invested in her already. He already loved coaxing her smiles. Watching her face light up in spite of the pain she was currently in. He particularly enjoyed that she was relaxed in his home, the fear slowly receding in his company.

"Grace, look at me."

She turned back to him slowly, those eyes of hers meeting his until he felt the impact all the way through his body, as if she'd shot an arrow and it was lodged in the vicinity of his heart. He had to resist putting his hand over his chest and pressing hard.

"It's up to you what you want out of the relationship between us. What you want to give back. I would hope that while I look after you, you would do the same for me."

For the first time, her face brightened a little. "I like that idea, Vittorio."

Her voice held a shy note, although he would never consider her shy. Just because she was the force behind KB Events and stayed in the background didn't mean she was shy. He knew she was thinking of his taking total control in the bedroom.

He pressed a kiss into the center of her palm. "When we have sex, *bella*, I have no doubt you'll give me everything I need or want."

She blushed, but she didn't protest. "I don't know the first thing about relationships, families, or being someone's fiancée."

"I know about families, *gattina*, but I've never been in a relationship or had a fiancée."

Shock registered on her face. "You've been in tons of relationships. I read the tabloids, the news, everything about you. I watched you at events. You always had a beautiful woman on your arm, mostly very tall, elegant models, which I most assuredly am not."

Grace had no idea what she'd given away to him. She'd clearly followed him in the tabloids, reading everything his family fed to the paparazzi. She'd been drawn to him before she met him. Immense satisfaction filled him. He liked that, more than liked it.

"When we attend a fund-raiser, the idea is to get as much money as possible for the cause. To do that, we generate publicity. Bringing a model or an actress with a following helps to do just that. Some of those women are friends, some were simply a one-time hookup. That isn't the same thing as a relationship."

"It's hard to believe that over the years you didn't find another woman you wanted to be in a relationship with."

He didn't have the luxury of explanations. He was a shadow rider and that meant no one, *no one*, other than family, and even then only *close* family, could know the truth about him. She had to be in completely. Committed to him. The pull, for him, had been instant and strong. He tried to keep their shadows separated but being in such close proximity to her these last three weeks, sleeping in her room with her, meant their shadows were becoming entwined.

"Nevertheless, Grace, it's the truth."

She nodded her head and then gave him a sudden little frown. "I thought you said you can't cook. This is delicious."

She was changing the subject in order to give herself time to think. He didn't want that, but she needed to feel comfortable and he wasn't about to push her any more than he already had. He was grateful for her response and the fact that she was thoughtful instead of snapping out answers when she hadn't had the time to consider all the things he'd laid out for her.

"You barely ate."

"I ate. Who did the cooking?"

He smiled at her. "Merry Dubois. She's a cousin as well. She married a man by the name of Marcellus Dubois while she was in culinary school. He was working on the building the classes were held in. Marcellus is the caretaker for the property, which is an enormous job. They live next door, our nearest neighbor."

He liked the couple. They were quiet and respected his needs to keep his home a sanctuary. If repairs had to be made, Marcellus always scheduled them to be made when Vittorio wasn't home. Merry not only did the cooking but supervised the cleaning staff as well. She also scheduled them when Vittorio wasn't home. The couple really looked after him as well as his home, and he appreciated them more than he could ever express to them.

"I do have a cleaning crew who come in and take care of the house, but Merry oversees them." He flashed her another smile, knowing she was attracted to him. Knowing he was unashamedly offering her his home, his lifestyle, in an effort to entice her to stay.

"Other than the fact that I can't use my arm at all, this feels like a fairy tale."

"Life with me isn't always going to be a fairy tale, but I can promise you I will always do my best to make you happy. That's important to me, Grace, making you happy."

"Just so long as it's okay that I make it a priority to make you happy."

His heart jumped, but he refused to let himself believe she was going to give herself to him. He was asking for things she didn't yet understand, and he refused to let her walk blind into a binding relationship until she knew exactly what she was getting into and was prepared to be fully committed. She had to want the same relationship, or he wasn't right for her. Already he knew she was the one he wanted, and it had nothing to do with their shadows coming together.

He liked her. He liked the fact that she was so courageous. He admired her. She had lived in terror and under the threat of unspeakable violence for years, and yet every single day, she had functioned, worked, kept her integrity while trying to protect those around her.

"It would be nice if you did."

Her eyes darkened in concern. "Vittorio, aren't you happy?" Her gaze swung around the room, taking in the high ceilings and the incredible view of the lake and then came back to rest on his face.

He wasn't going to give her less than the truth, not when he was asking so much of her. "Having money doesn't make anyone happy, *bella*. That's a myth. I present one face to the world and then come back to an empty house. It's beautiful and peaceful here, but it is still very much empty.

These last three weeks, you've made my life feel full and rich and given me a reason to get up every morning."

Grace tried to process everything Vittorio had told her, everything he was offering. The only time she ever had been happy was at work, pouring herself into KB Events, seeing to every detail, like a general orchestrating a perfect battle. She had no friends, she didn't dare. She didn't go out, because . . . she didn't dare. The only place she felt relatively safe was when she worked, and she often worked from home, making deals over the phone. Haydon wanted money, so he usually didn't interfere. Occasionally he would come to one of the events just to scare her into compliance—and it usually worked.

When Vittorio told her he wanted complete control in the bedroom, she honestly didn't think it would bother her. In fact, when he said it, her body had gone into meltdown. Still, she liked the idea that he would take his time to get her there. She was willing to spend the time it would take to see if they were compatible. He was worth it.

She was happy with Vittorio and felt safe most of the time. He gave that illusion, as if he was invincible and no one could best him. "You make me feel safe," she conceded. "And happy. I don't think I really knew what that was until just now. Realizing that just talking to you makes me happy. I even got a full night's sleep, although I feel bad that you're not sleeping in a bed."

"I like watching over you, Grace," he assured. He finished off the last of his coffee and stood. "I want to show you the rest of the house. You can call Katie and ask her to come out here for your meeting. I think she'd like to see for herself that you're alive and well. She has made inquiries several times a day, every day since you were shot."

She shouldn't have been surprised, but she was. Katie had often asked her to go out with her, a dinner or dancing. Katie loved to go clubbing, but Grace had been afraid to spend too much time with her outside of work. After Haydon had made his threat, she was extremely grateful she hadn't made the mistake. He would have really focused his attention and threats on Katie.

Now, he had a real target—Vittorio.

The thought made her heart pound and her hands clench in sudden fear. She couldn't stand idly by and let Vittorio get hurt because of her. She wanted him with every breath she took. She wanted the lifestyle he was offering her. She wanted him—Vittorio Ferraro. But there was Haydon, and Haydon never lost.

Grace sucked in a breath. Forced her hands to unclench. "I appreciate all that you've done for me, Vittorio, and all that you're offering. But I honestly think it best if we don't keep up this engagement."

"We already discussed this, *gattina*. You're getting spooked all over again. The announcement was made official by the family and has already been in the news. There isn't any taking it back. I know you're thinking you can protect me, but it doesn't work that way. In my world, I'm the one doing the protecting." Vittorio put his hand under her good arm and helped her out of the chair. "Merry will get the dishes," he added when he saw her looking at them as if she might clear the table.

Grace should have made her protest stick and she felt like a coward when she didn't. She couldn't help but feel cared for. It was his tone. His posture. Everything about him. She found him very hard to resist, and if she was truthful with herself, she wasn't trying that much.

CHAPTER SEVEN

The house opened from one room directly into the next, each with spacious, high ceilings. The foyer opened up into a library, living room, and sitting room that was a little cozier than some of the other spaces for visiting and relaxing with family or guests. The house had several living and family rooms, and Vittorio took Grace past the library straight to his favorite.

The sitting room faced the pool and had a large, open entrance that could be closed off if desired by glass doors and blackout curtains. The furniture consisted of the most comfortable deep, warm chairs, while the room had cool tile flooring and seagrass-textured walls. A covered porch ran the length of the swimming pool, which could be seen from the open doors, adding to the peaceful feeling Vittorio always got around water.

In the shade provided by the covered porch, several chairs and tables sat near an outdoor kitchen and barbecue combination for alfresco cooking. Before she sat down, Grace went straight to the open glass doors to take in the view. He stood behind her looking as well. The pool stretched out in a long, blue invitation, and beyond it was a rolling grass hill, scattered ornamental trees and the lake. The sun shone down on the surface, turning it into a crystal-blue jewel nestled among the trees.

"This is beautiful. I can see why you love this place. I can't help but feel relaxed and happy just looking at this view and hearing the sound of water."

He liked that he had added the hot tub above the pool so that water spilled in a series of small falls into the pool. The sound was soothing, and when he was working on learning not to burn everything he grilled, that constant song kept him centered.

"This is one of my favorite spots. I spend quite a bit of time here." He settled his fingers on the nape of her neck. Touching her and feeling her relax beneath his hand made him happy.

She tipped her head up, looking at him over her shoulder. "Can you barbecue?"

He leaned down to brush a kiss over the smirk on her face. "I have some skills with the grill, but I have to admit, cooking is not my forte. What about you?"

"I had plenty of time to get interested in various subjects when I was afraid to leave my home in case Haydon followed me and went after anyone I talked to. Cooking was one of them. Am I any good? Absolutely not, but I can bake."

"So, you're telling me we'll have to live on cookies?" He'd never thought he would have this—teasing with a woman, stripping himself bare and being accepted for who he was. She hadn't committed fully, but he could sense she wanted to.

"Something like that, yes."

The laughter in her voice warmed him. He led her outside, and she stopped to admire the gable and pillars all painted white. "Vittorio, your home is really incredible."

That was another point in his favor—she liked the house. "It's a house right now, Grace, but it has the potential to be a home." He wanted her to make it a home for him, for both of them.

She glanced up at him and then, at the urging of his hand pressing against the small of her back, made for one of the very wide, comfortable-looking chairs. He helped her into it and then pulled out her cell phone. "I thought you might want to call your boss."

Grace took her phone from him, but her gaze shifted just slightly from his. Instantly, he knew she was uncomfortable with something he'd said.

"*Gattina*, I took your cell phone because I didn't want the police to confiscate it. As no one could find it and they didn't ask me about it, I didn't have to lie. I did see messages from Katie Branscomb pop up, but I tried not to read them." He'd wanted to give her privacy. It was important that she learned he could be trusted. He didn't want to take over her life, he wanted her to surrender it to him. Invading her privacy was far different from her volunteering to tell him what was going on in her life.

"Katie is my partner, not my boss," Grace blurted out. "We both own the company equally."

Vittorio was silent, studying her averted face. The fingers of her good hand twisted into the material of her shirt nervously. He wanted to cover her hand to reassure her. He also wanted to strangle his mother. She would have known. She would have investigated both women before using the company. She might pretend she didn't know, but she could have told them quite a few things about Grace. She'd just chosen not to.

"I wasn't trying to lie to you, it's just that when we went into business, I knew that if Haydon found out, he would force me to take out loans against KB Events. It was my idea to name it that. Katie is the face of the business. She's really good with people and I'm not comfortable around them. Well, that's not exactly true, but . . ." She trailed off, obviously frustrated.

"You're not comfortable because you worry anyone

you're friendly with might become a target," he interpreted for her, and sank into the chair opposite her. "I can see why you'd want to protect your partner. How did you convince her not to tell anyone?"

"I told her I'd be partners as long as she never said a word to anyone. She wanted the partnership, so it worked out fine. Haydon isn't the type to look up business licenses. He eavesdrops on conversations, but he won't do research, there's never been a need. Over the years, he believed he had me thoroughly cowed." She grimaced. "Which, sadly, he did."

"You're too hard on yourself, *bella*." He indicated the phone. "Make your call."

She put in her passcode and instantly messages began popping up. "I've got several voice messages."

He read the underlying worry in her voice and instantly held out his hand for the phone. Without thinking about it, Grace put it in his palm. There were five messages, all from the same number. He glanced at her face. Her expression broke his heart. She looked stiff and scared. She believed the voice mails were from Haydon.

Putting the phone to his ear, he picked up her trembling hand and began to idly play with her fingers. At once, his touch appeared to be calming, just as he hoped it would be.

"You bitch. Do you think I'm going to let you get away with this? I'm going to cut out that bastard's heart and make you fucking eat it. But first, I'm going to kill his bitch of a sister and then the rest of the bitches in his family. One by one. I'll take away everyone he loves. You have one chance, you little whore. Get back to your apartment."

There were more profanities and threats, including disembowelment and more torture, on each of the other voice mails. He sighed, hit the off button and pocketed the phone. He handed her his cell and gave her the password. "Use mine to call her."

"I was right. It was him. What did he say?"

"Probably the same bullshit he always says to intimidate

you. He's going to murder anyone you're around. That sort of charming dialogue." He sent her a small, reassuring smile, his thumb sliding over the pulse beating so frantically in her wrist. "We expected that, right?"

"Vittorio." She said his name uneasily. There was stark fear in her eyes.

"You're safe, *bella*. He can't get in here."

"I'm not worried about me, Vittorio. You have a wonderful family. I haven't met them all, but the ones I have met have been so nice to me. They've treated me as if I'm part of your family . . ."

He brought her fingertips to his lips, his gaze holding hers. "That is because you *are* family to them. For me, this engagement is real." His thumb slid across her bare ring finger. "I suppose it won't be real to you until this isn't so naked." Bringing up their engagement did two things for him. He took her mind off her fear for his family and it also brought her one step closer to accepting that he meant his declaration that he wanted her in his life permanently.

A faint flush stole up her neck to her face, turning her pale skin a healthy rose. Her eyes shone a bright emerald green. The desire to kiss her was so strong, he had to call on every ounce of discipline he possessed.

"I'm fine without a ring."

"My fiancée needs a ring. I have a need to declare to the world that you belong to me." He kissed her fingertips because if he didn't, he would be kissing her lips. Her pouty lower lip made him want to sink his teeth in her. She was tempting beyond his ability to resist her. He sucked her finger into his mouth and stroked it with his tongue. She squirmed in her chair. Her mouth formed a perfect little O, and her eyes widened in shock, but she didn't pull away from him.

"I think it's best if I call Katie. Midnight Madness, a fund-raiser for Locals Helping the Elderly, is in three weeks. We have to get the details hammered out before the event. I believe you're on the guest list."

"I am?"

She lifted her chin. "You and a very famous actress, Anne Marquis. You remember her, blond, beautiful, willowy figure, in all the magazines. I believe she was nominated for an Oscar last year. I didn't see the movie but was told she gave an epic performance."

The urge to smile was strong, but he kept his face a mask. He wanted her, right there in that chair with her shoulder wrapped up and her arm useless to her. He wanted her with every breath he drew. His hand dropped to her thigh and stroked a caress there. It was difficult to resist the urge to strip her naked and take what was his.

"You've known all along you were helping to put on Eloisa's big event."

She nodded. The hint of accusation gave way to humor. "Yes."

"And you knew I was on the guest list with Anne, didn't you?" He kept his voice pitched low but changed the tone to one that promised retaliation.

She wasn't as fast to claim that knowledge. "Yes."

"So, you were just waiting for the perfect time to use that little bit of information against me, weren't you?"

Grace pressed her lips together to keep from laughing, but it was impossible to keep the laughter from her eyes. "Maybe," she admitted, feigning reluctance.

"Just for that, I'm going to kiss you."

He framed her face with both hands and leaned in to settle his mouth on hers. Heat exploded in his belly and raced through his body like a fireball. His tongue swept into her mouth, claiming her, and then he simply devoured her, taking over, silently demanding she follow his lead, that she give herself to him, surrender completely to him. He didn't ask. He took.

Vittorio gave her who he was, her man, dominant, taking over, insisting she follow his lead. He kissed her until neither of them could breathe. Until his body was so hard he thought he might shatter. Until he knew if he didn't stop it would be too late and all his careful planning would be for nothing. He forced his head up just enough to press his forehead against hers, staring into her eyes while he caught his breath.

Her breath matched his, uneven and ragged. Her eyes shone so brightly he felt a bit dazzled by the color. She looked adorably dazed, her lips swollen and very kissed, her skin slightly red from the shadow of stubble on his jaw.

"You make me feel alive, Grace. Every single cell in my body wakes up around you. My heart. Who knew it was even possible? I want you to be mine completely. I need you to give yourself to me the way you kiss me. More importantly, I need to be your man. The one who shelters you, protects you, gives you everything."

She didn't pull away from him, and he read acceptance in her eyes. He was getting closer to Grace at least thinking she might like his lifestyle. She liked the idea whether she wanted to admit it or not.

"I'm not certain it's exactly fair for you to be kissing me."

He ran the pad of his thumb over her lips, his heart feeling more than he'd known it was capable of. She turned him inside out without even trying. "Why is that?"

Her lashes fluttered and then veiled the emerald in her eyes.

"*Gattina*, look at me." He kept his voice gentle. She deserved gentle. He knew she wouldn't want him to think of her as a little lost kitten, but he couldn't help it. He'd rescued her in the parking lot, hissing and fighting, surrounded by wolves bent on devouring her, and now he had to win her trust in order to keep her.

He used his voice unashamedly. He knew it was a gift he'd been given and now, more than ever, when her long lashes lifted, he was thankful for the way his voice could compel others to do as he commanded. He waited, willing her to tell him whatever it was she'd been reluctant to say.

"I can't think when you kiss me."

Her confession wreaked havoc with his heart. He found

himself wanting to smile when his life had been one of duty and work, of constant training with few things that brought him real pleasure. He hadn't even known that there was so much more—not until his oldest brother had found Francesca. He had seen the difference in Stefano immediately and had wanted that for himself. Someone to care about him. Someone to be his center. Someone to make him feel alive and passionate about living.

He smoothed his hand over her hair because he had to touch her. "I can't think very well when I'm kissing you, either, but I like the feeling."

Her lips curved into a faint smile. She reached out as if she might touch his mouth with her fingertips, and he found he was holding his breath, waiting for her to actually make that first move toward him. At the last moment, she dropped her hand to her lap.

"I like it, too. A little too much."

Her confession was almost as good as knowing she'd wanted to touch him. Touching him would have been the beginning of her claim on him, but he'd take what he could get. He knew he was moving her too fast. He had to be patient, take more time so as not to scare her off.

Vittorio forced himself to sit back. "Just so you know, when you were in the hospital and I knew you were the perfect woman for me, I called Anne the first chance I got. I told her that I'd announced my engagement and didn't want anyone to think she was the 'other woman' trying to break us up. That scenario could help or harm her career, depending. Anne is a friend of our family. We've known her since she was a child, and she happens to still be very much in love with her ex-husband. He's also going to be at the event and she didn't want to face him alone."

He was gratified to see the instant compassion on Grace's face.

"You can't cancel on her, Vittorio. I'm behind the scenes and can't go with you anyway. This fund-raiser is very important. We can handle it. I'll talk to Katie. I'm certain we can use the two of you attending together as a promotion of sorts. Let me think about it."

Hearing the confidence in her voice, he could tell her mind was racing a million miles an hour working out the problem and trying to figure out how best to handle it. He knew better. There was no way to fight the tabloid stories. He would be annihilated in all the gossip magazines, as would Anne. Grace hadn't seen any of the articles about the two of them. He'd purposely kept them from her, but the tabloids had had a field day with the story about the heroic young woman getting shot, and her fiancé refusing to leave her side in the hospital. Add the Saldis' involvement and their reputation as a crime family, and once again the media exploded with speculation that the Ferraro family was mafia as well and that the two families were in some kind of war.

"We've got it covered, but thank you for worrying about her," he said and reached for her hand, kissing her fingertips because if he didn't, he'd be kissing her again. "Taviano is escorting her to the event."

Instead of looking happy, she frowned at him. "You have to go, Vittorio. It's important. This is a huge deal to your mother. She's overseen quite a few of the details personally."

He sighed. Eloisa dealt with the event planners when the Ferraro family name was involved in any of the fundraisers. She was very exact in what she wanted and if she didn't get it, there was hell to pay.

"Eloisa can be difficult," he admitted. "I'm sorry if she was in any way rude to you."

Grace didn't pretend she wasn't aware of Eloisa's temperamental disposition. "We deal with many clients who expect the impossible, and we give it to them. That's why our company is considered the leading event planners in this area. Katie is an amazing woman, and we take pride in giving our customers exactly what they're looking for."

"Does that mean Katie is the one talking to the difficult clients?"

She pressed her lips together for a moment and then answered vaguely. "Mostly."

"Bella." He pitched his voice low and gentle, aware he was treading on dangerous ground. "I need to know how much interaction you've had with Eloisa. My family told reporters that the two of us have been dating for months but had covered up the relationship. During that time, I attended fund-raisers with other women, but all of them can easily be explained. I worked more than usual, covering for Giovanni while he was hurt, so I wasn't in the spotlight as much as my other brothers."

He chose his words carefully. He couldn't very well say he was flying from one city to another under the radar, meting out justice to those the law couldn't touch. How was that going to go over? *One thing at a time,* he reminded himself.

"Your mother feels more comfortable talking to Katie," Grace said, clearly trying to be diplomatic.

"I know Eloisa," Vittorio said. "She's very abrupt, abrasive and rude, cutting people to shreds if she can't have her way. She's a bulldozer if you don't know how to handle her."

"Katie does very well with her," Grace said.

He brushed a caress over the back of her hand. "We're talking about you, *gattina*, not Katie. How much interaction have you had with my mother? I'd like a straight answer."

Silence stretched between them for a few moments. He let it, never taking his gaze from hers. He could see the reluctance in her eyes and knew his mother had torn into her on more than one occasion. Of course she would have. She would try to intimidate to get her way, and Grace was the detail person. She was the one to take the blame if anything went wrong. And she wasn't from a "good" family like Katie Branscomb.

"I stay in the background as much as possible," she admitted. "But sometimes, at big events, the caterers have some catastrophe that has to be dealt with and I'm the one to take care of it. Naturally, the client is upset, I expect that."

"Grace." He poured disappointment into his voice. "You're well aware of what I'm asking."

Her lashes swept down. "I don't want to say anything that might put your mother in a bad light, Vittorio. These events are stressful for those putting them on and she's very exacting, as she should be. She's asking her friends to donate large amounts of money to a cause she believes in. If she gets angry and yells, she isn't different from a dozen others who do the same thing when a small detail goes wrong. It's bound to happen."

He remained silent, willing her to give him what he'd asked her for.

She sighed. "I've had multiple encounters with your mother, and I can't say any of them were pleasant. She made it clear she thinks I'm incompetent. She likes to yell at me when she thinks she's not going to get her way. It doesn't matter what I say when I explain why she can't have what she wants. Once the person she wanted to sing had actually passed away a day earlier, but somehow that became my fault."

She tugged on her hand, but he refused to allow her to withdraw. Tightening his hold, he turned her hand over and pressed his lips to her inner wrist. "I can see I will have to work overtime in order to charm you, *mia bellissima gattina*, to make up for the fact that Eloisa is shrewishly difficult. I would only admit that to you, not to anyone outside our family. Just remember, when you're making a list with pros and cons, that I've had to deal with her since I was born, so have some compassion."

Her fingers curled around his. "I never had a mother."

"Neither did I, Grace," he admitted. "But I did have Stefano and he made up for it, even when he was a boy. He took care of us and made certain we were loved."

"Stefano seems like a very nice man. None of you are very approachable, but every encounter Katie's had with Stefano has been positive."

"How is it none of us ever came across you? That seems

so unlikely, given we've attended so many of your events."
His mother had. His mother had to have known she was a
shadow rider and she'd deliberately kept it from the family.

Her lashes fluttered again, a sign he now recognized that
meant she didn't want to tell him something. He waited,
pressing her hand to the heat of his thigh. She sighed and
capitulated.

"I stayed in the background. It wasn't that difficult. I
work behind the scenes, and I didn't want to be like everyone else. Watching you all, I could tell, even though you
were all hiding it, the constant vying for your attention and
fawning all over you when none of it was real was wearing
on you."

Abruptly he sat up. As far as he knew, no one had ever
noticed that they were anything but enjoying themselves at
their highly publicized appearances. They practiced their
expressions, their smiles, their charm. It was extremely important to be believable, yet Grace had stayed away from
them, not because she was intimidated, but because she felt
bad for them.

"Also," she continued hastily, as if she was afraid she'd
hurt his feelings, "I didn't want to be seen talking to anyone
for reasons other than work, because of Haydon. If he gets
a wrong idea in his head, it could be very bad for someone."

"I like that you noticed it isn't always easy for my family." He did. He wanted her to be included in his family.
"Just know that Eloisa is going to say very ugly things to
you. So far, she has to Francesca, Mariko and Sasha. She
says them to Emmanuelle all the time, and when she gets
going, to the rest of us. It's never easy dealing with her and
it never will be, but when she comes around here, I'll handle it. Most likely, after she's had a run-in with me, she'll
come at you at work. If that's the case—"

"Then I'll handle it," she said decisively.

He caught her chin, his smile genuine. Happy. Because
that was how she made him feel. "Damn right you will."
And then he kissed her, savoring her taste. Savoring the fire

that he could burn in. Most of all wrapping himself up in her acceptance of him. When he lifted his head, he pulled the small jewelry box from his pocket.

"I have a cousin in New York who makes jewelry. He has a gift for creating the perfect set of rings for each of us. He makes the rings without even knowing the women who will take us on."

"Vittorio."

He heard her nerves. The warning. Even fear. He brought her fingertips to his mouth when she tried to pull her hand away. "You promised you would consider what I was offering with an open mind. We've announced the engagement around the world, in every country we do business. It isn't as if we can just say we made a mistake."

"We could. We should."

There was panic in her voice. Her breathing immediately was restricted, and he realized she was on the verge of a panic attack. She tried to tug her hand away a second time and he clamped down, shackling her wrist with his long fingers.

"Grace, look at me. Right now. Take a breath and look at me." He poured authority into his voice.

Her green eyes flew to his. Clung, as if to an anchor. He watched as she took a deep breath and let it out. The panic receded enough that he nodded in approval.

"That's good. Keep breathing. Are you saying no to me? Because I'm asking you to marry me. Officially. I want the engagement to be real."

"There's Haydon . . ." she said faintly, her voice pitched so low he could barely catch the thread of sound.

"He's an excuse. Fuck him. What do you want? Tell me what you want, Grace. Do you want to at least give me a chance?"

She swallowed. Her gaze started to shift from his, but then she forced herself to keep looking into his eyes. Her nod was very slow in coming, but it was there. "Yes. If I could choose, then I'd want to choose you, but—"

"That's all that matters. Haydon doesn't dictate your life anymore, Grace." He opened the box and waited again, his pulse accelerating in spite of his resolution to remain centered.

Her gaze clung to his and then it dropped to the box where the ring nestled. Damian Ferraro had created a masterpiece, a ring unlike any of his brothers' rings. This one was all about love, open heart and passion. The center cut was a Burmese ruby, a pigeon's-blood red, set with shield-shaped diamonds climbing the platinum setting. The diamonds on either side of the ring matched the family crest in shape.

He watched her face, her expression. His cousin was considered a genius when it came to matching the perfect ring with his clients. And he'd done so for Vittorio's woman, even before any of them knew she existed. She let her breath out slowly.

"Vittorio, it's beautiful. It's the most beautiful ring I've ever seen."

He slid it onto her finger. It fit perfectly. No resizing. That was Damian. Somehow, he knew exactly what to make long before the riders ever found their brides.

She held her hand up to look at the ring. "Seriously, I've never seen a ring so beautiful. I don't wear a lot of jewelry as a rule. Earrings, but that's all, and none of the gems are real."

That was about to change, but he wasn't going to say that aloud. She would be going to places with him that would require her to wear certain clothes, shoes and accessories. Maybe it shouldn't be that way, but it was. He never wanted her to feel out of place. The women in his family would surround her with their protection, but he knew that she would meet many others just like Eloisa who would just wait for a chance to tear her self-esteem to pieces.

"I'm glad you like it, *gattina*. It suits you."

Her eyes shone so brightly he couldn't stop himself from leaning in for another kiss. This time, she kissed him back immediately, letting him take her over. Letting him deepen the kiss, accepting his going from gentle to a takeover without any reservation. Like before, she gave herself to him, surrendering, and this time he felt her tentative return, the foray of her tongue chasing his, sliding along his, sending spirals of heat down his spine, centering in his groin and racing through his bloodstream. She was the one. His only. He knew it with every fiber of his being.

Vittorio sat a distance from the two women, giving Grace space to conduct business and entertain her friend. He needed to be close enough to calculate just how tired Grace became during their conversation, or if she wanted out of the meeting. She didn't realize just how much she'd done just by getting up, showering and getting dressed. She'd been up for several hours already.

This would be their first test. Grace had no idea it was coming, that she would have to make the decision whether or not to allow him to dictate to her for the sake of her health. He chose something big right out of the gate, because if she could find it in herself to trust him to look after her when she needed it, she would trust him on much smaller things.

Merry brought out a tray with fresh strawberry lemonade and then left them with a brief, friendly smile toward Grace. Katie glanced his way, but he sat close to the glass doors, giving them the view of the pool and lake while he had a good side view of both of the women.

"I was so worried, Grace," Katie said. "I received an update every day, but not seeing you was very scary. There was so much false information." She glanced again at Vittorio. "Everywhere I look I'm seeing headlines that the two of you are engaged. He spent two weeks straight at the hospital. Now you're here. How would I not know?"

Grace looked at him a little helplessly. Immediately Vittorio got up and crossed to them, distracting Katie so his woman wouldn't have to answer. He perched on the arm of Grace's chair and lifted her hand, showing off the ring. "I asked Grace not to tell anyone at all, not even her closest friend. We would have been in the spotlight and you know how glaring and disruptive that is to a new relationship. I didn't want to chance losing her."

Katie gasped when she saw the ring, but when she lifted her gaze to Vittorio, he could see the wariness on her face. "I'm Grace's partner, not just her friend. I look out for her. Not saying anything for a year certainly allowed you to be with whomever you felt like."

"Katie," Grace cautioned.

"No, *bella*, she has a perfectly good point. The tabloids write all kinds of things about my family. They make two acquaintances walking together down the hallway of a hotel seem sleazy. Having lunch with a friend can turn into a love affair. That's what you're facing being with me. Every moment of your day, everything you do, will be scrutinized. I wanted to keep you away from that for as long as possible, and I'm grateful you have a friend who looks out for you."

Katie seemed to regard him with a little less suspicion and Grace hadn't had to lie to her. He kissed her fingertips. "I'll let you two get to it. I have some work to do, but I'll be right over there, if either of you need anything." He sauntered back to his spot, took out his phone and looked for all the world as if he was completely absorbed in what he was seeing on his screen.

"I didn't want to freak out too soon, but I didn't have any of your notes for the Midnight Madness—Locals Helping the Elderly fund-raiser," Katie said. "We're three weeks out and I need to know if we still have room for a couple more sponsors. I was contacted by three big restaurants just a few days ago. Have all the sponsors submitted their logos for the event program?"

Grace nodded. "Of course we have room, but we'll need their logos immediately. The print deadline is the day after tomorrow. I double-checked that the sponsors have turned their logos in, that's taken care of. Have Audrey personally get the logos from the three restaurants. We've kept the budget down to allow more of the funds to go to the organization and I don't want any last-minute glitches like a late printing."

Vittorio liked the way his woman spoke with complete assurance. She had complete confidence in herself and it was there in her voice. He managed to keep his expression blank and continued to feign interest in his phone.

"How many programs are we printing?"

"Mrs. Ferraro insisted this be kept small and intimate, as in five hundred invitations went out. Each person invited could bring one guest, so we're printing up one thousand fifty programs to be safe. Few people ever turn down a private invitation from the Ferraros. I do have extra security coming, but that was budgeted in. The programs are numbered, and we can use those numbers for the live silent auction."

Katie typed into her notepad. "What about the auctioneer? Has he been hired?"

Grace nodded. "I'm using the same one we did last year. He was a big hit and didn't charge nearly as much as that pompous Fred Manson. That man spent more time eyeing the women than he did working."

Katie flashed a smile. "I have to agree there. The more he drank, the more handsy he got. How many live auction items do we have?"

"We have seven very nice packages, one huge one, very attractive, that will command quite a bit of bidding, and two smaller ones that are still going to bring in a nice amount. We'll have the smaller two go first, building to the largest last. We want them to spend their money, Katie. That's why they're there."

"They're there to rub shoulders with the Ferraros," Katie whispered. "And now, because of your engagement, they'll want to go just to see you with Vittorio."

"Well, they won't. I'll be working. On the day of the event, I have to be ready to take care of all the problems."

He knew both women were looking at him, so Vittorio kept his gaze glued to the screen of his phone.

"Have you seen Eloisa?" Katie's voice dropped even more.

Grace shook her head. "No."

"She called me multiple times and I know it wasn't about the fund-raiser. I managed to avoid talking to her, but I can't forever. She's going to want a confirmation that you've been seeing Vittorio."

"If she does ask, just tell her that we kept things secret to avoid the tabloids."

"I don't envy you having to deal with her on a daily basis. I'm afraid she's going to be really ugly to you at the event. You know how she loves to publicly rip someone to shreds. She'll do it, Grace. You know she will."

"Vittorio isn't going to let that happen," Grace said.

Vittorio liked the confidence in her voice, but she was beginning to sound tired. He looked up. There was a bit of sheen on her skin. She was sweating. Her face had gone from pale to an almost grayish tinge.

"Eloisa is his mother. Boys always stick up for their mothers," Katie said, absolute conviction in her voice.

"I made certain to talk to the various donors about each item already, so I have confidence that there is interest in the items and we can get some lively bidding going," Grace said, trying to get Katie back on track. "And all the table items are numbered and ready to be laid out in order."

"We have to talk about the possibility of Eloisa making a scene in the middle of our event and how we'll handle it," Katie insisted. "You can't just pretend it won't happen. She can be vicious, and it will ruin our fund-raiser."

"It's her fund-raiser. If she ruins it—"

"She'll blacklist us, Grace. No one will care that it isn't our fault."

"We have so many things to discuss, Katie."

Vittorio stood up and pocketed his phone. "Katie, Grace is tired and needs to rest. I'm sorry we're going to have to call it a day, but you can come back tomorrow if you'd like. Give Merry a time and we'll fit you in."

"We're nowhere near finished," Grace said.

"I know that, *gattina*, but *you're* finished." He circled her waist. "Put your hand on my shoulder. When you stand, it's going to hurt like hell."

"Vittorio." There was protest in her voice, but she obediently put her hand on his shoulder.

Close to her he could see beads of sweat running down her skin. She looked close to tears. He should have intervened sooner. "Next time, *bella*, we won't have you up so long before you take your meeting. If you'll excuse us, Katie, I'll have Merry show you out. I've got to get Grace to bed."

Katie stood, really looking at her partner for the first time. "Yes, of course. I'll give it a day before I come back."

"Katie," Grace protested again, but her voice was weak.

Vittorio kept her walking along the patio. Inside the house, he swept her into his arms and carried her back to her room.

CHAPTER EIGHT

"Phillips sent Grace a series of text messages, each more threatening than the one before," Vittorio told his family. He passed Grace's phone to Stefano, wanting his brothers and sisters to read the texts for themselves. He waited patiently until the phone was back in his hands.

"He's definitely unraveling," Stefano said. "I don't need a psychiatrist to read those in order to assess his condition."

"I agree." Ricco slipped his arm around Mariko's shoulders. "He's losing it, and that means he'll make mistakes."

"But it also makes him more dangerous," Mariko pointed out.

Emmanuelle picked up the glass of water in front of her on the table. "I admire Grace so much, Vittorio. She's had to live with this monster all these years. She must be terrified to close her eyes at night."

Vittorio smiled at his sister. She was so important to all of them. She'd always been their personal ray of sunshine when they were growing up and Eloisa had made things so difficult for them. She had compassion and empathy for others and they all loved that about her. "I have that same admiration, Emme. She's an amazing woman."

"Have you convinced her the engagement is real?" Giovanni asked.

"The ring is on her finger, but we'll see. She wants to take her time making her decision. I don't blame her for being afraid. I'm moving her way too fast, but I'm not taking any chances. Phillips can't touch her here, so I want to keep her here, and I don't want to risk losing her by giving her too much space. Also, before I forget, Phillips put a tracking device on Grace's phone."

"Of course he did," Stefano said. "He can't watch her every minute of the day and he'd want to know where she is, who she's talking to or texting. He's likely cloned her phone as well."

"We can use that against him," Vittorio said.

"Has there been any sign that Phillips has visited Grace's apartment?" Taviano asked.

Vittorio nodded. "Emilio found his way in. The apartment building has a parking garage and one of the grills over the vent on the lowest level was loose. When he examined it, there were scratches around the screws holding the grate in place. He was too big to fit, so he sent Leone in. He's one of the Palagonia boys, doing his early training with Emilio, but he's only sixteen. Tall, gangly, hasn't hit the wide shoulders yet. He found all kinds of evidence that Phillips spends time spying on the occupants of the apartment building. He's left wrappers and other items behind."

Stefano scowled. "Leone's just a kid. Why the hell is Emilio using him for such a dangerous assignment? Phillips could have been anywhere in those ducts. If the kid had run into him, Phillips would have cut him to pieces."

"I said the same thing to him," Vittorio agreed. "He claimed he was certain Phillips wasn't there. Something about the way he puts the grill back on to cover when he's inside. We either trust Emilio to know what he's doing, or we don't. He's never let us down. Not once."

"I've got more bad news," Stefano said. "We just learned that Lando Gori was found dead, sliced to little pieces, his eyes and nose removed, most likely while he was alive. This little bastard is one sick fuck. How your Grace managed to survive when she knew about him is beyond me."

There was a short silence. Lando Gori was considered a top enforcer. Brutal. Dangerous. A very scary man. Phillips besting him, even getting near him, and then torturing him before killing him, would have been considered impossible.

"Lando had guards outside his apartment. He had one inside, in his living room, personally appointed by Miceli Saldi," Stefano continued. "Somehow, Phillips managed to get inside the apartment and into Lando's bedroom while the guard inside watched his porn. The detectives say Phillips took his time, took a good portion of the night and at no time did the guard hear a thing. Bradshaw mentioned the Saldis were nervous as hell."

"Shit." Giovanni shuddered and rubbed at his arms. "That man gives me the creeps. He's like a little rat, getting in and out of places without a sound."

"Have you talked any more to Grace about him?"

"No, but she did tell me the photographs he sent her were often of the people he was staying with. I've sent the photos to our investigators in order to run facial recognition and to ascertain if there are any clues in the pictures to help identify where he is. Or if the digital stamps will give location." Vittorio slipped Grace's phone back into his pocket. "If we can do that, we can go after him. Right now, we're dead in the water."

"I took a look at Lando's apartment," Ricco said. "Mariko and I thoroughly went through the ducts there. Unfortunately for Lando, the largest cooling duct led straight to his apartment first. Phillips was very comfortable there and left evidence of having spent the day there. He has life living in the crawl spaces, attics and ducts down pat."

Emmanuelle held up her hand, wrinkling her nose. "Ew. I don't want to hear any more. I know what you're going to say. That's disgusting. He must leave that when he's going away, otherwise the stench would lead to an investigation immediately."

"The point being, he's casual about his kills. He isn't nervous in the hours leading up to them. He's patient," Ricco said.

"Did you warn Eloisa?" Vittorio asked.

Stefano nodded. "I talked to her in person. She was livid over your engagement and practically accused Grace of knowingly harboring a criminal. She's gotten worse, not better since I married Francesca. After her last attack on Francesca, I completely banned her. I don't want Francesca upset in any way, and Eloisa has made her the primary target now that we're grown and won't put up with her crap." He looked at Vittorio. "I suggest you do the same, at least until Grace is on her feet."

"They've already met. I overheard her conversation with Katie Branscomb. As it turns out, Grace and Katie are partners."

"We just received that information," Giovanni revealed. "It's in your phone if you paid any attention."

"I've been getting so many updates so fast, I haven't had the time to read every report thoroughly. At first, I thought maybe Eloisa called Grace to spew her anger at her, because otherwise she would have known she was capable of producing the children she so desperately wants."

Stefano shook his head. "No, Vittorio. She wouldn't have told any of us."

A tendril of something red drifted through the tranquil colors in his mind. Vittorio had known all along. He was hoping his older brother would reassure him that wasn't so. "Why the hell would Eloisa not inform us there was an untrained rider, capable of giving us children? What the fuck does she have to gain by not telling us? It makes no sense at all. None."

"She made Francesca feel awful for not producing children," Emmanuelle pointed out.

"I could have met her sooner and protected her from all of this." Vittorio had watched Grace suffering. She hadn't complained about the pain in her shattered shoulder, but he could see the agony etched into her face. She'd been so white her skin was nearly gray. He could see silent tears tracking down at times. She hadn't been able to sleep lying down, and pain woke her intermittently. "She would have been safe from Phillips and the Saldis."

"We don't know for certain if Eloisa knew she is a rider, Vittorio," Emmanuelle cautioned. She put a hand on his arm. "She's so lost right now. She can't take Stefano banning her. It's a really big deal to her."

"She knew," Vittorio said with absolute certainty. "She met her in person. She knew. The big deal to her is that she no longer has Francesca as her whipping post."

Mariko ducked her head for a moment and then she lifted it. "Your mother is in pain. Not just lost, but in pain. I see it in her eyes. She lashes out at everyone because she's hurting. It's sad."

Ricco leaned over and brushed a kiss on the top of her blond head. "You are so forgiving, *farfallina mia*."

"We are not," Stefano said.

Vittorio echoed his older brother's sentiment. It was hard to forget their childhood and even harder to take Eloisa's attacks on their women. Emmanuelle was the one to always try to soothe her, but more often than not, Eloisa seemed to revel in tearing strips off of her. She found every reason to complain, mock and ridicule her. Nothing Emmanuelle ever did was right or good enough and yet she always helped her mother. Her brothers held Eloisa's treatment of their beloved younger sister against Eloisa more than almost anything else.

"Let's circle back to Phillips. There's no explanation for Eloisa or her treatment of her daughters-in-law. We know Phillips can't get to Francesca or Stefano," Vittorio said. "He won't be able to get to Eloisa, all the precautions are in place as they are in all of our homes. What about Lucia, Amo and Nicoletta? He might not know our connection to them, but we can't take any chances."

"I sent them all to Italy," Taviano said. "As soon as I knew our family might once again be under attack, I thought it best to remove them from danger. Amo and Lucia only know that we wanted them to take Nicoletta to Italy and Sicily. They were more than delighted to surprise her with a long vacation."

"I'm making certain my staff is protected," Vittorio said. "And also, Katie Branscomb. He's been in her home already. I had Tomas and Cosimo talk to her last week and explain the danger. I offered to put her up in the Ferraro hotel and she agreed to move there until this is over. They're with her now."

Vittorio glanced at his sister. Tomas and Cosimo Abatangelo were Emmanuelle's regular bodyguards, but lately they'd been used as roving guards, going to whoever needed them the most. Emmanuelle sent him a small smile as if she had it covered. Each member of his family present in his home had ridden the shadows to get there, which meant leaving their bodyguards behind.

"We'll keep someone on her," Stefano said.

"Thank you. Grace will be relieved to know she's safe. If he can't get to us through our homes, he's likely to come at us another way," Vittorio said.

"Grace's apartment is being watched so hopefully we'll know when he's there," Taviano said. "In the meantime, we've made it look as though Grace has been there on and off. Let's put her phone in her apartment as soon as the Grecos have the photographs they need."

"That's done," Vittorio said. "You can have the phone."

Ricco flashed Vittorio a grin as he took the cell phone. "It will make him crazy that he missed her. He'll need to camp there in the ducts, staring into her apartment."

"Maybe," Vittorio said. "He's cunning. He's been eluding the law for a very long time, which means he's extremely intelligent."

"True," Stefano agreed, "but those text messages prove he's unraveling. That means he's going to make a mistake. We have to be there to nail him if he does."

"What about the meeting with the Saldis?" Vittorio asked. "Is that still on?" He almost wished it wasn't, although he knew they had to get it over with. If war between the two families was coming, they had to know.

"Absolutely. Be at the hotel tomorrow at four."

"I'll be bringing Grace with me. She'll be able to meet Francesca if Francesca is up to it. It sounds like things have changed in the last few days."

Stefano nodded. "Doc wants her to stay off her feet as much as possible. He says things are fine with the baby, but she's had a little too much activity, meaning a few contractions. He's had a room with all the equipment he needs set up in our home. If the contractions continue or get stronger, he'll give her some medication to stop them. The meds would be hard on her."

Vittorio could see why Stefano had banned Eloisa, with her abrasive personality, from seeing Francesca. He stood up. "I appreciate you all coming here. Doc says Grace is almost ready to start physical therapy, which means I won't worry about her losing her arm."

"She's probably losing her mind being so helpless," Giovanni said and got up as well. "I know that was the worst for me."

"That's right, Gee." Vittorio said. "You don't get to use the shadows like a normal person, you have to drive."

"Normal people don't ride shadows." Ricco pointed out the obvious. "They drive. Guess what that makes you, brother."

"Don't say it," Giovanni said, and gave his brother the finger.

Vittorio waited until his family left and then he went to

find Grace. She was sitting in her favorite spot in the garden, looking out over the lake. She looked up when his shadow fell over her and then entwined with her shadow. The physical jolt of sexual awareness hit him hard, just as it did her.

She tipped her head back and smiled at him. Just that— she smiled, and his heart started tripping. Their joined shadows had already sent hot blood rushing through his veins. He had thought to hold a part of himself back until she made up her mind. Getting his heart broken wasn't on his list of things he wanted to experience. But the effect of her welcoming smile told him it was too late. He'd already fallen.

"I think that was the longest I've been away from you in over four weeks," she greeted. "It's weird because I've spent a lifetime alone, but I found myself waiting for you. I even thought about going to look for you. Isn't that strange?"

He shook his head. "I didn't much like being away from you, either." He crouched down beside her chair and framed her face with both hands. "I miss you when we're not connected."

Then he was kissing her. Her lips were soft, her mouth a hot spark igniting a stick of dynamite that seemed to explode, so the fire inside him raged out of control when everything else about him was always controlled. She took him to another realm where there was only pure feeling. Electricity snapped and crackled between them, sparking on his skin, while inside his body, blood turned to a molten stream, burning with need. His heartbeat pounded through his cock, until he was so thick and full he doubted anything could contain him if he continued.

He pressed his forehead to hers. "We have to stop."

"I don't especially want to."

He smiled in spite of his body making painful, urgent demands. "Neither do I, but nevertheless. Doc hasn't given permission for you to be doing anything but recovering."

Her eyes went wide, and she drew away. "You *asked* him? Discussed with him whether or not we could have sex?"

"Naturally. Oral sex, physical sex, rough, games, toys, positions, every kind of sex. I don't want you hurt."

"I can never look at him again." Her declaration was accompanied by that delicate rose color that swept up her neck to heighten the color in her cheeks.

He laughed softly, noticing she didn't protest that he thought they would be having sex—and as soon as possible. "He's a doctor, *gattina*. He knows men and women have sex."

She let her breath out. "What did he say?"

He couldn't help kissing her again, although it was dangerous to his fragmenting control. His woman was becoming a terrible temptress. She was learning fast, and every stroke of her tongue sent lightning strikes through his veins straight to his groin. Still, his role was to guard her health first, before his pleasure. He would have seen to her pleasure had the surgeon given the okay, but even that was forbidden for another week. Even after that, he would have to be careful.

"Is he still saying no?" she asked when he lifted his head. There was a note of teasing along with the deliberate seduction.

"I can see I'm going to have my hands full with you." He loved that she was willing to try seduction even though he couldn't allow her to succeed. It was becoming difficult to be with her and not think about sex.

He stood up to give himself a little reprieve, then instantly realized what a bad idea that was. His cock was at her eye level and her gaze went straight to the thick bulge. Her hand followed, fingertips sliding over the material covering his heavy erection.

"I could . . ."

"No, you couldn't," he said decisively. But he didn't move. The way she stroked him felt electrifying.

Her tongue touched her top lip and then moistened her

bottom one so that her lips glistened invitingly. He suppressed a groan.

"I've never actually had my mouth on a man's . . ."

"Cock," he supplied. "Never?"

"There was always Haydon to worry about. I never had the chance to see if I wanted to be that intimate with a man."

Her fingers kept stroking. Once she stopped to toy with the tab at the top of his zipper and then began dancing her fingers up the woven steel again. She lifted her green gaze to his and it was all he could do not to groan aloud.

"I want to be that intimate with you."

His Grace. She wasn't shy. The more those mesmerizing fingers caressed him through his jeans, the more his heart felt as if a hand was squeezing it tightly. Hot blood pounded through his cock. Hunger for her burned through him at her confession. Discipline was the only thing he had that could save them.

"Grace, more than anything, I want you. Right now. This minute. But the doctor said no, so it's no."

"What would it hurt if you helped me figure out how to please you, Vittorio? It isn't like I'm going to be really great at this. You'll have to give me step-by-step instructions."

Her green gaze clung to his and a slow smile only added to the seduction in her eyes. "It's not like I can YouTube on how to do it without my phone."

She was beautiful. His. "I don't deserve you, *il mia bellissima gattina*. You are fast becoming *vita mia*. I don't know what will happen if you decide you can't live with me."

Her lashes lowered, and she shook her head. Very slowly, with obvious reluctance, she removed her hand. The lashes lifted so he was looking into her unwavering green eyes. "I'm not going to pretend it will always be easy, but I can't imagine not being with you." She made a little face at him. "It is a little annoying to be told no when I really, really want something."

Relief was a fast current, running through him like a river. "What is it you want, *gattina*?" Her gaze began to shift, and he caught her chin. "Keep looking at me when you tell me, Grace. It pleases me to hear you say what you want, whether it's sexual in nature or not. When you look at me while you tell me, the pleasure is so much more."

"I wanted to taste your cock. To have it in my mouth." There was no hesitation. Her chin went up and her eyes sparkled like twin gems, the hunger in them making him want to push the denim from his hips and give her anything she wanted. "I want to give you pleasure."

"That's exactly what I want at this very moment as well, Grace." He ran the pad of his thumb over her lips. "A few more days, then we'll both be satisfied."

He sank into the chair next to her, much more gingerly than he would have ordinarily. Wanting Grace wasn't going to stop anytime soon. He stretched his legs out in front of him to ease the ache in his cock. "There is a tracking program on your phone, Grace. We're putting it in your apartment."

She was horrified. "No, Vittorio. You should have asked me. I need it back for work. You can't just decide to—" She broke off, her hand to her mouth as realization clearly dawned that he would be arbitrarily making some decisions based on what he felt was right for her safety or health. He'd warned her many times. Living with him wasn't going to be easy.

He waited in silence.

She turned her head to stare out over the colorful flowers to the lake just beyond the garden and beach. "My notes for the upcoming event as well as several others were in my phone."

"I'm well aware of that," Vittorio said.

Grace twisted back toward him so fast, a small cry escaped and he saw her wince. He caught her arm to steady her.

"Don't, Grace. You're going to hurt your shoulder for no reason."

"You copied it for me, didn't you?"

"As well as your contacts. I had to be careful. I sent everything to my computer geniuses to make certain I wasn't giving you anything that could infect a new phone." He pulled the phone from his pocket and handed it to her. "It's set up for you and all your contacts and notes are right where they were in your old phone."

"I'm sorry. I should have trusted that you would have done that."

"Why? Trust isn't given overnight, Grace, and I don't expect you to just blindly give it to me. The notes were important. I didn't find the tracking program. I'm not an expert in technology, but I have cousins who are. I took your phone to them, so they could get the photographs off your phone, the ones Haydon sent you of where he was living. We thought we might be able to figure out where he was by the various photographs. They're the ones who discovered the tracking program. No way was I bringing that back to you, so I just got you a new one and told them to take off everything to do with your work and make certain it was clean."

"Thank you. I should have known. More than once he took my phone from me and demanded to know my passcode. I thought it was to see my schedule, so he could threaten me by hanging around."

"He can't get to you now, Grace," he assured.

She stared down at the cell phone in her hand. "He gets very angry when he doesn't know where I am. I got used to him demanding my schedule."

Vittorio frowned. "I want you to really think back, *cara*. Even when you were children, was he always with you? Did he depend on you to do anything for him?"

She didn't answer right away. His thoughtful Grace. He liked that trait in her. The stillness in her. She brought a sense of peace to her surroundings. She'd lived in a potentially violent world every minute of the day since she became aware of what Haydon truly was. From that, possibly because of it, she'd developed inner tranquility, a place inside her that she could depend on when everything around her turned to chaos.

"He's older than I am by a couple of years, but he didn't talk much. When I first went into the foster home, he was already there. He was thin, and very small. Back then, I was extremely small, and I think he liked that I was littler than he was. It made him feel big. My other foster brother, Dwayne, was a bully. He liked to push us both around. I stood up for Haydon when Dwayne kept tripping him. That's where it started with us."

"No one had probably ever stood up for him before."

She put the phone on the table and reached for the pitcher of icy strawberry lemonade Merry had placed on the little table beside her glass. Vittorio's hand got there first. He would have to talk to Merry about expecting Grace to pick up a full pitcher of ice and juice. It was too heavy. He poured a glass for her and then went to the small, free-standing bar to pull out a glass for himself.

"Mr. Ferraro?" Merry's voice sounded strained, and he turned. She stood there wringing her hands, looking nervous. "Mrs. Ferraro is here."

Out of the corner of his eye he saw Grace stiffen. He wondered if she thought he was secretly married. The thought made him smile. The moment he saw the woman bearing down on them, her expression grim, her face a mask of anger, the smile disappeared. Instinctively, he put his body between his mother and Grace.

"This is ridiculous, making me stand waiting in the foyer like I'm some salesman. Your staff needs lessons on protocol. I'm talking to your mother, Merry, about your atrocious manners. When I come to my son's home, I don't expect to be told to sit and wait as if I'm some commoner visiting the king."

"Hello, Eloisa," Vittorio drawled. Deliberately he crossed the room, bent his head and brushed his mother's cheek with a barely there kiss.

She jumped back, recovered and glared at him. Her hand

went to her cheek and brushed at her skin, as if she could remove his mark on her. "Stop that, Vittorio. I know you do that to annoy me."

"It's a gesture of affection, Eloisa, which most mothers appreciate."

She glared at him, hands on hips. "Well I don't, so stop it." She looked past him to Grace. "It wasn't enough that you had Teodosiu Giordano panting after you, you had to go after my son. Vittorio does have a bigger bank account, but I think Giordano will suit a girl like you so much better."

Vittorio swung around. "Teodosiu Giordano expressed an interest in you?"

Grace curled her fingers around the tall glass of strawberry lemonade. "He asked me out several times, yes. I refused to go out with him."

"I'll just bet you did. Are you pregnant? Did he knock you up and throw you out on your ear so that now you are going after my son?"

"Giordano was an enforcer for Miceli Saldi for years. He came into a great deal of money and ended up a loan shark," Vittorio informed his woman. "This ties everything together so neatly." Deliberately, he ignored his mother.

"He's got to be the man Haydon owes the money to." Grace took her cue from him, not looking at Eloisa, refusing to be intimidated by her.

Pride burst through him. She was magnificent. She looked regal, even with her shoulder completely immobile, bandages holding her arm in place. Her voice was soft, but definitely, she was a woman in charge, speaking to him as an equal.

"I should have thought of Giordano. He would have been the first one a man like Haydon would go to for money." He turned his head and flashed a smile at his mother. "Thank you, Eloisa. You've solved part of the mystery. We needed to know who was supplying Haydon with cash."

Eloisa frowned. "Vittorio." Her voice was cautionary but cutting.

Vittorio ignored her and swung back to face Grace. "We've speculated for years over why Miceli would allow Giordano to leave his position as top enforcer and strike out on his own as a loan shark."

"*Don't* talk to her about our private family business." Eloisa nearly shrieked it.

Vittorio indicated the glass of strawberry lemonade and when Grace didn't pick it up right away, he did and held it to her lips. He brushed back her hair while she drank, his fingertips savoring the richness of the thick, silky strands. "This is all public knowledge," he assured her. "Anyone can speculate on Miceli's generosity to a former employee. The bottom line is, if you turned down a man like Giordano, he might think he could get you through a gambling debt. Did you know he was in the mob?"

Grace shook her head. "No, I thought the mob was more or less gone these days. You don't hear that much about it."

"It's alive and well. Just not as blatantly bloody as it used to be. Let's think about this, *bella*, put it into a timeline."

"Vittorio, I *insist* you talk to me."

He glanced over his shoulder and sent his mother a smile. "Please, do sit down, Eloisa. I'll have Merry bring you whatever you want to eat, or I can pour you a drink if you'd like, from the bar. I can make just about anything. Give me a minute. This is important."

"As if I'm not?" Eloisa snapped. "I *insist* that you speak to me now."

Vittorio sighed and turned fully around. "You have my full attention, Eloisa."

"Stop calling me that in that horrid tone. I despise the way you say my name."

"Would you prefer Mrs. Ferraro? Or Ms. Ferraro?"

"Stop being sarcastic, Vittorio." Eloisa all but gnashed her teeth. "You're putting off the inevitable. I have a few things to say to this little money-chaser. She works for Katie Branscomb, although how Katie, coming from such a good family, ever met up with her I'll never know."

"She's doesn't work for Katie, Eloisa, she is a full partner as well as Katie's friend, which you well know. You would never use a company without fully investigating them first. You pretended not to know because it suited you. Grace is my fiancée. We're getting married whether you approve or not." He kept his voice very calm. Very even. Compelling. "You may as well accept my decision because I won't be changing it."

"That's ridiculous. Just because she meets the criteria . . ."

Behind him he felt Grace's sudden stillness. He was aware she would demand a few explanations he wouldn't be able to give her. He willed her to stay silent and not ask questions. "You knew." It was a soft accusation. Anyone who knew him, other than his mother, would have tread lightly from that moment on.

"Of course I knew." Eloisa threw her head up, her eyes blazing with anger.

"But you didn't say anything."

"Because I knew one of you would do exactly this. Make a fool of yourself over her. Convince yourself you were in love. It's not real. She may meet the criteria, but she doesn't meet our standards."

"I would like you to leave, Eloisa. She's my fiancée. I am going to marry her and have a family with her. That alone should demand a little respect for her. You're insulting me and my intelligence by saying I don't know the difference between real and fantasy. Since I've had to endure your ugliness my entire life, I'm immune to whatever venom you choose to spew. However, and you'd better hear me, Eloisa, I will *not* tolerate you doing the same thing to my woman. She's my choice. She's always going to be my choice. I would like you to leave now."

"This is ridiculous. You can't possibly be throwing me out."

"I am politely asking you to leave my residence and not to return until you can be pleasant to Grace. The same Grace who saved my life."

Eloisa rolled her eyes. "I suppose you're very grateful to her. Write a check, don't marry her. And if you want to throw that in my face and imply that I should be grateful to her as well, I remind you that if it wasn't for her, no one would have been shooting at you."

"And I would remind *you* that had you told us about her, she would have been safe, and no one would have been shot." He leveled his gaze on his mother's face. He was finished talking.

Even Eloisa knew him well enough to know that look. She threw her hands into the air. "Fine. Make a fool of yourself. You boys all seem to want to follow in Stefano's footsteps. I haven't seen his precious Francesca. She's not working. She just spends her time like a princess in a tower. It makes me sick."

He took a step toward her. He had no problem picking her up and putting her out the door, but she took one look at his face and turned and strode out, without looking back.

Vittorio turned slowly back to Grace. She had the icy glass pressed to her forehead and her eyes were closed. That was a bad sign. Grace was no pushover. And she was intelligent. She wouldn't fail to miss his mother's accusations.

She lifted her long lashes and he was staring into her very speculative eyes. There was pain on her face, sorrow in her eyes. She'd believed in him more than she realized. It was there on her face. There was satisfaction in that knowledge, but he really detested the sadness his mother's revelations had caused her.

"Grace . . ."

"Just tell me, Vittorio. What criteria do I meet?"

"My mother is a very bitter, caustic woman. Don't let her hurt you."

"Eloisa Ferraro can't hurt me, Vittorio. You can. I need you to explain to me what criteria I meet."

"If I can't explain it to you?"

"I suppose you want me to blindly follow you without

any explanation whatsoever. That isn't going to happen. I suggest you tell me what she meant."

"I think, at this time, no matter what explanation I give you, your mind is closed."

Grace was silent. Her gaze shifted from his face to the lake. She looked so sad he wanted to gather her close to him and hold her.

"That's true. I think I'm overwhelmed with everything, and we're moving far too fast." Her gaze jumped back to his. "I don't believe in fairy tales, Vittorio. I let myself believe for a few minutes there, because I wanted it so much to be real. You're . . . extraordinary. You really are. Some woman will be very lucky to have you in her life."

There was no way for her to take the ring off and he was glad about that.

"Grace, don't. My mother is very good at saying the things she knows will hurt others. It's her special gift. She deliberately wanted you to feel as if you weren't important or loved by me. Our life is ours, not anyone else's. What we choose to do between us is for us alone. I'm telling you, stating it as a fact, that you're my choice. I love everything about you. I can name a dozen of your traits right now, if that would convince you, but you have to believe in me. In us. I can't give you that. You have to feel it."

She tilted her head and looked up at him, her eyes meeting his. "Is there truth in what she said? Do I meet some important criteria for you? Something that made you notice me?"

"The gunshot wasn't enough for me to notice you?"

She didn't buy his diversion. She waited, her gaze steady.

Vittorio sighed and crouched down in front of her, eye level. "Yes, Grace, there are criteria that all of our women have to meet, and you do. Was it the first thing I noticed about you? Not even close. I saw you explode out of the trunk of that car. You nearly lit up the parking lot with your fury. There were two big men, both carrying weapons, enforcers for Miceli. There was Haydon Phillips, trying to sell you for payment of his debts. None of that mattered to you. You were willing to take all of them on at that point. It was the sexiest thing I'd ever seen."

"I'm not going to let you distract me."

"I'm not trying to distract you. I'm telling you the truth. I fell in love right there in that parking lot without ever having been introduced to you. I overhead that you had taken loans out to help Phillips. At the time, I thought it was because he was your friend, not because you feared him, but regardless, to me, that showed your loyalty. Knowing you now, I know you would do something like that for a friend. Right down the line, everything I learned about you or observed made me believe you were absolutely the woman for me."

"And those all-important criteria that make me in the running to be married to a Ferraro?"

He sighed. "You're not hearing a thing I say. You don't want to hear me, Grace. Let's get you back inside. You look tired."

She didn't protest, not even when he cradled her in his arms rather than walk with her. He needed to feel as if he held her to him, rather than watch her move away from him. He already could feel her slipping through his fingers.

CHAPTER NINE

'm hoping Francesca can work her magic," Vittorio confided to Stefano as the private elevator took them from the penthouse suite. "Otherwise I'm going to lose Grace."

"What happened?"

"Eloisa. She deliberately said some things that she knew I couldn't possibly explain to Grace right now. I wouldn't mind so much, I could deal with that in time, but Grace is injured and that makes what Eloisa did reprehensible."

"She's got to be made to stop," Stefano said. "Seriously, Vittorio, she's getting worse, not better. If we don't find a way to stop her behavior, she's going to tear apart our family. What did she say to Grace?"

"She said it to me in front of her. She referred to Grace as meeting criteria and that's the only reason I noticed her. She pointed out that I wouldn't have looked at Grace for any other reason. I couldn't explain about shadows or riding to her, or anything about what we do. She hasn't committed to me. That could be disastrous."

Stefano stepped out of the elevator. "Francesca is a huge

asset to all of us. I'm going to text her and let her know there's a problem. Hopefully, Grace brings it up to her, so she can help smooth things over."

"Eloisa knew Grace was an untrained shadow rider for certain. I don't know how long she's known, but she did. I could see it on her face and she admitted it." Vittorio scrubbed his hands over his shadowed jaw. "Sometimes I want to strangle her. Why does she want to make our lives miserable?"

"She's miserable," Stefano said as they crossed the lobby of the hotel. It was beautiful, an elegant, well-cared-for space, with high ceilings and crystal chandeliers. Both ignored the sudden hush as several guests ceased talking and stared at them as they made their way to the hallway that led to the conference rooms. "Eloisa wants everyone around her to be the same. She was raised in a cold, unfeeling environment. It was all about work. She knows no other way and that's what she believes is the right way. The only way to stay safe."

"We have to have something to live for," Vittorio pointed out.

Stefano's sharp gaze leapt to his face. "You're my steady one, brother."

Vittorio shrugged. "I still have to have a home and without Grace, I'm back to empty nothing. Walls. Silence. You know what it's like."

Stefano stopped walking abruptly, just before they reached the conference room where they were meeting with the Saldi family. "Are you absolutely certain that Grace is yours? She's not just a woman who would be suitable because she carries the genetic code we need? Francesca is my world. Your woman needs to be yours."

"Grace is my Francesca," Vittorio assured. "If I lose her, I'll allow them to initiate an arranged marriage. It won't matter after she's gone because I'll never have what I need from anyone else. I feel that pull between us growing stronger with every moment I spend in her company. When I'm away from her, all I do is think about her. I want her happy and I know whatever it takes to achieve that, including letting her go, is what I'll do."

Stefano shook his head. "You don't let her go, Vittorio. You find a way to make her happy so that she wants to stay with you no matter what. What we do isn't easy to understand. For someone like Grace, a woman terrorized by a man who kills anyone who slights him, perceived or not, our way of life can be easily misunderstood."

"I'm well aware," Vittorio admitted. "Eloisa pushed my timetable up far too fast. Grace has just started physical therapy and I planned to slowly condition her to accept our way of life, not just blurt out explanations and force her to try to accept them."

Vittorio knew it would be impossible to explain what his family did. He was born a shadow rider and trained from the time he was two. There was no other job or interest for him. It was considered a sacred duty and no rider, if he was capable, would ever walk away from it, no matter how difficult. The life was lonely, regimented, dangerous and formidable. Now that he'd had Grace in his life, even for a short few weeks, he wasn't willing to go back to that stark, lonely existence.

Stefano pushed open the door and the two brothers stepped inside the huge room. "You might try explaining Eloisa. Grace seems a compassionate little thing. She might be distracted for a day or two."

"At least we had a mother," Vittorio groused. "If that's what one would call Eloisa. Grace never had one. She had a crap childhood." He detested that Grace had lived in terror. That she hadn't had anyone to comfort her when she was young. That the only person who had ever stuck up for her was a serial killer who since had made her life a living hell.

"You'll no doubt find a way to make up for it," Stefano said.

"Did you talk to Teodosiu Giordano? I'm certain he's the one loaning the money to Phillips."

Stefano paused just inside the door of the conference room. "I did. Personally. He's smooth, and he mixed lies with the truth. He admitted Phillips came to him and borrowed money on multiple occasions. He admitted he asked Grace out several times. He said he would again if given half a chance. He had no idea she was engaged to you, but for him that explained why she wouldn't go out with him. Phillips had come to him with a harebrained scheme to allow Grace to pay his debt with sex. He explained that wasn't what he wanted from her. I believed that much. I'm not so certain he wasn't in on the kidnapping. On the other hand, he was cool under fire and seemed a little angry that anyone would do that to Grace. That came across as real. So, bottom line, he's a question mark and someone we'll keep an eye on."

"Thanks, Stefano. I didn't want to leave Grace, not now when she's upset with me."

Ricco sat at the table, Mariko by his side. The couple looked up when they walked in. "Everything all right?" Ricco asked Vittorio. "I saw your lady. She didn't look happy."

"Eloisa."

"Of course. I should have known. Francesca will fix it," Ricco said with absolute confidence.

Vittorio hoped his brothers were right. She'd told him, after the disastrous conversation with Eloisa, that she was all right now sleeping in her room alone, and she worried about him sitting up all night. He hadn't protested, but he didn't like her separating them. He knew she had it in her mind that she was going to get strong enough to leave. The word *criteria* was right there between them.

Stefano glanced at his watch. "Mariko, you will stay in the shadows. Anything goes wrong, you're our ace in the hole. We'll be asking them to leave their bodyguards outside of the room, so we'll have to do the same. Sasha,

Francesca and Grace are safe upstairs and I have four men on them. Giovanni is our most vulnerable, so you cover him, Mariko. He's your first priority."

She nodded solemnly. "Consider it done."

"Speak of the devil," Ricco said as Giovanni and Taviano sauntered in.

"Am I hearing my name being used in a bad way?" Giovanni asked.

"Always," Stefano said and clapped his brother on the shoulder. "Sasha told Francesca the doctors are going to take the hardware out of your leg soon."

Giovanni nodded. "I'll have to go through therapy again before I can go back to work, but at least there's an end to this. I held off scheduling the operation until we're certain Grace is safe."

Vittorio sent his brother a smile of thanks. For all the downsides to being a rider, there was his family. Always there. Always ready to help and watch out for one another. His family was one of the biggest gifts he had to offer Grace.

"I want you close to this door." Stefano indicated the door that was secreted into the room on the wall just across from the head of the table. It was difficult to see the door and Giovanni would have to use his athleticism if anything went wrong to cross the short distance and dive to safety. "You're armed?"

"Of course." Giovanni looked offended.

It went without being said that all of them would be armed. The Saldis would be as well. Vittorio knew Stefano was going over the plan much like a general before a battle. His older brother always planned everything step-by-step, especially matters of his family's safety.

"Eloisa will also be in the shadows on the western side of the room. Mariko will cover the south. The New York cousins, Salvatore, Lucca and Geno, are here, and they will take east and north. Geno will find the fastest tube near Giuseppi and kill him first if they start anything." Stefano glanced at the door. "If things go wrong, Val is my target. No matter what, he doesn't get near Emmanuelle."

Vittorio had thought the same thing. Val had done enough to hurt their sister. Chances were, she would never trust another man. He'd used her, getting close to her on orders from his father and even bragged about it to another woman. Emmanuelle had not only been heartbroken, but humiliated. Still, she was coming to the meeting. Head high. A true Ferraro. If the Saldis were out for blood, the tables would be turned, and Val was going to be the first to die.

The cousins from New York emerged from three separate shadows, each wearing the signature Ferraro rider pinstriped suit. They shook hands and once again, Stefano looked at his watch.

"Salvatore, Emmanuelle will be seated closest to where you will be secreted. If things go to hell, she's your responsibility. She's deadly, and she'll be fighting her way to us, backing us up, but get her into the shadows. She's going to be their number-two target after me. I'm counting on you to protect her."

"On my life," Salvatore said.

Stefano once again went over where he had positioned all the riders and who their targets would be.

Emmanuelle hurried into the room. "I'm sorry I'm late, Stefano. I was upstairs with Francesca and giving last-minute instructions to Sasha." She sent Giovanni a smile. "Your wife is a woman to count on in a firefight."

Giovanni laid his hand over his heart. Emmanuelle threw herself into Salvatore's arms, hugging him hard. He kissed both her cheeks and then Geno followed suit. Lastly, Lucca hugged and kissed her.

"I should have known all three of you would come," she greeted. "Thank you."

"I don't really think Giuseppi would be stupid enough to try to wipe us out, but you never know," Stefano said. "Something's up. We just need to be careful. I've already given our cousins everything we have on Haydon Phillips as well."

"He's a scary little bastard," Geno said. "Have you locked your woman up tight, Vittorio?"

"She's upstairs with Francesca and Sasha," Vittorio said. "He can't get up there. The ducts have been protected and there is no way to use the elevator, or the elevator shaft. He's clever, though, and as more time passes and he can't get to Grace, I think he's going to try something he might not ordinarily try."

"He seems as though he can be very patient," Lucca observed. "I've read all the data they have on him so far and he waits months at a time for his revenge."

"But before, he's always had access to Grace," Salvatore pointed out. "I agree with Vittorio's assessment. I think in some way he relies on having her in his life. He seems to need her. He terrorizes her, he uses her to pay debts and he clearly was willing to sell her, but not for the long term, or permanently. He also expected he could control the deal."

Vittorio agreed wholeheartedly with Salvatore's conclusions. "Grace has been the only constant in his life. He wants to keep her isolated from anyone else. He's made sure she can't get close to anyone. She's the one person he isn't going to let go of. That means he'll come after her with everything he's got."

"And hopefully make mistakes," Ricco said.

"Caterers are coming," Stefano said, looking down at the text on his phone.

"That's our cue," Geno said. "Chances are, the Saldis have someone on the payroll."

Vittorio agreed. The catering company was one of the best, one they used frequently. Giuseppi Saldi would know every company the Ferraros did business with. It would stand to reason he would put someone on his payroll. The Ferraros always had people on the inside of companies the Saldi family used.

Mariko and their three New York cousins slipped into

the shadows in their assigned spots. Vittorio circled Emmanuelle's shoulders with his arm, drawing her close to him. "Emme, I would be a lot happier if you would join them. You could still protect us."

She went up on her toes and brushed a kiss on the hard line of his jaw. "I love you, Vittorio. You're the best. All of you. You're good to me, but I made this mistake. I set myself up as a target for the Saldi family. I knew I shouldn't have a relationship with Valentino, but in spite of all the warnings, I did it anyway."

She rubbed her face against his arm and then straightened her shoulders. "I'm a Ferraro. I can admit to making mistakes, no matter how foolish. I was sixteen when I fell for him. I'm not sixteen now. If he wants to gloat, let him. I stand with my family, and at no time did I ever give him one piece of information about any of you, or my family in general. He may have gotten my heart, but he didn't achieve his goal, so fuck him and Giuseppi."

There was no way his little firecracker of a sister was going to hide in the shadows while her brothers faced the Saldi family. Vittorio knew there was no sense in trying to talk her out of her stand. In any case, he would have done the same. "I'm proud of you, Emme."

She flashed him a smile and turned toward the door as the caterers began to filter in one by one. Vittorio knew that Emilio and Enzo were double-checking each employee as they approached the room. They also had a dog that would alert if there were any evidence of bomb materials in any of the carts or on their persons. The caterers were patted down for weapons. Their faces were run through facial-recognition software, checked against Haydon Phillips's face. Vittorio wouldn't put it past him.

The refreshments were put on the table along with small crockery and glasses. Wine was opened. The caterers left. Eloisa slipped into the room. She scowled at her oldest son, hands on her hips. "What is Giovanni doing in this room? He can't possibly escape if there's a problem."

"It's been handled," Stefano said.

"He shouldn't be here."

"He's a grown man," Giovanni snapped. "Don't start shit before this goes down."

"It wouldn't be going down if your sister hadn't decided to play the—"

"Don't," Vittorio commanded, his voice low, but carrying. He stepped closer, towering over her. "Do not say one word against my sister. You've caused enough trouble. Leave us, or take our backs, but for once in your life, hold your tongue or I'll put you out right in front of the Saldi family."

He was at his limit with Eloisa. She'd already jeopardized his relationship with Grace. More, she could have prevented what happened to Grace, but she had arbitrarily decided she didn't want Grace as a daughter-in-law. She was relentless in her desire to tear down Emmanuelle. He'd had enough and really, if she didn't stop, he was more than capable of picking her up and putting her out of the room right in front of Giuseppi and his family. None of his brothers would lift a hand to stop him.

Eloisa looked outraged. "How dare you threaten me. I'm still your mother, as much as Stefano tries to take that role." Even as she hissed the words at him, she backed away.

"Eloisa, you're on the western side of the room," Stefano said, indicating the position he wanted her in.

The conference room had been designed for the riders. Shadows fell across the walls and doorways, leading in all directions, thrown from the many overhead lights artfully placed. Their mother disappeared into the shadows, and Vittorio closed his eyes for a moment to center himself. The adrenaline receded, and he was once more himself.

Stefano put a hand on his shoulder just as the door opened and Emilio nodded at them.

"Bodyguards remain outside. You know what to do," Stefano said. "The trouble could start out there. Be watchful."

Emilio gave them all his deadpan look, as if to say *let them try.*

"Bring them in."

Valentino came into the room first. He scanned, taking in everything and everyone, his gaze coming back to rest on Emmanuelle. She didn't stand close to any of her brothers, but rather she was straight, her chin up, regal almost, and Vittorio was proud of her. He noticed Val's breath hitch, but his gaze moved beyond her to Stefano.

"I'm trusting you with my father, Stefano."

Taviano opened his mouth, but Vittorio shook his head. They all wanted to say the same thing. They'd trusted Val with their sister. They should have stopped the relationship. They'd protested, but they hadn't stopped it and she'd been broken by this man.

"I'm trusting you with my family," Stefano responded. Saying nothing and everything.

Vittorio always admired how Stefano could command a room with his sheer presence. He repeated back to Val his own words, yet his inflection meant something altogether different.

Val was silent a moment, taking a careful look around, even looking up, once more scanning the room for any hidden threat. He studied Stefano's face, and then looked at Emmanuelle, as if she might give him answers.

"Don't look at her," Vittorio cautioned. "Worry about yourself, not your family." He kept his tone low and mild, but there was a menacing promise in every word.

Val continued to study Emmanuelle's face. Vittorio glanced at his sister. He was proud of her. She didn't bend. Her shoulders remained straight, no expression on her face, and she looked right through Val.

Val's gaze shifted to Vittorio and then touched on each brother. He didn't look intimidated, but he did look upset. He shook his head and then glanced over his shoulder. "We're good."

It was difficult not to respect Valentino Saldi. In the midst of the hostility he couldn't help but feel emanating from the Ferraro family, he still trusted them enough to call in his adopted father. It was clear he loved Giuseppi and would defend him fiercely, but even if war was coming between the two families, he wasn't about to back down from trying to stop it.

Giuseppi Saldi entered. He was a man in his early sixties, in good shape. His black hair was streaked with attractive silver. He looked worn. Vittorio had never seen him look so beaten. He wore sorrow like a cloak. As a rule, Giuseppi could take over a room. He usually had a smile and his dark eyes were laughing. There was no laughter whatsoever in him. He went straight to Stefano and held out his hand. Stefano immediately shook it and indicated the conference table.

"I appreciate you meeting with us, Giuseppi, especially under the circumstances. We were so sorry to hear about Greta. I hope she's comfortable?"

Everyone knew Greta was the love of Giuseppi's life. She was in stage four pancreatic cancer, and Giuseppe spent all of his time with her. For him to take the time to come to the meeting meant it was extremely important to him.

Giuseppi nodded several times. "She was happy to see Emmanuelle." The man turned to look at her. "Thank you for going to see her. It meant a lot to her."

Emmanuelle inclined her head. "Greta is very loved by everyone who knows her."

Valentino swung around, looking from his adopted father to Emme. She didn't even glance his way.

Giuseppi smiled at her and turned back to Stefano as his brother entered, his brother's three sons behind him. "Pay no mind to Miceli. He's a hothead." It was an attempt at the humor he'd always shown.

Stefano accepted Miceli's handshake. "As is Taviano. We'll keep the two of them apart."

Miceli laughed. "He's been saying that since I was four. Now I'm sixty and he thinks I haven't outgrown that trait." He turned to Vittorio. "Before we start this meeting, I have to formally apologize to you. I had no idea Grace Murphy was your fiancée. No one knew of your engagement. I certainly have no idea what Ale and Lando were doing at your nightclub."

Vittorio, like all shadow riders, could hear lies. Miceli Saldi was lying. The look of apology on his face appeared sincere. His expressions and inflections were perfect, but he was lying. Vittorio studiously avoided looking at any of his brothers or Emmanuelle. They would hear it, the note that was just off enough to warn them the man was a blatant liar.

"How is she doing?"

"As well as can be expected with a shattered shoulder."

"I understand she works for the event planner. Martina uses the company for every charity or party she throws. She's met Grace."

"How is your wife?" That was safe enough. If the Saldis did have any psychic gifts, and it was entirely possible, Vittorio wasn't going to say anything that might be heard as a lie. Martina Saldi was a good woman. Vittorio had met her at numerous functions and she was always unfailingly polite to everyone. Even to Eloisa, who could be abrasive.

"Fine. Fine. She laments every day that our sons haven't married and done their duty to provide us with grandchildren." He waved his hand toward his sons, who had entered behind him.

Dario Bosco, Miceli's oldest, often worked as the primary bodyguard for his cousin, Valentino. His other two brothers, Angelo and Tommaso, spread out a little, taking up positions that didn't seem to be threatening, but would better protect their father and uncle should it be necessary.

"Our mother often says exactly the same thing," Stefano said. "I believe Martina and Eloisa have often had a conversation about grandchildren."

"Greta wished to see our grandchildren," Giuseppi mourned and sank into a chair to the right of the head of the table, exactly where Stefano had planned for him to sit.

The head of the Saldi family looked and felt so sorrowful, Vittorio felt sorry for him. Everyone who knew anything about the Saldi family knew Giuseppi Saldi was in love with his wife.

Miceli put a hand on his brother's shoulder and patted just before he took the chair next to him, facing Taviano and Vittorio. Ricco took the chair directly opposite Giuseppi. Giovanni took the chair directly across from Miceli. His body was nearly, but not quite, in one of the larger shadows cast by the chandelier overhead. Emmanuelle walked around the table, head up, royalty deigning to be with those far beneath her, coming around to take the seat beside Taviano.

Valentino took the chair directly opposite her, leaving two chairs open between Miceli and himself. Miceli's two sons, Angelo and Tommaso, immediately filled between their father and cousin, leaving Dario standing. Vittorio didn't like that Val's cousins were all but smirking when they looked at Emmanuelle, but she didn't appear to be in any way bothered by their looks, so he kept silent. This was Stefano's show.

Giuseppi took several food items and poured himself strong coffee. The others, on both sides of the table, followed suit. Vittorio didn't feel like eating. Sorrow was coming off Giuseppi in waves, but something else, some other strong emotion had crept into the room. The tension in his belly coiled, not like knots, but like a snake, waiting to strike. He couldn't tell where the source of danger was coming from, but it was in the room, spreading across the table and swirling around his brothers like a cloak of doom.

Stefano stood at the head of the table, his coffee cup close. "Thank you for taking the time to come to the meeting, Giuseppi. I know that every minute away from Greta is difficult for you."

"I felt this was important, Stefano, to clear up any misunderstandings that have occurred between our two families," Giuseppi said. "I explained to Greta and she agreed with me. We might have differing points of view, but we have always been allies with one another when necessary." Deliberately he referred to a terrible attack on the

Ferraro family—he'd sent his men to aid them. Of course, at the time, his son was in the line of fire as well.

"It has come to our attention that one of our employees at the nightclub has been working for the Saldi family. We have several men and women who have worked for us for years. Martin Shanks has always been a trusted manager and considered a friend. Timothy Vane is his assistant, also a trusted employee."

Vittorio watched Miceli and Giuseppi closely as Stefano talked. Giuseppi ate his food calmly but listened attentively. Miceli dropped his hand under the table several times and Vittorio envisioned him whipping out an automatic and spraying the entire Ferraro family with bullets. He felt that same tension coiling in his brothers, but none of them showed it, their faces expressionless as they ate from the abundance of food and drink.

"The cameras had been erased both in the parking lot and inside the club, but fortunately, we have cousins who are amazing with technology and they miraculously resurrected the video for us."

Vittorio knew the footage was recovered from the backup remotes.

"It clearly shows Timothy Vane escorting your employees, Miceli, Ale Sarto and Lando Gori, into my club, along with Haydon Phillips, who we now know is a serial killer."

Miceli waved his hand. "Ale and Lando went rogue on me. I would have fired them had I known they were dealing in trafficking. It came as such a shock when I found out. I questioned Lando myself. He was apologetic and begged forgiveness, especially for using your club for such a meeting. His reasoning was, it was the last place they would be spotted by any of their fellow workers. I do not employ this disloyal assistant Vane, nor would I. Clearly, Sarto and Gori were striking out on their own."

It was the biggest crock of shit Vittorio had ever heard. Miceli's voice sounded sincere, but the lie was too big to be covered by the superb acting. Vittorio watched the Saldi sons closely. Dario had taken the seat on the outside, beside Val. His gaze was on Taviano, as if he'd chosen the youngest male Ferraro as his personal target. Angelo was watching Giovanni closely. Tommaso had eyes only for Vittorio. That meant Val was on Emmanuelle. Vittorio didn't like it. If it came to a shoot-out with the Saldi family, he didn't know if his sister would hesitate before she pulled the trigger. If she did, Val would kill her. Could he get off a shot at Val and then manage to kill Tommaso immediately after? Even knowing Stefano had planned for such a shoot-out, he still went over the scenario in his mind, again and again, practicing until he knew he would be smooth and fast.

"Timothy Vane has been detained and is being questioned by the police," Stefano continued, his cold dark blue eyes boring into Miceli.

Giuseppi had turned in his seat to look accusingly at his brother. He didn't try to hide his expression or his skepticism.

"Haydon Phillips is on the loose, and if the cops can prove Vane aided him in any way, they'll put him behind bars. I've already questioned Vane and he had quite a bit to say. According to him, he was approached when he first was hired. The initial contact was made by a man named Harold Jenson. I believe he is in your employ, Miceli."

Rather than look outraged, Miceli laughed softly. "Stefano, let's be men here. You have those in my employ, in Giuseppi's and our businesses. We have them in yours. This is just business between us. We watch one another, but that is all. If Vane is one of these men Harold recruited, then yes, he's given money to tell us whatever he can about the mysterious Ferraro brothers and their lovely sister. That is all. There is no big conspiracy." He waved his hands dramatically and then picked up a cannoli and took a large bite.

Giuseppi nodded as if his brother had fixed everything between the families.

Stefano sighed. "Perhaps what you say has some merit,

Miceli, but conducting any business in our club is strictly forbidden. That is Ferraro territory. The lines are marked clearly, and we've set down the rules between our families long ago. Any infraction is an act of war. Your men have been conducting business in our club for some time now. Not just Ale and Lando, God rest their souls, but several others. In front of both of you is a list of names. These men are all on your payroll, Miceli."

Before Giuseppi could drag the paper to him, Miceli caught it up, crumbled it in his hand and threw it. The paper landed in the strawberry jam. "I've said I do not conduct business in your club, Stefano, and my word should be enough!" Miceli shouted the accusation, his face turning red.

Stefano stared him down, his gaze cool. Vittorio felt everything in him settle. He knew exactly what he would do. His first shot had to be a kill shot. At all costs, even with Stefano choosing to target Val first, Vittorio would take out Val Saldi to protect Emme. Tommaso was next in order to keep from being killed. All the while he had to be moving back to the shadows. Protecting Giovanni came third. Giovanni couldn't get into the shadows, not with the hardware in his leg. He would be exposed. Hopefully, their backup covering them would mow down their enemies before they fired off a shot.

Miceli's face turned even redder. "I don't care what you think, Stefano—"

Giuseppi had slowly stood, and his brother broke off, going quiet under his cold stare. "Stefano, it seems my family does owe you an apology. My son assured me that if you were making an accusation it wouldn't be without proof. The Saldi family keeps our word." He turned another cold look at his brother. "Conducting business in your club is not a sanctioned move. I will get to the bottom of this and we will pay restitution to your family."

"Giuseppi—" Miceli attempted a protest, but it was met with another cold stare and a shake of his older brother's head.

"No. When we say we will do something, when we negotiate and sign a treaty, we do so in good faith. Our word has never been questioned by the Ferraro family, nor has their word been questioned by ours. As head of my family, ultimately, I am responsible for not knowing what is going on right under my nose. I can only apologize, Stefano, and pay restitution."

Stefano inclined his head. "You have been caring for Greta."

"There is no excuse. Perhaps I need to step down and turn the business over to my son." He sank into his seat, looking older, his handsome face lined with grief. "There is no stopping cancer, Stefano. It doesn't matter the money or power, nothing stops it."

Stefano put a comforting hand on his shoulder. "I'm sorry, Giuseppi. I can't imagine losing Francesca. Greta has always been a bright star to everyone she touches."

Miceli gripped his brother's other shoulder. Vittorio didn't buy the murmured words of sympathy. He glanced at Taviano. His younger brother knew Miceli's condolences were false. Miceli was angry that Giuseppi would apologize to the Ferraros. He had knowingly conducted business in their territory, in one of their establishments, and he'd done so on purpose.

"I feel very bad having to continue with the list of proof," Stefano said, "but I can't let you think the nightclub was the only place the Saldi men were conducting business. I want it all stopped. Harold also recruited Bruno Vitale to sell drugs out of his family's flower shop. Bruno was using the shop to ship drugs out as well through the postal service, which is a federal offense. He will be dealt with by us, but in doing so, two of the men bringing him the drugs to sell began to harass and threaten my ward, Nicoletta."

Dario whipped his head around to glare at Stefano. "Names," he snapped abruptly. "Do you have proof of this?"

"I don't make accusations without proof," Stefano said. "Nicoletta told us what happened. She was threatened by these men because she saw them bringing the drugs into the shop and she protested. One of them pushed her into the wall. Fortunately, she was taught to defend herself and she was able to get away and call for help."

Vittorio flicked a look at Taviano's grim face. While Grace was in the hospital, Vittorio had heard there was an attempted assault on Nicoletta at the flower shop. The family had been elated that she'd coded in the alarm she had on her wristwatch. Taviano had been the first to get to her and had stopped the attacker's pursuit. Later, Taviano had confirmed he'd retaliated.

"I imagine these two men who were stupid enough to put their hands on your ward are the ones who have disappeared," Giuseppi said dryly.

"I wouldn't know about that," Stefano said. "I was out of town at the time."

"Nicoletta is not just Stefano's ward," Taviano said. "She is also, and more importantly, my fiancée. It seems that not only was Vittorio's fiancée targeted, but mine as well."

Dario shook his head. "That's impossible. Nicoletta isn't wearing your ring. There's been no announcement."

"We do not bring attention to our women if we can help it," Stefano said. "The media attention is brutal as you well know."

"What I know is, you spend half your life screwing women on the pages of a tabloid," Dario snarled, his dark eyes challenging Taviano. "This is bullshit."

"What's bullshit is the Saldi family conducting business in our territory," Stefano snapped. "And threatening our women. I want it stopped. If it doesn't stop, I can only assume you are declaring war between our families."

"It will stop," Giuseppi said. "I want the list of names, everyone you have, along with the proof. I need to put a stop to this now. A hard stop to it." He glared at his younger brother. "This has put our family in a bad light. Our word is our bond. Our honor."

Stefano inclined his head. "I want all drugs removed

from my territory. I also want your word of honor that no trafficking of any kind, especially human, will *ever* be conducted in our territory."

"You have my word," Giuseppi said solemnly. "I speak for our family."

"I want the word of every Saldi in this room," Stefano said. "Specifically, I want to hear them say it aloud to us."

Vittorio felt the warrior in him rising. He felt every one of his brothers go on alert as he was doing. Stefano's demand bordered on insult. He was all but declaring he didn't believe Giuseppi spoke for his family.

Val protested immediately. "My father has given his word of honor."

"Perhaps, but it wasn't Giuseppi's men invading my territory, selling drugs or kidnapping women to sell them to the highest bidder," Stefano said coolly.

Vittorio watched Val out of the corner of his eye, but he kept his gaze fixed on Tommaso. At Stefano's demand, Tommaso flicked a quick glance at his father. Miceli rose with great dignity. He inclined his head at Stefano.

"I take full responsibility for what is clearly a mutiny in the ranks of my men. Lando Gori and Ale Sarto have always been trusted employees. More like family. I gave them more and more duties while my sons attended college. Now, my boys are home again, and I have spent time with them that was missed while they were gone. It is clear that there has been some kind of mistaken attempt to take in more territory. Perhaps I didn't make it clear to these men that the Ferraro territory was out of bounds. I can give my word as a Saldi, for me and for my sons, that we will not conduct any business, drugs or trafficking in the Ferraro territory."

He looked dramatic. He sounded utterly sincere. He also had that note in his voice that told Vittorio he was lying. Vittorio flicked a glance at Stefano, who inclined his head at Miceli, who sank gracefully into his seat and folded his arms across his chest.

Val rose. "I will never, under any circumstances, conduct family business, including the sale of drugs or trafficking of any kind, including women, in Ferraro territory." He kept his gaze on Emmanuelle's face. His voice rang with sincerity.

She paled but she didn't even deign to lift her lashes to look at him.

Miceli's sons made their promises. Dario sounded sincere, and Vittorio couldn't hear any lie, but Angelo and Tommaso echoed their father's strange, off-putting note.

Stefano was gracious after that, turning all smiles, although a bit grim.

Giuseppi rose. "Thank you for your patience, Stefano. Again, I apologize for my family's indiscretions. I must get back to Greta, so if you will excuse us, I have quite a lot to do before I can see my wife." The last was said almost as an accusation at his brother. "If you don't mind, Stefano, again I would ask that you provide another copy of the list of names of anyone who has been involved in this conspiracy, as well as the proof."

"I have it right here for you," Stefano said and handed over a second copy of the list. "Thank you, Giuseppi. I'm very happy that you cleared this matter up between us."

Val rose hurriedly and went to the door, his hand on the knob, blocking his father from leaving the room before he cleared the other side.

CHAPTER TEN

Y ou seem so sad."

Francesca sounded so compassionate, Grace was afraid she might burst into tears and spill her every fear to a complete stranger. Stefano had brought Francesca to two functions, and he'd hovered so close to her, watched over her like a hawk, so much so that Grace had been mesmerized by the couple. Stefano had rarely left his wife's side, and when he did, she was surrounded by his brothers and sisters. Mariko and Emmanuelle were close to her at all times. Grace had wondered what it would feel like to be part of that family and so loved by them all.

Francesca half sat in her bed, looking astonishingly beautiful for a woman on bed rest. The room was enormous and included a sitting area. Before he had gone downstairs to the conference room, Stefano had arranged the furniture so that there were very comfortable chairs for Sasha and Grace to sit in while visiting with his wife.

"This is like a fairy tale," Grace admitted. The two

women were looking at her for some explanation and she felt as if she had to give them something. They'd been welcoming to her, clearly happy to see her. She hadn't expected that kind of unreserved reception. "But it isn't real."

Vittorio had escorted Grace up to the penthouse of the Ferraro Hotel where Stefano and Francesca resided. As always, he had his hand on the small of her back, making her acutely aware of him. Sometimes his touch was so hot it felt as if he were burning a brand through her skin right to her bones. She never moved away from him, and she could have. She just didn't. She'd told him she didn't need him to sleep in her room, and he didn't, but that meant she couldn't go to sleep and she was tired. Her eyes felt sandy and swollen from crying most of the night. All for a dream. A fairy tale.

"What do you mean by 'it'?" Sasha asked. "What's not real?"

Grace sent her a smile, fighting the urge to cry. She'd been indulging herself in her room, staying there, hoping Vittorio would leave her alone so she could get used to being without him, but then when he did, she was devastated. It made absolutely no sense.

"I don't know how this thing happened between Vittorio and me. I really don't. I woke up in the hospital engaged to a man I don't really know. And he doesn't know me. He can't possibly think he's in love with me, and I should have known better to believe any of it."

Grace pressed her fingers over her mouth to stop herself from blurting out another word. What was wrong with her? She was acting completely out of character. She'd stayed in her room, hiding from the one man who had shown her any kindness, because she was afraid. What did she think? That a man like Vittorio Ferraro was playing an elaborate hoax on her? That was absurd. She just knew she couldn't take rejection from him, so it was easier to leap on the first legitimate excuse to run. Her jumbled fears weren't making any sense.

"If I talk about this, I'm going to turn into a crying machine and I'm supposed to be cheering you up, Francesca," she added.

"Vittorio is an honorable man," Francesca said, ignoring Grace's effort to change the subject. "In spite of what you read in tabloids, he is a man of his word. You can believe anything he tells you. If he says he wants to marry you—"

"Eloisa said I met the criteria and that's why he wants to marry me," Grace blurted out before she could stop herself. "She said he wouldn't have looked at me otherwise. When I asked him, he admitted to me there is a criterion and that I did meet it." Grace couldn't keep the challenge out of her voice.

There was a small silence while Sasha and Francesca exchanged a long look. It was obvious that they knew what she was talking about.

"Vittorio didn't explain?" Francesca asked cautiously.

Grace shook her head. "No, he refused to."

There was another long look between Francesca and Sasha. Grace sighed. "It's clear you know what Eloisa meant."

"What it means, Grace," Francesca's voice was gentle, "is that because you meet those criteria, Vittorio is free to fall in love with you. I know it sounds archaic but think in terms of the royal family. They have certain duties they are born to take on and with that comes tremendous responsibility. They aren't allowed to marry just anyone."

"I am not royalty," Grace denied. "And I don't want a man to choose me simply because I meet a certain criterion."

"Do you really believe that Vittorio Ferraro, who could have just about any woman he wanted, would choose you if he wasn't capable of loving you? Do you think he wants a loveless marriage?"

When she didn't answer, Sasha took over. "Do you believe Stefano loves Francesca?"

"That's obvious to anyone who sees them together."

"What about Ricco? Does he love Mariko?" Sasha challenged.

Grace thought about the times she'd observed them together. Ricco had been very much like Stefano, rarely leaving his wife's side and focusing completely on her in much the same way Vittorio focused on Grace. Butterfly wings began to flutter in her stomach. Deep inside she began to have a niggling doubt.

"Yes, I believe he does."

"You probably haven't seen Giovanni with me," Sasha said. "But I can assure you, he's very much in love with me. When we're together, his attention is wholly focused on me. It doesn't matter how many beautiful women throw themselves at him, he never notices. And guess what? We meet those criteria Eloisa so quickly pointed out to you."

"Not to me," Grace corrected absently. "To Vittorio, where I could hear her." Vittorio did focus completely on her. Even now, after she'd told him not to sleep in her room, everything he did was for her.

He had set up a room with the equipment needed for her physical therapy and was already talking to the physical therapists. He brought her breakfast and made certain she had everything she wanted. Katie came to go over work with her. He escorted her personally to the back patio, so they could look out over the pool to the lake.

He touched her often. Just a brush of his fingers, but each time he did, he sent heat spiraling through her body and secret fingers of desire dancing down her spine. Sometimes, she wanted him with every breath she drew. Other times she was upset at the disappointment and hurt she saw in his eyes. Every cell in her body urged her to soothe him. To make everything between them all right, but she knew that was her personality. She was a nurturer. A pleaser.

She was good with details and she noted everything about Vittorio. She knew he didn't like shoes worn in his house. She knew how he took his coffee and when he preferred tea or Scotch. She could tell when he was restless and needed to retreat to his private training room, or when he preferred to meditate. She recognized the signs in him when he struggled to keep from kissing her, or maybe even taking their relationship further, but he respected the boundaries she'd set. She almost wished he didn't.

"Grace, any number of women might meet those criteria. We don't know. I, personally, couldn't care less," Francesca said staunchly. "I will admit, like you, at first I was worried he hadn't chosen me for me, that we moved too fast, but then it didn't matter, because he was everything I ever wanted in a man. Don't get me wrong, Ferraro men are no picnic to live with. You have to be committed to them. Wholly. If you take him on, Vittorio has to be your world, because you'll be his. That isn't always comfortable."

Sasha nodded. There was a hint of worry in her eyes. "Vittorio is a wonderful man and he'll always look after his wife and children, but don't let this go any further if you don't really love him. He needs that. A woman who will love him so completely that she'll want to be his universe. Like Francesca says, that isn't always a comfortable place to be."

"I'm very aware of that," Grace acknowledged. "I just hate that he has to take care of me. If I wasn't so needy—" She broke off. What was she saying? She wanted him. That was the truth. She wanted the fairy tale, even if her prince was admittedly a little on the dark side. A little shiver crept down her spine. He'd never shown that side of him to her, but he'd alluded to it and she was aware, on some level, that it was there.

"Has he intimated in any way that he doesn't want you there or he doesn't like looking after you?" Francesca asked. "I can't imagine that. I think Vittorio would enjoy looking after you."

"He says so. I think, after having Haydon in my life for so long, I'm terrified of trusting anyone. Other than Katie, who I met by accident in college, I haven't believed in anyone. Not ever."

She hadn't. She'd been conditioned not to go near anyone else. She'd met Katie in school and they both had done papers on event planning. After they found that out, they met for coffee and discussed their ideas. When Haydon had objected and made overt threats toward her, Grace had pointed out that if she didn't have a job that paid well, she wouldn't have a place to live. She'd implied he wouldn't, either, and he'd left her alone. Katie had ended up sharing her dorm room through college.

"Do you love Vittorio?" Francesca asked.

It was far too soon. A month? Five weeks? Part of that she'd been out of it. It had been the best month of her life, in spite of the pain. She looked for him. She listened for him. Every cell in her body was completely tuned to him. Was that love or obsession? Was it just turning to a man to help her out in a terrible time of need?

"I haven't had time to find out. He asked me to give him a chance and I was. I told him I would, but then Eloisa came along and I lost my confidence."

Francesca sighed. "Don't fall into the trap I did. Eloisa tried to drive a wedge between Stefano and me. She does a good job of undermining my confidence whenever she sees me. I wish I was more like Mariko, who ignores her, or Sasha, who puts her in her place. Instead, I let her words hurt me and then Stefano loses his mind."

"Vittorio threatened to put her out of the house, and I think he would have."

"He would have," Francesca and Sasha said in unison.

Grace found herself laughing. "I'm beginning to know him enough that I believe when he says something, he means it."

The smile faded from Sasha's face. "I hope you always remember that. Ferraro men show their true colors to the women they fall in love with. I can't imagine that Vittorio won't let you see him as he truly is with what he needs and expects from his woman."

Francesca glanced at her sister-in-law sharply but then sipped water from a straw and subsided onto her pillow. "Do you have any idea how exhausting it is doing absolutely nothing? I've taken up knitting and it's a mess. I heard crocheting was easier, but I doubt it. I really admire and have mad respect for women who knit." She indicated the bag that was on the side of the bed.

Sasha took out the ivory-colored yarn and held up the shapeless blob that was supposed to be some kind of handmade item. "What is it?"

"Give that to me," Francesca said and tried to snatch it out of Sasha's hand.

Sasha burst out laughing. "I'm showing this to the boys."

"Don't you dare. That awful Taviano will have it framed and hung in my baby's room and then torment me day and night over it."

Grace wanted the camaraderie the Ferraros unfailingly showed to one another—and now were extending to her. Vittorio was offering her that. Was she really so afraid that she wouldn't even give him a chance—give them a chance? She didn't want to be that girl, the one curled up in a little ball. The one under the covers in the fetal position. She'd been there hundreds of times and every single time she'd told herself to stand up. This time, win or lose, if she just stood up, she had the very real opportunity, which would never come again, to be with a man she'd dreamt of.

She wanted someone to care for her the way Vittorio was offering. Someone who would keep her safe and protect her from the worst of life. She'd had the worst for too long and she wanted a buffer. The idea of an exciting and different sex life made her hot and damp with excitement. She was unashamed that she wanted everything he was offering and was willing to trade a little of her freedom for it. In her mind, Vittorio gave her wings. He set her free to soar high, but in safety.

"Do you know something?" Grace leapt out of her chair, jarring the hell out of her shoulder but she didn't care as realization dawned. "Most of my life, I've thought about Haydon every single minute. I've been terrified of him. Terrified for anyone I spoke to that day. If I laughed when I was talking to a client. Or to the catering company. Anyone. The point is, he was always uppermost in my mind. I haven't thought about Haydon practically at all. Just the last few nights when Vittorio wasn't sleeping in my room."

She didn't care how that sounded to them—if they believed she and Vittorio were already having sex. What sane woman wouldn't have sex with him? She was elated. In his way, by taking her phone, wrapping her in a cocoon, making the decisions about who could speak to her and who couldn't, he had already given her freedom. *I haven't thought of Haydon.* She hadn't been afraid. She already missed the closeness she'd had with Vittorio. "Vittorio is on my mind. I think about him every waking minute."

Francesca practically beamed at her. "That's good, Grace. I'm so happy that Vittorio could do that for you."

"Me too." She touched her arm and found herself laughing. "Ow. I don't think I'm quite ready to jump out of chairs."

"Vittorio wouldn't be happy with you," Sasha said. "Lord only knows what he'd do if he saw you do that." She and Francesca exchanged a knowing look and then burst out laughing.

"I'm not sure I want to know." Suspicion edged her voice, but there was excitement, too. She couldn't help it. Vittorio was a very sexual man. He'd said there weren't punishments like she'd read about in books, but she knew there would be something he would do if he wasn't happy and for some insane reason, the thought excited her.

A light flared bright red through the room. At once the smiles faded from their faces. Sasha was up immediately and pulled weapons from under the bed. "It's all right, Francesca, Stefano said to expect this, remember? We're good." Her voice had gone from laughter and fun to businesslike. "Grace, we need to stay in this room. The panic room is right behind Francesca's bed. I'll need you to help me get her into it, if the alarm is given a second time. Vittorio wants you in the panic room with Francesca if it comes to that."

"What about you?" Grace asked. She tried to keep her heart from accelerating. It was impossible, but she breathed deeply in order to stay calm. Like Sasha, it suddenly was important to her to take care of Francesca.

"I'll be on the inside with the two of you."

"Coming in," a man's voice called out.

Sasha pointed the shotgun toward the door. "Get behind me."

Grace didn't argue. She had just moved to the bed to sit beside Francesca when the door swung open and a man in a suit stepped through, followed by another. The two men looked grim, but somehow reassuring.

"That's Drago and Demetrio Palagonia," Francesca whispered to Grace. "Brothers. Related to Stefano. Emilio trained them, so you know they're very good." Her face had gone pale.

Grace didn't know about Emilio or his training, but if Francesca and Sasha were so convinced, she was willing to be, as long as Haydon wasn't slipping through the duct system.

"No one has breached our security, ladies," Demetrio said. "This is just a precaution." He looked directly at Grace. "It is an impossibility for anyone to crawl through the ventilation system. If they were to find a way to do so, they would trigger any number of alarms. Most likely, they would be deceased before we could get to them."

He didn't elaborate on how the intruder would become deceased, and Grace didn't ask. She couldn't help but look around the master suite, noting each vent and the proximity to the bed. She felt very protective over Francesca, especially knowing she was pregnant and already having difficulties.

Francesca hadn't taken her gaze from Demetrio's face. "If this is a precaution, nothing more, then why did the alarm go off?"

* * *

Vittorio was up out of his chair and off to the side of the door, ready to block it once the Saldi men were through so that Emme, Giovanni and Stefano were safe. He hadn't liked the look that passed between Angelo and Tommaso. Dario had seemed intent on staring Taviano down, but then everyone knew Dario had a thing for Nicoletta and Taviano's announcement of his "understanding" with Nicoletta had been met with hostility.

Valentino went through the door first, signaling to his father's bodyguards. He stepped aside and waved Giuseppi through. The man stepped into the wide hallway that opened directly into the lobby with confidence, still shaking his head, annoyed with his brother. Vittorio saw a shadow move high up on the second floor and alarms went off in his head. He glimpsed several people leaning out over the bannister to point at the chandeliers. A few moved up the circular stairway.

The stairway had been built very reminiscent of eras gone by. The Ferraro Hotels were known for luxury appointments, but also the mixture of elegance and modern technology. One man stood in the corner to the right of the stairs where he had a perfect view of the entrance to the conference room. He was lifting his arm and pointing an object toward the door and Giuseppi.

Without thinking, Vittorio shoved Miceli back into the room and dove for Giuseppi, calling out a warning to Valentino as he did so. Vittorio was a big man and enormously strong. He hit the older man hard, driving him to the floor and rolling toward Emilio. Shots rang out, but Emilio's knee dug into his back as his cousin covered both men. Enzo had taken down Val a second after Vittorio hit Giuseppi.

Screams broke out in the lobby. Bodyguards on both sides first pointed weapons at one another and then up toward the stairs.

"Don't fire!" Stefano yelled. "Too many people!"

The shooter grabbed a woman as she ran past him, trying to shoo her teenage son out of the way. The boy ran back down the staircase a few stairs and then crouched low, still in harm's way. Emilio eased his knee out of Vittorio's back and then helped him up. Vittorio gently aided Giuseppi. Vittorio's momentum had taken them down the wide hallway and away from the lobby. He peered through the archway into the lobby and up the stairs.

"Are you all right?" He wasn't looking at the older man; he studied the shadows falling around the shooter.

"Yes, yes. Thanks to you. Where's Valentino? Was he shot?"

Stefano directed the bodyguards, "When it's safe, take Giuseppi and Miceli and their sons back into the conference room. Make certain no one gets near them." He clapped Giuseppi on the shoulder as he walked past him, but he didn't stop. He walked into the lobby to the bottom of the stairs and looked up.

An eerie silence had taken over the hotel. All eyes were on Stefano. "Why don't you let her go?" In the distance was the sound of sirens.

"That's not going to happen," the man called down, his accent very heavy. "If I let her go, they'll shoot me down immediately."

"No one is going to shoot you down."

"They will. I know too much. They're after me and I didn't get the job done."

With all eyes on Stefano, Vittorio slipped back into the darkness of the corner. His family was in place in the shadows inside the conference room. Taviano, Emme and Giovanni were with the Saldis in plain sight, but they were guarded by their mother and cousins. He didn't have to worry about them. Stefano was deliberately placing himself in danger in order to allow Vittorio to get into position to take the shooter down.

Vittorio spotted the shadow he needed. It was one of the thinner ones that moved like lightning, so fast one's body felt as if it were torn apart and could never catch up. The shadow, thrown by a hanging crystal branch dripping with what looked like icicles, went all the way up the stairs, beyond the shooter, to disappear into the darker corner behind him.

Vittorio would have one moment when he was exposed as he stepped from his corner to the shadow, but all eyes appeared to be on the drama playing out between Stefano and the shooter. Emilio suddenly glided between Vittorio and the others, giving him the opportunity to come in behind him. One step. The tube caught at him, dragged him inside so hard he felt wrenched apart, his body seemingly flying to pieces.

The shock was always greater than one expected, even with all his experience. He streaked past his brother and up the stairs. A teenage boy crouched six stairs from the top, almost in plain sight of the shooter. He huddled there, shaking, holding on to the bannister as if he might leap over at any moment. Vittorio caught a glimpse of the shooter's human shield as he sped past. The woman had stark terror on her face. She was moaning, the tears streaking her makeup so it ran down her face, making several dark lines.

He halted just behind the shooter in the mouth of the tube, waiting for his body to come together, for the terrible wrenching to subside so he could breathe again. He studied the man. He was older than expected. In his late forties or early fifties. His accent had been Sicilian. What had he said? He knew too much. They would shoot him down. They needed this man alive. They needed to be able to question him.

He waited, knowing Stefano would distract the shooter to give him time to get into position to free the woman and strip the gun away.

"I'll come up. You let her go and take me hostage. This is my hotel and I can't very well have my guests accosted. I won't resist in any way. I think that's a fair deal." Stefano set one foot on the stairs.

Vittorio couldn't help but admire his brother. In one short moment he had saved the hotel's reputation. Everyone would want to come where the owners put their life on the line for their guests.

Behind him, the doors of the hotel opened, and police burst into the lobby, rushing up behind Stefano. Stefano turned to face them, his hand up in the air. "Just hold it right there."

For a moment, chaos reigned as the SWAT team poured into the lobby, weapons drawn. There was more yelling and some screams. Vittorio stepped out from the shadows, behind and just to the side of the shooter. As he reached to strip the gun from the man, two shots rang out, one after the other, and the woman slumped in the shooter's arms, blood dripping from her throat and the middle of her forehead.

At once screams rivaled with gunfire as the police opened up with their weapons, mowing down the shooter. Vittorio turned and dove for the tube as the shooter was flung backward. The teenage boy waited as the cops rushed the stairs. One tapped him on the shoulder and he turned and ran down the stairs, looking as if he was weeping.

Stefano was waiting at the end of the hall. Relief was palpable the moment Vittorio stepped out of the shadows in front of him. "Are you all right? Were you hit?" He ran his hands over his brother's chest. "That went to hell fast. What the fuck happened, Vittorio? Who shot her? The shot didn't come from behind me."

Vittorio shook his head. "I don't know. I was concentrating on trying to strip the gun without him pulling the trigger. It was small caliber. I barely heard it. It sounded more like a pop, pop to me. The only one close was a kid . . . a teenage boy. I think he was the woman's son. She waved him back when the shooter grabbed her. He was crouched on the stairs and was terrified. We should find that kid and make certain he's all right."

Stefano swore softly. "I thought for sure you were hit, too. My heart nearly stopped." He gave a sigh. "This bites, Vittorio. The cops are going to be all over this, especially when they see we've had a meeting with the Saldis. We might as well just invite them to investigate us all over again."

"They're not going to let any of us leave."

"Get Val and Giuseppi back into the conference room with the others where they'll be more comfortable. There's food. Drink. See if they need anything else. I'll make sure the police know that Giuseppi has to get back to his wife as soon as possible."

"They'll be nasty about that."

"Not if Art Maverick or Jason Bradshaw are here. They're decent men and good detectives. Neither one will hold Giuseppi here for no reason when they know his wife is dying."

Vittorio knew that much was true. He wanted to get to Grace, but he'd been seen behind the shooter and the police were going to keep him downstairs as well. Stefano was going to catch the brunt of the investigation. As head of the family and the one trying to talk the shooter into giving up his hostage, he would be the one talking to the police and the reporters. Vittorio didn't envy him.

"Let's get it done." Talking to police and reporters was just something the Ferraros had to occasionally put up with. Vittorio put his hand on his brother's shoulder. "I'm going to text Grace and let her know we're all okay. She'll be worried."

"I'm letting Francesca know, although I've been keeping Demetrio and Drago apprised of the situation," Stefano said. "Things didn't look good between you and Grace."

"They haven't been for this last week. If she doesn't come to me soon, I'm going to have to force the issue. She isn't sleeping, and that will impede her shoulder healing. Eloisa, as usual, managed to fuck things up for me."

"I think she makes it her life's work to fuck up our relationships." Stefano was watching over Vittorio's shoulder and he turned slightly to see Art Maverick come into the building with his partner, Jason Bradshaw. The two detectives were assigned their neighborhood along with Little

Italy, so they were very familiar with both the Ferraros and Saldis.

"I'd better get Giuseppi and Val into the conference room, if they weren't taken there already," Vittorio said. He hastened to the little alcove where Val had taken his father to sit, their bodyguards surrounding the two men. Vittorio ignored the posturing of the bodyguards. "Giuseppi, Maverick and Bradshaw are in the building. Let's get you into the conference room and Stefano will have them question you and Val first so you can get out of here."

"Do you know who the shooter was? Or why he tried to kill us?" Val asked as he helped his father stand.

Vittorio noticed the older man trembling. Giuseppi wasn't that old or frail. Was he ill? If he was, neither Val or Giuseppi would admit it to a Ferraro. "I didn't have time to look at his wallet if he had one," Vittorio said. "Someone shot that woman. Stefano thinks they were shooting at me."

They proceeded from the alcove to the conference room. The door was open and Miceli and his sons were standing, trying to take in everything that was happening with their bodyguards attempting to shield them.

"It wasn't one of us," Val said, almost belligerently. "We brought a small contingency and your men were watching ours the entire time."

Miceli dropped back to allow his brother and nephew into the room. He caught his brother in his arms and hugged him. "Did the fall hurt you?" He managed to glare at Vittorio. "You were hit very hard."

"He saved my life," Giuseppi said. "I'm certain of it."

"There was no way to tell who the shooter was aiming for," Miceli said. "It could have been anyone."

Vittorio had to concede that he was right, although his gut told him that Giuseppi had been the primary target. "I agree, Miceli. You may as well make yourselves comfortable. No one is going to be able to leave until everyone's been questioned. If anyone is armed or carrying anything illegal on them, now is it the time to get rid of it."

Emmanuelle hugged him tightly. "Vittorio, that was a little too close for comfort. Too close. Whoever shot that woman might have been trying to kill you."

"They didn't, honey," he reassured her.

"What was Stefano thinking, offering to exchange places with that woman?" she asked. "He can't do things like that. I could have taken her place. It's not like I'm pregnant."

Val made a sound that had both of them turning to look at him. His vivid green eyes were narrowed and boring into Emmanuelle. "That's bullshit to think that way, Emme. You're not expendable because you don't have children. That's your mother talking."

Giovanni slid between Val and Emmanuelle, a fluid, easy motion that didn't seem intrusive but was. He kept his back to Val, while looking at his sister. "That poor innocent woman had nothing to do with whatever beef that shooter had with one of us in this room. Or all of us. As head of our family, of course Stefano would make the offer. It also allowed Vittorio the time to get to the man from our private stairway."

Vittorio had known, sooner or later, one of the Saldis would ask how Vittorio managed to get up to the second story without being seen. Giovanni had easily answered the question as well as cut off Val's access to Emmanuelle.

She never even glanced at Val, treating him as if he didn't exist. "You're right. I just panicked when I heard him. Francesca is so fragile right now. She doesn't think of herself that way, but she has to be so careful. The drug they're putting her on makes her shake night and day. It's crazy."

She poured herself a cup of coffee and turned back to Vittorio. "I'm going to talk to Grace and explain about Eloisa." She glanced in the direction of the shadows on the far side of the room where her mother was hidden and unable to reveal herself. Fortunately, the room was long and Eloisa wasn't able to hear the conversation.

Vittorio ruffled her hair. "There is no explanation for Eloisa, but thanks, honey. I've made up my mind to talk to her. The charity event is this coming weekend. We have to be on the same page by that time. It only gives me a few days to prepare. I have the feeling that Haydon Phillips will try to hit us there. It's the first time he can really get to her."

All the while talking to his sister and brother, Vittorio was aware of the Saldis in a little group together talking quietly at the opposite end of the room. Val kept casting annoyed glances toward Emmanuelle, but he stayed by his father's side. Somewhere close, Taviano hovered, blending into the background, forgotten.

In the shadows were the cousins and Eloisa, listening to every word the Saldis had to say to one another. If they, in any way, were responsible for the attack in the Ferraro hotel, and they talked about it, the Ferraros would know. If not, their speculations might reveal answers.

"It's getting a little dicey," Giovanni said. "As if Phillips wasn't enough to worry about, we've got this shooter and the Saldis."

"Miceli was lying his ass off," Emmanuelle whispered, her voice very low. "I think Giuseppi was very genuine, but then I've always liked him and Greta, so maybe I'm prejudiced. He hasn't been paying a lot of attention to what's going on around him since Greta got sick."

"Has Val been taking over?" Vittorio asked her the hard question.

Emmanuelle's chin went up and for the first time she looked across the room at Val. Their eyes met, but she didn't look away. "I wouldn't know. Since I heard him tell another woman that he'd been ordered to make me fall in love with him but really, did she think he wanted a spoiled baby who didn't know jack about sex, I haven't had anything to do with him."

Vittorio froze. Very slowly he turned his head to look at the man who had shattered his sister's heart. Ferraros notoriously fell in love once. Right or wrong, Valentino had been Emmanuelle's choice. To do such a cruel thing would never occur to any of them.

"He actually said that? Those words?"

"Vittorio," Emmanuelle cautioned. She put a deterring hand on his arm. "I told you this before."

Vittorio exploded into action, throwing Saldi bodyguards out of his way to reach Valentino Saldi. He was like a fierce, destructive tornado. Trained in hand-to-hand combat, in every style of fighting, he went through the bodyguards easily, getting his hands on Val in less than a second, his fists and feet doing damage before the other man had a chance to raise a defense. He had his opponent against the wall, slamming his fist into him repeatedly before Dario reached him to try to get him off Val. Dario went flying, and Vittorio hardly had glanced at him.

"Stop." Giuseppi stood. An imposing figure. A voice of absolute authority. "Vittorio. Val. Stop this now. There can be no fighting between us."

Vittorio was always aware of everything around him, even when he was in the midst of annihilating an enemy, but nothing was going to stop him, not even Giuseppi, whom he had some respect for. He wanted to smash Val into the ground. Beat him into a bloody pulp. He wouldn't have stopped, but Ricco caught his bloody fist in midair before it could once again slam into Giuseppi's heir's face.

"Enough, Vittorio. He's had enough."

"It's never going to be enough as far as I'm concerned," Vittorio said, contempt dripping from his voice. Holding Val up, he smashed his fist into his ribs.

"Vittorio, he's not worth it," Emmanuelle said softly, laying a restraining hand on his arm. "Please stop."

Vittorio instantly stepped back, allowing Val's body to slide down to the floor. Not even looking at the fallen man, he turned, taking Emmanuelle with him, to go to Giuseppi. "Forgive me, Giuseppi. It is a matter of family honor."

Giuseppi had to be the one to have ordered Val to seduce Emmanuelle, but he still looked puzzled as his gaze moved from his son to Emme. Dario and Angelo crouched beside Valentino.

"Do you need an ambulance?" Ricco asked, his voice strictly neutral.

Giovanni handed Dario a bucket of ice and a cloth.

"No. We'll take care of this," Dario snapped, glaring at Vittorio over his shoulder, the promise of retaliation on his face.

"See, Giuseppi," Miceli said, his voice low, but carrying. "There is no peace between our families. There is no reason for this attack."

"There was reason," Val said, his voice husky and edged with pain. "Just leave it alone."

Vittorio couldn't give a damn what the Saldis thought or whether or not Val acted like a man and took what was coming to him. No one was going to treat Emmanuelle the way Valentino had and get away with it. As far as he was concerned, the Saldis were the enemy and always would be. In his opinion, a war was brewing between the two families and there was no reason to pretend it wasn't.

CHAPTER ELEVEN

Grace glanced down at Vittorio's hands as he reached for her elbow to help her up. Her breath caught in her throat. "Vittorio." She breathed his name, shocked at the smashed skin and knuckles as well as the swelling.

"It's nothing," he said, dismissing the fact that it was clear he'd been in a fight.

She nearly winced at the curtness in his voice. Vittorio had never been curt with her. Not once. He was always gentle in everything he did and said. She had driven a wedge between them and she wasn't sure how to make things better. She wanted to, especially after talking with Francesca and Sasha.

The Ferraro family was there in force, even their cousins from New York. They were astonishingly handsome men, just like those in Chicago. She figured their looks came from a long line of good genes. Eloisa was conspicuously missing.

"He was defending my honor," Emmanuelle said. "I think

they were all spoiling for a fight, and I said something I shouldn't have . . ."

"Emme. Stop." Vittorio's voice was commanding.

Grace had never heard him use that particular tone. The way he spoke shut down all conversation in the room.

"I've got to get Grace home, so if you'll excuse me, we'll be taking off now," Vittorio added.

"You're not staying for dinner?" Francesca protested.

"No, honey, I'm sorry." Vittorio softened instantly and bent to brush a kiss along Francesca's temple.

"Will you bring Grace back to visit? I really enjoyed seeing her."

"When I get the chance."

No one but Grace seemed to notice his hesitation. It was a tiny thing but one more blow she felt deeply. He looked tired and unhappy. She desperately wanted to find a way to get him to sleep better and take that look of melancholy from his face. She knew she was responsible for putting it there in the first place. She just hadn't expected to miss him so much or that his despondency would affect her quite so completely. She actually hurt with the need to make things better for him.

She said her good-byes and stepped into the private elevator with Vittorio. The moment the doors slid closed, she turned to him. "We watched the entire event playing out on the hotel security screens in Francesca's room. It was really frightening. You moved so fast to save Giuseppi Saldi. I couldn't help being proud of you but terrified for you at the same time. When you covered his body with yours, you were completely exposed to that gunman."

She couldn't keep her voice from shaking or the little bite of accusation out of it. She'd been terrified for him, so had the other women, which hadn't eased her mind. Demetrio and Drago wanted to turn off the screens, but Francesca had refused.

Vittorio looked down at her from his superior height, making her feel small and fragile. He was a big man all over, his chest, arms and legs heavy with muscle. He was a good foot taller, easily more, and she was slight in comparison. His indigo eyes drifted over her face, making her want to squirm. She did squirm under his focused scrutiny.

The elevator doors slid smoothly open and they were met at the Ferraro private entrance to the hotel by Emilio and Enzo. The car was right there, Enzo holding the door open. Vittorio and Emilio both looked carefully around before Vittorio helped her to slide onto the cool leather of the back seat. He slipped in beside her and Emilio closed the door. Only then did she realize that Enzo wasn't driving. He was in the front seat and they had a driver she didn't recognize.

She glanced behind them to see Emilio entering the passenger side of a second car. When they pulled out of the parking lot, Grace realized they were following a lead car. That had never happened before. When she looked up at Vittorio's set features, she decided not to ask any questions until they were home. Maybe he wouldn't answer. Maybe she'd lost her chance to be a part of him, but she was determined that when they reached his home she was going to try—and not because his family was amazing and she'd give anything to be part of it, but because she was certain Vittorio Ferraro was the most extraordinary man she'd ever meet and she would forever regret being a coward if she didn't give what had been growing between them a chance.

She stayed quiet, looking down at her hand, the one on which she spent an inordinate amount of time wiggling her fingers to celebrate the fact that she could. Physical therapy was painful, but she rejoiced in the ability to finally work at getting better. More, Vittorio sat in the room with them, watching, and more than once, when she thought she might throw up because the pain was too much, he had stood up and simply snapped, "Enough." No one ever dared contradict him and her shoulder was immediately iced, and she could breathe her way through the pain enough to let it recede.

The more she sat there quietly on the ride back to the

house, his warmth enveloping her, feeling safe and secure because he took care of her when she was unable to, the more she realized how much she wanted that. How many men would actually give her that kind of relationship without being totally controlling? Vittorio had never once made her feel as if he was controlling her. He made her feel as if she was the most precious, treasured woman in the world and he was determined to watch over her.

Without thinking she moved closer to him, fitting under his shoulder. His body was always warm and the moment she moved close, he put his arm along the seat and then curved it around her shoulders. That felt good. He hadn't done that in what seemed a very long while. She rested her head against his chest without looking at him. She was afraid of what she might see if she did. She didn't want the mask he wore around others. She wanted the true intimacy he had given her, the real Vittorio, the real man. He had offered her that man and she'd been so afraid she'd rejected him.

"What's wrong, *gattina*?"

His soft inquiry nearly stopped her heart. She hadn't heard that voice in over a week—the one that was for her alone, the one that sent desire dancing down her spine or heating her sex to a welcoming liquid honey. He hadn't called her his special nickname for her, either. She hadn't realized how much she wanted either until that moment.

He touched her face and she realized it was wet. Tears tracked down her cheeks. She turned her face into his chest and he fit the back of her head into his palm, saying nothing else until the car slowed and then stopped. That simple gesture had felt intimate and caring as well, as if he offered her silent comfort and yet didn't want to call attention to the fact that she was crying. She detested making a spectacle of herself in front of his bodyguards, or anyone for that matter. She liked to stay out of the spotlight.

The house was a mixture of more than one style of architecture. Its nine thousand square feet stretched out in three clearly different sections, rather like welcoming arms. At the very center of the house was a tall turret held up by the structure itself, stone and white square pillars. Beneath the high turret was an open patio with a stone floor and two sets of glass doors that opened into a dining room from one and a sitting room from the other. The tower was surrounded by long, narrow, multipaned windows that opened outward.

Elongated arms or wings extended out on either side of the elegant turret. The drive allowed the family car to circle to a sheltered entry extending out from the right-side wing. It was covered, but more importantly, secluded, preventing anyone, even someone with a pair of powerful binoculars or a scope on a rifle, from seeing the members of the family or their guests exit the car and enter the house.

As soon as Emilio opened the passenger door, Vittorio was out, but he reached back in to help her slide from the car. Exiting a vehicle was still difficult. Grace felt top-heavy with her arm and shoulder still so stiff and painful, preventing any real movement. As always when they walked anywhere, Vittorio had his hand on her, in this case, right on the small of her back. She felt the heat of his palm burning through the thin material of her shirt.

Mariko had helped her shower and dress that morning, but she was getting much more adept. She still had her arm in a sling when she wasn't doing physical therapy, but dressing one-handed was getting to be a little easier. There was more movement in her shoulder and the more she worked the fingers on her hand, the more she was able to.

"You look tired, Grace. I'm going to take you to your suite and run a bath for you. I've texted Merry and she'll have a late dinner ready for us by the time you're out."

"I was hoping for the opportunity to talk to you," she admitted. It cost her to ask, which surprised her when she was so assertive in her work. She didn't want to say anything that would drive Vittorio further from her.

"I'd like that, *bella*. Let me run your bath, get you in it and I'll take care of my hands. I don't want them swelling too much. We can talk over dinner."

She nodded, grateful there was a little more time to think about what she wanted to say. She was tense and hopefully, a bath would allow her to relax. There was a special plastic casing that fit over her shoulder and arm to prevent the bandages and sling from getting wet. It had to be fitted to her and she couldn't do that.

She knew Vittorio had been the one to help her in the hospital but having him help her when she wasn't looking her best was disconcerting. He didn't offer to call one of the female members of his family or Merry to come help her. She knew if she protested his help, he would stop instantly, but she didn't want him to go, not even for the sake of her modesty. She hoped that by giving him this, he would understand she really wanted to fix things between them.

She watched Vittorio cross the room to the elegantly appointed bathroom attached to her bedroom. The room was exceptionally large with golden faucets in the double sink as well as in the deep bathtub. Grace stood a little helplessly watching him, unsure of herself. Uncertain what to say or do. He dumped lavender and honey salts into the water, his wrist checking the temperature. He did things like that for her almost without thinking.

"You do know, Grace, that you have every right to ask what Eloisa was talking about. You haven't done anything wrong. I don't want you to think you have."

Her heart accelerated. He looked so casual draped there on the side of the tub, one hand under the spray of water, testing it. "I could have handled things better."

He sent her a faint smile, but it was the first she'd had from him in a week and she wanted to celebrate.

"We both could have handled things better. Let me help you with your clothes. I'll get you settled and then take care of my hands. By the time I've showered, you should be ready to get out. I've had a button installed that you can push if there's an emergency, right here beside the tub. I'll come immediately."

"So will security, no doubt."

She got another smile, and this one made the butterflies in her stomach take wing.

"No doubt," he agreed. He dried off his hands and crossed to stand in front of her. His fingers found the buttons of her blouse. "I'll admit that I've discovered I can be a jealous man and I don't exactly want other men looking at your body, but if you're in trouble, I'd rather we both have to put up with it than take a single chance on anything harming you."

Her entire body grew hot with every brush of his hands on her through the thin material. She had never considered jealousy a good trait, but the way he said it, that soft, low tone that seemed to find its way inside her, coupled with her growing knowledge of him, she didn't mind in the least. Vittorio wouldn't display jealousy unduly. She would have to really do something blatant, flirt outrageously or even go out with another man before he would react. She was certain enough that she could enjoy his tone and the way he so gently pushed the sleeve from her good arm and then, after unhooking the sling, slid the blouse off her injured shoulder.

She stood in front of him in just her jeans and a lacy bra. She was on the thinner side and lately, because she wasn't eating much, her ribs tended to show. She knew that bothered him because he traced each one with his fingers, a small frown on his face.

"The doctor said you needed to eat more, *gattina*. I think you've eaten less. Every tray brought to you, no matter what Merry fixed, had most of the food still on it. Is there something you prefer to eat that I haven't thought of?"

Her pulse jumped and then began pounding. His hands were at the waistband of her jeans. She tried to be casual, as if she'd been stripped naked by a man every day of her life. He was looking down and the wealth of gleaming, thick black hair, a little on the shaggy side, was an invitation. Tempting her like the devil when she knew she should be good. She didn't want to be. She wanted his touch. His kisses. She wanted the two of them to be as intimate in the bedroom as they had been when talking together.

He looked up and her heart contracted. *"Gattina?"*

Grace ruthlessly pushed away the need to sink her fingers in his hair and shook her head. "The food is wonderful. Truly. Merry is a great cook. I just haven't had much of an appetite lately."

His gaze dropped again to her jeans and the task at hand. He hooked his thumbs in her waistband and slid them over her hips, taking the little lace panties with them. She knew they were damp, and her face flamed a wild rose. There was no stopping the blush and she knew it was covering every inch of her body.

He put the jeans and panties aside and reached around her to unhook her bra. "Grace, wouldn't it be more comfortable for you not to wear a bra until your shoulder is healed?"

She stood completely naked in front of him and when he dropped his gaze, she saw his chest rise with a swift intake of breath. His eyes lifted to her face. There was no hiding the raw desire etched into his expression. It darkened his indigo eyes until the blue was nearly black. He pinned her hair on top of her head and stepped back.

"You're so beautiful, woman. You take my breath away." Abruptly, but gently, he removed her sling and the brace that supported her arm in between her physical therapy sessions.

Grace wanted to hug the knowledge to herself that he still wanted her. She might be too thin, but he still found her beautiful and desirable. He slipped the casing on her shoulder and arm and then unexpectedly cupped her right breast. One thumb slid over her nipple, stroking caresses until she thought she might go insane.

"I'm not above seducing you to get what I want," he confessed.

She didn't tell him, but his voice alone could seduce her. Having his hands on her was beyond exciting. Exhilarating. She wanted more. She wanted to feel as if she belonged to him.

"I'm not above letting you," she admitted, tearing her gaze from the mesmerizing and rather erotic sight of his big hand claiming possession of her breast, stroking her nipple into a tight peak.

The expression on his face was extraordinary. Once again, he was wholly focused on her. On her body. On the way she reacted to him. His expression was cut into sensual lines and the look sent a shiver of excitement coursing through her.

"This isn't safe." He bent his head slowly, giving her every opportunity to step away.

She couldn't move, not if her life depended on it. She had never wanted anything more in her life. His hair brushed her skin. If felt like a million strands of silk heightening every nerve ending. Then his mouth was on her left breast, his tongue teasing her nipple. She gasped at the fire spreading through her, rushing to pool low. She felt the empty clench of her sex, the sudden slickness between her thighs. He suckled gently at first, but then the fingers on his other hand began to roll and tug her nipple. His mouth worked her mound harder, teeth scraping and sending little strikes of lightning arrowing downward.

Then his teeth tugged on one nipple and his thumb and finger did the same to the other. She arched her back, giving him better access. Her arm slid around his head, trying to cradle him to her. Her knees went weak, legs turning rubbery, threatening to give out on her. Her body turned to fire. Flames raced through her veins, and a fireball grew in her core, spreading need and hunger through her until she was no thinking person. Only pure feeling, every nerve ending alive.

She heard the moan that escaped. She sounded as needy as she felt. Nothing in her life had ever felt so good and yet at the same time, so frustrating. She needed . . . more. Her fingers finally sank into that thick, silky hair, fisting there, claiming him.

His tongue lapped at her nipple and she closed her eyes,

knowing he was going to save them both. "I don't want saving," she whispered, meaning it.

"Neither do I," he murmured against her bare skin. "It's the last thing I want. You have to be sure, Grace. I know you're what I want, but you have to come to terms with your fear and accept the relationship because when you do, you have to know you're giving yourself to me. Putting yourself in my hands, trusting me always to do the right thing for you. For us. For our children. You take your bath and we'll talk over dinner."

She reluctantly allowed her fingers to loosen in his hair so he could stand up. He stood just enough to brush a kiss over her lips. She knew she was pouting, but her entire body was on fire. The only good thing was he had a large bulge in the front of his pin-striped trousers that told her she wasn't alone in her frustration or need.

"Tell me what you need from me, Vittorio." She walked on shaky legs to the edge of the tub. He had his arm around her the entire way. Looking down, she could see the marks of his possession on her breasts. She could still feel every nerve ending sparking like little electrical shocks to her body, needing more. Her nipples were twin hard peaks, blatantly telling him she wanted him.

"I need you to commit fully to me. You have to know for certain, without any doubts, that I'm the man for you." He lifted her with casual strength, careful of her shoulder as he placed her in the bathtub. He kept hold of her until she sank down into the hot, soothing water.

She *loved* the bathtub. Showering or bathing had always been fast and efficient. The entire time she'd felt vulnerable, afraid any minute that Haydon would come in and harass her. She didn't like the feeling that he was spying on her all those years, but there was nothing she could do about it. He enjoyed taunting her with his ability to move in and out of any house or apartment. Or that he could find her wherever she was. He loved holding it over her head that he could get into the home of anyone she talked too long to.

"Can anyone do that, Vittorio? No one knows the future. You could stop wanting me."

"That would be impossible for me. I know this relationship started in an extreme way, but it's real. What I feel for you is real and it's only growing. I hope it's the same for you, but only you can determine that. I'm willing to wait. I'm willing to let you have as much time as you need, but the truth is, all obstacles are in your mind. If you let yourself believe in me, I'll take care of us. I believe absolutely, without a shadow of a doubt, that you'll take care of us just as well."

He placed a gel pillow behind her head and one under her arm. "I'm heading for my shower. I'll be back in a short time. The water should stay hot for you." He ran his hand very possessively over her shoulder, down to her breast, caressing the soft skin once again before abruptly leaving her.

She had no doubt that he'd be back before the water had time to cool. What did that say? She closed her eyes, although he'd dimmed the lights in the bathroom as he went out the door. Of course he had. He saw to everything. He thought of everything. She'd never felt she had the luxury to lie in a bathtub, the hot water soothing her body, and she wouldn't have anywhere else. She relaxed because of Vittorio.

Grace tried to think what possible criteria she met that other women didn't. Francesca and Sasha had been casual about it, as if it wasn't any big deal, but they had intimated that whatever the Ferraro men required, there weren't all that many women who met their needs. Did they have some built-in radar for a woman who might keep up with them sexually? Just the thought as well as the admission to herself gave her a full body blush. From the moment she'd laid eyes on Vittorio Ferraro, she'd been awakened sexually. By that, she had to admit, her entire body had come alive. Every single nerve ending. Muscles she hadn't known about.

It was strange to her that she didn't feel the same way about the other Ferraro men. From the beginning, Vittorio was the one who'd captured her interest, and then her heart. She'd read the tabloids as well as any news article. She'd searched the Internet for anything at all on him. Some things she'd dismissed as pure gossip, but it hadn't mattered. The compulsion to read everything had been too hard to resist. She would have kept pictures like a stalker, but Haydon would have realized her interest in Vittorio and she didn't want that.

She knew from every article that the Ferraro men had ferocious sexual appetites. That couldn't be all made up. Maybe their criteria for a bride could match them so that they never had reason to stray. She didn't like that thought. Francesca couldn't have sex, not with her pregnancy. Stefano was never far from her. She couldn't imagine him cheating on her. So, it wasn't about sex. She almost wished it was, because she could have checked that box. Once the door had been opened, she found herself wondering about all kinds of sex, and in every erotic fantasy, Vittorio had been her partner.

Criteria aside, what did she need in a partner? If she took out fantasy and really tried to look at the man Vittorio was, would she want him? Strip away the hot body and the gorgeous eyes. His voice, so smooth he could stroke her skin with every note. Take away the fact that he was the wealthiest man she knew, what was there about him that she craved? Needed?

Safety was paramount. She knew that. She knew she would always need to feel safe because she never had. The feeling that her partner wanted to form a family unit with her, she'd never had that, either. She wanted freedom to do her work and follow her dreams with her partner's full support. At the same time, she didn't want to have to be the "bad guy" all the time. She was at work. She didn't want to confront anyone at home. She liked the idea of her man taking charge when she was home. That relationship appealed to her along with most of what came with it. It both excited her and scared her a little, which she liked. She craved the feeling of being a man's whole focus in every aspect of their relationship. Some would say it wasn't healthy, but it was for her. It was what she knew she needed when she'd never been anyone's anything before. She wanted to be her man's everything.

The huge question was . . . as she got older, would she still need it? If Haydon Phillips was out of her life, would she want the same things in a relationship? She would sexually; she knew the idea of Vittorio taking charge was more than exciting. She liked being taken care of. Was it because she'd never had care as a child? Maybe. That was a real possibility, but did it matter the reason? She might have been born wanting total care from her partner.

She knew she was the type of woman who would always look after her man and her children. She was a detail person. Meticulous about details. She noticed everything around her and what made people comfortable and when they weren't. That was what made her so good at her job. She would be even more so at home with the people she loved, if given the chance.

Her eyes flew open. She wanted the chance to care for Vittorio Ferraro in the same way he cared for her. That didn't mean making decisions she didn't want to make. Or forcing herself to make demands in the bedroom. It meant seeing to the details that made *him* happy. Giving him whatever it was that made his life full and contented. If anyone was capable of doing just that, it was Grace Murphy.

"You ready to get out of there, *bella*?"

His voice cut through every doubt, if any lingered. She wanted to hear that voice for the rest of her life. She knew he only saw her. That tone was reserved only for her. She forgot about being embarrassed that she was naked. She knew he liked looking at her body and she didn't mind in the least giving that to him—or tempting him.

"I'm ready."

"I've got your clothes laid out. We're going to eat on the back patio. I've set up a small table and the screens are in place so we'll be insect-free." He let the water out and reached for her, his hands around her waist.

She put one hand on his shoulder. He was in his casual clothes, this time soft drawstring pants and a thin button-up shirt he left unbuttoned. As usual in his home, he was barefoot. Her sex clenched and this time the heat moving through her seemed like lazy molasses that spread slowly, taking over her veins one by one until it reached her core, settling there like a smoldering fire waiting to flare.

"I love to sit out there and look at the water." She did, it was her favorite place in the evening.

She stood still while he dried her off. He took his time, sliding the towel sensuously over her breasts and then stopping to suck her nipples into hard peaks before proceeding lower. He crouched, so she had to steady herself with one hand to his shoulder as the towel slid back and forth between her legs creating a terrible burn that kept building when his tongue drew a line up her thigh and then flicked her clit. His hair set fire to nerve endings and then he was standing.

"You could keep going. I wouldn't mind."

His eyes drifted over her, noting her color, her breathing, the peaked nipples, with satisfaction. "We're going to talk, Grace."

She knew there would be no swaying him, but she also knew her hunger for him was going to continue to grow as the evening progressed. She couldn't be with him and not crave him. Now that she'd felt his hands and mouth on her, that craving had grown stronger.

On the bed was a filmy, very short gown. She looked at him but didn't protest when he pulled the sleeveless hole over her injured arm up to her shoulder. With extreme gentleness, he slipped the gown over her head and then her other arm. He had to pull the forest green stretch lace over her breasts. It clung like a second skin, feeling so sexy her nipples peeked out through the open lace. He drew it down over her ribs and settled the fabric over her hips. The lace ended just under her bottom, barely covering her mound or her backside.

"I've sent everyone from the house," he assured as he picked up a longer filmy robe that fell to the back of her thighs. "Do you feel the need to wear this? I would prefer not, but I don't want you to be uncomfortable."

The robe wouldn't cover a thing, but she knew psychologically, it might give her more confidence. Vittorio was leaving it up to her, but he'd made his preference known. She had already made up her mind she was going to jump into their relationship with both feet. She wanted to make him happy, see to every detail she could, and this was a very small one. She loved the feel of the stretchy lace of the gown on her skin. It made her feel sexy. Mostly, she liked the way he looked at her.

"I don't think I'll need it."

Grace was shocked at the amount of pleasure she got from watching his face. He was very pleased and the desire for her darkened in his eyes to a raw, hungry lust that made her press her thighs together. The burning between her legs increased.

"Dinner is going to get cold if we don't get out there, and I want you to eat tonight." He stepped back to let her walk just in front of him.

She had never considered that just walking in front of a man could make her feel sensual with every single step. It didn't matter that her shoulder still felt a little heavy and awkward, she wasn't even aware of it, because she found herself totally focused on Vittorio. Every breath she drew, every step she took, she was aware of him close to her. His hand found the small of her back, branding her there with his heat. The breath hissed out of her lungs in an excited rush.

His hand slipped lower, shaping the curve of her butt, resting there possessively so that deep inside that smoldering fire burst into flame. He stroked a caress from the top curve of her bottom to the dip between her cheek and thigh, tracing along that line briefly, and brought his hand back to claim her again. Her body went slick and hot.

Inside the room created by the fine mesh, candles were lit, so that light danced across the small table. He pulled out a high-backed chair with a wide seat and helped her into it. The lace pulled up nearly to the top of her hips, exposing her lower half. She glanced down to see liquid drops gleaming on the fiery curls at the junction between her legs. His hand dropped to her thigh, almost casually. She went very still, but she didn't pull away, her heart beating fast.

His fingers slid into the curls, lower still to caress her clit and gather up the droplets. She couldn't look away, mesmerized by the carnal look on his face. Her heart was nearly pounding out of her chest. She could actually feel blood pounding through her clit. He brought his fingers to his mouth.

"I've wanted to taste you from the moment I saw you leap out of the trunk." His voice was that low, intimate husky *growl* that aroused her every time she heard it.

He licked his fingers slowly. Savoring the taste. Never taking his eyes from hers. It was the sexist thing she'd ever seen. Her entire body reacted. She could barely breathe, hot, aroused, completely under his spell.

He slipped into the chair across from her, but the table was so small, he could reach out and touch her. "I hope you're hungry. Merry outdid herself. She knows you haven't had much of an appetite lately, so she made certain this was very light fare."

She suddenly had an appetite, but not necessarily for food. Vittorio had fallen silent, those dark indigo eyes fixed on her face. Waiting. She realized he was waiting for her to speak. "I'll try."

He sent her a small smile as he placed a tostada on her plate. "This is white bean with blackberry salsa, one of Merry's favorites. Pumpkin dukkah with avocado slices, which are good for you and she says you are particularly fond of. Both the salsa and the dukkah are homemade. I think you'll love them."

He took the wrapping off a small bowl of salad. "This is tempeh salad with plum and charred artichoke hearts and bok choy. She went to a lot of trouble for us tonight."

She touched her tongue to her upper lip as he poured red wine into glasses. "I chose the wine. I think you'll like it. If not, we can choose something else. There's an extensive wine cellar here and we should be able to find you something."

Grace picked up her fork. The food did look delicious and sounded even better. She took a tentative taste of the salad, aware of Vittorio's gaze on her. She sent him a small, embarrassed smile. "Are you going to keep watching me?"

"Yes. Why?"

"It's a little unnerving. No one's ever paid so much attention to me before."

"I like looking at you, especially right now, in your lingerie. I knew that color would be especially beautiful on you. The candles play over your breasts perfectly and light up your skin as well as throw flames in your hair."

The way he talked, so matter-of-factly, as if he was discussing the weather and not her body, made her hot all over again. He sounded as if he were stating facts, admiring a beautiful art object rather than a flesh and blood person.

"You'll have to get used to me looking at you all the time, *gattina*, because I intend to indulge myself as often as possible."

"You do?" She barely could croak out the question. Her voice didn't sound like her own.

He nodded slowly. "Just knowing you're here in my home with me pleases me, but knowing I can look at your body anytime I ask, and you'll indulge me, arouses me. Thinking about that gives me great pleasure." He ate two more bites while she stared at him a little helplessly. "You would indulge me, wouldn't you, Grace?"

She knew she would. She knew she would be equally as aroused by giving him what he wanted. It was a powerful thing to be wanted with the kind of intensity Vittorio showered on her. She nodded. "Yes." Her voice was very low, but to her astonishment, she sounded blatantly sexual. She felt sexy as hell sitting across from him when she'd never, not once, felt that way in her life. She knew he made her feel that way because he saw her that way.

"I like the idea of walking into a room and you're there, naked, waiting for me. Just waiting quietly." He looked around him. "This house is all about peace. I like it quiet. I meditate often. Do you meditate?"

"I've tried. I thought it might help me cope better with the stress of Haydon. I tried to learn from reading books."

"I rise early as a rule." His gaze drifted over her, dwelling on her breasts and then sliding lower. The glass tabletop enabled him to look at the green lace pulled up to her hips.

She pushed her thighs together almost involuntarily, her face burning. Her body was slick with need and with the candlelight playing over her, it would be impossible for him not to notice.

"Don't do that. Widen your thighs, Grace." He spoke in that same low tone, the one that got to her, but also was more of a command than a statement.

She found herself obeying and the moment she did, her sex clenched hotly, and more liquid slipped along her upper thighs.

"So beautiful. I could eat you for breakfast, lunch and dinner. You've set up a craving that is never going away." He leaned across the small table. "I would very much like another taste, *bella*."

She froze, uncertain what he meant her to do. He didn't help her out at all, rather he lifted his wineglass to his fantastic mouth that she was now fantasizing over, and drank the red liquid, his eyes on her face.

More than anything, Grace wanted to meet his every expectation, because every look, every gesture, every suggestion was so sexual, so intimate, she was more aroused by the moment. She wanted to feel beautiful, desirable, but it was more than that. He made her feel as if she belonged to him. That every single part of her belonged to him. She'd always wanted something different and more complex than she knew most people had in their relationships, but she hadn't known what it was. Now she did.

Vittorio didn't ask again. He remained silent, but he set his glass down, his eyes on her face. Very slowly, Grace put down her fork, her gaze locking with his. Her hand moved to her neck, fingers feeling the pulse beating so frantically there. Her fingertips traveled down her body, between the curves of her breasts, lower along her belly, absently traced her belly button.

The heat in his eyes flared. Smoldered. Lust was stark and raw. His gaze followed the movement of her hand as it slid over the green lace and then into the damp, fiery curls. He waited. Unmoving. Daringly, just to please him, because she knew that was what he wanted, she stroked her clit and then curled one finger inside the damp heat of her body.

Her breath hitched as electricity sizzled through every nerve ending. His breath hitched as well, and she saw his face darken, lines of lust cut deep. He looked like sin itself—the devil tempting her when she was doing her best to tempt him.

"All the way for me, Grace." His voice was a little husky, but as commanding as ever.

She pushed her finger deeper and then turned it, making certain to coat the digit with her liquid heat. She pulled it out slowly and held it out to him. The liquid glistened as the candlelight played over it.

"*Mia bella ragazza, sei cosi coraggioso.* I never thought it would ever be possible to find you." He circled her wrist with his hand to steady her arm. "In all honesty, I didn't think there was a woman in the world for me. You couldn't be more perfect." He leaned closer and took the tip of her finger between his lips, his eyes on hers as he slowly sucked it deeper into the hot cavern of his mouth.

The bottom of her stomach seemed to drop to the floor. She really was afraid she might spontaneously combust.

He sank back into his chair and once again picked up his fork. "You have to eat, *gattina*, and we really have to talk."

CHAPTER TWELVE

Vittorio watched the frustrated sexual need build in Grace's eyes. He reached across the table to take her fork when she just sat there looking at him, a little dazed and as adorable as she could be. He forked a bite off her plate and held it to her lips until she opened. She could have been stubborn, but that wasn't his woman. She tried for him.

He'd made up his mind years earlier that he would never have the life he wanted or even needed. He would do his duty as a rider and he'd be faithful in a loveless marriage. That was a matter of honor. He had a code he lived by and he wouldn't break it because he wasn't happy.

Now there was Grace. An unexpected gift. She was far more than he'd ever fantasized or dreamt about. She was courageous and beautiful. Intelligent and no pushover. He wanted a woman who could stimulate him intellectually. One who would run his home and see to those details. He also wanted a woman willing to follow him and, in their home, give over control to him. He had thought such a woman probably didn't exist.

"Before we take our relationship any further, Grace, I'd like to clarify a few things. I don't want you to think I'm just controlling things in my household because I can. There are things that I've come to know I need in order to function. This isn't about me imposing my will on you. It's about me living in an environment I can handle, do my work and survive intact."

Just revealing that much could get him in trouble. He rubbed at the faint shadowing along his jaw. No matter how often he shaved, it was always there. Her gaze followed the motion of his fingers, but she took another bite of her tostada. He didn't want her to question him too much about his work, but like most people, she bought into the fact that the family owned many businesses and those businesses had to be overseen.

The fact was—he was virtually an assassin. Riders meted out justice, but at the end of the day, they were still sent out to kill—and they did. The safeguards were in place, several of them, to ensure no mistakes were made but, even knowing whomever they were sent after had committed horrendous crimes and gotten away with it, they had to live with the fact that they killed. Over and over. They had to be apart from the rest of the world. They had to live a lie.

"I need a certain balance in my world. My preference would be that my woman would want to adhere to my lifestyle. I want her by my side as much as possible. I'm not a man who would get tired of my woman because she was with me too much. There isn't a 'too much' for me. When I get up in the morning to meditate, I would need my woman to also get up to meditate with me. I want her to eat breakfast with me. I want her to exercise when I do."

Grace's expression didn't change to one of alarm as he'd feared. She was listening, and he could see she was carefully thinking over everything he was telling her. He felt a little as if he was holding his breath. He already knew she was a match for him sexually. She'd just proved to him that she was. She sat wearing what he'd asked her, giving him everything he asked without question. She was a natural for him, as if she'd been made for him. Now he was asking even more of her. He couldn't imagine that any woman would want to be with a man with his kind of needs, but she wasn't running.

"In other words, you would prefer that we do everything together."

He took a bite of his food before answering. "As much as possible, yes." He barely tasted the tostada, and blackberry salsa was one of his favorites. He had years of practice keeping his expression blank. Although he felt as if he couldn't keep his breath, it never showed on his body. If someone had taken his pulse, it would have been steady. He sounded matter-of-fact, but this was one of the most important conversations he'd ever have in his life.

She nodded. "I have to admit, I would want a close relationship as well. I honestly didn't think men and women wanted to spend time together once they were committed. The people I've talked to seem to think they have more to talk about if they go their separate ways."

"That could be, but it won't work for me. I hope it doesn't for you."

"And if we have children and I'm exhausted from staying up all night?"

"*We're* exhausted. You won't be taking care of our children alone. Clearly things will change, but we'll talk it over and manage the differences as they arise."

She smiled and tried the salad. "Merry is amazing."

"She is," he agreed. "There's more, Grace, and it's important that you really think about what I'm asking of you before you commit to me. I'd rather lose you now than later, after we're so entangled it's a nightmare to separate. I don't believe in divorce. It isn't something my family easily does. If we take a vow, it means something. The consequences would be . . . brutal." He knew she would think, as most people would, that he meant dividing their assets and if they had children, sorting that out.

"I would never go into a relationship with the idea that I can easily get out," Grace told him, putting her fork on the table in order to pick up her wineglass. Her hand was a little unsteady as she brought the glass to her lips.

"When we're alone in this house, and that will be most of the time, I would expect my woman to do as I ask her." He watched her closely.

She blinked. Looked up at him. "In what way?"

"In every way. If I asked you to meet me outside wearing nothing but that little robe that's lying across your bed right now, I would expect you to do it."

A soft rose flush slid over her skin and she pressed her thighs together. It was a subtle reaction, but one he'd hoped to see. She reacted in the best possible way. The idea didn't make her want to talk about rights and equality but was seductive to her. He resisted the urge to scoop her up and kiss her until neither of them could breathe. He knew that wouldn't be fair to her. His lifestyle wasn't for a moment or two. It was what he would expect for their lifetime.

"The thing to think about, Grace, isn't whether or not you need this lifestyle, too. Deep down, where it counts, before you ever commit to me, you have to know that this is something that will satisfy you sexually and in every other way. It can sound exciting, but then get old very fast. Sometimes it will feel one-sided. You won't always agree with me. Or want to do the things I ask of you."

She put her wineglass down. He noted she'd drunk more than half. "I might be afraid."

Her voice quivered, and Vittorio wanted to gather her up and hold her on his lap to comfort her, but he forced himself to remain where he was. "I expect that you will. I also would expect your trust and your communication. You have to tell me that you're afraid. You have to say when you don't like something we do. For a relationship to work between us, I need to know how you're feeling at all times."

She nodded, her gaze fixed on his face. He liked that she was giving him her full attention when he needed her to.

"That being said, it doesn't mean we won't go there, only that we'll discuss it more and we'll take things slow until you get to a place you're no longer afraid."

"What happens if I don't do something that you want me to do?"

"Then I would be very disappointed."

Her lashes lifted and she looked directly back into his eyes. His heart lurched at what he saw there. She didn't like the idea of him being disappointed. He had to find a way to make certain she would always look at him that way.

"So, no whips."

"I would never, in any way, hurt you. My woman is the one I love and respect more than any other and I would never want to see her hurt." He meant that, but didn't agree that there wouldn't be whips.

Vittorio wasn't a man who would ever enjoy seeing tears in his woman's eyes—Grace's eyes. He had already passed being interested in her or falling for her, he was there. He'd been in her company for nearly six weeks now and he knew he wanted to spend a lifetime with her. He was giving her an out while he could, and it wasn't easy. Listening to himself talk about his needs made him feel selfish, and he was afraid the things important to him would drive her away, especially since he couldn't explain why he needed precise obedience and complete control in his home to keep him sane.

"That's a good thing." She finished off her wine and put the glass down, once more picking up her fork to shove her salad around.

Clearly the tempeh wasn't her favorite and he made a mental note to tell Merry not to serve it to her again.

"Having said I'm not into giving my woman pain, that doesn't necessary mean there won't be whips." He poured a teasing note into his voice but watched her closely.

She sat up straighter. "Vittorio, I'm not into pain at all."

"That's a good thing. I just told you I'm not into inflicting it on my woman. I want to bring you pleasure, not hurt you. Sometimes, *gattina*, playing can be very sexy."

She was silent for a moment and then she visibly relaxed. "I'll have to trust you on that."

He was very pleased with her answer. He took a sip of his wine, wondering what he'd done right for the universe to send him such a gift.

"What about you, Grace? I'd like you to tell me the things that you feel you need in a relationship."

"I want to feel loved," she said without hesitation. "I want to know that my man loves me and isn't looking at other women when I'm not with him. You're extremely wealthy and used to women throwing themselves at you. You've dated gorgeous women and had any number of them. I'm not so certain I can measure up. I'm not exactly experienced."

He sat back in his chair and studied her face. She was nervous about having sex with him and yet she'd still dressed the way he'd asked and when he'd made a very sexual demand of her, one most women might hesitate to do, she had been courageous enough to do it. She had really given thought to his deliberate mention of whips in the bedroom, and then put trust in him. He wanted to frame her beautiful face between his palms and kiss her senseless as a reward.

"You're so naturally sensual, *bella*, you never have to worry about inexperience. Haven't you heard the things I'm telling you about me? I want things my way in the bedroom. That means inexperience on your part is a plus. It allows me to teach you what I like and want. I can promise you that at the end of the day, I can give you everything you could ever want."

She rubbed at the sling holding her arm, something she did when she was growing tired of the weight on her sore shoulder.

"Do you want dessert? Merry made her famous raspberry-lemon tart just for you." He was tempting her on purpose, even though she was growing tired. He wanted her to get stronger and heal faster. The doctor had said she would need additional calories in order to not lose any more weight with the rigorous demands of physical therapy.

She nodded. "And coffee?"

He shook his head. "That would keep you up all night. You need to sleep."

She ducked her head. "I haven't slept much since I asked you not to stay in my room."

He waited, deliberately not answering her. He had known she wasn't sleeping. Even the doctor had commented on it, worried that she was wearing herself out. There was a short silence and finally she lifted her head.

"Why didn't you tell me?" He kept his voice pitched low, conveying his disappointment in her. "Your health is paramount, Grace. You know that."

"Yes, I know, I'm sorry. I was very confused about what your mother meant when she said I met some criteria that you needed for a partner. I was hurt," she admitted.

"I'm sorry that hurt you, but you should have told me you needed me in your room to sleep." He collected her plates and put them in a small bin Merry had given him for the dishes. She had eaten little of the salad, but half of the tostada. "Just so you know, the criteria my mother referred to don't hold a candle to all the requirements I just laid out for you. As for being faithful, I've told you, that is something that is part of my code I live by. I would never take a vow with a woman and break it. Tell me what else you need to make you happy."

"I want the kind of relationship where my man is my best friend. He's the first person I want to share anything with, tell anything to, be with above anyone else."

He flashed an encouraging smile. "I'm on board with that entirely."

"I want children and I want my man to really be a father to those children, really participate in parenting. It's imperative to me, since I never had it, to know my children will feel loved and important to us all the time."

Vittorio nodded solemnly. "I agree one hundred percent. I didn't have stellar parenting. Neither my mother nor father was interested in any of us."

She looked a little shocked. "Vittorio. You're so close with your siblings. I knew there was a problem with your mother, but your father as well?"

He shrugged. "We had Stefano."

"But he's only a few years older than the rest of you."

"He took his role seriously. Keep going, *gattina*. What else do you need? You need to be able to tell me anything."

She took a deep breath. The action lifted her breasts, drawing his attention. He'd been studiously avoiding looking too much at her sitting there, appearing vulnerable and sexy. He already wanted her with every cell in his body, but she kept wreaking havoc with his brain.

"I want to work. I love what I do, and I'm good at it."

She had already indicated as much to him, so he stayed silent.

"I'm good with the routine you already have in the household because it's important to you, and anything you need of course would be important to me," she added.

"Why?" He pushed her. He knew he was asking a great deal of her to reveal more of herself to him, but he'd put himself on the line for her. Few women would have been happy with what he'd asked of her. "I know it takes courage to look at yourself and ask for what you need, but this is us. Our relationship, which is no one else's business. I will always take care of you, Grace. Always. Any secret you have is mine. Anything I tell you I trust stays with you. We're in this together. I'm already so proud of you for going this far with me."

He knew stripping oneself of armor and baring one's darkest secrets was uncomfortable and scary. Even terrifying. Her chin went up and his heart jerked hard in his chest. His cock matched the action against the material of his drawstring pants. It was a good thing they were loose because he was full and hard, his erection pulsing with urgent demands.

"I like pleasing you and really, *really* don't like disappointing you. It's the worst possible feeling," she confessed in a low voice.

His heart jumped. If nothing else had gone before, he would have known she was the right woman for him just from that admission alone.

"When I'm with you, I find I want to make you happy. When I'm away from you, I'm thinking about making you happy and what that would take. I try to see all the details, how you like your home to be, your clothes, your coffee. Small things. Just so I know and can make certain you have them. Right now, you've been doing everything for me, but I want the chance to do things for you."

His smile broke free before he had a chance to check it. High wattage. The real thing. He couldn't help it. She was magnificent and too good to be true.

"I like doing things for you, Grace. I'll continue to do those things and more. Does that make you uncomfortable?"

She shook her head and turned her attention to the raspberry-lemon creation Merry had made for them.

"I like verbal answers, *bella*," he reminded. "It doesn't seem important now, but it will be later when we're having sex and I need to hear that you're okay with whatever we're doing."

Her head came up, the color sweeping up her body, turning her breasts rosy. Her nipples peeked right through the lace, drawing his attention.

"Whatever we're doing?" she echoed faintly.

"Yes. We'll be doing the things I want to do. The things I demand of you. You haven't told me what you need from me in the bedroom. Here, in our home. I have to know what your needs are in order to fulfill them."

Her color deepened even more. She took a deep breath and tilted her chin at him. "I need you to tell me what to do. What you want from me. For some reason, when you do, I get more aroused than I ever thought possible. When you tell me what you want in or out of the bedroom, it makes me feel more in control and more powerful. I know what it takes to please you and I like being able to give that to you."

She couldn't have given him a more perfect answer. Vittorio could barely breathe with the need to hold her. Just to feel his arms around her and know she wanted him to belong to her in the same way he wanted her.

She took another deep breath. "And I don't just want to be compatible. I want to be loved. Really, deeply loved. I want my man to fall so hard he won't ever find a way to get up. I want to love that man with that same fierceness and passion." She looked him right in the eyes. "I want everything or nothing at all, because I'm not willing to settle."

He leaned toward her. "Grace, I know a few things about you from living with you these last few weeks. You have high self-esteem and you are very self-aware. I trusted you to know what you need and to tell me what those needs were because you are very aware of who you are and what your strengths and weaknesses are. You gave me hope when I hadn't had any whatsoever; listening to you talk to Katie, I knew you were aware of other people's needs and you worked hard to make certain those needs were met. You have a solid center in the midst of a horrific situation, and you've even achieved peace of mind in spite of Phillips, which is a fucking miracle."

He reached across the table and caught her hand, his thumb sliding over the ring he'd put on her finger. "I want you to marry me. I don't want you to get away."

She took a deep breath. "Just because we're compatible doesn't meant you'll feel—"

"Stop." He sat up, letting her go, his command harsher than he intended. He made an effort to soften his tone. "It would be impossible for a man like me to know those things about you in such a short time, and yet I do because everything I've described as your characteristics are spot-on, right?"

At her nod, he continued. "If those are the traits in a woman I've searched the world over to find, it stands to reason I would already be falling in love with her when I found a woman with just those attributes."

She blinked those long, feathery lashes at him. "You are?"

"I am. Are you finished with your dessert?"

She looked down at her plate. She'd eaten most of the slice. "Yes. I'm getting tired, and I don't want to be tired." Her uninjured hand slid along her thigh, rubbing back and forth.

He got up immediately and went around the table to help her out of her chair. In such close proximity, he found he couldn't wait one more moment, doing what he'd wanted numerous times throughout dinner. He framed her small face with his large hands and bent to take possession of her mouth.

It was a takeover. His tongue found entry and he swept inside, taking control, kissing her the way he wanted. Claiming her as his. He was rough, demanding and possessive. He wanted her to feel his brand of love. Complete. Encompassing. Reverent. Carnal. All those things mixed together. Fire spread hot and liquid through his veins to pool in his groin. His cock ached for release, made its own imperative demands, so hard and thick he wasn't certain he could take a step. He forced himself to lift his head and was happy when her mouth chased after his. He swept his hand down her body to settle between her legs, even more gratified to feel her slick, welcoming heat. She'd need all of it to accommodate him.

"We're heading back to your room, Grace, but only until the doc says you no longer have to wear that sling to support your arm. You've only got another week, then we'll move your things to the master bedroom."

Grace nodded. He could see there was still a little apprehension in her eyes, but he couldn't blame her for that. He was asking a lot of her and he hadn't even talked to her about what he did as a rider and how that could possibly affect both of them should anything go wrong between them.

She turned toward the door but then glanced at him over her shoulder. "We can't leave the dishes out here."

He blew out the candles and then gave her his full attention. "I've got that taken care of."

"Of course you do." She sent him a smile and walked ahead of him to the door.

He reached around her to put his hand on the doorknob. Lowering his head to her shoulder, he bit the sweet spot between it and her neck. "You should have trusted that I took care of that detail, *gattina*."

She gave a little yelp at the sting and then shivered when he soothed the bite with his tongue. "I'm usually the detail person, and I'm still getting used to the fact that you're willing to take that on for me."

He pressed a kiss over his mark on her skin. "It will take time to work things out between us, but we'll get there. Trust is given over time, not immediately. I don't expect that."

It had taken Vittorio a long time to accept the dominant traits in himself and what that would mean when expecting a partner to live with him. He didn't want to ever be overbearing or in any way hurt his wife or children. He took time to find the things he needed to keep his life balanced and peaceful, as well as to develop compassion and humility. He might be dominant, but he refused to be domineering.

He'd learned to be a clear, good communicator, one who listened attentively with an open mind and tried to find every solution before resorting to imposing his will. His voice was a gift he could use when needed and it helped to persuade and soothe a difficult situation. He hoped it would help with their children. He knew it would be every bit as important for him to be honest with Grace as he wanted her to be with him. If he wasn't, how could he expect her to be?

He had pride in who he was, because he'd taken the time to train his mind just as he had his body. He had a strict code he lived by and loyalty was at the top of the list. If his woman put herself and her well-being into his care, he took that seriously and knew the gift she was giving him. He wasn't about to let her down through self-indulgence.

He was very aware his hold on Grace was tentative. She wanted him and the lifestyle he offered her, but he could tell there was a part of her she was holding back. That was expected as well. She was an intelligent woman and she wasn't just going to hand herself over to him because she was tempted. He loved that about her because it meant when she did fully surrender, he'd earned it and he had a much better chance of keeping her when he had to tell her he was a shadow rider and what that meant for both of them.

He swept his hand from her shoulder blade to the curve of her bottom and then rested his palm there, making her hyperaware of him. He felt her reaction as she walked back to her room, the slight trembling of her body, the little hitch in her breath.

"Do you object to walking around the house with just lingerie such as this on?" Deliberately he stepped closer to her, letting her feel his heat.

She shook her head. He remained silent, and she cast an anxious glance up at him. He met her eyes. Waiting.

"No. I'd definitely have to get used to it and wouldn't want anyone else in the house but the two of us."

Her explanation came out in a little rush. She'd continued walking so her face was averted, but once again, he saw that slow blush that was full body. He found the way her color rose when she looked at him both sexy and endearing. Just that sight alone did unexpected things to his body. He dropped his hand and caressed her left cheek.

Reaching around her as if to open her door, he let his body press tight against hers, so she would feel the thickness of his cock and know he wanted her as much or more than she wanted him. "If I ask you to wear something for me, you'll have to trust that I'll keep you safe, Grace, whether someone's in the house or not."

Her breath hitched, and she glanced at him over her

shoulder. He swept his hand down her back from the nape of her neck to the curve of her bottom, but she didn't protest.

"There will be many occasions that I will use something like handcuffs or ropes. I like the idea of having you helpless and me giving you orgasms over and over. I've fantasized about that." He made the confession against her ear, his lips brushing her skin, his breath warm. "Does that excite you or make you afraid?"

He opened the door and used his body to urge her forward. Her trembling increased, her color going from rose to a beautiful shade of red.

"Both." Her voice shook.

"Mia bella gattina, sei cosi coraggioso." He murmured his admiration as he came up behind her and took her hand gently out of her sling. "I'm a very lucky man. Very few women would have the courage to be so honest with me. Without honesty between us, I would never be able to give you everything you want or need." He caught at the stretchy lace, bunching the material in his hand and slowly drawing it up over her hips and rib cage.

Her breath was coming in fast, ragged pants of anticipation. He wanted her there, but he needed to take her even higher. Those breathy gasps caused his cock to throb and ache. Her music to accompany his seduction of her. She was giving him more than he possibly could have asked for this first time with her. She was focused wholly on him, his every movement, the way he walked, his bare feet, his open shirt, his very breathing, and that drove his own need even more.

"Stay relaxed for me," he instructed as he pulled the sexy little gown higher. "I'm taking this off your good arm and then carefully off your injured shoulder before anything else. When I've got it off, use the bathroom and get ready for bed, although you won't need clothes."

Grace stood there for a moment, nearly bringing her hand up in an attempt to cover the fiery patch of curls at the junction of her legs. She stopped herself, and he leaned down to brush a kiss across her mouth. She'd stopped herself for him.

"Looking at you gives me immeasurable pleasure." It was true. "I'm going to be doing a lot of that."

She smiled, but it was a small smile, as if she wasn't quite convinced, but he knew, over time, she would be.

He turned her toward the bathroom. "I love watching you walk." His palm cupped her cheek and then released her. She took the cue and moved across the room to the bathroom. He couldn't take his eyes off of her. She was mesmerizing. Sensual. She didn't know it and that was half the temptation.

He kept the lights off, although he had the drapes wide open. The view of the lake was incredible, and the surface served to enhance moonlight and send it through the long bank of windows. He wanted to be able to see his woman and judge just how she was feeling at any given time.

He had the covers pulled back exposing the bottom sheet. He shook her meds into his hand and waited for her return. When she came back, he put her hand back in the sling and offered the pills to her.

"I drank wine tonight."

He had consulted with her doctor, who had assured him one glass of wine wouldn't hurt her. She wasn't taking pain pills so much as anti-inflammatories. The combination wasn't going to bother her. He remained silent, still holding out his hand with the pills on his palm.

Grace took them from him. "You already talked to the doctor, didn't you?"

"Would I take a chance on harming you?" he countered.

She smiled up at him. "You amaze me that you're willing to see to every detail. By the time I get off work, I'm so exhausted, I honestly forget to think about myself. These past few weeks I've been leaving it all up to you and you haven't let me down once. In fact, you take better care of me than I do." She swallowed the pills down with the glass of water he had sitting on her nightstand.

Vittorio took the glass from her and pointed to the bed. She made a face at him and hesitated.

"It's awkward getting on the bed. Doing it in front of you is really embarrassing."

He frowned, not understanding. "You've been insisting on getting on your bed without help every night for more than a week. I was in the room, sitting right over there. I asked you every night if you needed help and you said very clearly you didn't."

For a man like him, watching her struggle had been pure hell. More, he'd been up-front from the beginning what kind of man he was and what he required. When she had refused his help, she'd refused him as a man.

She looked as if she'd been struck. Her eyes grew bright and her face flushed. She took a step closer to him. "Vittorio." Her hand shaped his face. It was the first time she'd touched him intimately, the care in her touch. "I never meant to hurt you. It felt wrong to ask for your help when I was so confused and unsure of why you had chosen me."

"Why wouldn't I choose you, Grace?" He didn't want her to step away. The tips of her breasts were just above his cock and he wanted the two scant inches between them gone, so he could press against her.

"You have to remember where I work, Vittorio. I'm an event planner. I'm hired to put on events for your family. We move in completely different circles. You date movie stars and I carry around a serial killer."

She made an attempt at humor, but he didn't like it.

"I know you don't think you're in any way beneath me."

She dropped her hand to her side and ducked her head.

He caught her chin. "You don't get to hide from me. That's part of our rules. We're honest with each other, even brutally so. Am I wrong in thinking you have high self-esteem?"

She pressed her lips together. For a moment he caught a flash of amusement in her eyes. "Evidently too high. I considered you to be a spoiled playboy with too much money.

I kind of put you in a category of super-beautiful, but a little useless."

His eyebrow shot up. Truthfully, he wanted to laugh. "Useless?" he echoed.

"Not as bad as some of your brothers," she added hastily.

He did laugh. She was priceless. "*Some?* Which ones of my brothers were more useful?"

She did laugh then. "I can see no matter what I say, I'm going to be in trouble. I'm extremely thankful you aren't really heavily into whips."

"My hand, however, is wondering how your very pretty ass will feel under it. And remember, *gattina*, I like it when you blush. Red looks good on you."

"It definitely doesn't. I'm a natural redhead, and we don't ever wear red. It would clash."

He spanned her waist with his hands and lifted her onto the bed. "Sit right there for a minute and tell me what was different about climbing into bed last night, from tonight." He shrugged out of his shirt and very carefully laid it over the back of one of the two chairs in front of the long built-in fireplace.

"I'm naked."

Deliberately, he ran his gaze over her body. Her breasts rose and fell with each breath. She looked vulnerable and excited, so perfect he could barely contain his desire, and he was an extremely disciplined and controlled man. "You are naked. I just noticed."

She laughed, and the sound of her laughter played over his body like the touch of fingers. His cock felt as if it might shatter into a million pieces. He didn't care. It was the most wonderful feeling in the world when he had never felt quite like it with anyone else. She made everything new and different. She was well worth the long wait and the worry that he'd never have anyone right for him.

"You're not."

"I'm not, am I?" He touched the front of his pants, rubbed over the thick length of his burning cock. The heat was tremendous, his need of her growing every moment he was with her. Still, he took the time to be playful with her. He wanted her on edge, slick with hunger, but he didn't want her afraid. Sometimes being a little fearful could heighten her pleasure, but not this time. Tonight, he was going to take his time and make love to her. He'd meant what he'd said when he'd told her he didn't want to ever see her hurt or with tears in her eyes. He knew never was a long time, but he would still do his best to make that promise count.

She laughed just as he knew she would. "You have a beautiful body, Vittorio. I noticed you at all the functions you attended. I couldn't help watching you. You've probably had several stalkers and I'm fairly certain I could be counted among them."

He liked that. He liked that a hell of a lot. "You noticed me."

She rolled her eyes. "Seriously? Every woman notices you. I think the men do, too, even the straight ones. You're that good-looking."

"But you took great care to stay out of my way."

"Spoiled useless rich boy, remember? I had fantasies. Hundreds of them. I couldn't take the chance that you would ruin even one of my illusions."

He stepped close to the bed. "Widen your legs for me." She did so, and he stepped between her thighs. "What else went on at these events that I didn't know about in reference to me or my family?"

"You want me to tell you event-planner secrets?" There was laughter in her voice, but he heard the underlying reluctance. She thought he wouldn't like what she might say.

He ran the pad of his finger from her collarbone to the top of her breast where he traced back and forth. "There aren't any secrets between us."

"You have secrets."

It was a challenge. His Grace was more than intelligent. She was very quick. "Yes, but I intend to tell you every single one of mine. What's the harm in telling me about anything to do with me?"

He kept his eyes on her face. Willing her to take the next step. They were still dancing around each other in the guise of teasing, but he needed her to take the next step to trust him with things she wouldn't normally tell him.

"I don't want you upset with Katie. I'm the one coming up with all the irreverent nicknames for certain clients."

He remained silent, disappointment slicing through him. They weren't at that point yet, and he knew above all else, patience was key to getting her to trust him wholly. He shook his head, annoyed with himself for trying to push her beyond where she was ready to go.

"Vittorio." She whispered his name and there was an ache in her voice.

She didn't like disappointing him, and she knew she had. He leaned in and pressed a brief kiss to her mouth. That alone made him feel as if she'd given him a great gift. She might not trust him all the way yet, but she definitely cared enough that when he wasn't pleased, or he was disappointed, she was upset.

"It doesn't matter, *gattina*, it will come with time. We'll get there." He was confident they would.

"It *does* matter." Grace surprised him with her fierce reaction. "I'm embarrassed that I can be childish at work. I want you to recognize that I'm a professional. I love what I do and I'm seriously good at it."

"I've listened to you and Katie every day for the last week. I'm very aware you're professional."

She ducked her head again, and his heart sank. He didn't like her disappointed in herself when she clearly was trying—really trying. He willed her to keep going. This was an important moment in their relationship even if she didn't recognize it as such. He was patient, remaining silent. Waiting. He concentrated on the rise and fall of her breasts. Her skin was soft, very pale, almost glowing in the moonlight spilling over the lake and pouring in through the bay of windows.

She touched her tongue to her lip and then looked up at him, meeting his eyes. "I should trust you enough to know you aren't petty enough to retaliate against our business, or Katie, because I like to play silly games."

Vittorio was elated that she made her confession to him. She didn't quite know that he wouldn't hold whatever her game was concerning him against him, but she wanted to extend him that trust. Her work was very important to her. It was the one thing she'd had that Haydon Phillips hadn't been able to take away from her, and she'd made it a success. She didn't want him to belittle it, hurt it, or in any way think less of her regarding her business.

"When clients are difficult, I make up names for them, and then use acronyms in order to make us both laugh."

He couldn't help but smile. She made the confession as if she'd committed some terrible sin. "I see. I have one of these acronyms?"

"SURB."

He caught on immediately. "Spoiled useless rich boy," he translated. That wasn't bad enough for her to have waited so long to tell him. He thought over what she'd revealed. *When clients are difficult.* He'd never been "difficult" at any of the charity events. She had invented a game to ease the sting when difficult clients were ugly to Katie or her. "What did you call my mother?"

She sighed. Her fingers twisted in the sheets. He couldn't help himself. He caught her hand and pressed her palm to his thigh to give her courage.

"She was known as QBSITDROH." She rattled off the letters fast as if she'd used them often.

He raised an eyebrow. "That is quite a mouthful."

"Your mother is not an easy person to work with. She deserved a name befitting someone who could raise her level of contempt, sarcasm and venom. It was necessary to find a way to laugh."

He could hear the apology in her voice. That wasn't what he wanted from her at all.

"You'll have to teach your special name to my sisters-in-law. They occasionally need a humorous way to cope. What does it stand for?"

"Queen bitch spawned in the deepest recesses of hell." She looked up at him quickly as if expecting him to be angry.

Vittorio couldn't help himself. He burst out laughing. "I have a very healthy respect for my mother, but no one can quite reach the particular level of vitriol she can when dealing with anyone in any situation. Very imaginative and apt."

He framed her face and kissed her, taking his time, letting her fire consume him.

CHAPTER THIRTEEN

Kissing Grace turned his world upside down. Once he started, Vittorio never wanted to stop. She tasted like wildfire, hot, spicy and yet sweet, a runaway sensation that took him down the dark path he desired. No one had ever come close to taking away the harsh reality of his life—not until he'd found Grace.

She occupied his thoughts day and night. He studied her with the same complete focus with which he'd trained. He knew everything about her that he could possibly learn in the weeks he'd been with her. Every expression. The way she moved when she was tired. The habits that gave away her moods. He knew how she liked her coffee or tea. She had a certain expression that crept over her face when she didn't like something but was determined to go through with it.

He kissed her gently, with no demand, determined to go slowly, but in spite of his determination and all of his discipline, there was no way to keep from deepening the kiss. She set up an addiction, a craving he was never going to get over. The way she surrendered to him was the most amazing feeling in the world. She gave herself completely to him. Pleasure washed through him until his pulse thundered in his ears and beat through his cock. He'd never felt more alive, or more in need of his woman, not even after coming out of the shadows after a mission when the adrenaline poured through his body.

Vittorio had known, almost from the first glimpse of her as she leapt out of the trunk, all fury and fire, furious with her foster brother, that the passion in her would be wild and explosive.

He guided her down to the mattress, so she was lying on her back, legs over the edge, all the while his mouth refusing to leave hers. He kissed her repeatedly, long drugging kisses, wanting to consume her, devour her, seeking more of her surrender. Demanding more. All the while his hands began a slow exploration of her body.

She was exquisite. The feel of her skin, soft beneath the pads of his fingers. He splayed them wide to take in as much of her as possible. He went slow, refusing to hurry, no matter the demands of his body. He savored her, letting himself absorb the feel of her surrender to him, everything about the experience with her. The rise and fall of her breasts. How they looked, twin alluring mounds, the curves drawing his eye as he lifted his head to take in her body.

He liked having her under him, at his mercy, her body open to him, his hands moving over her possessively, letting her know who she belonged to. Grace was elegance, her body fine-boned, her rib cage delicate and small. Her hips flared, matching the sweet line of her breasts. He traced every line of her body, every curve, memorizing her, etching her into his brain, taking his time, appreciating every inch of her.

Grace was very responsive to him. Shivering. Moaning. Every sound served to heighten his pleasure. Her nipples peaked so that he couldn't resist the temptation and he flicked his tongue over them and tugged and rolled just to hear her soft cries. He spent time on her breasts, filing away every shudder of her body, every buck of her hips. He wanted to know what she liked and what she didn't. Every trigger point that brought her pleasure. There was no reason to hurry and every reason not to. He wanted this first time to be perfect for her. This was about loving Grace and showing her how he felt about her.

Grace stared at Vittorio's brutally handsome face. There was nothing soft or feminine about it, not even the long sweep of lashes that framed his strange, blue eyes. He was utterly masculine yet managed not to be brutishly so. She knew surrendering to him meant giving him everything. He'd laid out very carefully what he wanted in a relationship and expected her to live with his rules.

A million butterflies took flight when he spoke to her in that velvet tone. She craved the life he offered to her. She loved her work and her mind grasped details. Planning dream weddings and fairy-tale parties to fulfill people's fantasies was the perfect job for her. She needed to make others happy and she was meticulous about getting every detail perfect and right for them. They told her what they wanted, and she found the best way to provide that dream event for them.

It was always at home, when she was alone with herself, the way she'd been her entire life, that she was lost. She had no purpose. No focus. No center to balance her. Now, this man, Vittorio Ferraro, an amazing, sensual, intelligent man, offered those things to her. He was exactly what she needed—and wanted.

Grace sank her fingers into the thick mass of hair spilling onto his forehead. She loved that she could touch his hair. She'd fantasized over doing just that. When she inhaled, there was that elusive, masculine scent that appealed to her. It was faint, but there, all spice and woods, something she found hard to describe, but she knew she'd be able to find him blindfolded, with a hundred other men in the same room.

His hand was on her bare belly, fingers splayed wide, the tips touching the underside of both breasts, causing her breath to come in ragged pants. There was no hiding from him. He knew what he did to her. He'd kissed her and that was all it took for her body to go soft and pliant, melting into his, desperate to have him inside her.

His fingers moved back and forth over her stomach, stroking mesmerizing caresses there that soothed the fear in her yet fed her fierce arousal at the same time. Her fingers curled into his hair as he pressed a kiss to her belly button and then swirled his tongue there. She gasped, and her hips bucked involuntarily when his teeth scraped her skin and then nipped, causing a little sting.

"Are you paying attention, *gattina*?"

"Yes." She was, but she could barely get the affirmative past her throat. Flames licked at her skin along the path his mouth took. She was acutely aware of him kissing, licking and biting his way down her body to the tangle of fiery curls covering her mound.

"Vittorio." His name came out a moan.

"Lay still for me, *bella*. We have to be careful of your shoulder. If you keep squirming around like that, I might have to punish you."

Grace couldn't stop squirming, not when his breath felt hot between her legs. He caught each leg behind the knee and pulled it back, holding each with his arms but leaving his hands free. He slipped off the bed so that his head was between her legs. He turned and licked up her thigh, making her gasp at the sensation. Fingers of desire danced up and down her thighs. Her hips bucked again when his hot breath bathed her sex.

It was too much, and he hadn't even gotten started. "You said no punishments," she managed to gasp, her entire body shuddering with need.

"I might have misspoken." His tongue swiped across her entrance, collecting liquid heat and driving her up the wall.

She cried out and curled her fingers tighter in his hair.

Nothing, *nothing* had ever felt that good. "So, handcuffs are in . . ." She could barely get the words out, air refusing to move through her lungs.

"And ropes. I've been studying for several years now, and lately have really picked up the art of shibari from my brother. He uses his skills mainly for art while I . . ." Implying he didn't. Teasing her.

She laughed because he made her feel as if she was his everything. His mouth. His hands. Those eyes of his moving over her body and then settling on her face when he delivered his playful, but truthful statement. Her laugh turned to a gasp as he kissed his way up her other thigh, using lips, teeth and tongue. Every single nip sent lightning flicks through her bloodstream.

She couldn't think. At. All. It was impossible. Her world had suddenly narrowed to Vittorio. His hands kept her thighs apart easily, giving him full access to her, and his mouth felt suddenly ravenous. He was doing what he said—having her for dessert. Her body responded in a way she'd never experienced, coiling tighter and tighter, the pressure tremendous.

"Vittorio." She breathed his name, unsure if she wanted him to stop or to continue, but there was no laughter in her anymore. A dark shiver crept down her spine. He'd said he'd have her for dessert and he'd meant it. She knew he'd meant it when he'd talked about ropes and handcuffs.

Grace's body shuddered, somewhere between excitement and fear of the unknown. Little flames licked at her thighs, everywhere his skin touched hers, as if he'd set off an inferno and she was catching fire right along with him. Deep inside, she felt her heartbeat. Pulsing. Aching. Heat spread through her from the inside out. All the while the pressure kept building. The coiling inside tightened. Swelled.

Everywhere Vittorio touched her on her skin, he left pulses of heat, tiny flickers of electricity that crackled and zapped. She'd never felt so sensitive. He wasn't touching her breasts, but she felt that buildup moving through her entire body, so that her nipples were stiff and aching. Her breasts throbbed to that heartbeat deep inside. The sensations were becoming overwhelming. She sobbed his name. It broke from her like an amulet that would keep her safe.

"Let go, *bella*. Just relax and let go."

His voice was velvet soft. Low. Compelling. Impossible not to obey. Heat exploded through her. She felt the gathering wave begin somewhere deep and spread through her like a wildfire, swamping her, encompassing her entire body. The sensation took her over, rushing like a freight train. Her back arched. Her toes curled. A cry escaped her throat and there was no repressing the sound. Her body pulsed, alive, shocked, the sensation beyond her wildest imagination.

Vittorio kissed her inner thighs and rubbed his face down each one, leaving behind the burn from the shadow on his jaw. He stood slowly, his gaze fixed on her face as he loosened the drawstring of his lounge pants and let them drop. One hand circled the girth of his cock, just as her lashes lifted. Her eyes widened, and she let out her breath in a little rush.

"Are you on birth control, Grace?" He hated even asking her. He didn't give a damn if she got pregnant, but they hadn't discussed it yet. He hadn't told her he would want a child sooner rather than later. He didn't want her to feel as if he was marrying her just because she could give him the rider the rest of his world demanded.

"Yes."

"I don't want to use a condom. I've never had unprotected sex with anyone. I go in regularly anyway, just to make certain I'm clean. I got a clean bill of health right after I met you." It sucked having to bring up the fact that he'd been with other women. "Tell me if you're uncomfortable with me going without a glove."

"I'm not."

He could barely breathe. He hadn't expected to feel so differently. Everything was different with Grace. Her absolute trust and faith in him. The feel of her skin. The scent of her. The sound of her cries. He found his need of her had grown beyond anything he'd ever experienced. Her body was hot, and the moment he pressed the head of his cock into her, he was surrounded by hot, liquid flames, squeezing down on him, drawing him deeper into that fiery paradise while at the same time, fighting to keep him out.

"*Gattina*, relax for me."

She was so tight, he doubted if he could move through that constricting channel. He could feel her heartbeat right through his cock. Or maybe it was his, pulsing and throbbing. The sensation of being inside her was both heaven and hell. Looking down at her face, that exquisite, beautiful face, for the first time in his life, he felt overwhelming love. It was all-encompassing and heightened the sensations pouring over him as he relentlessly pushed deeper, feeling her channel gripping and milking his cock. Silken heat wrapped him tight, strangling him. A million hot tongues rasped over him.

Vittorio threw back his head, but not so far that he couldn't keep eye contact with her. His hands settled on her hips, as her body opened slowly, reluctantly for him. She squirmed just a little and he caught the faint sheen of tears.

"Relax for me, *gattina*. Talk. I need to know what you're feeling."

"It burns. Stretches." She gasped the explanation.

He had been pressing steadily, but gently forward. He stopped immediately to give her body time to adjust to his size. "That will subside. This is going to be a little uncomfortable at first, but that will ease once you're used to me."

It was difficult to wait. The feeling was so perfect. Scorching hot. Tight. That pounding pulse, sending a million flames flickering like licks of lightning through his body. He breathed away the need to slam deep, but his fingers tightened on her hips, holding her there when she kept moving. Squirming. Adding to the building need in him.

"I'm good."

He'd never wanted to hear two words more. Still, he

studied her face, waiting for the tension to recede. "That's my girl."

She'd never looked more beautiful, with her skin flushed a soft rose. Her breasts heaved, every movement sending a jolt through them, so they swayed invitingly, drawing his attention. He could see her stomach muscles rippling and her thighs tightening with every forward press.

He wasn't going to prolong his entry. He waited until she was exhaling, and he buried himself deep, moving right through the thin barrier and claiming her body for his own.

Grace cried out, pain flashing through her. Instinctively, she tried to crawl away, even though she'd been expecting it.

"Grace."

That voice. Intense. Compelling. Impossible to ignore. She opened her eyes and stared up at his face. He looked like carnal sin. The devil himself tempting her. There was a dark lust in his eyes, etched into the lines of his face, but there was also something else, another emotion that made her body relax for him. The more she relaxed, the more the pain subsided.

"Just stay still and breathe with me."

"It's gone. It's okay." Already her body was going back to responding to his. It was impossible not to feel the heat. The heartbeat they shared. She wanted him to move. She needed him to move. The hunger in her was building all over again, the pressure winding and coiling tighter and tighter, just from looking at his face.

"Lift your legs. Wrap them around my hips."

She liked hearing him tell her what to do. It was so much easier than trying to figure it out. She wanted to feel the sensations he was offering, and she wanted to give him something equally as pleasurable or even more back. She needed him to give her instructions when she really didn't have a clue. He slid his hand from her hip, down her thigh to the back of her left knee and urged her leg up. He helped her wrap it around him. She followed suit with the other leg and hooked her ankles, so she was wrapped completely around him.

He pushed forward, burying himself even more. She hadn't known she could feel so full. So perfect. Eyes on his, she felt him withdraw. She didn't want him to, but then he surged forward, driving through her tight muscles, the friction over the sensitive bundles of nerves sending fire streaking through her body. She cried out again, unable to stay silent. He smiled at her, looking more like temptation than ever before. She didn't care, she wanted everything he could give her.

Vittorio began to move in Grace, one hard surge after another, watching her carefully, seeing the buildup, the tension winding through her as each hard stroke took her closer and closer to the edge. Deliberately, he didn't tip her over. He kept moving in her. Letting himself go just a little, enough that his body felt the way she clamped down on him harder, like a vise, surrounding him with that hot silk, wrapping him up and squeezing until he thought his head might come off.

Little sounds escaped her throat, becoming louder and longer as he pumped into her, testing her a little more with each hard thrust. The sounds turned to aching sobs of need. Her nails bit into the comforter as she fisted it. He wished those nails were in his back. He loved the sight of her, breasts jolting with each surge. Her little body undulating as he drove deep into her. Her eyes shocked. Dazed. Dark with her own desire. Her mouth open, breath escaping in ragged pants. Just the sight of her nearly took him over the edge.

He stood above her, her hips in his hands, his legs adding to the strength of each surge into her. Streaks of fire danced up his back, roared in his belly and rushed down his legs. Her body gripped his cock like a fist. Squeezed. Milked. Scorching hot. His breath exploded out of him and he took her over the edge.

Her body paused for one moment in the brutal milking

of his and then the fireball hit, a giant wave of pure flames roaring through him, through her, sweeping them both up into its path. His cock jerked hard, over and over, as her sheath constricted and strangled his shaft, the heat nearly too much, but only adding to the incredible fierce beauty of the moment.

"Fucking paradise," he whispered and let himself go with her over the edge.

He was flung far out somewhere he'd never been before. There was only Grace and the passion washing through him. Every cell in his body was alive. Every single nerve ending was on fire. The sound of her cries was a kind of music playing in his head, reaching the crescendo as his seed rocketed deep into her.

The entire time, he kept his gaze on hers, forcing her to stay with him. To look at him. He wanted to see that beauty steal over her face. He wanted her to know he was the one giving her that feeling of utter euphoria. He needed her to know who he was—her man. Her lover. The man she trusted to always take care of her, have her back, give her everything.

Her eyes moved over his face. A little shocked. Very dazed. Incredibly sexy. She knew. He saw the knowledge there. He was her everything just as he needed to be. There was so much more, but theirs was the kind of relationship that had to build slowly and come from a place of trust. Little by little he'd introduce small things to her to see what she liked or didn't like, what she could accept or not. He knew he was embarking on the adventure of a lifetime and happiness elevated the endorphins pumping through his body.

Vittorio felt his legs turning to rubber, and he slowly allowed his body to reluctantly begin to withdraw from hers. He was still semi-hard and the action triggered another huge quake in her, so that for a moment her body gripped his, refusing to give him up and squeezing down hard on his most sensitive part. It felt like paradise all over again.

Vittorio collapsed over her, reveling in the way his body

shuddered and jerked, giving her every last drop of his seed. The hot splash triggered a multitude of aftershocks so that her body bit down hard time and time again, strangling him, prolonging that feeling of utter paradise. He'd been careful, gentle even, and he'd still come harder than he'd ever come in his life.

He pressed his body deeper into hers, giving her his full weight, basking in the feeling of her small body beneath his much larger one. The feelings of conquest and possession mixing with love were a heady combination. Those traits were deep in him and she accepted him without judgment. How could he not be in love with her?

He kissed her eyelids and trailed more kisses down her cheek to the corner of her mouth. His tongue teased the seam of her lips until she opened, and he caught her breath and swallowed it down. Her breasts were heaving beneath the crush of his chest, but she kissed him back, one arm sliding around his neck, while she simply put her other hand on his rib cage.

He took his time, kissing her long. Kissing her hard. Moving from gentle to rough. He let her take his weight longer, mashing her soft breasts into his chest and resting his hips in the cradle of hers. She didn't fight him, didn't try to get out from under him although her air was restricted. She relaxed into him, her body seemingly melting into his. He lifted his head to frame her face, watching her struggle a little to breathe, but pulling in air determinedly. She had given herself to him and she was still doing so. Reluctantly, he eased his body off of hers, so she could breathe properly.

He'd been extremely careful of her shoulder, keeping his weight off that arm, but he narrowed his eyes, watchful to make certain she wasn't in pain. Finding no sign of discomfort, he kissed her neck, teased with his teeth, scraping back and forth before biting down. She yelped, and he instantly soothed the mark with his tongue. "You're perfect, Grace."

Her eyes shone up at him. That dazed, shocked look was

receding slowly. "That had nothing to do with me and everything to do with you. I had no idea I could feel like that."

He kissed his way to her throat and then over the curve of her right breast. "That was just the start, *bella*." He licked along the upper curve and then pressed a kiss there. "There's so much more I have to show you."

His teeth scraped back and forth along that inviting curve. He watched her face. Felt her agitation as her breasts rose and fell in anticipation. She knew. She was waiting for it. Holding her breath. Needing. He slipped his hand between her legs and bit down gently. Her back arched, thrusting her breasts up like an offering. Hot liquid seeped from her body to his fingers. Her hips bucked. He licked at the mark he left there.

"I can't believe something can feel that good," she whispered.

"There's so much more," he reiterated. "Let's get in the tub. I don't want you sore."

"Can we go out to the hot tub after I clean up a little?" She looked ruefully at the smears of blood and semen on her thighs. "I've been wanting to get in it since I first saw it. I love the idea of going out at night and sitting under the stars."

He considered how tired she was. There was no way he would ever be able to keep his hands off of her if he sat with her in the hot tub. Warning her was the best policy. "Honey, if we go out to the hot tub, I'm going to be fucking your brains out. There's no way I'll be able to keep my hands off of you."

She gave him a siren's smile. "I would hope not."

She hadn't even winced at his language. He loved that she let him be who he was, no matter what. If anything, his choice of words sent another flush of heat spreading through her body. Her breathing was elevated all over again. He loved her beyond words.

Vittorio slipped off the bed. "Just stay there."

"I'm kind of a mess."

"I like you lying there, legs sprawled apart, a mixture of the two of us running down your legs. You look as hot as sin. I especially like seeing that I'm your only. I want to keep it that way. I had no idea I could be so primitive, but suddenly I am."

She put her uninjured arm across her eyes. "I can't believe the things you say to me."

He turned back to her, one hand on the doorjamb leading to the bathroom. For a moment his heart stood still.

"Or the way they make me feel," she continued, without looking at him. "I want you in me all over again just because you said that."

"That's going to happen sooner than you think." He wet a cloth with warm water and after rinsing himself off, took the cloth to her. "Lie still and let me get this for you."

"I can do it." She started to sit.

Vittorio put a gentle hand on her chest. "I want to clean you. Later, I'll teach you how I'd like you to clean me." Again, he kept his gaze steady on her face. Her eyes never left his. "I'm going to be asking so much of you, Grace. I have to be able to feel as if I'm giving you back as much or more." It was a confession, plain and simple. He took great care to be gentle as he wiped away the evidence of her innocence.

"I don't see how you could possibly ask more of me than you've already given."

"I'm asking for your trust in all things. That alone is worth any price. I'll ask for things in our bedroom that might frighten you at first, but that's where that trust needs to come in. You have to know that I'll take you higher each time but never go so far that you can't handle it. I also will have to talk to you about things regarding the Ferraro businesses, and you'll have to accept them and never speak of them to another soul outside our immediate family." He watched her face as he referred to the one thing he feared the most.

In the bedroom, he could reward her ten times over for

her trust in him. It was the revelations as to what he really did for their family that he was afraid she wouldn't be able to handle. His shadow and hers had become entangled in spite of his efforts to keep them apart. Although, truthfully, he hadn't tried that hard. He knew if she rejected him, the consequences to him would be dire. She would simply forget the things he told her, believe he had proclaimed her his fiancée in order to take care of the bills and her until she recovered and then they would break up. He would lose everything—including his ability to ride the shadows.

He reached for her hand and helped her to sit. Immediately she stroked her hand down his belly as if she had been waiting to touch him all along. Her fingers lingered low and his cock reacted, jerking hard, letting her see how appreciative he was of her touching him.

"I like being yours, Vittorio. I'm very aware it won't always be easy. I can see it on your face sometimes that you would insist on your way at times, and I might not like it."

He nodded, more aware of the heat from her breath spreading over the sensitive head of his cock. She sat on the bed, her thighs still spread wide, and he was standing inside them. If she tilted her head up, her mouth was exactly where he needed it to be. Without conscious thought, he shifted even closer, so he was facing directly toward her. Immediately her gaze dropped to his cock, her eyes widening.

Her hands came up to cup his sac, driving the breath from his lungs. First her thumb stroked and then the pads of her fingers with exquisite gentleness. "I had no idea you were so soft here."

"I like that I'm the only man you've ever touched intimately, Grace." He rested one hand on top of her head, careful not to put any pressure on her, no matter how much he wanted to. At the stroke of her fingers on his balls, his cock was hardening all over again. "If you keep that up, we're not going to make it to the hot tub."

"Really?"

Her tongue darted out and moistened her lips. He had to suppress a groan. She was sexy without trying. Her gaze shifted from his growing cock to his eyes.

"What would we be doing instead? It has to be something very impressive in order for me to give up a night in the hot tub under the stars with you."

Her teasing voice and the look of growing hunger was as sensual as the flush on her skin and the stroking of her fingers. He wrapped his hand around one of hers and squeezed gently, showing her how to roll and caress his sac. Then he took her fingers and stroked his shaft before wrapping them in a fist at the base and pumping up and down while squeezing hard.

"I'd want to stay right here and have you learn to suck my cock just the way I like it. Your mouth would be tight and hot and your tongue would lash and dance, until I was so hot I'd have to pull out and take you again."

"Why would you have to pull out?"

Her hand had picked up the rhythm he showed her and he let go. She didn't hesitate or falter. Her gaze was fixed on his cock while she worked him.

He fisted her hair, tugging a little until she looked up at him. "You aren't ready to swallow yet, that will come with time. I want you to enjoy every single thing we do together. Sucking my cock is fantastic for me, but only if you love doing it. If you're not getting anything out of it, *bella*, it takes away from my enjoyment."

"No matter what, I'll love it because I know it makes you feel fantastic."

His heart threatened to beat right out of his chest. She meant it. He could hear lies. All riders could hear lies, and she absolutely meant what she was saying.

"Do I get a choice on what I'd like to do?"

His throat nearly closed. "Yes."

"Then I'd like to stay here and see how much of you will actually fit in my mouth. You're really quite intimidating, but on the other hand, you're beautiful. I've never thought a man was especially beautiful until I saw you."

Red silk spilled from either side of his fist, a fiery cascade of her long hair, a perfect handle for him to guide her.

"Use your tongue. Don't worry about going slow or fast or doing anything right. Just explore. I consider your body mine. I want to play. I want to make love to you. I want to fuck you so hard neither of us can breathe. I hope you get to a point where you feel the same about me. My body belongs to you alone. All of it. It's yours to explore. I'm hoping you can't stop touching me any more than I can stop touching you."

Grace seemed to take him at his word. She let go of his shaft and caught his hips, urging him closer to her. The moment he stepped right up against the bed, she leaned in to kiss his belly. Her hands stroked his rib cage, fingers trailed over the ridges of his abdomen. He found himself holding his breath. Waiting. Anticipating. She was naturally sensual, although he could see she didn't have a clue she was. Her featherlight kisses trailing down his belly had him sucking in his breath as one of her hands cupped his balls again, fingers working his sac very gently.

She moved lower, her breath heating the flared head of his cock. Her head dipped and everything in him stilled. She licked up his sac, fingers and tongue working in tandem, until she sucked one ball into the heat of her mouth. Fire shot up his spine. His entire body jerked. Her fingers slid farther around him, massaging his perineum with a firmer glide. Several times she licked her fingers as she continued working on his balls.

His cock jerked eagerly, lengthening, thickening until his girth was even more intimidating. He murmured encouragement to her, his hands once more fisting in her hair. He had to hold on to something in order to keep from exploding. Breathing deeply, he concentrated on keeping his legs from turning to jelly.

She settled her fist around the base of his cock. Tightly. He waited. Counting his heartbeats. He felt her breath again. Her tongue flicked out and tasted the pearl drops leaking on the flared head. Holding his cock close to her mouth, she looked up at him and smiled. She was so close her lips moved against his shaft, sending a lightning strike straight through his groin. It was all he could do to keep from forcing her head over his cock. He'd never in his life wanted a blow job more than he did right at that moment and she hadn't yet done anything to his cock.

"I don't think you have to worry that I'll enjoy myself." Grace took a long lick up his shaft as if he were an ice-cream cone. Her tongue lingered over the sweet spot just beneath the flared head. She flicked her tongue experimentally. "I like your taste. It's different. Salty, but good."

Again, she wasn't playing him. Her voice held that note that told him she was giving him the strict truth. He couldn't help himself. He tightened his hold in her hair and guided her head that scant distance. "Then get to work before I embarrass myself."

She opened her mouth and settled it around the sensitive head, her laughter vibrating through him. The sensation was almost too good to be true. His entire body shook, and he had to impose strict discipline to keep from forcing her mouth to envelop more.

Her tongue began a slow dance, as if she took him at his word and was exploring. Experimenting. She sucked hard and then was back to licking up and down his shaft and under the head. One hand moved from his balls to caress his inner thighs and then once again stroked fire along his perineum. The assault on his senses had his body straining and she had barely done anything to him.

"Look at me." His command came out more of a growl than his usual soft dictate.

Her long lashes lifted and those green eyes of hers stared into his.

"I want you to take as much of me as you can fit into

your mouth and suck. Use your tongue." He spoke through clenched teeth. If she didn't get to it soon, he really was going to lose it.

His life was about discipline. Nothing had ever threatened his discipline the way she did. She was completely inexperienced and had no real idea what she was doing, but her instincts were perfection. Small beads of sweat broke out on his forehead. His hips moved restlessly. His body screamed with urgent demand.

"Keep looking at me. I want to see your lips stretched around my cock. It's so fucking sexy." It was. Everything about her was sexy.

She obeyed him, slowly opening her mouth and drawing him in. He let her do the work, feeling the suction, the tight hold pressing around him. Her lips had to stretch to accommodate his size. No way she could take much, but her hand worked him, each tight slide sending flames dancing up his cock. Then her mouth suckled strong until he thought the top of his head might blow off. Her tongue took over, flicking, dancing, swirling up and over the head and then under it. Then she licked, getting him wet and starting all over again.

There was no way to last. None. She'd done him in almost from the moment her hand had brushed his body. She was no pro at sucking his cock, but she didn't need to be. She was Grace. *His* Grace. He could see her enjoyment shining in her eyes. She was giving him this by giving him herself. Everything she did was for him. Every stroke of her tongue. Her tight suction and the artistry of her tongue.

He pulled at her hair, pulling her off of him with more regret than she'd ever know. "We're going to stop right here, *gattina*."

"No!" she wailed, and he could see the instant rejection of his command in her eyes and with the sudden pout.

Vittorio had never seen that particular expression and he wanted to kiss it off her face. "Yes. When I say enough, *bella*, I say it for a reason. Stand up and turn around. Ordinarily, I'd want you on your hands and knees, but we're being every careful of that shoulder and arm. Right now, lie on your stomach, legs over the bed."

She complied readily, and he leaned over her to make certain her arm was comfortable. Her feet didn't quite reach the floor if her hips were on the edge of the bed. He liked that. It gave him far more control. Placing his hand on the small of her back to keep her from moving, he guided his very wet and hot cock to her slick entrance. He wasn't nearly as careful entering her as he had been the first time. He simply drove through her reluctant folds, one hard invasion, the flames rushing over him as her body protested, trying to keep him out of that scorching hot paradise.

Grace sobbed his name and he didn't stop. That glorious cry drove him on, the desperate need in her almost matching his own. He settled his fingers around both hips and, using his strength, pulled her smaller body into his and surged forward with his hips. Over and over. He closed his eyes and threw back his head, savoring the fact that he could go deeper, that he filled her, stretched her, gave her that burn that was everything she could want.

Her body clamped down, gripping his cock almost viciously, so that when he surged in and out of her, the friction grew, sending both to amazing heights. He had no idea how many times he brought them both to the edge, but when he finally tipped them over, her moans had turned to cries and her body swept his into something close to real paradise. He couldn't believe the feeling of complete euphoria. For a moment he floated there, while flames licked over his body and centered like a firestorm in his cock.

Vittorio had to fight for air, but the sensations running through his body were worth the lack of ability to breathe. He let himself collapse over her, and when he could he kissed the nape of her neck and then down her spine. She didn't move.

"I think we're done tonight, *gattina*."

"No hot tub?" Her voice was muffled.

"Bed. Not hot tub. And I'm sleeping with you." He waited for her reply. He was sleeping with her and he'd find the energy to convince her if necessary.

"All right."

Her soft consent earned her more kisses and then he cleaned them both up and tucked her into bed, curling his body around hers. She fell asleep immediately and he wasn't far behind her.

CHAPTER FOURTEEN

You'll have to excuse me, Grace," Vittorio said, brushing a kiss across her knuckles. "Please go ahead and continue your physical therapy while I see what kind of crisis my family is involved in this time." He poured amusement into his voice, when he didn't feel in the least amused.

Grace blinked up at him, suspicion in her expression. It was hell not being able to lie to her, especially when every Ferraro was certain that a war was brewing. It wasn't bad enough that they had to contend with a cunning serial killer, they had to worry about a family whose history was steeped in violence.

"Everything is going to be okay," he assured before she could protest. He deliberately glanced at the physical therapist, knowing she would take his silent cue and not ask any questions when they had a stranger in their midst.

She nodded, and he kissed her just because he loved that she followed his lead, even when she didn't want to.

"Please be careful of tiring her out," he cautioned the therapist. "There's no need to push her so hard that she's in pain afterward." He put a warning in his voice. No one wanted to cross him. His beloved Grace might think he was the sweetest man on the planet, but the rest of the world was much more careful around him.

Vittorio shut the door and immediately hurried down the hall to the room Merry had set up for his family to meet with him. Giovanni had to drive, but the others arrived via the shadows, even Eloisa, and that wasn't a good sign.

He greeted his mother first, simply out of respect that she had given birth to him, but his greeting was cold. He couldn't help it. Stefano had been more of a parent when he was ten than she'd ever been. Vittorio wasn't too happy with her after the problems with Grace she'd caused him— deliberately, he was certain. He gripped his brother's hand and accepted the hug Stefano always gave him.

"Thanks for coming here instead of having me drag Grace out."

Eloisa rolled her eyes. "I don't think there's such a thing as an independent woman anymore. Is she so afraid of losing you that she can't be without you for a day? That's going to become a problem, Vittorio. You have serious work to do and nothing can interfere."

"I don't like my woman far from me, Eloisa," Vittorio answered. "It's my preference and she understands that and gives that to me. Fortunately, as an adult, I can choose the kind of lifestyle I want, and I don't need anyone's approval."

She winced at his tone. The "least of all your approval" was implied. Stefano's voice carried absolute authority, but Vittorio had recognized early on that he had a gift. His voice could be compelling, or commanding, and those in a room reacted to it. He could calm others down, arouse or infuriate, all with his tone. He used a reprimand, dark and threatening, to let her know she'd better stop before he retaliated in a way she wouldn't like.

"You're really going to marry her, aren't you?" Eloisa changed tactics.

"Absolutely I am."

"Even with this serial killer stalking your family."

Stefano sighed. "The implication being that Phillips being a madman and targeting all of us is Grace's fault?"

"Of course not," Eloisa snapped. "But she did bring him straight to us."

"That's a good thing," Taviano weighed in. "Who better to bring such a man to than us? We're shadow riders and we're supposed to mete out justice to those the law has been unable to reach."

Eloisa turned on him with a hiss of annoyance. "You have managed to make yourself scarce. I've called you dozens of times in the last few days. You didn't even have the courtesy to return my calls."

Taviano glanced at Stefano. Vittorio didn't blame him for the uneasy look he sent his older brother. Eloisa was a pain, but she was their mother and Stefano demanded they all respect that. She was also a fellow shadow rider and for that alone, she needed to be respected. She wasn't, after all these years, going to step up and be a real mother, but none of them would have accepted that from her anyway. Still, Stefano insisted they answer her calls and put up as best they could with her lectures.

Stefano sent Taviano a hard look, one that promised they would be having a private conversation after the meeting. Taviano acknowledged the look with a nod, because none of them would ever disrespect Stefano.

"I'm sorry, Eloisa," Taviano said. "I flew to Los Angeles to take care of business there and then represented our family at the meeting in New York for the Internet company we're considering buying. However, I should have made the time immediately."

Vittorio knew Taviano was pointing out the obvious, not to Eloisa but to Stefano. They all, including Taviano, knew it wouldn't be considered a good enough excuse.

"You announced to everyone at the meeting with the Saldi family that you were engaged to Nicoletta. That is impossible. The girl is . . ." Eloisa trailed off to search for the proper word.

"Be careful," Taviano cautioned. "She belongs to me. You don't have to like it, or sanction my choice, but she's mine and I'll defend her with everything in me."

Eloisa threw her hands into the air. "Have all of you gone insane? I realize there are very few choices for you to make, but better an arranged marriage from a good family than scraping the bottom of the barrel. At least Sasha has a proper pedigree. Her lineage is one of great value to the riders. And Mariko has tremendous value. Her ancestors, at least on her father's side, are some of the greatest riders in history. Even Francesca is better than the choices you and your brother are making. I feel as if you're children, deliberately defying your mommy because you don't like her. Just remember, you will be saddled with these women for a lifetime."

"I'm sorry you don't like my choice, Eloisa," Vittorio said. "But she will be my wife and therefore a member of this family. I expect you to treat her with respect. You don't have to love her or even see your grandchildren when we have them, if you don't want to, but when you're around Grace, I want her to feel as if you know she's a member of our family. I also expect that you give her business your full support."

"*Her* business?" Eloisa all but spat the words at him. "I believe it's called KB Events for a reason. Katie Branscomb is the face of the business. Grace is a mere, very replaceable partner, and a not very good one at that, as I've pointed out to Katie on many occasions."

"Actually, Eloisa," Vittorio said, his voice pitched low. Ultra-calm. He knew every single family member could hear the lie in her voice. Eloisa had to know that. "Grace is a full partner for a reason, yes. Katie is the face of the business, talking and hand-holding difficult clientele, while Grace sees to every detail. It's Grace that gives you the perfect event every time. I'm surprised you didn't figure that out. Grace, because of Haydon Phillips, protected everyone by staying in the background, but as you're usually so good at realizing what's really going on, but didn't, I'll have to tell Grace she was particularly clever." It was a compliment and yet not.

Eloisa scowled. "I can barely believe such a thing." Her voice was caustic.

"You know damn well she's a full partner for that reason, Eloisa," Stefano snapped. "You investigate everyone. There's no way you wouldn't know."

"Exactly," Vittorio confirmed.

Unrepentant, but clearly reluctant to go into her reasons for lying, Eloisa shook her head and then turned her attention to her youngest son. "When did you ask Nicoletta Gomez to marry you? She's too young for you."

"She's old enough."

Vittorio noticed Taviano avoided his mother's question and realization dawned. Taviano hadn't asked Nicoletta to marry him. He'd proclaimed they were engaged and his voice had rung with truth only because he intended to marry her, not because they were formally engaged. He intervened before their mother could follow up.

"Stefano, what's happened that we all needed to be here?"

Stefano glanced at his watch. "Giovanni is pulling up now and we'll start as soon as he gets here. There's been a few unsettling developments between the Saldi family and ours."

Vittorio moved closer to his sister. Emmanuelle was seated in one of the larger wide-armed chairs, her legs drawn up tailor-fashion, a look Eloisa detested and often reprimanded her daughter for. Emmanuelle looked young and defenseless. Sad and very vulnerable. His heart went out to her and every protective instinct rose.

At Stefano's revelation, Eloisa immediately looked at her daughter, her face a mask of accusations.

"Don't." Vittorio rarely used absolute authority in Stefano's presence. "I've gone beyond calm to something else. Just don't." It was all the warning she was going to get.

Emilio opened the door to allow Giovanni into the room. He closed it after, no doubt standing in front of it on the other side to ensure they weren't disturbed.

Giovanni greeted them all. "What's up?"

Stefano waved him to a chair. The room had been set up with comfortable furniture in a circle with a table filled with refreshments in the center. Giovanni threw himself into the only chair available.

"As you all know, I gave Giuseppi the names of those suspected of working with their family in our territory. When we went to question those people, they had disappeared. Bruno Vitali was found murdered this morning, his body rolled in a carpet from his apartment and stuffed in a dumpster not far from his home."

A collective gasp went up. Eloisa half rose. "I should go to Theresa. She must be beside herself. Has she been told?"

Stefano nodded. "Yes. Art Maverick and Jason Bradshaw caught the case and they called me, although, of course, I'd already been informed as soon as he was found. They know our family looks after Signora Vitale. Emmanuelle, Sasha and I went with them to tell her. As expected, she went to pieces. Sasha is with her now." He glanced at his brother. "Sasha didn't know until we got there what was going on."

Giovanni nodded. "She told me she was going on an errand with you. I knew she was safe, so I didn't ask anything else."

"I left Tomas and Cosimo with them. I'm not taking any chances with Phillips on the loose."

"Bruno was Theresa's last living relative here," Eloisa said. "She has cousins in Sicily, but no one in the United States. Bruno was so young."

"He agreed to work for the Saldis, Eloisa." Stefano's voice was gentle. "He betrayed our family for money."

"But to kill him when his grandmother has no one else . . ." Eloisa trailed off, looking down at her hands. "No matter what we do, how long we dedicate our lives to fighting murderers and rapists, there's always more."

Vittorio turned his full attention to his mother. She sounded so tired. *Weary* was a better word, as if her exhaustion wasn't just physical, but mental and emotional as well. He understood. They lived in the shadows, giving up their lives to training, killing, and living alone without much hope. They had all the money in the world, and to the world appeared as the spoiled useless playboys Grace and her partner thought them. In reality they led lives of extreme discipline.

Eloisa's life had been harsh. There had been no love in her marriage, no one to care for her and now she wouldn't accept care, not even from her children. If anything, she did everything she could to drive them further away. None of them understood, but the two people most compassionate with her, Emmanuelle and Francesca, were the worst treated. He might feel compassion, but not in the way Grace would. He would never allow Grace to put herself in the position Francesca had, where Eloisa tore her to pieces. He was far too protective already over his woman. He could feel sorry for Eloisa and even understand, but Grace wasn't going near her.

"Do the police have any idea who killed the kid?" Ricco asked.

"No, and neither do we at this point. Uncle Alfeo and Aunt Rachele are investigating Bruno's murder." Alfeo and Rachele Greco were actually their mother's first cousins so therefore their first cousins once removed, but the family never split hairs over how they were related. They referred to the older couple as their aunt and uncle. "We will find out."

"You know the Saldis are behind it, don't you?" Eloisa demanded, glaring at Emmanuelle as if her daughter was somehow responsible.

"No, Eloisa, I don't." It was Stefano who answered. "It looks bad, but until *all* evidence is in and I have a chance to weigh it, I am not taking our family to war, and neither will you."

"Theresa will come to us, and she has every right. Her grandson was under our protection." Eloisa made a choking sound that had all of them sitting up straighter. She coughed to cover up the shocking sound of emotion.

Emmanuelle stirred as if she might get up to go to her mother, but Vittorio put a restraining hand on her shoulder, preventing her from rising.

"He was under our protection, yes," Stefano agreed. "We had multiple talks with him about selling drugs in our territory. We actually, at Theresa's request, handed out a few lessons. He tried to lure Nicoletta into the same business, but that didn't work out in his favor. Bruno, of his own free will, chose to go into business with someone else and he was killed so he wouldn't talk to us, or because he double-crossed them. He was quite capable of something like that. He had few scruples."

"That doesn't mean he wasn't ours," Eloisa insisted.

Stefano nodded. "That's why we're investigating, Eloisa."

"She'll need care. For all his sins, Bruno did see to her care," Emmanuelle said.

"The Laconis own the kitchen shop. Their daughter Angelina is a nurse and I've asked her to oversee Theresa for now. Our family will pay for her private care. I've asked Angelina to find a second nurse willing to help her with round-the-clock care. Also, the Laconis have a son, Pace, in high school. He'll help Anita Laconi keep the Fior A Bizzeffe open for now. Theresa needs the income and the Laconis can use the extra income. We'll see about selling the shop for Theresa and adding whatever amount she needs to her account."

"We'll take turns visiting her," Vittorio said. "Make all the funeral arrangements for him. I can talk to her if you'd like, Stefano."

"I'll do it," Eloisa said. "She's been my friend for more than forty years. She was one of the first people my mother ever took me to visit." Her voice broke and she shook her head.

"Unfortunately, Bruno was not the only victim," Stefano continued, covering up for his mother's unexpected show of emotion. "This was undoubtedly a purge of employees. There is no way it is a coincidence that Bruno and three others disappeared and then their bodies were found a day later."

"Who?" Ricco asked.

Eloisa turned fierce eyes on him. "Where's Mariko? She's a rider and should be here. She may be a woman, but she is every bit as good and deserves her place here. I think she's earned the right to be a Ferraro."

Ricco leaned toward his mother. "I agree one hundred percent, Eloisa. Thank you for acknowledging that my wife is a true member of our family. All of us believe the same way. She's guarding Francesca."

"Of course. In the middle of a war, where is your wife, Stefano? I would think she would be here, instead of lounging at home . . ."

"Enough." Stefano rose to his feet, his face a mask of fury. "She's at home *exactly* where she needs to be, fighting for the life of our child. You will not say one more word, not one, against the woman I love and respect with everything in me. She's made my life worth living. I'm sorry yours wasn't and your children didn't make up for your loneliness, but you let yourself become a bitter, nasty woman striking out at anyone who shows you the least bit of compassion. For once in your life you listen to what I say. If I hear you utter one more word against my wife, I will banish you from this family. You will leave our territory and you won't be spoken of again. If you think I won't do it, you try me."

Emmanuelle went white, shaking her head, eyes over-bright, and again Vittorio had to keep her from jumping to her feet.

The room went completely silent for several seconds. Vittorio kept his eyes on his oldest brother. Stefano had lost more than one child and now, with Francesca struggling to keep the one she carried, he wasn't to be trifled with. The family was one rider down and all of them were exhausted, never a good thing for riders and he knew it. He was sending his brothers and sisters into the shadows to carry out harsh justice when they were already tired. Now they faced a war with a major crime family, one they'd had a truce with, even at times an uneasy alliance. Stefano was responsible for all of them and the pressure on him was tremendous.

"I'm very sorry, Stefano. I had no idea Francesca was pregnant or that she was having trouble carrying. At times my idea of tough love is ludicrous. I can't even call this that. I struck out because I'm so upset on Theresa's behalf, and I don't deal with my emotions well. There will be nothing more said about Francesca."

Vittorio noticed she didn't promise not to speak about any of the other women, but his mother's apology was so shocking he didn't point it out. Again, there was a stunned silence.

Stefano slowly lowered himself into a chair. "I accept your apology, Eloisa, and will pass it on to Francesca. In the meantime, we need to get back to work. There are three more bodies, all discovered around the same time in various locations. Each of them was stuffed in a dumpster behind one of our buildings. Bruno was the first to be found, behind Petrov's Pizzeria. Benito discovered the body and called me as well as alerted the police. Bruno's body was desecrated."

"You mean he'd been tortured," Eloisa clarified.

"That too. They were making a point. That was why he was found a day after he disappeared. They took their time with him." Stefano's voice was grim. "They removed body parts and shoved them in other places. It would have been a horrific sight for Theresa or one of the waitresses at the pizzeria to see."

"Who else?" Ricco asked.

"Timothy Vane. We hired him a few years ago. He was promoted to assistant manager under Martin Shanks. Vane's body was found in a dumpster wrapped in a carpet. He had been tortured and cut to pieces as well. He was the one giving his okay to allow the Saldi enforcers into our club without alerting us. He claimed to any waitress, bartender or security man who asked that we had given our approval. He put something in Martin Shanks's drink to make him sick, so he'd go home that night. It wasn't the first time."

"How long has he worked for the Saldis without our knowledge? Do we have any kind of timeline yet?" Vittorio asked.

"He's still under our investigation. He was a bit careless spending his extra money, so we should have that information fairly quickly. It's ours, not to share with the police. Our official answer is we have no idea what is going on or if, because the three we knew of worked at the club, it might be related to Grace's kidnapping."

"The cops know we had a meeting with the Saldis at the hotel," Taviano pointed out.

Stefano shrugged. "Old friends getting together. Nothing more. The second man working at the club the Saldi family employed was a security guard named Ezra Banks. He's the one who wiped our security cameras. Vittorio's presence scared the hell out of him and lucky for us, he knew nothing about the remote backup."

"Background with us?" Ricco asked.

"He worked for us for three years. Was introduced to us by Vane."

"How long has he worked for the Saldis?" Taviano asked.

"My guess?" Stefano said. "The entire time. Rigina found him from the times the cameras had been sabotaged. She went back two years on his shifts. The cameras were messed with on his shift about six times last year and four more this year. We'll take a leap that each of those times, he allowed someone known from the Saldi family into our club. He was found in the dumpster directly behind Masci's. Fortunately, Pietro found him and called me before calling the police. Ezra had been done the same way, tortured and then cut in pieces, his body parts placed in wrong places."

Emmanuelle made a small sound in her throat and Vittorio moved to the arm of her chair, making it casual, dropping his arm around her shoulders, staring at his mother, daring her to say something derogatory, but she didn't even look up.

"The carpet, by the way, was taken from Luciu, Lola and Merci's interior design store, Puglia's House of Design. Their store was broken in to and four carpets were stolen. Bruno's carpet was from his apartment. Vane and Banks each accounted for one of the carpets from Puglia's."

"Was the third body they found someone from the club?" Vittorio asked.

Stefano sighed. "Vittorio, you were the one who said at least three employees had to be involved for them to pull it off and it appears that you were correct. Vane, Banks and, unfortunately, Clay Pierson. I don't know why that one feels like such a betrayal."

"Because it was," Vittorio supplied. He pitched his voice low and kept it soothing.

Stefano shrugged. "He was offered a lot of money. According to Rigina, each time Banks sabotaged the footage, Vane and Pierson were both working. The investigation is still ongoing, and they're scrutinizing every employee now, but they've uncovered evidence that each of them at one time met with Harold Jenson, Miceli's *consigliere*. When questioned, Jenson claimed it was no more than a casual meeting, but nothing Jenson does is casual."

"Where was Pierson found?" Giovanni asked.

"Berardo found him in the dumpster behind Giordano's butcher shop. I was grateful he went to the garbage first thing and not Claretta. These bodies were in very bad shape."

"But they took a fourth carpet," Vittorio said. "Another employee we don't know of, or a warning to us?"

"I think the dead bodies put in dumpsters behind the buildings we own might be a warning," Taviano said. "I'm so fucking glad I sent Lucia, Amo and Nicoletta to Italy. Did you have the dumpster behind Lucia's Treasures searched?"

"Lucia and Amo are in Italy?" There was obvious relief in Eloisa's voice.

Emmanuelle put her mouth close to Vittorio's ear. "Sometimes I think she cares more for the people in our territory than her own children."

Vittorio kissed the top of her head, aching for her. Her heart had to be completely broken. Somewhere deep inside, she had to be holding out hope that the Saldis were not preparing for an all-out war with the Ferraros. "Sometimes it does feel that way, honey. Always know, you're very loved."

"I do know," Emmanuelle said.

"We're still searching other dumpsters as well as for any missing employees in any of our establishments or the shops in our territory," Stefano continued.

"Would they have two dealers in that small of an area?" Vittorio asked. "One in the club for sure, and then Bruno already."

"What other purpose then?" Ricco asked.

"Not gun running," Giovanni said. "If they were selling guns, who would they be selling to other than our family?"

"They went after Grace," Eloisa said. "Human trafficking? Right under our noses? Would they dare?"

Vittorio thought it over in the ensuing silence. "They were using the club for their dirty work and that had to be deliberate. Maybe trafficking."

"Have any of our girls or boys disappeared?" Eloisa asked. "If so, who is looking into it?"

"I was," Emmanuelle said. "Two of the girls from the local high school. They were friends with Nicoletta and hung out at the flower shop with her."

Vittorio happened to be looking at Taviano. His features

hardened perceptibly. He went from looking young to appearing a dangerous, lethal and very pissed-off man.

"Two friends of Nicoletta's have gone missing and you didn't tell me?" Taviano snapped. "What the fuck, Emme?"

"Sisters. Twins. Eva and Marta Giboli," Emmanuelle conceded. "Their mother, Rita, asked me to look quietly into their disappearance. She thought they'd run away from home. Their father lives in Tuscany and they've never met him but whenever she insisted they do chores around the house, they threatened to go live with him. She was afraid they might have."

"And you didn't think it was worth telling me?" Taviano repeated, glaring at her. "Nicoletta is a hellion. If her friends were running away, wasn't it possible she might have been considering following their example?"

Emmanuelle sighed. "Seriously, Taviano, I just got the call from her yesterday and started the investigation. I couldn't talk to Nicoletta because she's in Italy. Rita didn't see fit to call me until *yesterday* evening. She feared her friends would think she was a bad mother if they knew the girls had run away to be with their father."

"Oh, for heaven's sake," Eloisa snapped. "I've always wanted to slap that woman. She doesn't have a brain in her head. How long have the girls been gone?"

"Almost two weeks."

"Did she talk to their father?"

Emmanuelle shook her head. "She refuses to talk to him, but she's certain the girls are with him. She wants me to get in touch with him. I tried, but no one answered his phone."

Stefano scowled darkly. "That's insane. She waits almost two weeks before she contacts anyone and won't ask her ex-husband if the girls are with him? What the hell is wrong with her?"

"I have no idea," Emmanuelle said.

"Put the Grecos on it immediately. I want an answer in the next hour. If they aren't with their father, and they've been taken, the odds of getting them back are slim to none after two weeks."

Ricco swore under his breath. "Maybe she needs parenting classes, or better yet, if the girls are safe with their father, just leave them there."

"I think we're all in agreement there," Eloisa said.

Vittorio didn't point out how ironic it was that Eloisa was furious with Rita, although he had to admit, his mother might not have been nurturing, but she saw to their training and would have gone looking in a heartbeat had they disappeared.

"I've texted the Grecos with all the information," Giovanni said. "They're on it."

Vittorio settled back in his own chair, ignoring the way Eloisa rolled her eyes. His mother thought they all spoiled Emmanuelle. He didn't think Emmanuelle had ever been spoiled in her life, although the brothers loved her and tried to protect her when they could. Certainly, she would need help avoiding Val Saldi. He hadn't given the impression he was going to give up.

"We need to either find another body wrapped up in the missing carpet or figure out who they plan to hit next."

"They could just be fucking with us, stealing another carpet," Taviano pointed out.

"Or they were going to use it for Bruno's body, but it was more convenient to take the carpet out of his apartment," Emmanuelle said.

Stefano looked around the room. "Did Merry set up the coffeepot?"

"Behind you," Vittorio said, indicating the coffee station.

"I'll get it," Emmanuelle offered and jumped up.

"Thanks, honey," Stefano said. "I've got every dumpster in our territory being searched. Any suspects for another Saldi contact in our territory?" He swiveled around to regard his sister. "You have the most contact with everyone, Emmanuelle."

"Francesca had taken over the visiting as well as sitting

on all the committees to represent our families. Have you asked her?" Emmanuelle placed a cup of coffee in front of Stefano and then her mother before going back to the station for more.

"Not yet. She's been down the last few weeks, and I know you and Sasha have been visiting so Sasha could take over those duties for Francesca."

"Honestly"—Emmanuelle put the mugs in front of Ricco and Giovanni—"I was so busy trying to remember every detail of every family for Sasha that I wasn't paying as close attention as I should have been."

Eloisa heaved an over-exaggerated and very loud sigh.

Emmanuelle clenched her teeth as she handed Vittorio his coffee and set another cup in front of Taviano. Vittorio winked at her. She managed a faint grin as she turned away to get her own coffee.

"I'll ask Francesca," Stefano said. "But you take some time to think back to each visit. More than likely, because you know them so well, you'll notice a detail that will nag at you about someone. I don't care how ridiculous it sounds, you tell me."

"I will," she said immediately.

"We're going to have to consider that Miceli Saldi is staging a takeover from his brother. Giuseppi has been very wrapped up with his wife's illness these last few months and has left himself open for a takeover."

"Or it's possible it's his own son and he's throwing the blame on Miceli," Eloisa pointed out with a glare at Emmanuelle. "That's the problem with having power and responsibility and falling in love. It's selfish."

"There is always that possibility as well," Vittorio said before Stefano could reprimand Eloisa. "We have to consider any possibility, no matter how remote."

"I agree," Stefano said. "Or a third party may be setting up both brothers." Stefano turned his attention to Vittorio. "Where are you in your relationship with Grace? Where is she on her recovery?"

"She's doing physical therapy on her shoulder and arm. The doc says she's coming along faster than he'd hoped, so physically, she's much better."

"And your relationship?"

Vittorio knew Stefano wanted to know if there was a danger of Grace rejecting him. "The reference Eloisa inadvertently made in front of her to all of us needing women meeting a certain criterion set me back a bit. She asked questions I couldn't answer immediately." He made certain to keep his features expressionless when he wanted to smirk. Eloisa made mistakes and she would detest that, in her need to slam Grace, she'd been careless with her choice of barbs.

Stefano turned cool eyes on his mother. "You actually made a reference to someone outside our family that could endanger us?"

Eloisa nodded. "Yes. I apologize to all of you for such a slip."

Stefano drummed his fingers on the table. "Have you been to the doctor since Phillip died?"

Eloisa sent him her blackest scowl. "I don't believe that is any of your business, nor is it the business of anyone sitting at this table other than me."

Stefano leaned toward her, his eyes boring into her. "This is a business matter and when you start making mistakes, when *any* of us starts making mistakes that could jeopardize all shadow riders, that has to be addressed and you know it. You'd be the first one to demand it, Eloisa. You suffered a trauma. We all did. There are going to be repercussions to us. We train physically and mentally, but there is no way to factor in emotions. See a doctor. And I want a report. That's essential. If you need counseling, get it. We have a rider here who is a counselor. She set up shop a few months back, as you well know."

Eloisa held his gaze defiantly for several seconds. Vittorio felt sorry for her. Having one's son dictate after years of being the top rider in the family was most likely humiliating. Still, Eloisa knew he was right and she nodded.

"Continue, Vittorio."

"I haven't talked to her about what we do, but I will as soon as I think she can handle it."

"It has to be soon," Stefano warned. "You've spent so much time together, it might already be too late."

At Eloisa's swift intake of breath, Vittorio looked at her face. For the first time, she looked older. Eloisa was a beautiful woman and appeared far younger than her years. He knew it was already too late. He'd seen the way their shadows tangled together.

"One last thing," Stefano continued. "The victim at the hotel, Mrs. Lanie Kandar, was traveling alone. She has no children. Her husband was killed in a hunting accident about ten years ago and she never remarried. No other children. She lives and travels on the insurance money left to her as a result of her husband's death. She had no known enemies."

Vittorio had been certain nothing would be found in the woman's past that might explain why she was shot, but he was surprised about the boy. "If the boy wasn't hers, who did he belong to?"

"That's a good question. The investigation showed the bullet that killed Mrs. Kandar was not fired by any of the policemen present. None of us fired the shot. The Saldis were inside the room, at least we thought they all were. If they had any others secreted around the hotel, they weren't spotted by the security cameras."

Vittorio drummed his fingers on the arm of the chair.

"Stop," Eloisa hissed between clenched teeth. "That's a terrible habit picked up from your brother. It gets on my nerves and I can't think."

Vittorio immediately ceased but shot his brother a worried glance. Eloisa had always been edgy, but it seemed as if she was getting more so in the last months.

"Did the police question the kid? He was closer to the shooter than anyone else, he might have seen something we didn't." When Stefano shook his head, Vittorio knew immediately what the answer was. "The police never found the kid, did they?"

Stefano shook his head. "What are you thinking?"

"He was small, but up close he looked older. Haydon Phillips assumes different personas. It could have been him."

"Working for the Saldi family? No way," Eloisa said. "He tortured their enforcers. They'd kill him on sight."

"Working for himself," Stefano said. "He couldn't have known about the Saldi meeting with us. No one knew about it."

"Unless he had them bugged. I'm beginning to think he's capable of anything," Vittorio said. "On the other hand, it's worrisome that he was on his way to the second floor rather than hovering outside the door of the conference room or trying to get close enough to one of us to kill us. What was he doing there? Especially if he didn't know about the meeting between our two families."

Stefano handed his phone to Giovanni. "I'm headed home now. Vittorio, do your best to wrap this up with Grace. Get her on board."

Vittorio tried not to laugh. That was so like Stefano.

Emmanuelle rolled her eyes. "She isn't a boardroom, Stefano. She's a person."

"Exactly. A woman. He has a certain reputation."

"Which is working against me at the moment."

"I have faith in you. I'm heading home. Ricco, put in a call to security at the hotel. I want a complete overhaul. I want floor by floor inspections. Let's find out what Haydon was up to."

"We don't know if it was him," Eloisa pointed out. "We don't want him to get us off our game and make mistakes."

"We have to go on the premise that it was Haydon," Taviano said. "He's a cunning little bastard, and he wants one of us so he can prove to Grace that he can get to her and anyone she cares about. He's been terrorizing her since she was a kid, keeping her under his thumb. No way is he going to let her go."

"It's all a game to him," Giovanni said. "He thinks he's the smartest man in the room."

"Maybe he is," Vittorio said. "But that doesn't mean he can win against all of us."

CHAPTER FIFTEEN

Grace laid her head back and stared up at the explosion of stars. They were spread across the clear night sky, looking like glittering diamonds. Around her, small puffs of steam rose from the hot tub to drift lazily around her. Her shoulder ached from the laps in the pool she'd done in order to strengthen it, but there was satisfaction in knowing she was finally able to actively work on repairing the damage.

Vittorio picked up her foot, put it in his lap and began massaging the sole and toes, relaxing her further. He had a way of touching her that relaxed her body immediately. He'd made love to her dozens of times. The moment he could, he had his staff leave, and he loved to strip her naked, or have her dress in very beautiful, elegant, but transparent lingerie. She learned very quickly he liked looking at her body.

"You do know, if I were to get pregnant, I'm not going to look the same." It came out before she could censor.

His long fingers continued the massage, and silence ensued. She looked up cautiously and met his eyes. There was always that moment when she first made eye contact where she had the sensation of being held captive. She knew, no matter how long they were together, how many years passed, every time she looked at him, she would feel that same thrill, have that same sensation of a slow somersault in her stomach.

"Where did that come from?"

His tone was strictly neutral. She was coming to understand, Vittorio never got ruffled. He was always calm. Always centered. He spoke in that soft, low tone that carried absolute command, but he didn't raise his voice.

She gave what she hoped was a casual shrug. "I was just thinking about how much you like to look at my body. After Merry leaves, the first thing you like is for me to strip, or to put on a see-through but gorgeous outfit."

"Does that bother you?"

Vittorio tipped his head to one side and his hair fell across his forehead. Whenever he did that, she always had the urge to push the wayward strands back. She indulged herself. He touched her often and in intimate places. When they walked, he always had his hand on her hip or the small of her back, sometimes on the cheeks of her butt. She hadn't yet been brave enough to claim him by voluntarily touching him unless they were having sex. Then she indulged her needs. Right now, she felt very brave reaching out and brushing at his hair with her fingertips.

He lifted his head and caught her finger in his mouth, drawing it in to suck on it. Her stomach plunged. Rolled. Heat exploded deep. Her sex clenched. She would never get enough of him. *Never.* He was the most sensual, gorgeous man in the world and she still couldn't believe he was hers. She kept waiting for the proverbial shoe to drop.

His tongue curled around her finger as he drew it out of his mouth. "The question requires an answer, *gattina.*"

She had to wrack her brain to remember the question, that was how easily he could make everything go out of her head. "I like that you want to look at me," she admitted. She did, but it took getting used to. "I never thought of myself as beautiful. I think, like most women, I see every flaw I have, so at first, I was a little uncomfortable." She still was uncomfortable, especially if he laid something out—like tonight—that was something she considered risqué. Still, it didn't matter. If he wanted her to wear it, she would, because she loved to see the look on his face when she complied with his wishes. Pride. Approval. Pleasure. Possessiveness. He looked at her as if she was the most beautiful woman in the world.

"You have flaws?"

She laughed. "I'm not pointing them out to you if you're blind to them." She couldn't imagine that, since he saw every little detail.

"I like when you wear what I've bought for you. It especially meant something to me tonight. I know you were a little reluctant when you first put it on, but you looked so sexy, you took my breath away. Thank you for at least trying it."

Hearing the ring of sincerity, she hugged his compliment to her. She felt she didn't give nearly enough in their relationship. He was always giving to her. He had smiled a lot less after the meeting with his family days earlier and she'd done her best, without knowing what was causing him undue strain, but so far, she didn't feel as if she had succeeded in lightening his mood. Wearing lingerie seemed a small thing to give back if it pleased him.

She looked at the small table where the leather outfit was folded neatly and waiting for her to reclaim it after she got out of the tub. She'd done her laps naked and was still without clothes in the hot tub. She was fairly certain Vittorio would have been comfortable in a nudist colony, and he was slowly getting her to be the same way.

"I like giving you the things you ask for," Grace admitted. "Although you don't ask me for much."

"As for you getting pregnant, Grace, you know I want children. Having a family of my own is important to me. Having said that, if, like Francesca, you have problems, or you can't have children, I would much rather go through my life with you and no children than alone or with someone I didn't feel this way about. Have no worries. I will love your pregnant body as well as any changes that come after."

"And if I gain a ton of weight?"

He shrugged. "I guess we'll both be doing a lot of swimming if it bothers you. Whatever it takes to make you happy. You want to lose it, I'll instruct Merry to make meals that will help and I'll exercise with you."

She believed him. "I think you're so perfect, Vittorio, that I can't believe you're real."

"No one is perfect, Grace, least of all me. I'm a Ferraro, remember? Our lives aren't anything like people believe them to be." His voice was pitched low. Compelling. Almost sad.

Grace knew that was the truth. Vittorio was completely attentive to her. Totally focused on her. She would never have believed him capable of only being with one woman, not when he had the worst reputation ever. She had read so many tabloid stories on him it was ridiculous, and he wasn't anything at all like the stories she'd read about him. He wasn't wild, nor was he a partier. He seemed serious most of the time and he was completely devoted to her.

"Something is wrong, Vittorio. Why don't you just tell me?" she invited, hoping he would tell her whatever had happened at the family meeting that had gotten him so far down.

"Not in here. Let's dry off and go inside. I could use a drink."

That shocked her. Alarmed her. Vittorio drank the occasional Scotch, but it was rare. He had a glass of wine with dinner, but no more. If anything, he avoided alcohol.

She stood up the moment he let go of her foot. Whatever was wrong, she was determined to help him. Water poured off her body, ran down her skin in little rivulets. Drops caught on the tips of her breasts and held there for a moment, catching Vittorio's eye. He leaned down and licked at her nipple, sending a shock of electricity running from her nipple straight to her clit. He got out of the hot tub first and then put both hands on her waist and lifted her out. When he lowered her to set her on her feet, he licked over her left breast and then suckled for a moment, his teeth and tongue wreaking havoc and leaving marks on her fair skin.

Grace stood while he dried off her body. He always dried her off after a shower or bath, his hands gentle but arousing, the towel sliding over her curves and inflaming every cell and nerve ending in her body until she felt like she might die if she didn't have him.

He handed her the small triangle that was nothing but leather laced together. The thong disappeared between her buttocks and the tiny triangle was partially open where it laced together, showcasing her fiery curls rather than hiding them. The black leather corset was cupless, just cord lacing up the front with straps and buckles up the back and a buckle that went around her neck.

Vittorio buckled the corset in place and then reached around her to cup her breasts as they thrust out of the two holes. He tugged and rolled her nipples until they were standing up for him. She felt boneless and wanton, her body needy for his. She was instantly slick. Blood pounded through her clit and pooled low. Her skin was flushed and her breathing ragged.

Vittorio was always sensual, and he made her feel sensual. The way he looked at her made her feel beautiful. It was an unfamiliar feeling to her, but one she wanted to keep. He made her aware of her body at all times, that he was masculine, and she was feminine.

They walked inside and then down the wide hall to the first sitting room. The views of the lake were beautiful. There were glass sliding walls on three sides of the round turret, and she could look out in any direction and see a wide expanse of water.

Vittorio used the remote to start the fireplace and indicated one of the deep, very comfortable-looking chairs. She sank into the seat and all but sighed. She had the feeling that she could live there for months without knowing what each individual piece of furniture was like or what each room was used for. She was always discovering new things, almost as if she was on a great adventure.

"This house is so incredible, but it's really what you've done with it that makes it so special." The house was intricate and complex with the sprawling mix of styles, the turret and patio beneath it the center, and the arms going out in either direction. Inside, Vittorio preferred simplistic designs, sometimes almost stark, but his décor worked and was always the most comfortable, with chairs she wanted to sink into and just stay in.

"I'm glad you like it. I was hoping you would."

"How could I not?" She brushed back the tendrils of red hair spilling around her face. She'd put it up in a topknot, the way she did whenever she was going to take a bath or sit in a hot tub, but it was already trying to slip loose.

The moment she lifted her hand to her hair, her breasts rose and fell, drawing his immediate attention. Grace held her breath, watching his eyes, watching the way the firelight caressed his face. He looked haunted. She leaned toward him, uncaring that her breasts spilled forward, swaying with her every movement.

"Vittorio, I can tell something is wrong. Just please tell me. If you've changed your mind, I won't lie, it will break my heart, but saying it straight out is far better than me having to guess."

Vittorio sat back in his chair and steepled his fingers. "Why would you think that, Grace? Even for a minute? You should have every confidence in yourself. Surely I've managed to convey how much you matter to me."

The disappointment in his voice and on his face brought the unexpected burn of tears. His response wasn't exactly a reprimand, but he was right, and she felt the sting like a lash. Of course he'd be disappointed when he'd done nothing but show her that she meant the world to him. There wasn't a moment that they were together that he wasn't touching her, kissing her or telling her she was incredible.

He made it very clear he respected her job. He was unfailingly kind to Katie and always left them to their work after making certain they had refreshments. As the Midnight Madness charity event was coming up very fast, things were getting intense. Grace had to see to a multitude of details, as she always did before any event, large or small. Vittorio, no matter how busy, and he had an office he worked out of—although she didn't know what he did—always saw to her comfort as well as that of her guest.

"Grace?" Vittorio prompted. "Tell me where this insecurity is coming from."

He deserved an answer, she just wasn't certain she had a clear one for him. "I'm sorry, Vittorio. You certainly aren't the cause of my insecurities. I was just thinking, as we came here from the hot tub, that you make me feel so feminine and sexy."

"You *are* feminine and sexy." His voice was dark with lust. "You're also clever and smart. You're strong. You're the epitome of a woman, and I know I'm extremely lucky to have you. I want you to get to a place where you know that, too."

She nodded, knowing he wouldn't like that she didn't give him a verbal answer. Vittorio required a spoken answer so there was no miscommunication. He didn't ask many things of her and answering shouldn't be that difficult—but she didn't always know why she withdrew and curled into herself.

"Grace."

One word. Her name. He could say a multitude of things just by his inflection alone. Always soft. Always low, but so much meaning. This was a clear warning.

"I feel strong and worthy of you most of the time. I do. You give me confidence all the time and you do show me that I'm important to you."

"I show you that you're the center of my world, Grace, because that's exactly what you are. I don't like you to question that because it means I'm failing you in some way."

Horrified, Grace shook her head. "Vittorio, no. It isn't you. You're amazing, truly wonderful. Every single day I wake up I'm astonished that I could actually fall asleep. You gave me that ability. I can't remember a time when I felt safe, and you've given that to me as well. I lived my life in total terror, now it's a form of paradise. Believe me, I'll never take you or how we live here for granted."

She ducked her head for a moment, afraid how he would take the rest of what she had to say. "There's always going to be a part of me that is that little girl no one wanted. Not my parents, not grandparents, not a foster family. No one came forward to adopt me after the first family when there was an accident that killed the father and the mother turned to drinking." She'd been young, but she remembered the pain of being taken away and put in another home. It had been wrenching and frightening and she'd felt as if something was wrong with her that no one wanted her.

He moved then, kneeling between her legs on the thick woolen rug. His fingers curled around the nape of her neck and he kissed her so gently there were tears in her eyes when he lifted his head.

She loved him. Beyond anything, she loved him. She didn't know when it had happened, but she knew how. He was so good to her, it was impossible not to love him. When he touched her as he was doing, his hands on her body, fingers caressing her skin, giving her comfort and yet letting her know she was not only loved, but desired as well, she couldn't help but fall hard for him.

His arms slid around her waist and he laid his head in her lap, as if he was the one who needed solace, and she was coming to think he did. Her heart melted, and her fingers tangled in his hair. He was scaring her just a little bit. What could be so bad that he was reluctant to tell her? She stroked caresses through his hair and over his temple, waiting. She knew he would tell her eventually, so she stayed quiet, reveling in her ability to just touch him the way she was doing.

It took a few minutes and then he sat back and looked up at her. "I want you to remember that I love you. I not only love you, Grace, but I need you in my life. I know you don't yet realize how much, or even comprehend it's the truth, but I can assure you, I need you far more than you'll ever need or want me. I want you to keep that in mind."

She took a deep breath and let it out, suddenly worried. He was serious. He stood and went across the room, his body totally fit. Totally naked. He was confident in his body and had every reason to be. She could tell he'd all but forgotten he wasn't wearing clothes. He didn't need them—like she did—for armor.

Vittorio crossed to the small bar on the opposite side of the room from the fireplace. "Do you want a drink?"

He poured straight Scotch into a crystal glass. She noted he didn't use ice. The amber liquid swirled in the glass when he put it to his lips. He shocked her a little when he drank the contents.

"Water would be good." She didn't think it would be a good idea for both of them to be drinking, at least not if Vittorio kept it up. Inside, she began to coil tighter and tighter, the tension making her wish she was wearing something other than her sex kitten lingerie.

He handed her a glass and went back to the bar. "What have you heard about my family?"

That was getting into very dangerous territory. Everyone knew of the Ferraro family. They seemed to live their lives out in the tabloids. Their exploits were legendary. Her tongue touched her upper lip and she rubbed her palms over her thighs. "There are rumors," she conceded. "But your family is famous, Vittorio, and shrouded in mystery. People make up things because they either want to tear you down or live through you vicariously."

"You've been around my family a few times."

It was the first time she'd heard a hint of bitterness in his voice. He finished off the Scotch in the glass and poured himself more.

"You must have formed opinions regarding the rumors."

"You'll have to be more specific. Which of the ten thousand rumors are you referring to?" She didn't want to have this conversation. Her heart already was accelerating. She wished she hadn't agreed to come inside. There had been a cool breeze coming off the lake. She moistened her lips again. "Can you open the door?"

He sent her one all-encompassing look, his gaze dwelling on her bare breasts. "I don't want you to get cold, Grace. It won't do your shoulder any good."

"I'll keep that side to the fireplace," she promised. "I like the breeze on my body."

"I like it on your body, too." He stepped around her chair to go to the glass wall. As he did, he reached out and stroked her left breast, fingers tugging her nipple as he slipped past her.

Grace felt the jolt of lightning all the way to her toes. A single touch from him was all it took, his fingers flicking her nipple. His eyes dropping below her waist to dwell on the tiny triangle of leather, split by the lacing so her fiery curls could be seen. Instantly, she went damp and needy.

He folded the thick glass of the pocket door back to allow the night into the room. She inhaled deeply, drawing the night into her lungs, hoping the air would clear her head enough to let her listen with an open mind to whatever he had to say.

"Let's not do this dance, *bella*. Everyone knows the Saldi family is a family of criminals. They pass that legacy from father to son."

She watched as he paced restlessly across the room and then went back to the bar to pour himself another drink. She opened her mouth to protest, thought better of it, and remained silent.

Vittorio pressed the glass to his forehead. "Our family contends with those same rumors. In fact, we're investigated on a regular basis. Because of the incident at the hotel, we will most likely come under scrutiny again."

She would hardly call what had happened—a woman being shot to death—an incident. That seemed a little disrespectful, although she didn't know how she would refer to the death. Again, she remained silent, just watching him. He was mesmerizing as he paced back and forth, the crystal glass pressed to his forehead, his body fluid, prowling across the floor like a feral tiger, caged and restless.

"People come to us, to my family. They have for hundreds of years, to fight against families like the Saldis. When they can't get justice, or they're threatened, they seek an audience with those we refer to as greeters."

She frowned. That wasn't what she'd been expecting. "Greeters?" She echoed the term, knowing it was important.

"The things I'm telling you, Grace, can't go out of the family. We're tied together. You're one of us now and you need to know, but no one else can know, not your closest friend, not your business partner. No one. The things I tell you can't go beyond this room. When I say it's life or death to keep our family legacy secret, I'm not being dramatic."

Katie was the only friend she had, and they weren't yet that close. Grace didn't dare, even now, show her a close friendship, although Vittorio had her guarded and the family had put her up in the Ferraro Hotel, so Haydon couldn't get to her. She knew better. Haydon was patient and eventually his potential victims dropped their guard, then it was only a matter of time.

Grace nodded her head to show Vittorio she was listening. She narrowed her eyes when he took a small drink of the Scotch. She didn't know enough about alcohol to know if that was a lot he drank, or a small amount, but either way, it was more than she'd ever seen him drink.

"Remember the 'criteria' my mother went on about that got you so upset?"

"Of course." She still was a little upset about it. A woman didn't want to think a man wouldn't even look at her unless she met some standard the family had set.

"Have you ever noticed your shadow?"

She sat up very straight. Of course she'd noticed her shadow. It was strange. It had always been strange, and as she'd grown, she'd come to terms with it. Unlike others, her shadow had strange arm-like appendages shooting off of it everywhere. Like tentacles. An octopus. Those feelers would reach toward other shadows to connect them. Sometimes, when that happened, she could almost feel what another person was feeling. Most of the time it was nothing. Sometimes she could hear lies. With Vittorio, every single time it happened, she would get a very physical reaction. A *huge* physical reaction, a surge of greedy need so strong it could shake her.

"Yes." She answered in a whisper, because he clearly expected a verbal answer and her voice wouldn't climb above that low, husky sound.

"Have you noticed my shadow is the same as yours? As is Stefano's and all of my brothers' as well as Emmanuelle's?"

She had only noticed Vittorio's shadow. She hadn't been paying attention to his brothers'. She was glad she wasn't the only one with a peculiar shadow, but she hadn't thought that much about it. She glanced at it now, thrown from the light from the flames dancing in the fireplace. Her shadow and Vittorio's were connected. More than connected. The tubes had intertwined to the point that it appeared to be one shadow, not two.

"Yes." She wished he'd just say whatever it was he needed to say, but she couldn't help staring at their shadows, thrown on the wall across from her.

"If I tell you a lie, or someone else does, can you hear that lie?"

Grace frowned and rubbed the bridge of her nose. "Most of the time. I don't rely on it, but a red flag goes up if I think I hear a lie."

"I can hear lies. My family members can. Greeters are usually older family members who can hear lies. By the time they become a greeter, they are adept at telling the difference between a lie and the truth."

"I don't understand." She frowned, trying to figure out where he was going with his revelation. She half expected he would tell her the Ferraro family was as immersed in crime as the Saldi family. Or that he traveled the world on family business, sitting on boards for banks or hotels, and she would have to stay in their home alone. She was prepared for almost anything but the direction he went.

"If you came to us and petitioned for a meeting for help, you would first see two greeters. They would serve you tea or coffee, whatever your preference, and they would make small talk with you. Just have a light conversation."

She knew immediately why. By conversing about the weather, a job, just everyday things, whoever was listening would be able to ascertain a rhythm to a voice. The way a person breathed. Their heartbeat. That would help indicate if they suddenly told a lie.

"When they were ready, the greeter would ask you why you have come to see them. At that point whoever has petitioned for help would lay out their problem. It can be anything from as trivial as a lost purse to what you are dealing with. If you were the petitioner, you would tell them about your first meeting with Haydon Phillips and everything that happened after that. You would tell them about your suspicions—that he is a serial killer, but you have no real proof. You would supply whatever you do have—names, dates, cities. And then you would tell them about how he terrorizes you and how he lives in other people's attics and spies on innocent families."

Her breath caught in her throat. Where was he going with this? She found herself very tense and couldn't quite relax no matter how much she told herself to. Maybe it was because for the first time in her relationship with him, she knew he was tense. He didn't take his eyes off her as he talked, but every now and then he sipped at the Scotch.

She had been around Little Italy for a while, and even at times had entered the Ferraro territory, but the only thing she'd heard was that there was little crime there and it was dangerous to cross a Ferraro. Everything else she'd heard on the news or read in tabloids or magazines.

"At the end of the interview, without telling you whether or not they will accept the job, the greeters rise, indicating the meeting is over and they will contact you. Little is said because there is always danger of someone attempting to record the interview, or perhaps an undercover cop will try to slip through. We're very careful. Cell phones aren't allowed in the interview room, although the room looks like a very cozy sitting room."

She was intrigued in spite of everything. "What happens next?"

"If the greeters determine that the petitioner is telling the truth as he or she knows it, and they believe there is a valid case, the petition with all details is turned over to two teams of investigators. One will investigate the actual crime or crimes. When necessary they call on another team that can handle anything on the Internet. The second team of investigators does a complete workup on the petitioner. Until both teams and the greeters are satisfied, no one touches the case."

Private investigators? They supplemented the police detectives? She couldn't imagine the sophisticated Ferraro family getting down and dirty in the trenches. She frowned, trying not to jump ahead with her imagination.

"Investigators are also members of our family. They can hear lies as well. That is a requirement in our family if you want to be a greeter or investigator, but they can also persuade people to talk to them with their voices. Those they speak to about any crime find they want to tell the investigators as much as possible. Both teams take their time and investigate thoroughly. No one wants to make a mistake. Sometimes, things are let go because one person isn't absolutely certain and all parties, both teams and the greeters, have to agree the crime or crimes were committed and someone has been wronged."

"You have the ability to persuade others to do what you want, don't you?" His voice. That beautiful, compelling voice. Black velvet. Magical. He soothed an entire room. He could calm anyone down.

"I have an ability. It's a little different than the investigators', but yes, if you want to call it persuasion, I guess you could use that description. I think of it as energy and I keep mine low and hopefully soothing in a bad situation, one that is escalating. I want to defuse it."

Grace stood up and wandered over to the open doorway to stand in the midst of the breeze so that it cooled her suddenly heated skin. He had persuaded her to wear the leather corset. To marry him. To give herself into his keeping. She had wanted to wear the daring lingerie for him, something she never would have considered on her own.

Vittorio came up behind her, his body tight against her back, his arms coming around her. She reached up and took the nearly empty glass of Scotch out of his hand and drained the contents, nearly choking when the burn slid smoothly down her throat to settle in her belly. He buried his face against her neck, his teeth scraping gently, his lips sliding over the pulse there while his hands cupped the soft weight of her breasts.

"What are you thinking?"

"That you're very good at persuading me with that voice of yours. You speak to me and I would do almost anything to please you."

"Is that my voice, or because of the way you feel about me?"

Was there disappointment in his tone? Hurt? Her stomach knotted in protest. She leaned her head back against his chest, letting him lift her breasts, the pads of his thumbs brushing caresses over her nipples. There seemed to be a direct line from her nipples to her sex, because every stroke sent darts of fire streaking through her body, sizzling through her veins so that the blood pooled hotly. He could do that so easily.

"I believe it is because of the way I feel about you. I like making you happy. You always manage to make me happy and I like to give that back to you." It was more than that. She loved giving back to him. She knew she was a pleaser. It was in her to give and she was perfectly fine with who she was. That trait made her very, very good at her job. She hoped it would make her an excellent partner as well. "But, I am susceptible to your voice."

She turned in his arms to look up at him. "Tell me the rest. It's very intriguing." She had no idea where he was going with it. She still didn't believe, not for one moment, that his family helped the police in their investigations. She had seen interactions between the Ferraros and the detectives. It was a very uneasy alliance.

He hesitated and then pressed his forehead to hers, looking into her eyes. "Once you know this information, you have committed fully to me. We don't divorce. Not ever. It isn't done, not without severe repercussions to both of us. Understand that, Grace."

She couldn't see how she could understand unless he told her, but she didn't have plans of running away from him, so she nodded. Vittorio dropped his arms and straightened abruptly. He stepped outside onto the patio and looked up at the stars as if he could find an answer to whether or not he wanted to trust her further. Abruptly, he spun around and stalked her when she backed away from him. He looked like a tiger about to pounce on his prey.

Vittorio caught her hand and drew her back to the chair. She sat down at his silent command and looked up at him expectantly.

"When everyone has absolutely agreed and there is no possible margin of error, the reports are turned over to what is known in our family as a rider. A shadow rider."

Just the way he said it, or maybe it was the title itself that made her heart plunge, but whatever it was, she was suddenly afraid.

"There are portals in the shadows. Have you ever slipped into a shadow and realized no one noticed you there? Has that ever happened to you?"

It had. Multiple times. There had been a strange sensation, one she didn't care for, as if her body had been wrenched apart, her chest flying away from her and her body scattered in molecules throughout the shadows. It was just a weird sensation she couldn't account for, but every time it happened, others would walk right by her and not realize she was standing there. Once, Haydon had almost walked into her.

She moistened her lips and nodded slowly because he was waiting for an answer. She always answered him truthfully. That was their agreement. There would be honesty between them, even if it was difficult. "It's happened. But I don't know what you mean by a portal."

"We refer to the tubes as portals because the shadow itself can transfer us from one place to another."

Automatically, Grace shook her head. "That's not scientifically possible."

"Nevertheless, we've done it. I can step into a shadow and be gone from one end of the house to the other. My brother Giovanni was shot and had to have hardware, pins and bolts, just like you have in your shoulder. Because of the hardware, he can't ride the shadows, so he drives a car here when he comes. The others don't want anyone, especially Haydon, to know they've left their homes, so they use the shadows. It's necessary to make him think, if he's watching, that we're all going about our regular business."

She stared up at him, trying to change what he said, or change her comprehension. She just wasn't hearing him correctly. "You are telling me that you and your family are capable of moving in this house, from one end to the other, using a shadow? Not walking in that shadow, but you step in, can't be seen, and you come out in another room."

"That is correct. We were trained from the time we were two years old. It isn't easy. The energy force feels like a strong magnet pulling the body apart. You actually feel as if you're flying apart. Skin, bones, blood, your very cells. It isn't a pleasant sensation."

She'd felt that exact sensation. "You can really do that?"

He nodded slowly. "I know it sounds insane, but I do it all the time. I can step into that shadow cast by the fireplace." He indicated one that danced on the wall and carried over to the other side of the room. "Once I do, it will take me to the spot by the door where it merges with the light."

She knew he was going to demonstrate and she wasn't certain how she felt about it. If he really could do it, it was the coolest thing ever and she wanted to be able to do it. "If it's true and you could teach me, maybe I could actually get evidence on Haydon, enough for the cops to arrest and convict him."

"A man like Haydon Phillips won't stay in prison and you know it, Grace," Vittorio said gently. "He's too good at what he does. The man can be anyone and he's slippery. I've read the reports on him, and we've got just about everything possible on him from the time he was first put in a foster home until he shot you."

She stared up at him, the firelight dancing across her face. When she looked down, she was surprised to see the shadows flickering across her bare breasts. She'd almost forgotten she wasn't wearing much in the way of clothing. "He said his parents loved him, but were too poor to keep him."

"He lied to you. You know he lied to you because you heard those lies, *cara*."

She flinched at the gentleness in his voice. She'd heard the lies, even as a child, but something had always kept her from challenging Haydon, even way back then. She had stood up for him the first time their foster father beat him. He'd been shocked, but after that, he'd seemed to genuinely try to shield her. For a time, she thought of him as her only family. That hadn't lasted long.

"You had us investigated? Both of us?"

"That's how it works. I didn't give a damn what was found on you, Grace. You were mine no matter what and I made that clear."

"Even to your mother."

"Especially to Eloisa. You are capable of having children that can ride shadows. That's what she was talking about. That's what is important to her. I want children, but if we can't have them, we'll have a good life without them."

His voice rang with truth. She studied his face. He was still wary. She could see it in his eyes. He hadn't told her anything to put that look on his face. He had, several times, reiterated that if she knew what he did, what his family did, there was no going back, the consequences to both of them would be dire—at least that was how she interpreted what he said.

"Are you going to show me?" She invited him because she was suddenly certain he was telling the absolute truth, but whatever he hadn't revealed was going to shake her. She was certain of it.

Without waiting, Vittorio stepped into the largest shadow. Because they were so connected through their shadows, she felt the jolt. That sensation of flying apart. Vittorio completely disappeared and reappeared outside on the patio.

Grace found herself smiling and then laughing. "That's so cool, Vittorio. I wish I'd known how to do that. I could have gotten away from Haydon and actually lived my life. I love that you can do that. That our children will be able to do it."

He walked in, that wary look still on his face. "This isn't an easy life, *bella*."

She heard the warning and forced herself to learn it all. "Once you get your reports from the investigators, Vittorio, and everyone concludes the petitioner isn't lying, why do they turn the results over to the shadow rider?"

"A shadow rider is considered the most important person in the family. When I say family, I'm talking extended family. All the businesses, the bankers, the jewelers, the hotels and casinos are all run by Ferraros. We have family spread throughout several states. There's a reason for that. Riders are considered so important that, although they are trained in every manner of self-defense, they must have bodyguards with them when they move around a city."

"And you're a rider. Stefano and Ricco, all your brothers and Emmanuelle. That's why you all have bodyguards."

He nodded and sank to the floor at her feet, pushing her legs apart to sit between them. His hand moved up her right leg slowly, her ankle, her calf, and then caressed the back of her knee to slide up her thigh.

She gasped at the sensations pouring into her. She didn't want to lose track of what they were discussing, and she knew he could so easily sidetrack her. "You can't distract me, Vittorio. You still have some revelation you don't want to tell me, and you need to just get it over with." She looked down into his face. So gorgeous. It wasn't just his beautiful, very masculine features, it was the way he was inside. "I'm in love with you. There isn't anything that you can tell me that is going to change that."

His eyes met hers in a kind of wary challenge. "And if I told you a shadow rider is essentially an assassin?"

CHAPTER SIXTEEN

Vittorio cursed himself under his breath in both Italian and English. What a complete idiot to blurt the fucking truth out when so far, he'd been careful, choosing every word so she would understand. He could have said a shadow rider administered justice, but no, he had to just come right out and call it what it truly was. He killed people. There was no getting around it. Cousins called him in from New York or Los Angeles and he did his duty. He killed a criminal the law couldn't touch.

He didn't take his eyes from her face. She continued looking down at him without blinking, her green eyes wide, looking so shocked he wanted to kiss the look off her face. Her red hair fell in a long slide out of the messy knot she liked to wear in the bathtub or hot tub. Her breasts rose and fell, betraying her agitation. Finally, she shook her head.

"That can't be true, Vittorio. I don't believe you."

"Why wouldn't you believe me? You've believed everything else I've told you and you can hear lies. Do I sound like I'm lying?" He did his best not to sound bitter.

He had accepted his life. He was born a rider. He was a damn good rider and more, he was good at his job. He was fast, and he dispensed justice without the criminal feeling pain—even if he felt they deserved it. He was always able to keep his emotions under control. Sometimes the things he read in the reports or saw in person gave him nightmares, but what he did, he wouldn't do unless he was absolutely sure the criminal had committed the crimes. Still, one could feel bitterness when their entire life was duty and the only thing they'd ever asked for themselves might walk away and take everything with them.

She took a deep breath and shook her head a second time. "Honey, you need to go a little slower. You jumped over something and I'm not computing what you're saying. I know the heart of you and I'm not wrong. I can't be wrong. I gave you my absolute trust. I put myself in your hands. I have to believe in you."

He'd shaken her. Shaken her faith in herself. Shaken her faith in him, but she was determined to hang on, to see it through.

He rubbed her leg because he had to touch her. Had to stay connected. "You're right, *vita mia*. I did jump us forward. I'm risking everything telling you about my family. For the first time that I can remember, I'm totally fucking things up when I need to explain everything very carefully to you."

She leaned toward him. "Start again with the shadow riders. You're given a report that says absolutely Haydon Phillips is a serial killer. What do you do?"

"The report is given to Stefano. He's the head of the family."

"Not Eloisa?"

He shook his head. "She was replaced by Stefano years ago. She was—difficult. As riders, you have to have absolute faith in the head of the family. He has the last word in everything. Every single thing. We all defer to Stefano, which means he carries a tremendous burden. He's responsible for our safety. For our reputations. He has to make absolutely certain those reports are correct and, in fact, the investigation continues even after the report is given to the shadow riders."

Vittorio continued to stroke her leg. Her skin was soft. She never once pulled away from him and he needed her right then. He needed her acceptance of him in spite of the truth he'd blurted out like a madman. His fingers danced up her leg to the tiny strip of leather covering her sex. He stroked the tight red curls between the laced cord that held that tiny strip in place while his mind sought for the right words.

"I love you, Grace." He had shown her. He'd implied it. He wasn't certain he had ever said the words to her, but he knew he meant it. He hoped she knew it, too. He touched her with love. He looked at her with love, he knew because every time he saw her, his heart melted, or clenched or just plain ached with love for her.

Her green eyes remained absolutely steady on his face. "I love you, too. I do. I know I do, but we have to talk about this. I want to slow down and go back to Eloisa. I'm not an over-the-board feminist, but I do believe in equality, and if Eloisa is your mother, no matter how difficult, she is still head of your family, isn't she?"

His first gut reaction was instant denial, but he was used to taking his time before reacting, and he realized she thought Eloisa wasn't at the helm of the riders because she was a woman. He shook his head. "A woman can easily hold the position as head of a family of riders, but to be in that position, one has to have both compassion and wisdom. Eloisa is all about duty. Our lives are ones of duty. It doesn't matter if we're sick or weak, or unwilling. She expects every rider to pull his weight no matter what is happening in his or her life."

Vittorio continued to stroke her soft inner thigh, realizing that for the first time in his life, he needed the connection with a woman. He had never felt a need bordering on desperation until he faced losing Grace. He'd always had his family, his brothers and sister, and they had formed a unit so strong, when he was younger, he hadn't thought he would ever need anyone else. Loneliness taught him otherwise. Grace had filled all those lonely places, replacing them with laughter and conversation. She'd given him the purpose he needed there in his home to maintain his balance in a world of stark duty.

"I had a younger brother, Ettore, born just eleven months after Emmanuelle. He had respiratory problems when he was born, and the problems worsened as he grew. He was always weaker, although he tried so hard to follow the dictates of our training regimen. We all started instruction at age two. Everything is about training from that point on. For Ettore, it became a nightmare of being yelled at and being unable to do something so simple as breathe. The worse his respiratory problems became, the more was demanded of him to make him stronger. No matter what the rest of us said, or did, he was expected to keep up."

He didn't realize his fingers had closed around her thigh like a vise. She didn't wince, not even when his grip bit into her leg. He let her go the instant he realized what he was doing. "I'm sorry, *mia amore*, I have a difficult time when it comes to those memories. All of us do. "

Her fingers sifted through his hair, her touch soothing. "You didn't hurt me."

He was a very strong man. He hoped what she said was true and he rubbed at the smudge marks left behind on her skin. "Ettore's life was a nightmare. Nothing he did was ever good enough. We tried to shield him, but one had to be perfect in all things. Always. If you fell below Eloisa's high standards, your life was hell. Ettore lived in hell."

"What about your father? Couldn't he stop her?"

"Phillip couldn't care less about any of us. He wasn't a rider, not in the sense of one who dispensed justice. He wasn't trained. It was an arranged marriage and the two barely spoke. He certainly didn't bother with us, and he would never have gone against Eloisa in training us as riders.

Stefano took care of us. He wasn't that much older, but he still acted as our parent, both mother and father."

"That explains a lot about him," Grace murmured.

"Stefano tried to tell Eloisa that Ettore couldn't be a rider, that his body wouldn't take the punishment. You can be torn apart and it can be just too hard on a rider, but Eloisa insisted. No child of hers would dare be less than perfect. She sent him into the shadows when he had just turned sixteen. Stefano wasn't there to stop her."

He closed his eyes, memories of that terrible day washing over him. Choking him. He turned his head away from her, not willing for her to see that losing Ettore was still a raw wound that would never be healed, no matter how much time went by. "Stefano brought his body out and we buried him, but he took over as head of the family of riders. He'd always been the parent to us, and we all lost faith in Eloisa's leadership. She was so driven to show the other rider families that we were perfect that she risked Ettore's life."

"I'm so sorry," Grace murmured. "I really am. I understand the dynamics of your family a lot better. Even after seeing you do it, it's difficult to believe someone could use shadows to get from one place to another. It's easier to believe that there really is a way to move through the shadows when I listen to you talk. It's clearly a way of life to you and there are obviously other families besides yours that are capable."

"Mariko is from Japan. Her family, on her father's side, were legendary riders. They're all gone now, but she's a strong rider."

The grip grief had on him was lessening and he turned back to her. "I know Eloisa is harsh and can be as cold as ice. She shreds people and she must have done so to you when you tried working with her, but she saves her best work for us."

Her hand cupped the side of his face and she leaned down. He kissed her. Her mouth was everything he needed. Hot and wild. Tantalizing. That elusive, incredible taste he was addicted to. She transported him instantly into a world of sensation, of feeling, every cell in his body alive. Electricity arced between them, little strikes crackling against his skin, spreading flames over him. Dark, erotic images filled his mind as a dark erotic taste filled his mouth. Heat spread throughout his body, fire burning down his spine and roaring like an inferno in his belly.

She continued cupping his face gently in her hands. He simply pulled her from the chair right onto the floor with him, kissing her over and over. She was . . . salvation. Everything good. She lit up a room just as she lit up his life.

Grace did what she always did when he kissed her—she gave herself to him. Surrendered completely. His hands moved over her body, claiming everywhere he touched and she arched her back, giving him full access to any part of her he claimed. She took away sorrow and anger, replacing it with acceptance and love.

Vittorio kissed his way down her throat to the swell of her breast before lifting his head. "I don't know what I'd do without you."

Grace cuddled into him like the kitten he often called her. He loved when she did that, when she stayed close to him.

"Tell me what happens when Stefano is given the report on the criminal and petitioner," she urged.

He knew it was important she know every detail. She had to accept their way of life, or he would have to give her up. Their shadows were tangled already, so much so he knew if she didn't accept him and they had to be untangled, he would never be a rider again. She wouldn't remember him or their relationship. This was the most dangerous moment of all to him, but Vittorio knew he had no choice. He kept his arms around her, holding her to him, as if he could physically keep her.

"Stefano would turn the reports over to our cousins in New York or the ones in Los Angeles. We don't work in our own cities as a rule. There can be no ties back to our family.

That's for the protection of everyone. Obviously, it doesn't always work that way, but for the most part, we're careful never to have anything personal touch us."

"I still don't really understand."

"If we're called to go to New York, two of us very publicly board our private plane. A third will ride the shadows so there is no evidence of him or her ever leaving the city. The two in plain sight make certain the paparazzi take multiple pictures. Cousins meet us at the airport and escort us to some club where we party hard in front of the media. More pictures. Pictures with the cousins are taken."

"You set up alibis." Grace rubbed her face on his chest and then pressed her ear over his heart. "That's why you're always in the tabloids, you make certain you're seen."

"Exactly. No one would ever suspect us and if they did, we're in plain sight. Nothing to hide. It works very well."

Grace was silent for a very long time, staring into the fireplace. She leaned up against his chest, her head resting on the heavy muscles there, the silk of her hair sliding over his skin. It was impossible for his cock not to react to her when he was already naked, and she was in leather and lace. Her buttocks were bare and his erection immediately found the crease between her cheeks, nestling there, while his arms surrounded her, hands beneath her breasts.

"If I had come to you about Haydon, what would happen to him?"

"Once we had ascertained he was in fact a serial killer and the law couldn't touch him and we found him, a rider from New York or Los Angeles would ride the shadows to where he was. He would never see the rider, or even know he was there. The rider uses a technique, breaking the neck cleanly, so there is no suffering. That is why it is important not to allow it to be personal if at all possible. You always want the visit to be about justice, not revenge."

His heart pounded. This was the moment he could lose her. He was very aware of her stillness. She didn't move. His hands cupped her breasts and yet he was barely able to feel the rise and fall of that soft weight. He didn't say a word. Not yet. She needed to think about what he'd said. Weigh it in her mind. Make her decision. If it went against him, if she compared what he was to what Haydon was— and it was very possible—he would attempt to defend himself then.

He closed his eyes, rested his chin on top of her hair and breathed evenly to keep himself centered. He was asking so much of Grace. Every time he turned around, he was asking just a little more of her, when their relationship was so new. He had no choice, or he would have waited, but she couldn't marry him and come fully into the family until she accepted what he was. He couldn't change the fact that he'd been born a rider. Worse, if she accepted him and agreed to marry him, he would still have to tell her that their children would be trained as riders. He wouldn't blame her if she didn't want that life for them.

"If I had known about your family and the possibility of stopping him, I might have been able to save lives."

Her voice broke his heart. He tightened his arms around her, although he couldn't help the surge of relief pouring into him. "Grace, you didn't know about us and you are in no way responsible for any lives Haydon Phillips took. You did your best to protect those around you, so much so that you sacrificed your own quality of life." He brushed kisses in her hair and over her temple.

"I don't know if it's wrong or not," she mused. "Taking justice into one's hands is considered vigilante work, but . . ." She trailed off. "I honestly don't know if it's wrong. Even if the cops suspect Haydon, how do they find proof? He's so smart and he can be anyone. He plays his roles so well. As for finding him, where would you start? I've tried to question him about parts of the city or coffee shops, or just anything to give me an idea of where he might be, but I've never even gotten close. He has more than one house he lives in, with more than one family. It's so creepy and I worry about the children in the homes all the time."

"Does he always choose a home with children?"

"Yes. If there's a teenage boy, I really worry. Simple things can trigger his anger. Dwayne Mueller, the biological son of the foster parents who were so terrible, used to do terrible things to us. If a boy were to remind Haydon of Dwayne in any way, I know he would retaliate against him. The boy might just simply get in a fight with his sibling as kids do."

Vittorio felt the little shiver that ran through her and he nuzzled her neck and shoulder in an effort to comfort her.

"I wouldn't be horrified to learn Haydon was dead. I might be horrified to learn that you were the one who killed him."

He closed his eyes. "Why is that?"

"I don't like the idea of you doing dangerous things, and clearly riding shadows is very hazardous and risky. And you have to live with what you do. Killing other human beings can't be easy, whether it's personal or not."

He could tell by her tone that she was still puzzling things out in her mind. Trying to decide if what he did was right or wrong. He could tell her there was no answer to that, but she would have to come to that conclusion on her own. At least she wasn't condemning him out of hand. She hadn't compared him to Haydon and that was his greatest fear.

She reached a hand back behind her to hook around his neck. "You scare me a little, Vittorio. You lead a difficult life no one knows about. People think things of you that aren't true and are rather insulting."

"People's opinions of me don't faze me. We were raised from a young age to know our lives weren't entirely our own. We belong to the family. A hundred years ago, our family was nearly wiped out and those left had to be scattered, leave their country in order to survive. We never have all riders in one place openly. We make certain someone will be able to avenge all deaths should some enemy decide to try to wipe us all out again. We are taught that is our duty and we accept the responsibility."

She turned her head to look at him over her shoulder.

Her face was soft with love. There was admiration and respect in her eyes. His heart clenched hard in his chest and his stomach did a slow roll. His cock jerked hard, aching and dripping with need. Careful of her shoulder, he slipped out from under her, laying her out on the thick rug in front of the fireplace.

"Stay with me, Grace. Be mine. All in. Everything." He skimmed his hand from her throat, between her breasts, down her belly to her fiery curls. "I don't want to be alone anymore and you're my only. My everything. Tell me yes."

He bent his head and took her mouth roughly. He threw gentle to the wind. He didn't feel gentle. He knew he'd won. He *knew*. Grace was too compassionate not to give herself to him. She was already in love. She would never abandon him, not when she knew he was alone. Not when she knew his mother and father had been cold and unfeeling. Or that he'd lost a younger much beloved brother. Grace would never have it in her to leave him.

He tasted triumph in her surrender. Heat rushed through his veins and roared in a fireball in his belly. He took everything she offered and demanded more. She gave him more, her tongue dueling with his, her flames mixing with his until the two were so explosive he feared they might start a fire right there in the sitting room.

He kissed his way over her chin and then reached for the buckle behind her neck, slowly unfastening it, his gaze drifting possessively over her face. "You're so beautiful, *gattina*, you're a fucking miracle." He bent to nip her chin with his teeth, his tongue easing the sting when her eyes went wide. "You didn't answer me."

Her tongue moistened her lips, leaving them gleaming in the firelight while he pulled the straps from around her neck.

"I'm uncertain about what to think, Vittorio."

She had her adorable frown on her face, so he kissed it right off just the way he was always tempted to. When he let her up for air, she looked bemused. Slightly dazed.

Wholly his. She might not have said it yet, but her complete surrender was there on her face. He pulled her gently into a sitting position and reached around her to unbuckle the corset. Only two buckles held it in place and he didn't have to look to free them, his fingers deft on the metal. Loosening the leather garment, he tugged until it was gone and then he eased her back down onto the rug.

"Say you're going to stay with me, Grace. Give me your word." He murmured the demand against her right breast and then he was devouring her while his hand worked her left breast. While his mouth was rough, using his teeth and tongue as well as suckling strongly, his fingers were gentle. When his fingers rolled, tugged and pinched her nipple or kneaded her breast, his mouth turned gentle. He changed the rhythm, so she couldn't get used to the feel of either. Her feet went flat on the floor, knees up, hips bucking wildly.

"Vittorio." His name only. A gasp.

"Say it, *bella*. Say you belong to me and you always will. Make it a sacred vow so I know you'll never break it."

He kissed the valley between her breasts, the heavy shadow on his jaw leaving a trail of red as he chafed the sensitive skin. He turned his head, nipping and then laving with his tongue, following the curves around to the undersides of her breasts to add to his marks of possession.

"I can't think when you're doing that."

"Doing what?" He kissed his way to her intriguing little belly button, swirling his tongue there, and then claiming every inch of her belly and rib cage. He rubbed his jaw lower, marking her skin, and then used his teeth, small nips that made her slick with need. "You're not talking to me, and I need to hear actual words."

Her breath was coming in ragged pants. His cock was raging. It took only moments to open the laces of her leather thong and drag it off of her, leaving her body completely bare. Vittorio brought his palm once more from her throat to the junction between her legs. "You're hot as hell, woman. So beautiful like this."

Seeing her needy and so hungry for him was erotic beyond anything else. When his cock was in her mouth she had much the same look. Adoration. Love. Hunger. She was sinfully sensual. He moved into her, caught her legs behind her knees and pushed them forward so they were nearly even with her ears, exposing her wholly to him.

"I wish you could see yourself right now." He bent his head and swiped his tongue through her wet folds, collecting the nectar he was so addicted to.

Her body shuddered, and she gasped. He lifted his head. "I haven't heard what I want to hear."

"I can't think straight. You're making it difficult."

He smiled wickedly at her and bent his head again. A moan escaped her, and he felt the muscles in her belly ripple beneath his spread palm. Smiling, he attacked, sucking, drawing out what he craved and then when she cried out, flattening his tongue and stroking until she was nearly sobbing. He changed tactics and flicked her clit hard with his tongue until she was close to exploding. He pulled back, wiping his face on the insides of her thighs.

"Vittorio." She wailed his name.

"I am listening, *mia vida*." He blew on her gleaming curls and then lower still.

"You know I'm staying."

"You may have said so in the past, but there was no vow. I didn't hear a vow." He lowered his head and indulged himself all over again.

He loved the taste of her, but he also loved that she was so sensitive and responsive to him. Within minutes she was gasping out his name, her fingers curling in his hair, begging him. He loved that note of desperation in her voice. He had never played when he was with a woman, but Grace made him feel as if they had all the time in the world to enjoy themselves. She made him feel as if she gave him the freedom to play. To tease her. To enjoy every square inch on her body.

"I'm loving you, Grace." He whispered it to her against

her belly, unable to contain the truth. The feeling was over-whelming and so huge it spilled out of him until he had no choice but to tell her. "I'll never stop."

She went still, her hips quiet, and her gaze widened to drift over his face. "I never want you to stop, Vittorio. No matter what, I'm staying with you for as long as you want me. We'll see it through together."

He let himself look his fill, drinking her in, and then he couldn't look anymore because his eyes were burning. He lowered her legs to the floor and rose over her to find her mouth with his, sharing her taste, half expecting her to turn away, but she didn't. She kissed him, that slow burn he needed from her, igniting a hundred explosions in his belly, all the while conveying absolute love.

"I want you on your hands and knees, *gattina*."

Her eyes searched his and then she moved, rolling over obediently, her face to the fireplace. He rubbed her but-tocks, loving the look and feel of her. His hand settled on the nape of her neck, pushing her head toward the floor very gently.

"I'm going to take you hard and fast. It will be rough. You have to protect your shoulder, Grace, so lower yourself all the way down and put more weight on your good shoulder."

She turned her head to look back at him but lowered her upper body more until she was resting on her elbows, her good shoulder taking most of her weight. He rubbed her bot-tom again, tracing his finger along the seam of her cheeks and then leaning in to nip with his teeth until she gave a little yelp and pushed back toward his hand.

He knelt up behind her, his cock heavy in his hand. He wasn't going to last nearly as long as he would want to. Not with the firelight playing over her body the way it was. Not with her kneeling, presenting herself to him the way she was. He pressed the thick, flared head of his cock into the scorching heat waiting for him. She gasped, and he looked down at her face.

She was looking at him with her green eyes, those long

feathery lashes framing them. There was that look he would never get enough of—the one that told him she definitely belonged to him. Watching her face, he slammed home, driving through her tight folds to bury himself as deep as possible. A streak of fire threatened to engulf his cock in fiery flames as her sheath closed around him, seeking to grasp and hold him tight enough to strangle him.

The air rushed from his lungs. He heard her sharp little cry, abruptly cut off as she gasped for breath. He caught her hips in his hands and began to move. Hard. Fast. Just like he'd promised her. Deep every time. The scorching heat was almost too much. Her channel was so tight he wasn't certain if he was feeling pleasure or pain. It didn't matter, because the combination was perfection. He couldn't stop. He wanted to live right there, with the fire burning him clean.

It was too good. He knew it even as he resolved to prolong his time inside her. Every bit of his discipline seemed to fly out the open doors into the night as he slammed into her over and over, riding her hard, never wanting this time to be over. He felt her muscles clamp down and then her sheath was rippling around him.

"No." He groaned it, knowing she would take him with her. He was too close. There was no pulling back.

Her breath whistled out of her and the wave grew larger and stronger, sweeping him up, pouring all around him until her body was a vise. She burned him in a silken fist that refused to let up, only tightened more, so much so that he felt her every heartbeat pounding into his cock. Blood thundered in his ears. Roared through his veins. Roiled in his belly and centered in his groin so that his release started in his toes and swept upward, consuming him. Destroying him. Killing him. He felt every wild jerk of his cock in tune to the rhythmic clamping down of her scorching channel around him. Over and over, hot jets splashed her walls, coating her, triggering heavier shocks.

The explosion was all-consuming, enveloping the two of

them, sending them soaring. He held on to her tightly, his cock shuddering, his body trembling, as hers rippled and pulsed around his. Her cries were a soft counterpoint to his guttural and very harsh gasp of her name. Grace. His woman.

He had the presence of mind to ease her legs out straight so she was lying flat on her belly as he collapsed over top of her, still pulsing, still buried in her. She took his weight, even though there was no give in the floor beneath the rug. His lungs refused to draw air as her body continued to milk his. Pleasure swamped him. Stayed. His heart beat too loudly. Too fast. Chaos reigned in his brain. His world had narrowed to this one woman, her body and his connected just as their shadows were. Sharing. Riding that wave of pure passion together.

The night breeze came off the lake, stealing through the open glass door to play over their bodies. Teasing his buttocks and back. Drifting over his head to ruffle his hair.

She lay very still, her sheath clamped around him. Very slowly, her small muscles began to ease their death grip around his cock. He couldn't find the strength to move. Each little movement of her body sent ripples through both of them.

"If you weren't so heavy, I could sleep here." Her voice came out muffled and a little breathless.

"If I was a gentleman, I'd attempt to move, but I'm not. And I can't." He used what little air he had left in his lungs to separate from her, rolling as he did so, to get his weight off of her. She wasn't asking, and it wasn't exactly a complaint—he knew Grace would have let him lie on top of her until she really couldn't take a breath.

He rolled over onto his back beside her, looking up at the ceiling. "You're a fucking miracle, *gattina*." He couldn't tell her that enough. It was the truth.

"That was both of us, so I would have to say you're the miracle. I don't know what I'm doing, remember?" She rolled over onto her back and lay close to him, their thighs touching. Her red hair looked like gleaming silk in the firelight. Her body was covered in a fine sheen, and every breath she drew was a temptation to sin.

He threw one arm over his eyes. It was dark, the only light came from the flames of the fireplace dancing over them and the moon reflecting off the surface of the lake.

"That isn't what I meant, Grace." He forced himself to roll to his side and prop his head up in one hand. "You said you'd stay with me even after I told you what my family does."

Her gaze flicked to the side, meeting his eyes, but she didn't turn her head. "I do love you. I think you knew that before you told me. You didn't have to. You could have kept it a secret. It's not like too many people would believe you could travel through shadows. I'm still not clear on how."

"I had no choice." He couldn't help but touch her. He laid his palm on her stomach, right over her belly button where he hoped their child would be nestled someday. "There are consequences if our shadows tangle together too much. We spent quite a lot of time together and I didn't hold back my feelings at all. I didn't even try." He made the confession in a little rush.

"What consequences?"

"If we ripped apart our shadows, I would be unable to be a rider. I was born a rider and I trained all my life, it's who I am; it would be the worst thing that could happen to me other than losing you. You wouldn't remember we were in a relationship. You would have thought we were together in order for me to help you because you were shot in the parking lot of our nightclub."

She went silent. He was used to her taking her time before her response, but he was very tuned to her and tension in her had gone up several degrees. He kept breathing. Stayed conscious of the air moving in and out of his lungs. He kept his energy low, nonthreatening. No fear. No anger. Just breathe. He kept the mantra going in his head. She had said she would stay and Grace Murphy was not the type of woman to go back on her word.

"You lead a difficult life, Vittorio."

"I suppose that's true. It's the only one I really know, so for me it doesn't feel difficult. Grace." He turned her head toward him deliberately, forcing her to look at him. "I swear to you, you'll be happy with me. I'm the same man you fell in love with. We talked, remember? I know what you like, and you know what my preferences are. We fit. You'll be happy in my family. They'll welcome you. Eloisa will back off. She snipes at all of us, but she's also intensely loyal."

"I'm not worried about Eloisa, Vittorio. I'm worried about you."

He bent his head to brush a kiss across her mouth just because he detected a slight trembling of her lips. "I'm extremely good at what I do."

"You live life on the edge all the time. You hunt and kill criminals."

"I bring them to justice when no one else can."

"It doesn't matter how one words it, that's what you do. There is excitement in that. It's high adrenaline, right?"

He studied her face while he gave her a nod of confirmation. "Yes. It's a rush. It takes a while for the adrenaline to recede and in the meantime, I'll warn you now, the rush goes straight to my cock. I'm going to come home to you and want a day or two of constant sex every way I can get it. That's a fact."

"So an adrenaline rush and hot sex for days after." She turned her head straight so she was back looking at the ceiling.

"Talk, *bella*. You need to voice your concerns. We promised each other."

"I've seen the things you do. Skydiving. Driving race cars. Flying planes. Climbing mountains. Sailing. It's all there to read about over and over in the tabloids and magazines. I've read them all, every story about you, and I looked at the pictures. The proof those articles weren't made up. You really do all those adrenaline-junkie sports."

"I do."

"I don't."

"You didn't," he corrected. "You will."

"I wouldn't know how. I'd be terrified. I'm a boring person, Vittorio, and within a month, you'll be bored out of your mind."

"That's been your hesitation all along, hasn't it?" He rubbed her belly, those muscles flowing like silk under her skin.

"You have to admit, it's a genuine reason to be concerned."

"You already agreed to try the things I want in the bedroom. Some of those things are bound to scare you, but you'll trust me to make things good for you, right?"

"That's different."

"Trust is trust, Grace. If you trust me to take care of your body when we have sex, it isn't a leap that you'll trust me to take care of you inside the house, right? You're already doing it."

She nodded warily, sensing a trap.

"Then it won't be a huge leap if you trust me to take care of you outside the house. I want you to learn to fly a plane. To climb a mountain. To scuba dive. I want to share my world with you, all of it. You have to trust that I'm going to go slow and careful with you, introduce you to things I know you'll love."

Vittorio rolled over top of her to blanket her body. He framed her face with both hands, so he could look into her eyes. "You're my world. You. You're my life. Do you really believe for one minute that I would put you into a dangerous situation I couldn't control? You would be trained properly before you were ever allowed to try anything. I would always be with you. I wouldn't chance losing you. I want us to share adventures together. You learn to trust me all the way, Grace, so you know you're always going to be safe with me. Can you do that for me?"

Her eyes moved over his face. She swallowed. Hard. His

heart clenched in reaction. His woman. She was going to give him this. To please him. Because he was hers to take care of and she knew he needed her trust more than anything. Trust was intertwined with love. The more he felt her faith and belief in him, the more he knew she loved him.

She nodded very slowly. "I'll try whatever you want me to, because I know it will please you and that's important to me."

He kissed her gently. "Thank you, Grace," he murmured when he finally lifted his head. She'd kissed him back without hesitation, although she breathed shallowly and he knew he had to shift his weight off of her.

"I'm very tired, Vittorio. I need to go to bed. I have the feeling I'm going to need a lot of sleep to keep up with you."

He felt the rush of happiness and let himself feel it. Happiness hadn't been in his life. He enjoyed his family, but he hadn't felt complete. Whole. And he hadn't been happy.

"I'll get you cleaned up, *gattina*, and then carry you to bed." He loved performing that little ritual after sex for her and he knew the more he did it, the more it would become normal for her. He kissed her again and got to his feet.

CHAPTER SEVENTEEN

Vittorio got the alert from Stefano as he came out of the physical therapy room, Grace tight against his body. They'd planned to go swimming together, something the doctor said would be very good for her shoulder and she was already addicted to doing. Midnight Madness was coming up fast and she was pushing herself in order to be in the best shape she could in order to pull off the event successfully.

"What is it?" Grace asked, looking up at him from under her veil of long lashes.

He tightened his arm around her, locking her to him. "My brother. The family is on their way for another quick meeting." That was the truth, but not all of it. He wasn't certain how much he should tell her. She'd accepted what his family did, she'd even accepted that he was a shadow rider, but talking about being an assassin—whether it was for justice or not—and actually carrying out the order were two very different things.

She continued to look up at him as they walked down the hall toward her room. "This is about Haydon, isn't it?"

"I don't know for certain." That much was true, but he had a gut feeling and his feelings, so far, had never been wrong. "Most likely," he conceded. "I'll tell you when I find out."

Once in her room, he closed the door and turned to frame her face. "It's almost over, Grace. We're going to get him, and his reign of terror will be over. You can live free."

Her green gaze moved over his face for what seemed like forever. He found himself holding his breath. She reached up with her injured arm, her fingers brushing his five-o'clock shadow, sending fingers of desire dancing down his spine as if that intimate touch could be felt all over his body.

"I'm already living free, Vittorio. You gave that to me. I breathe easy when I'm here. I feel safe when I'm with you. I know he's out there, but the longer I'm with you, the more I believe I'm safe and I feel it."

He wrapped his arms around her and brought her in tight against his body. "I'm having your clothes moved to the master bedroom today. Merry's arranged for three women we trust to come in and make the move for us."

Alarm turned her eyes a dark emerald. "Wait." One hand went defensively to her throat.

He smiled down at her. "I've been sleeping in your bed for a while now, *gattina*. Why would you object?"

The tip of her tongue moistened her lips. "It's my space."

He threw his head back and laughed. "Are you thinking that if you're annoyed with me you could just kick me out of the bedroom?" Vittorio never took his gaze from hers. His beautiful woman. She lit up his world.

"Well," she hedged. Her nod of assent was slow. "I did have that in mind, yes."

"*Bella*, you're priceless." Laughter welled up and he didn't try to stop it. Happiness was something he wasn't used to, and it felt good to just bask in it. She was going to be the best mother, the best partner. She would give their children a happy childhood filled with laughter and fun.

She glared at him. "It isn't funny that I need the room to be mine, so I can kick you out of it." She took a step away from him to look around at the large space.

"What's funny is just how you think you're going to get me to leave. I'm twice your size. Size does count in these situations," he was compelled to point out.

She gave him her snippiest look. "I will ask you to be a gentleman and leave."

"*Gattina.*" His voice was very gentle. "We talked about what kind of man I am. There will be no throwing me out of the bedroom. If you're upset, we will talk it out. I think this is about you having your own space, not your own bedroom. You don't mind me being with you at night, sleeping the way we do."

His body was always tightly around hers, so much so that there was no getting a thin piece of paper between them. He liked it that way. He wanted to feel every inch of her soft skin. He enjoyed being able to stroke caresses over her breasts, or feed there, his mouth hungry for her, his fingers curling into her to feel her waiting reception. He loved waking up to her mouth on his cock and the feel of her hair sliding over his thighs. He wasn't giving that up.

He wasn't going to get into the fact that if he was in that room with her, aside from his need to spend as much time with his woman as possible, he knew he could protect her. Should Haydon find a way to penetrate his security, he would still be there to keep the man from getting to Grace. It was important for that alone that they stay in the same bedroom.

She wrapped her hand around the bedpost. "I think that's partially right. I do want to sleep with you at night and yet at the same time, I like knowing I have my own place."

He heard reluctance to take the conversation any further. "I've had a room fixed up for you. You clearly need an office here at the house. It has a private bath as well as a sitting room. Having your own office will allow you and Katie to have privacy when you need to discuss details of upcoming events. The phone and Internet systems are fast and reliable. And don't worry, I didn't have it painted some bizarre color. I should have clarified, I had the phone system installed but the rest is up to you. I thought you might have fun designing exactly the way you want the interior to look."

She practically beamed at him. "I've always wanted an office. It will make things so much easier, and knowing Haydon can't get in and look at anything I've put together about clients and vendors will be such a relief. Thank you for thinking of that."

He loved making her happy. He'd have ten offices built on the property if he could get that particular smile from her. Still, there was something bothering her she didn't want to tell him, and he couldn't have that. He needed to know when she was upset over something.

"I want to know why you're reluctant to share the master bedroom with me." He made it a statement. "Tell me, Grace." He made that an order.

She made a small face at him. "It shifts the balance of power to you." She made the confession in a little rush. "Everything about that room screams you. I think you can fit two of my rooms into it, and this room is enormous. The colors are all you and sort of . . . intimidating. The bed looks as if you might really be able to tie me to it, although I looked through the entire house and didn't see any kind of dungeon, so hopefully I'm perfectly safe." She ended on a nervous laugh.

He stepped close, forcing her to look up. One finger went under her chin so that she had to look him directly in the eye. "Just so you know, you're never going to be perfectly safe from anything sexual I demand. Tying you up or not is my option no matter where we are." He brushed a kiss across her lips, smiling as he did so because her eyes had widened and looked slightly shocked yet filled with a dark lust and clear anticipation. "It doesn't matter what room we're in. I want you in the master bedroom with me. Always. We're moving you today." He waited. Watching her expression.

She nodded slowly. "I'd better start before I get my swimsuit and go swimming."

"First, you aren't lifting a finger. I've instructed the movers to begin immediately as soon as we're out of here. Secondly, there's no swimming until I can go with you. I'm not taking chances that something might happen while you're in the water."

A storm of protest crossed her face and her eyes turned ominously dark. "*First*, nothing at all is going to happen when I'm doing laps. I'm swimming slowly, just like the doc ordered. I don't need a babysitter in the pool. Before I came, did you swim alone in your pool?"

Her chin had gone up and he couldn't help himself, he leaned into her and bit down gently until she yelped at the pressure. "It doesn't matter what I did or didn't do, *gattina*. It only matters what I want for you and above all, that's your safety. You're not swimming alone. That's a rule I expect you won't break."

She looked positively mutinous. He wrapped his arm around her waist and brought her in tight against him, locking her there. His mouth came down hard on hers. He was rough, indulging himself, kissing her until she couldn't breathe. Until he couldn't. Until he was certain air wasn't strictly necessary. He loved kissing her.

Somewhere along the line, he'd become addicted to her taste—to the fire roaring in his belly the moment his mouth was on hers—to the flames pouring like a liquid inferno through his veins when he was kissing her. His woman, kissing him back, was a miracle. She felt like a living flame in his arms. He got lost there, swept up in the magic that was Grace.

He lifted his head reluctantly when his watch vibrated,

letting him know his family was arriving. They had all agreed to travel to his home using the shadows, so Haydon had no idea where any of them were, other than Giovanni, who had no choice but to arrive in a car. Mariko used the shadows to get to the hotel, so she could stay with Francesca. His family always met in the same conference room overlooking the herb garden. The garden was closed in with fences. Ropes of wisteria in purples and whites rose up from every inch of fencing to further hide the room with its glass wall from the outside world.

"I would like you to sit outside on the patio and contemplate the perfect wedding for us. What is your dream wedding? Have you already pictured it in your head? Do you know what you want? Now would be a good time to write down the details."

He turned her toward the door. Her face paled as she looked up at him. He kept them walking right out into the hallway. The matter with his family had to be urgent for everyone to be told to arrive immediately.

"You're going too fast, Vittorio. You need to slow down. We're just beginning to know each other. We can't get married so soon."

She sounded breathless. Shocked. Scared. He chose to address the scared. "Grace, you have to get used to trusting me. You're wearing my ring on your finger. You've made your promise. We've lived together for a couple of months now. A little more. You know you're in love with me and you know that I love you. I am not going to wait to marry you. There's no reason not to do it as soon as we can. Haydon Phillips aside, and we're going to find him and remove him from your life, what reason is there to wait?"

"Haydon is a *huge* reason, Vittorio. We absolutely can't have a wedding ceremony until after he's in custody or dead. Seriously. You have no idea how dangerous or how sick he is."

"I do know. I made it my business to know. I've read every report that's been prepared on every single death you suspected he was involved with. I've studied the reports. I know more about him at this point than he knows about himself. My investigators have put together timelines and traced his travels, using the pictures on your phone. They can place him right at the murder scene of three of the victims at the same time the victims were killed. Somewhere along the line, a year or so ago, he began messing with the camera, making it harder to trace him."

"He probably figured out that his whereabouts could be traced using the photographs. He's like that. He doesn't need a formal education. He was always smart, he just didn't want anyone, including teachers, telling him what to do."

He slid his palm down her arm to take her hand. "Let's go. The sooner we get this over, the sooner we can swim." He led her outside. "Merry will bring you refreshments. The three women will move your things to the master bedroom. All you have to do is plan your perfect dream wedding."

Merry had already, at his texted instructions, brought a pitcher of strawberry lemonade, a bucket of ice and a tall glass. Beside it was Grace's iPad with the planner program on it. She slipped into the chair without arguing further with him.

"I shouldn't be long." Vittorio kissed her again, taking his time. He could hurry everything else in his life, but he was never going to make the mistake of hurrying his time with Grace. She was too important, and everything else could take a back seat. His watch vibrated impatiently, telling him his older brother was ready for him, but he ignored the summons.

The third time, he lifted his head. "I love you very much, Grace Murphy." His thumb slid over the little indentation in her chin. "Marry me soon."

She nodded slowly, looking a little bemused. "I will, but just know you're cheating by kissing me. I can't think straight."

He was having a little trouble himself. Mostly, his body was making urgent demands, which circumstances forced him to ignore. His watch vibrated again and this time he imagined it trying to shake his entire arm. Giovanni must have arrived. He'd been so into kissing his woman, he'd ignored the car.

"You're the expert, *bella*. Plan us a spectacular day. I never thought I'd look forward to my wedding, so give us both our dream day."

"Men aren't usually especially thrilled for a wedding that's considered spectacular by a woman."

He loved the amusement in her voice so much that he brushed kisses across her eyelids. "This man does." Anything for his woman. He wanted "spectacular" for her. "Emilio and Enzo are close and while I'm in the meeting, their sister, Enrica, is here if you need anything."

He preferred being with her himself but had three of the best and most experienced bodyguards the family had to watch over her while he was in his meeting. He strode down the hall and entered the designated conference room. His family was already seated around the table.

"I take it something's happened," he greeted.

Stefano indicated the remaining chair. "The Grecos think they've found the house where Haydon Phillips is staying," he announced without preamble. "In the last eight hours, we've had several breaks. We're finding out the whereabouts of the family, so we can go after Phillips safely. He will be less suspecting in broad daylight."

Vittorio's pulse jumped. The thought of freeing Grace after all the years of terror was a heady one.

"Before we focus on Phillips, the two missing girls, Eva and Marta Giboli, are in fact with their father. He met them at the airport when they called him, and he flew with them back to Tuscany. They intend to live with him. Eloisa, I would prefer that you deliver the news to their mother and make her understand that it would be best to leave the girls there. They're old enough to choose and if she insists on getting the State Department involved in getting them back, tell her our family will testify that she didn't bother to come for help for over two weeks."

"I will be more than happy to deliver the message," Eloisa agreed.

Vittorio flicked a glance to his mother. She looked more rested than she had in weeks. She always looked young, too young to have as many children as she'd given birth to. Stefano had tried to talk her into retiring full time from shadow riding. She still took the occasional job, especially since Giovanni's injury had left them one rider down.

Stefano inclined his head and continued. "John Balboni, as you know, owns the local hardware store. He and Suzette have been struggling a little to keep the business afloat and it didn't help that he was shot during the attack on our family, although we paid all the bills. The exact nature of just how bad they were struggling wasn't brought to my attention until recently. We considered options for them, but in the end, hadn't found the right answer to the problem short of loaning them more money. They're already into the family for three hundred thousand."

"John and Suzette's store has been in the community for over thirty years," Ricco said. "As long as I've been alive."

"Which is why we tried to keep them going," Stefano said. "John's body was found in the dumpster behind Fior A Bizzeffe this morning."

"No," Eloisa whispered. "Not John. Poor Suzette." She half stood as if she might go to the woman immediately.

"Sasha is with her. She's certainly getting a baptism of fire," Giovanni said, shaking his head. "I left two bodyguards with her, but all this makes me very uncomfortable. Something bad is coming our way."

"This is insane," Ricco said. "John? Why John?"

"The Balbonis have very poor business practices," Taviano said. "I went over the books twice with John and he just kept ordering double the amount of merchandise needed. His reasoning was he didn't want to run out of anything, but in the end, he literally rents another storage facility in order to put everything into it and then he forgets he has it. In my opinion, he has a problem. He can't stop ordering items he doesn't need. It's almost a hoarding situation. Nothing I said deterred him. Suzette got it, but John seemed oblivious to the fact that he was the one bringing the store down."

"That is exactly what made John the perfect target for the Saldis," Stefano said. "Clearly they're studying our people for weaknesses."

"Unless someone's telling them," Eloisa said. "Giving them details in casual conversation." Her gaze flicked to her daughter's set face.

"If that's happening," Vittorio said smoothly, as if he didn't see the look his mother shot Emmanuelle, "more than likely, the information would be given at the butcher shop when Val Saldi or his men are delivering to Giordano's. Berardo loves to gossip. He would definitely talk to the deliverymen, but it would be an innocent conversation. He would never give information away deliberately, especially if it was something that might get a friend killed, and he was very good friends with John."

"I agree. The information was most likely gotten at the butcher shop," Stefano said. "The point is, John was found wrapped in a carpet, his body tortured in the same way the others' were. Sending a message to anyone working for the Saldis to keep their mouths shut. He wasn't taken until after the others were. They took the carpet, but he wasn't missing. He and Suzette were there on the street when the dumpsters were being searched."

"Did you speak to anyone who might have seen them?" Vittorio asked.

Stefano shook his head. "I turned the investigation over to Renato and Romano."

Vittorio was well aware his two cousins had voices considered the most powerful in the family when it came to persuading others to remember details, tell the truth and *want* to give any information to the brothers.

"What about the cameras?" Giovanni asked.

"Rigina is looking at all of them now," Taviano said. "We make certain all cameras on the streets are working at all times. We might get lucky. There didn't appear to be any tampering done to the ones under the eaves of the businesses."

The placement of more cameras under the eaves of businesses along the street had been Taviano's idea. He was very good with electronics.

"Which implies . . ." Vittorio urged a response.

"The cameras each store owner was required to put in and maintain outside their buildings' fronts and backs were tampered with on the buildings up and down the alley. Someone knew those cameras were there, but didn't know about ours," Taviano explained.

"I can't believe Suzette wouldn't know what John was up to," Eloisa said. "She and John have always told each other everything. I can talk to her. We've been friends for many years."

Vittorio couldn't imagine his mother being friends with anyone, let alone for years. He didn't look at his sister, who had remained silent the entire time. John had been the one to help Emmanuelle learn to use a hammer and nails when she wanted to put up shelves in her bedroom herself. Of course, she'd gotten in trouble. Her parents hadn't praised her for the good job she'd done, that had been Stefano and the rest of her brothers.

Vittorio wished he was sitting closer to Emmanuelle, but he'd entered the room late and the only chair open was across from Stefano. That left Emmanuelle sitting between Taviano and Giovanni but across from Eloisa. Eloisa always targeted her daughter when she was upset.

"I had Emme talk to her," Stefano said. "She was able to get some information, but Suzette never saw the men who talked to John. She knew they had and she admitted to making the decision with him to deliver packages."

Eloisa scowled at Stefano. "You sent Emmanuelle to talk

to Suzette instead of coming to me first? John and Suzette have been my friends for years. It was my place."

"No, it wasn't. You're not thinking clearly, which is exactly why I didn't send you, Eloisa," Stefano said. "Emmanuelle handled it with sensitivity, although personally, I wanted to shake Suzette. She didn't think it was a betrayal to work for the Saldis because they didn't ask for information about us."

"Where were the packages delivered?" Vittorio asked before Eloisa could attack Emmanuelle, which she clearly was about to do.

"Suzette swore she didn't know. They were given to John after hours and he took them. She said we could follow the car's GPS. It was always on. John liked gadgets. The contents were downloaded by Rosina before the car was turned over to the police," Stefano said.

"She had no idea what was in the packages?" Ricco asked.

"No, John handled everything," Emmanuelle spoke for the first time. Her voice was tight, and she didn't look at any of them. "Suzette didn't want to know. She wanted the money, so she pretended what they were doing was all right. She claimed she didn't believe it was illegal or that it was a betrayal. She couldn't even say for certain someone in the Saldi organization had approached John. She didn't actually see or hear anything, because she wasn't there. John shared the information, so it's hearsay."

Eloisa made a sound in the back of her throat. Her eyes narrowed on her daughter. "You interrogated Suzette and that's what you got out of her?"

"Yes, Eloisa, that's what I got and those were my conclusions. Suzette admitted she wanted the money and she encouraged John to do whatever was asked of him. She didn't want to know what it was, but she wanted him to do it."

"That's ludicrous. What woman wouldn't want to know what her man was up to? Oh, wait, that would be you, my own daughter, having an affair with the enemy. What did you think Valentino Saldi was up to, Emmanuelle? Did you really think he *loved* you?" Eloisa's voice was a sneer. "Because you didn't notice all the other women in and out of his life? Because I noticed, and I believe I pointed them out to you."

"Eloisa." Stefano's voice was pure warning.

"No, let her," Emmanuelle said. "She may as well spew all her hatred and venom at me instead of anyone else. Maybe if she does it enough she'll find a way to be a decent human being." Her chin went up when she faced her mother. "You did point out all the women, thank you, Eloisa, and yes, I did think Val loved me. That was my mistake. But at no time did I betray our family. I'm not worried whether or not you believe me, I only answer to Stefano."

Eloisa opened her mouth to retaliate, her scowl of disapproval along with her flush at her daughter's sudden defiance darkening her skin.

Vittorio intervened. "That's enough, Eloisa. Emmanuelle has done nothing wrong. You've always disapproved of her . . ."

"Because you all *baby* her," Eloisa nearly screamed. Her hands were two tight fists on the table. "How is she going to be strong enough to have the tools to survive if you don't let her fall now?"

"Don't worry, Eloisa," Emmanuelle said in a very low tone. "I've fallen over and over. I got back up and I will every time. I'm a Ferraro first. I always will be. I don't regret loving Val. I don't believe loving anyone is wrong. He made the mistake, not me. It's his loss. I'll cope. But I didn't do anything or say anything that would have led to John's death." She made it an absolute statement.

Vittorio turned everyone's attention elsewhere before Eloisa could respond. "Until that investigation into the GPS on John's vehicle is complete, we're just spinning our wheels. What are we doing about Haydon Phillips?"

"The Grecos used the photographs to pinpoint Phillips's

location when he took them. There is always latitude and longitude embedded in the metadata," Stefano said immediately. "Apparently, he turned the location finder off, but didn't go into the file's properties to disable the GPS."

Vittorio frowned. "That doesn't make sense. He turned off the location finder so no one could see where the photograph was taken, but didn't go into properties to make certain the GPS feature was disabled? Phillips is thorough. I can't imagine him missing that."

"Not everyone knows everything about digital cameras," Taviano pointed out. "We have to keep up with the latest technology and we're always required to learn as it comes out."

That was true. It just seemed to be such a lucky break. On the other hand, Vittorio knew most of the serial killers apprehended were caught on a lucky break. Detectives could pore over evidence, but it was that one thing the killer didn't count on that tripped them up.

"The house is owned by a man by the name of Byron Fields. He's a lawyer for Beta Corporation, a business we do some work with. It's small, but they're very good. They gather data on other companies and sell it to anyone interested after their initial client has had their report for ninety days."

"Double-dipping," Eloisa said with a sniff of disdain.

"Or smart business practices. Sometimes a company, when they see the information up on an auction block, buys it back themselves," Giovanni said. "Beta Corporation has made some good money in the last few years. They've done well in the stock market. Their investigators are very good at finding out secrets."

"What's the plan?" Vittorio asked. He wanted to rush out that instant and make certain he could put an end to Haydon Phillips before the night was over.

"Byron's wife is a schoolteacher and she's at work. So is he. They have three children. One is in middle school and she's in her classroom. The boy is in elementary and he's in his classroom. The youngest is three and in preschool. She's being babysat at the house until noon and then she'll be taken to her school. The sitter won't pick any of the kids up until three and then she takes them to various after-school programs."

"It doesn't matter if the family is in the house or not," Vittorio pointed out. "We enter houses all the time with others in them. I can go now and get this over with."

"That's true," Stefano said, "but we need to know he's in there. We've got Raimondo with a broken-down car a block from the Fieldses' house. Hood's up and he's working on it himself."

"Raimondo?" Eloisa inquired.

Vittorio sighed. The bodyguards were all related. Close relations. It was so like Eloisa not to know them. "Raimondo Abatangelo. He's Tomas and Cosimo's younger brother. Good kid. Looks the part. Right age."

She sent him an exasperated look and put her hands in the air as if that wasn't enough information to clue her in. He knew better, but he rarely rose to Eloisa's bait.

"Raimondo sent word that a man appearing to be homeless entered the house after waiting until the sitter drove away. Raimondo is still there, watching to make certain he doesn't come back out, but here's the thing. The 'homeless' man had a key. He entered from a fenced-in side yard where the neighbors would be less likely to spot him. The dog barked but appeared to be tied up."

"Is that normal? The dog kept in the yard tied when it's fenced?" Ricco asked.

"Dogs can be escape artists," Giovanni said. "They dig."

Eloisa gave a little shudder. She'd never allowed her children to have pets of any kind. "How do you want this done?"

"Vittorio will take Phillips down," Stefano said. "We'll make certain the family stays away. If for any reason they look as if they are going home while Vittorio's there, we'll arrange a delay quickly. Taviano will back Vittorio up just for safety reasons."

"We can't have a dead man stinking up someone's home," Eloisa said.

"We'll leave him there and send an anonymous tip to the police in a day or two. All of us will need to be seen everywhere. We'll get looked at because we're tied to Phillips through Grace," Stefano said.

Eloisa rolled her eyes, but she didn't deliver one of her many barbs as they all stood up to go. She traveled by shadow back to her home and then Henry, her chauffeur, along with two bodyguards, took her downtown to shop.

Giovanni was the only one with a vehicle and he sauntered out to his car as if he didn't have a care in the world. Sasha was with Suzette and he drove straight over to the Balbonis' home and, in plain sight of every policeman watching, got out and went up the three brick steps to enter the house.

Stefano made his way home first and then got into a car with his bodyguards to be driven downtown. He made certain the window was down and his face could clearly be seen at every traffic stop. He entered the building across from Beta Corporations.

The others one by one did the same, each getting into a vehicle and going to a place of business near one of the schools where the children or their mother were. The Ferraro family members just had to be seen.

Vittorio went to Grace. "I'm going to be gone for a short time, *mi amore*. I'll be back as soon as possible. I would prefer that anyone making an inquiry be told that I'm not available as I'm on a conference call, but I'll be happy to speak to them as soon as I'm off."

She looked up at him with her clear, far too intelligent green eyes. "Do you expect company?"

"Not that I know of, but it is possible." He waited. She would be part of their world and that meant secrecy at all times. She couldn't tell a soul anything he told her. Trust worked both ways and he was trusting her with his life and the lives of his family members.

Grace was used to keeping secrets and she nodded slowly. "Just be safe, Vittorio."

"Always." He bent down and kissed her gently.

Grace kissed him back, surrendering immediately, giving him everything he could ask for. He tasted passion, but more importantly, he tasted love.

He turned away from her and went back to his room and changed his clothes from the casual ones he wore in the house, although those clothes were made of the same materials as his suits. No Ferraro would be caught out in public in casual clothes. He caught the nearest shadow that would take him, like a thoroughfare, into the city. The tube was fast, and he barely could make out the various branches he had to dive into in order to reach his destination.

He had to use smaller shadows for a short while, moving from one to the other until there was a large one he could take that led to the suburbs. The address was in a nicer part of the city. It was a gated community, which Vittorio found rather ironic since the family had a serial killer living in their attic. From what Rigina and Rosina had written in the report Stefano had sent to each of their burner phones, some of the pictures had been taken in other residences within that same small community. The residents thought themselves safer behind that gate, but they weren't.

He spotted Raimondo just down the street. How he had gotten through those gates was anyone's guess, but he was trained by the best and it would have been easy enough for any one of their bodyguards to find a way in that appeared legitimate should the cops ask any questions.

Standing across the street, Vittorio studied every shadow leading to the house. The dog had settled down and was very quiet. He didn't want to chance disturbing it. Sometimes, when they moved past, even though an animal couldn't actually see them, the sensation was so disturbing, the dog would bark ferociously, or in some cases, fearfully.

There were several shadows leading to the front door. He couldn't chance being seen; he would have to ensure whichever shadow he took would take him into the house. The blinds were drawn so there was no way of seeing inside. From across the street, inside the mouth of the tube, he couldn't hear anything that was going on in the house.

Making up his mind, he took a breath and stepped into the largest shadow cast from a tree in the front yard. At once the tube pulled him into what felt like pieces, his body flying apart. The sensation of the dark cylinder spinning around him, over his head and under his feet as he streaked through, added to the sickening feeling.

He shot through the tube, the speed hurling him through so fast it was difficult to see. They'd trained from the time they were little to see under dizzying conditions, a glimpse enough for their brains to catalogue and sort out where they were and what they actually saw. Right now, he was across the street, over the lawn, up the side of the porch to the front door and inside. Abruptly the shadow ended, and he was forced to put the brakes on too fast as he was nearly hurled onto the floor of the front room.

Vittorio waited until his body adjusted to the motionless position after the wild ride. He listened for a moment. The house was eerily silent. Once he heard a creak, but it wasn't overhead, as it should be. The noise sounded like it came from the back of the house. It was possible Phillips was moving around, making himself at home, now that the family was gone.

Vittorio stepped into a shadow that led from the front room to the hallway. The tube extended nearly to the back of the house, thrown by an overhead light left on, illuminating the way. He rode the shadow as far as possible and took one that brought him to the kitchen. The room was empty, but he could see this was where one of the entrances to the attic was. A trapdoor was built into the ceiling overhead. He could see the frame cleverly concealed by the design painted on the ceiling.

Vittorio took his time, ensuring that Phillips was in the attic and not somewhere in the house itself. He had already chosen his entry point for the attic and it wasn't from inside the house. He retreated, going back to the front and then traveling around the house to a side yard, away from the dog and herb garden. A tree cast a perfect shadow going up the side of the house to a large grate that vented the attic. He rode straight up and into the large area without hesitation.

Phillips had made himself at home up there. There was furniture, overstuffed chairs and a low couch that had seen better days. Food wrappers were scattered on the floor, and a half-opened cooler had food items in it. Water bottles full and empty were near the couch. Phillips lay on the sofa with his back to Vittorio, curled almost in the fetal position.

Vittorio stepped from the mouth of the shadow he was in to a smaller one that took him right up to the sleeping serial killer. This man, wrapped in rags, had killed several people, torturing them first. He had impacted Grace's life severely, terrorizing her deliberately. Vittorio stood in the shadows, hearing the sounds of the outside world, the cars going by. A lawnmower. Someone calling out a greeting to someone else. The world kept moving, but here in this attic, time had slowed.

He studied Phillips. He wasn't moving at all. Not a single muscle. There was no restless turning over. Strangely, he'd just arrived, not more than a few minutes before Vittorio and yet he was already asleep. Soundly. Vittorio started to move forward out of the mouth of the shadow, but an alarm skittered down his back and he locked himself into position, carefully studying the body.

The body. Phillips was dead. There was no rise and fall of the rags around him to indicate he was breathing. There was no sound to give it away. Vittorio took a careful look around the attic. There was no one else there, he was certain of it. He was alone with the body. He rode the shadow that would take him closest to Phillips. Out of habit, he didn't step from the mouth of the shadow, not wanting to leave any trace of his existence there behind.

He got very close, but stayed concealed, taking his time, examining the body. He leaned over it. Phillips's face was grizzled, his jaw covered in gray and black stubble. Lines creased his skin. Wrinkles. His nose was large and mottled from far too much alcohol. Vittorio's heart jumped. This man was definitely not Haydon Phillips. More, he had just died.

Haydon Phillips had known the photographs he'd sent to Grace would lead back to his hideout. He was certain the police would find his home in the Fieldses' attic. He had deliberately lured a homeless man to the house and then killed him, leaving the body for the police to discover when they got there. He had no idea the Ferraros were the ones tracking him.

He'd been there minutes before Vittorio, waiting for the homeless man, leading him up to the attic and then killing him quickly. Vittorio smelled blood mixed with alcohol. He leaned closer and immediately saw that blood had pooled beneath the victim, soaking into the couch cushion. His throat had been cut. Caught between his right sleeve and the back of the sofa was something that looked like a piece of paper, or a photograph. Vittorio debated, but then, because he wore gloves, removed the item.

Flipping it around, his heart dropped. The photograph had been taken at the Ferraro Hotel. It was taken in the foyer of the penthouse. Stefano's penthouse. Haydon Phillips had been inside Stefano's home.

CHAPTER EIGHTEEN

I don't like this," Vittorio said for the tenth time to Emilio. "There are too many people and no way to cover everyone."

Emilio looked at him with cool eyes. "My worst nightmare," he admitted. "I don't like that Stefano insisted I come to help protect the family here, when he's a sitting duck with Francesca in the hotel. She can't move fast. I doubt she would agree to make a run for it. And where is safe? That little bastard seems to be able to go anywhere he pleases without getting caught."

Vittorio took a slow look around him. Midnight Madness felt just as if it had been aptly named. The huge ballroom was decorated like the outdoors, the ceiling covered in stars, the heavy drapes covering the walls midnight blue with stars scattered over the tops of them like gems in the night sky.

Doors stood open in order to allow guests to spill outside onto the enormous patio where food and drink had been set up. The inside and outside areas merged seamlessly, and the music poured into both spaces without intruding. Vittorio knew it was that way because Grace had spoken to the band several times until she got exactly what she wanted.

Couples danced under the artificial stars with their luminous lights beckoning. He wasn't entirely certain how Katie and Grace had pulled it off, but the décor was elegant and beautiful, carved ice sculptures and flowing waterfalls with the same luminous lights as the stars had pouring into fountains.

The event was in full swing. Vittorio recognized most of their guests, celebrities from movies and television to powerful political figures. The Saldis had a presence. Of course they'd been invited. Midnight Madness was an annual charity event that raised several million dollars each year. Teodosiu Giordano was there as well, but he had merely said hello and drifted off with the lady he'd brought with him. Eloisa wouldn't leave out major contributors, although Giuseppi and Greta couldn't come due to Greta's illness taking such a toll on her.

Watching his woman work behind the scenes so that everything ran smoothly for their guests was an eye-opener. Grace didn't miss a beat. She was always polite. Always. She started with a smile, but when things didn't go *exactly* as she had specified, things quickly got done under her watchful eye. She orchestrated dozens of things for the guests, making certain their names were at the right table and they were seated beside those they particularly liked. She made certain enemies were tables apart. She had an eye for developing trouble and stopped it before it got out of hand.

"I've checked with Stefano numerous times," Emilio continued their conversation. "He says he's fine. He claims he doesn't believe Phillips made it into his home." There was a note of worry in his voice, something unusual for Emilio. "I personally went over the security measures at the hotel. If he did get in there, and the photograph was clearly of Stefano's foyer, he's much cleverer than I am. I couldn't figure out how he did it."

"They are being especially careful of anything Phillips might put in the vents that they could breathe in," Vittorio responded. His gaze remained on Grace as she talked animatedly with the caterer. Twice she clapped a hand on his shoulder and laughed, the sound even prettier to him than the music playing. "He thinks Phillips bribed one of the hotel maids into taking a picture of the foyer. Stefano is still investigating, but it sounds plausible, given all the security measures we put in place."

"This is the perfect place for Phillips to hit, far less risk. I wouldn't put it past him to go at Stefano and Francesca in the penthouse, but it is far riskier, especially now that he warned us. And why *would* he warn us?" Emilio asked. "He's tipping his hand. Why? Just to be able to thumb his nose at us? To show us how smart he is? Uh-uh, the slimy bastard is up to something."

"I think so, too," Vittorio said, frowning as Grace shifted closer to the caterer. It was very obvious she knew him well. He wasn't used to sharing her company with anyone, let alone other men. He'd never been a jealous man. He didn't think it was an attractive trait. To him, jealousy said one didn't trust one's partner. It also said the person feeling that emotion had little confidence. He was a confident man, but honestly? He didn't like the close proximity his woman was sharing with the man who had brought the food and beverages.

Vittorio began drifting toward Grace and the caterer. "Haydon Phillips is an intelligent man. He's astute and calculating as well. He wouldn't taunt us without a reason. He left that picture for us, not the cops."

"How did he expect you to see the photograph immediately? The cops might have played it close to their chests and not even showed you right away," Emilio pointed out. "Why would he think you'd get the message, whatever he was trying to tell you?"

"He called the murder in anonymously. He even reported

a strange car in the neighborhood and gave the license plate of Raimondo's truck. Luckily, Raimondo had a real reason for being there. His mother knew one of the women living in that gated community and she'd called to ask if our family knew anyone willing to do some yard work. She couldn't afford the price the gardener was asking and her yard needed work. Raimondo said the gardener was price gouging the elderly in the community."

A muscle ticked in Vittorio's jaw. He detested when anyone took advantage of the elderly. "I'll make certain the gardener knows not to do that again." He would pay the man a visit personally and the interview would be quite pleasant the first time. He would make it clear if he had to come back, it wouldn't be so pleasant the second time.

He studied the dancers as they whirled past him. He knew them all and nodded several times as he made his way to Grace's side. The moment he was there, he swept one arm around her waist, pulling her beneath his shoulder, even as he turned her to take her mouth with his. It didn't matter that she had perfect makeup and lipstick. He kissed her like he owned her. Hard. Hot. Possessive. She didn't fight him. She surrendered. The instant she did, he found himself caught in her spell and he gentled the kiss.

When he finally lifted his head, he didn't know who was more bemused, Grace or him. Either way, the kiss had done the trick. Those who witnessed it knew he was staking a claim on her. He wasn't the type of man to act in any way possessive toward a woman, not the way he was acting with Grace.

"Vittorio, this is Rene Bisset. He's one of the best chefs in Chicago."

Rene caught her hand and pressed his lips to it. "One of the best? I *am* the best. Don't let her fool you. She is trying to keep my ego from inflating my price."

"That's because your food is amazing, and you keep pricing yourself out of the running for my events and you're always my first choice."

Vittorio reached out, took Grace's wrist from Rene with exquisite gentleness and pressed her palm over his heart deliberately. "The food is delicious. It would be such a shame to lose you." His tone implied even more than his words.

The Frenchman snapped to attention, a smirk on his face. "I see this ring. It has blinded me." He reached for her hand again and this time, just studied the ring. "Magnificent. A ring befitting our girl."

Vittorio couldn't help smiling at Bisset's audacity. "Is everything the way you wanted it, Grace?"

"Of course. Rene never disappoints." Grace stroked the caterer's ego even more.

Bisset beamed. Vittorio, for no good reason he could think of, clenched his teeth. Rene reminded him of a slick shark, circling his woman. Instead, Vittorio gave him a charming smile and leaned down to look Grace in her eyes.

"Are you finished here, *mi vida*? Perhaps you have time to dance with your man."

Grace rubbed his chest, right over his immaculate tux. The one with the thin stripes. It was a distinctive design few wore—mainly the Ferraro brothers and Emmanuelle. Tonight, his sister wore a beautiful gown from one of the leading designers. It was made of a special fabric and had the same thin strips running through the black. The dress clung to her figure, and the fabric moved with every step she took, as if alive.

Vittorio could see Emmanuelle in the distance, making the rounds as he needed to be doing, making a point to talk to those with large bank accounts in the hopes that they'd open their pocketbooks and support the Ferraro causes. He didn't wait for Grace's reply but turned her toward the crowd milling around their assigned tables and making trips to the dance areas.

Inside the ballroom, nearly every couple was dancing. A few stood around the edges watching, but most took the opportunity to dance with one another. The music was upbeat but deliberately romantic, calling to anyone listening to get on their feet. Vittorio thought Grace may have put some form of compulsion in the décor and music because the night took on a magical quality as he walked with her through the crowd and out to the patio to get to his brother Taviano.

A tall blonde, a notable actress, stood close to Taviano. He had his arm around her waist and he bent down often to hear what she had to say. The two of them laughed often and naturally. They looked very much like a couple who were comfortable with each other.

"Anne Marquis looks stunning tonight," Grace said. She waved at several other couples, murmuring her hellos and calling them by name.

He should have known his woman would know the identity of every person attending the event. It was her event and her guest list. She had to have gone over it a hundred times. Not to mention, Eloisa tended to invite the elite every time, so her charity made a lot of money, but it narrowed the guest list.

"Anne has always been a favorite of our family," Vittorio said as they neared the other couple. They were stopped numerous times, and he knew that was because everyone wanted to see that it was true—he was engaged to Grace Murphy. "A really good friend."

"I'm glad Taviano is escorting her. They look so good together."

Vittorio scanned the patio in an effort to catch a glimpse of Anne's ex-husband. She'd been so in love with him and his betrayal had nearly wrecked her. She'd called Emmanuelle, who had gone over to her house and removed any pill that might tempt her to do something crazy in her grief. Then they'd stayed up for two straight nights talking. When Anne had fallen asleep, Emmanuelle had guarded her, taking phone calls and redirecting them to Anne's agent.

Her ex-husband, Moritz Mischer, the owner of a famous winery, had a piece of eye candy on his arm. The girl couldn't hold a candle to Anne. She was wearing a gown cut in a vee down the front all the way to her navel. The back had a similar cut to the very middle of her buttocks, but the back had thin strips of material, a ladder holding the back in place. Her laugh was overly loud, and she clung to Mischer and sent Anne poisonous glares.

Anne didn't look across the patio at them. She seemed completely absorbed in her conversation with Taviano. Emmanuelle made her way to the couple and the two women hugged. Vittorio noted with satisfaction that Mischer couldn't take his eyes off his ex-wife, who looked elegantly stunning as usual.

Candy Chardonnay had been the model Mischer's winery had hired to do commercials and posters. She'd legally changed her name to Candy Chardonnay when she'd begun her acting career in the porn industry. Moritz spent a good deal of time with her and when she'd offered him all kinds of favors he'd taken her up on them. Unfortunately, for him, Candy had also arranged a very public way for Anne to find out. The paparazzi just happened to be there when Anne opened the door, exposing Candy on her knees, her head in Mischer's lap. She had looked up and smiled for the cameras, a very distinct and iconic contrast to Anne's sorrow and horror and Mischer's shock. That contrast ensured the photograph was in every tabloid possible.

Mischer was unaware Candy was behind the exposure, but the Ferraro family, at Anne's request, had done an investigation. Rigina and her sister uncovered the phone calls Candy had made to the paparazzi, promising them a very juicy story on Anne and her husband. She had called Anne anonymously and told her she had to hurry to the winery, that Mischer was hurt. Anne had rushed there.

Vittorio continued moving Grace expertly through the crowd, winding his way toward his brother and Anne, all the while scanning every possible hiding place and checking out the caterers in their uniforms, balancing trays as they moved around the people, offering hors d'oeuvres. No one bumped into Grace. Vittorio protected her shoulder at all times.

"How are you feeling, *gattina*? I saw you pick up a few things that are heavier than the five pounds the doctor is allowing you."

She nodded. "I realized that at the last minute. I'm used to just getting things done without constantly asking for help."

He transferred his hand to the nape of her neck, smiling carelessly at a senator and his wife. He leaned down to focus completely on his woman, his body posture protective, showing his friends and family who mattered the most to him. "I'm not going to lecture you on following Doc's orders because clearly you're trying to. But I did see Eloisa pull you aside and talk to you. You didn't say a word to her, but I could tell from the way she looked that she was tearing strips off you."

Grace looked up at him, the expression on her face wary. "This is my business, Vittorio. You agreed I would handle my business. Your mother hired my company to put this event on and we pride ourselves on delivering exactly what the client wants. She ordered a plant called *Lotus berthelotii*, more commonly called parrot's beak, to be on every table and going up the trellises. The plant is gorgeous. The flower is known for its lobster claw–like petals that resemble a parrot's beak. We ordered them, of course, far in advance, but the plane carrying them lost an engine and had to make an emergency landing. There was no way to get them here in time, so we substituted another very rare flower of equal beauty."

Vittorio looked around him. Flowers were everywhere. They were beautiful and had a faint, elusive perfume that was subtle but added to the romance of the evening. The flowers were a blue-green hue, large vines hanging on trellises and down the ceilings in the ballroom, adding a tropical feel. Each table had a single clump floating in water with candles as a centerpiece.

"The jade flower is found in the Philippines and really is a vine, but the color, almost turquoise, is rare and beautiful. It was extremely difficult to get it flown in, but I know a few people, and for this worthy event, we made it happen. Katie knows how to sweet talk. In any case, parrot's beak flowers are a different color. Apparently, it was the color and not the rarity your mother would have preferred. We tried calling to ask her when we couldn't get the parrot's beak, but she didn't return our calls even when we said it was an emergency."

He brushed his fingers down her soft skin because it was impossible not to touch her. She wore her hair up, a red flame so intricate he longed to take it out, one pin at a time, and watch the strands fall around her. He had chosen her dress for her and there had been a minor protest, but it was beautiful, and she knew she would look amazing in it. The slip was from fabric made in France by the Archambault family, cousins of the famous riders. The green was a perfect match for her eyes and brought out their color and shine. Like the rider suits, the fabric seemed alive, breathing with every step as it clung to every curve, but was lightweight and stretchy.

The overlay was translucent with white embroidered roses scattered across the fishtail gown as it dropped to the floor. The green slip beneath was low across the curve of her breasts, but the translucent overlay had a rounded neck and long sleeves. The fitted silhouette was gorgeous, the slip contrasting with the embroidered lace. Scattered over the roses were tiny glimmering diamonds, catching the light to add glimpses of fire to the gown to match the fire in her hair. Vittorio knew Grace would never have touched the gown had she known the cost, but he knew it was perfect for her. He thought she was the most beautiful woman in the room. It was sexy and yet elegant, exactly as he'd envisioned her when he'd seen drawings of it.

He cupped her face, his hands framing the beauty there. "I appreciate that you think it's your job to put up with

Eloisa's bullshit, but it isn't. This isn't her event alone. The Ferraro family puts it on jointly. She might talk to the planners, but she can't fire them without the vote of the entire family. If you're worried about that . . ." His thumb slid over the little indentation on her chin.

She shook her head. "Eloisa lives for these events. She enjoys them, every step of the planning all the way to the final night. She has a vision and usually, it's one that is beautiful and successful. We might help her tweak it a bit, but she visualizes what she wants better than any other client we have. Each event has been better than the one before it and raised more money for her causes. If I have to put up with her haranguing me over flowers that should have been here, I'm okay with that."

He bent to brush a kiss over her upturned mouth, his heart clenching hard in his chest. "I know you're okay with it, but I'm not. You're mine. My woman. You're going to be my wife very soon. She doesn't get to abuse you any more than I want her to abuse my sister."

"Your mother vents. She expresses her frustration in anger. She isn't good at pulling her punches. It's clear she has few friends and no one to talk to when she doesn't understand what is happening around her. All of you are grown-ups now . . ."

"Don't think of her as being an empty nester." Abruptly he let his hands slip away from her face as he straightened, his mouth hard, his eyes warning her there were some things he wouldn't tolerate. Eloisa abusing her was one of them. "She never wanted children and when she had them, she didn't take care of them. She left that to her oldest son, who was barely school age. Eloisa doesn't see us as children."

"Maybe not, Vittorio, but when you were older, she interacted with you. She had someone to talk to."

"To criticize," he corrected.

She smiled at him and slipped her hand into his. "Perhaps that's her way of talking. In any case, as long as it pertains to this business, we're going to agree to disagree."

Vittorio swallowed down his decree. He shouldn't have made the bargain with her. He should have just announced he was the one in charge and gone on from there. Now he didn't have a leg to stand on, even when he knew how really bad Eloisa could get. Sasha hadn't put up with her continual criticisms, but Emmanuelle mostly did, which only encouraged Eloisa to leap on her daughter and tear her to shreds emotionally every chance she got. She did the same to Francesca. She tried with Mariko, but not often, respecting her as a rider. Now she had Grace to kick around, but Vittorio wasn't having it.

"I'm going to warn you this once, Grace. I might not have a say when it comes to your business. I don't like it, but I promised you, and I keep my promises. Any other time she gets out of line, I will be the one dealing with it. And I expect you to tell me immediately every single time it happens." He held her gaze until she reluctantly agreed.

They reached Emmanuelle, Taviano and Anne. Vittorio immediately introduced Grace to Anne. Anne held out her hand and Grace took it. "Such a pleasure to meet you. Vittorio has told me so much about you."

"None of it's true," Anne proclaimed with a wide smile. "You can't believe a word he says." She leaned over to brush both sides of Vittorio's face with a kiss.

Vittorio could see the sorrow in her eyes. "Have you been dancing yet?"

"We were just about to," Taviano said. "Would you care to join us?"

A very handsome man hovering near them smiled at Emmanuelle. "Dance with me, Emme?" He was tall, with dark hair and very dark brown eyes.

Vittorio tried to place him. He looked to be older than Emme by a few years. "You might want to tell me who you are before you take my sister anywhere."

The man turned to him. "I'm Elie Archambault. I was in the military with Demetrio and Drago, same unit. My father is French, my mother American. He died some years ago and she brought me to the States with her."

Vittorio recalled one of the famed Archambault riders dying of cancer some years earlier.

"My father was my mother's world. When he was gone she was so grief-stricken that I came with her," Elie added as if Vittorio would need more of an explanation. "She passed when I was eighteen. I joined the military and had a good career, but I was injured and had to leave. I needed a job when I got out, and Demetrio suggested I come here and train with Emilio as a bodyguard." He sounded almost bored, as if he'd repeated his story several times, and Vittorio was certain he had.

Elie had accompanied his grief-stricken mother home rather than have her be alone after her husband's death. Vittorio liked him more for that.

"You could have told all that to me, not my brother," Emmanuelle pointed out. There was clear suspicion on her face, as if she believed Elie had been ordered to ask her to dance.

Elie's cool dark eyes slid over her. "Your brother asked. You didn't." He turned on his heel and took a step away.

"Wait." Emmanuelle had to take several steps to catch up. "I would love to dance with you. I should have said so immediately, but you surprised me."

Elie turned back to her slowly, those dark eyes drifting over her. "You look beautiful. Like royalty. I don't know why you'd be surprised that a man would want to dance with you."

"You're aware of the possible situation going on tonight?" Vittorio asked.

"Emilio apprised all of us of it. I'm on a break. I wouldn't have asked her while I was working."

Out of the corner of his eye, he saw Emmanuelle let out her breath. She visibly relaxed at Elie's declaration. Vittorio tightened his fingers around Grace's hand and indicated Elie and Emmanuelle precede him to the ballroom. The music had changed to a slower, dreamy number and the moment the three couples were on the floor, Vittorio swung Grace into his arms. He'd been aching to hold her.

"I'm supposed to be working," she reminded, her voice muffled against his chest.

"You're supposed to be making sure your man is happy, which, at this very minute, he is." Vittorio brought her even closer, welding their bodies together so they flowed over the floor in perfect harmony.

If he could get lost when there was potential danger surrounding him, or anyone he loved, it would have been right there, in that moment. The music, the stars overhead, the fragrant turquoise flowers cascading on trellises from ceiling to floor, all added to the complete magic. He lifted his head for one moment to look around him at the other couples dancing. The event planners had created the perfect moment for everyone, giving them a chance to indulge in a romantic interlude with someone they were hoping to get to know better, or someone they loved.

Grace felt perfect up against him. Her body moved under the dress, a sensual flow that built a smoldering fire in the center of his groin and made for a lazy spread of heat through his veins. Her steps matched his flawlessly, but he didn't want to break the spell woven around them to ask her if she'd ever taken dancing lessons. She'd learned somewhere.

He noted his sister talking with Elie as her partner kept her safe from anyone bumping into her. For the first time in a long while, Emmanuelle looked relaxed and, if not happy, definitely interested in whatever Elie had to say. That was a good thing. He wondered if he should suggest to Grace that Elie be seated at Emmanuelle's table. He didn't look the part of a bodyguard. He was tall and lithe rather than sinewy, but Demetrio would never have suggested he look for a job with Gallo Security unless he thought the man was capable of working at the level Emilio would demand. He must have been taught to be a rider, with his father a famous member of the Archambault family. They were renowned as riders.

Vittorio moved his hand down Grace's back. His palm was hot against the thin material of her dress. He wanted to touch her skin so badly he could taste desire in his mouth. His cock pushed hard against her body, making it known how she affected him. She just seemed to melt into him, her body soft and flowing, surrendering to him, in just the way she did when she kissed him—or made love to him.

He whirled her around, so they were in the dark and his hand could slide over her tempting ass. He cupped her there and pressed her deeper into him. "You make me happy, Grace. It's that simple. I've never felt like this before."

She tilted her head to look up at him. "You make me very happy, too."

A couple came close and Vittorio spun Grace away from them, looking down to see who had gotten so near when they didn't need to. To his astonishment, Eloisa danced with a man who had worked for their family for years. Henry Watson had his arms around her, their steps absolutely in synch, as if they had been dancing together for years. He'd never seen his mother dance before. His father, Phillip, had danced at numerous charity functions, but never with his mother. Vittorio glanced at Taviano to see if he was witnessing what Vittorio considered a historic event. Grace and Katie had really created magic in order to lure Eloisa into a man's arms for a spin around the dance floor.

Taviano sent him a smirk and then nodded his head slightly toward the left. Vittorio rubbed his chin on the top of Grace's head and shifted his gaze in the direction his brother had indicated. Moritz Mischer danced with Candy. Candy was all over Mischer. She rubbed her body blatantly over him, her hands sliding up and down his as they moved together around the dance floor. He looked very uncomfortable. Her laughter was loud and to Vittorio's ears sounded taunting, as if she knew Anne was close.

Taviano turned Anne so she faced away from the couple. His hand twisted hers gently to bring it over his heart and as they matched steps perfectly, elegantly, he bent his head to hers and whispered in her ear. They appeared to be a couple in love.

"You Ferraros definitely know how to play to an audience," Grace said. "Anne is an actress so I expected her to look as if she was totally into your brother, but his acting skills are superb." She eyed him as though she thought he was acting.

Vittorio bent his head to kiss her. "Her ex is with the loud, very drunk woman dressed in purple just over there but getting closer." He whispered the information against her ear.

Grace turned her head and he whirled her around so she could get a better look. Candy teetered drunkenly on her heels and caught at the lapels of Mischer's jacket.

"I can't believe he traded Anne for that woman." Grace was outraged on Anne's behalf.

"He doesn't look happy. In fact, he's paying more attention to Taviano and Anne than to his date."

"He's a ridiculous man not to know what he had and treasure it. Anne and Taviano are seated at the Ferraro table. I hope all of you will look out for her."

Grace would have glared at Candy and Mischer, but Vittorio whirled her around once again, trying not to laugh. He knew his woman was a little stick of dynamite when she got going. He'd seen her furious.

"We'll definitely look out for her," he reassured.

"The goal with Taviano isn't to make her ex-husband jealous, is it? She doesn't want to get him back, right?"

Vittorio looked down at the anxiety and fierceness on Grace's upturned face. His heart did that curious melting thing he was becoming used to when he was around her. "You're such a ferocious little thing when you need to be. I think of you as my beautiful kitten, and then you roar, and I have to change my assessment. Are you saying if I made such a mistake as to allow another woman to tempt me . . ."

"Cheat, Vittorio, just use the right word. Break your vow. No self-control. It cheapens you as a man. I realize men in positions such as yours, men with power and money, have women throw themselves at them, but if a man took a vow and promised the woman he's supposed to love and respect above all others, and then cheats on her, he isn't worth anything. Nothing at all. It shows he isn't any kind of a man. So, no, I wouldn't take you back. I don't need a man to take care of me. I've been taking care of myself most of my life, even my own emotional needs. I'd walk away because I would always think less of you."

He loved her snippy little voice. She meant every word.

"My man could fail in business and I would never leave his side. But that? Cheating? It just says he's really nothing and he doesn't respect himself or me. I'd rather live on my own. I can support myself and be happy with my work."

He bent his head to press his lips against her ear. "What about sex?" His voice was deliberately sensual, and his lips brushed that little shell with every word. Grace shivered in his arms.

"There are really wonderful toys that make up for a *lot*, Vittorio, so if you're thinking of going down that cheating road, know that I will replace you with a girl's best friend."

"I thought that was diamonds." He swung her around, keeping their bodies between Taviano and Anne and Moritz and Candy.

Moritz was definitely trying to get next to Anne. Candy was louder the closer they got. Henry whirled Eloisa right between the couples, putting another obstacle in the way, thwarting Mischer's plan. Then Elie danced Emmanuelle between them as well. All the while, Taviano kept his head bent to Anne's as if they were having an intimate conversation and knew nothing about the drama playing out on the dance floor.

Vittorio felt eyes on him and he turned his head to meet Valentino Saldi's angry gaze. The man was furious. He glared at Vittorio, and then at Emmanuelle. Val didn't try to approach them, which was good. Vittorio didn't want a public fight on record, but there was no doubt in his mind that the Saldi heir was very angry with the way Emmanuelle and Elie danced together.

Elie made no bones about showing his interest in the princess of the Ferraro family. She was intelligent, beautiful, elegant, sensual and very lethal. Emmanuelle danced at fund-raisers all the time, but she never leaned into a man, or looked up at his face as if she wasn't aware of the dancers around her. She laughed at something Elie said, and Vittorio knew it was genuine. Emmanuelle didn't laugh often. None of them did, but he knew when she was acting, and it wasn't that. For the first time since she'd gone out to meet Val at the age of sixteen, she looked to honestly be interested in another man.

"I don't like the way Val is looking at Emmanuelle," Grace said softly. "It's too late to change tables. Emmanuelle always requested that the Saldis be seated at the table left of the Ferraro table. Val sat at the end, closest to where Emme sat. Those arrangements were never changed."

Vittorio cursed under his breath. "Are you certain you can't change the seating?"

"I'm sorry, honey, people are already sitting down. The food is being served and the silent auction will start. I wish I'd known."

"My mother knew." Damn Eloisa and her games. She thought she was driving home to Emmanuelle what happened when you allowed yourself to love the wrong person. Vittorio knew the risk was too great to take the chance of Val talking to Emmanuelle. Val had gifts. Maybe the others didn't acknowledge them, but Vittorio knew the Saldi heir had a voice similar to his own. He could charm and persuade. Emmanuelle was particularly susceptible to his voice.

Vittorio knew they could lose Emme. She would never betray her family, and she had too much pride to go crawling back to Val, but if she thought she would never be free to love anyone else, she might take her own life.

They lived with violence every day. It was never easy to get up and face what they did when they were alone. They all tended to live wild in order to combat that terrible emptiness that was always eating away at them. Emmanuelle was sensitive. Compassionate. She was romantic. If Valentino didn't leave her alone and allow her to find another good man, Vittorio knew their beloved Emmanuelle would take matters into her own hands.

"This is a bad scenario." Vittorio voiced his worry aloud.

"I could easily add Elie in the mix. Would Emmanuelle be upset if I did that?" Grace asked. "I think he's the kind of man that if you took him aside and explained that her ex is right on the end of the table, he would take Emmanuelle's usual seat and we'd move her one seat down. It would be difficult for Val to talk over the top of Elie."

He liked the plan. Emmanuelle might not, but Elie would do it. He was in the employment of the Ferraros whether he knew it or not. All the businesses eventually were under a Ferraro umbrella.

"Let's do that," he agreed.

Grace started to slide out of his arms, but he tightened them around her. "Wait until the end of the song. I'll get us close to Emme and Elie and explain what you're going to do. You slip away at that point and get it done."

She nodded. "No worries. I just have to get to the kitchen and print up a name plate on our fancy gold and silver paper. Give me five minutes."

Vittorio shot another glance at Valentino. The man hadn't taken his furious gaze from Emmanuelle. He clearly was willing her to look up and spot him. Beside Val, his cousin and bodyguard, Dario, was also looking at the couple. It was clear he was angry as well, but his gaze was on Taviano.

Grace was looking, too. "The man with him seems very upset at Taviano."

Vittorio wasn't surprised that she noticed. She had to be alert and observant when she was constantly worried that Haydon Phillips would show up in her life any minute and take her world away from her.

"Thàt's Dario Bosco, Val's first cousin. He's Miceli's son, although Miceli never married his mother. He often bodyguards for Val, although he's also an heir apparent to the Saldi empire. He has a bit of a thing for Nicoletta. Taviano told him to back off, that he was engaged to Nick."

Her eyebrow shot up. "Is he?"

"Not yet, but he will be."

"I love these events," Grace said. "All the drama and undercurrents of a play or a movie. I should write books."

"An exposé on the Ferraro family," Vittorio said, but he didn't really feel the humor. He'd had too many years of the paparazzi invading his life and trying to ferret out every secret his family had.

"Not your family. You're not nearly as wacked as some."

Grace's voice rang with truth and he was immediately intrigued, looking around the room as if he might spot the craziest of their circle.

Her laughter should have elevated his mood, but the knots in his gut began to tighten. To magnify. The music faded and reluctantly he allowed Grace to slip from his arms. He preferred to keep her right at his side, but when it was impossible, he had several of their guards with eyes on her at all times. Nevertheless, he texted them to ensure they took over watching the woman he loved.

He made his way to Emmanuelle and Elie, who were standing on the edge of the dance floor talking in a low tone.

"I hate interrupting," he said as they both looked up.

"Where's Grace?" Emmanuelle asked immediately, scanning the room.

Vittorio knew the moment she spotted Val and Dario at the entrance to the ballroom. She flicked them a quick look and then her gaze went straight to her brother's face. "You're here because of them."

"Grace and Katie didn't know to change the table arrangements."

Emmanuelle scowled. "I reminded Eloisa."

"The reminder wasn't passed on."

Emmanuelle looked down at her feet. Vittorio willed her to come up with the solution herself. He didn't want to put her on the spot, not if she really was interested in Elie. He knew if she was, and Vittorio forced Elie to sit with her, she would be stilted and standoffish.

"I'm sorry," Elie said. "I don't know what's going on, but if I could help in any way, I'd be happy to do so. And if you'd rather talk privately . . ." He indicated he would walk away.

Emmanuelle didn't drop her hand from where it was tucked into the crook of his arm. She looked up at him and took a deep breath. "I know I'm acting like a coward, but I would very much like it if you would sit at our table with me during the meal. I'm sure Emilio would approve. Vittorio can ask him."

Elie's gaze didn't leave Emmanuelle's face. "The reason?"

Vittorio liked that he didn't just simply agree. He wasn't a man to be pushed around. Emmanuelle definitely needed to be with someone strong.

"I've been seeing Val Saldi on and off for several years. Recently, I broke up with him after finding out some very disturbing things. They were facts, I don't listen to gossip. In any case, he's been trying to explain things to me and I don't want to hear his explanations. If you would prefer not to get mixed up in my mess, I understand completely."

Elie was silent a moment, studying Emmanuelle's face. Vittorio knew what the bodyguard saw. His sister was beautiful. Right now, she looked vulnerable, almost fragile. He couldn't imagine any man passing up an opportunity to help her.

"It would be a pleasure to have dinner with you, Emmanuelle," Elie said. "Let's go find our seats."

CHAPTER NINETEEN

Vittorio seated Grace beside him at the elegant table with its tropical rain forest centerpiece that included the turquoise flowers from the Philippines. Grace was very uncomfortable and had tried to get out of sitting with him several times. It was their first real argument, and, in the end, there was no way to compromise—he wanted Grace by his side at the family table and she complied with his wishes.

He understood. She was working. This was one of KB Events' largest functions. Grace didn't sit and eat with the patrons, she worked. She made certain everything ran smoothly behind the scenes. He wanted it understood by her and everyone else that she was with him. She was a Ferraro for all intents and purposes and everyone—especially his mother—needed to give her that respect at all times or they would be dealing with him. No matter the argument she used, he refused to budge when he knew she was in terrible danger. He knew she couldn't be there long, but even a few minutes would establish in everyone's mind what he needed. Then, he planned to be at her side when she worked.

He dropped his hand to her thigh beneath the cover of the spun lace tablecloth. She looked up at him, touching the tip of her tongue nervously to her upper lip and then biting down on her lower lip. He leaned down and brushed a reassuring kiss on her mouth. He loved her mouth and was tempted to kiss her the way he wanted, but technically, with her working, he needed to show some restraint.

He rubbed her thigh over the lace and slip, feeling the heat of her skin and the way the muscles beneath the material jumped and quivered. "Nice solution, *gattina*. Thank you. I want Emmanuelle to enjoy herself as much as possible."

She had added Elie Archambault to the table seamlessly, his name on the elegant foiled paper as if it had always been there. There were five couples at the table and she'd exchanged Eloisa's and Henry's place cards for the end of the table nearest the Saldi table and had given Emmanuelle and Elie the two places across from Vittorio and Grace. Anne and Taviano were across from Sasha and Giovanni.

"Nice arrangement. I approve wholeheartedly."

"Eloisa is always very specific about where she wants to sit," Grace said, looking the epitome of innocence. "Under the circumstances, I knew she would want to help her daughter, so I exchanged her place with Emmanuelle's."

As if she heard, his sister looked up and blew Grace a kiss. Eloisa and Henry walked up behind Emmanuelle and Elie. Vittorio noted his mother and Henry were holding hands. She scowled as she peered at the names etched in the golden nameplates. Her scowl deepened as she looked across the table at Grace. Vittorio held his mother's stare, daring her to make a public issue of the change. Henry said something and tugged at her hand. She went with him to the two open chairs at the end of the table.

Talk swirled around them. Giovanni and Sasha engaged with Emmanuelle and Elie while Taviano and Anne began a lively conversation with Eloisa and Henry.

"I feel as if the entire event is going to fall apart because I'm sitting here instead of watching everything from a distance," Grace murmured somewhat rebelliously.

"Be patient. You hired three extra people to help Katie with just this moment. You have your cell right there. In another few minutes you'll be able to go around and check every detail for the auction."

She glanced at her watch and then nodded.

He took her hand, noting that it was shaking, and pressed it to his thigh, high up, close to his wayward cock that was already reacting to the close proximity of any part of her. He rubbed his thumb over the back of her hand.

"I love watching you work, Grace. I think what you do is worthwhile and you're extremely good at it. Bottom line, you're my woman and when we attend any event, one of yours or someone else's, you're going to be by my side or I'm at your side. Either way, we're together. I don't mind going with you to check all the details you need to attend to."

He didn't pretty up the demand. He had warned her what he was like. She had known before she ever agreed to really give them a chance. He would dictate in certain matters. This was a big one. He'd said her work belonged to her, and it did, but at any big event such as this one, he would be at her side.

"I'm well aware that this is something that really matters to you, Vittorio, or you wouldn't be pushing so hard. I'm giving this concession to you because I want you happy." She cupped the side of his face. "That's important to me."

Her thumb slid over his lips and he sucked it into his mouth, his tongue swirling around it. She blushed.

"Vittorio." His mother said his name in a way that might mean a reprimand, or just a way to get his attention.

He took another moment to enjoy scraping his teeth over the pad of Grace's thumb and watching the color rise in her face. He moved her hand higher up on his thigh, so her fingertips touched his throbbing cock just because he loved the color sweeping into her face.

"Yes, Eloisa? I missed what you were saying, but if it's about the decorations, I agree completely, the entire thing is beautiful. More than beautiful. It feels like a fantasy land. I especially love the jade plants. The color is amazing and the way they drape down from the ceiling is pure genius." He turned back to Grace. "Did you think of that, *bella*?"

"I love those flowers as well," Emmanuelle said. "Eloisa, was that your choice? She always chooses the flowers, Vittorio. Her ideas are so good she should be a designer." The compliment was genuine. Emmanuelle had no idea there had been any problems with the flowers.

"Eloisa always wanted to be a designer," Henry said. "For as long as I can remember, she was brilliant at it. Of course, you were never allowed."

"Henry." Eloisa's tone was different. Almost an admonishment, but not quite.

Servers were putting plates of food in front of guests. Eloisa waited until they were gone. "Originally, I had ordered a flower called parrot's beak, but the plane lost an engine. Grace substituted the jade and the color is exquisite. I couldn't have found a better second choice myself. She's done enough events for us that she knows my tastes."

Grace blushed again, but Vittorio wasn't certain whether it was from his mother's unexpected compliment or the way he had picked up her hand, nibbled at the fingers for a moment and then, once again, taken it under the table to place her palm over the burning thickness of his hefty erection. The moment Grace touched him, his cock jerked in response.

He picked up a fork. The food at the events KB planned

was always first class, which was a plus. "Is there anything in the auction lots that you particularly liked, Grace?"

She sent him a smoldering look of pure reproof, but she didn't pull her hand away. She picked up her fork as well. She'd had a lot of practice eating with her nondominant hand and did so smoothly. She started to answer him, but she abruptly closed her mouth, pressing her lips together. He laughed. She retaliated by stroking caresses over his aching cock.

Out of the corner of his eye, he saw Emmanuelle's gaze go in the direction of the Saldi table. Immediately, his sister looked away, her color rising just a little as if she couldn't control it. Elie picked up her hand and began absently playing with her fingers.

Vittorio gazed directly at Val, hoping to warn him off with a look. Val was watching Elie's fingers moving over Emme's with a look of something close to pain. He started to rise, and the woman seated next to him put her hand on his arm and leaned in, her breast resting on his arm as she whispered in his ear. Val didn't turn to look at her, he kept watching Emmanuelle and Elie and now there was anger.

Elie wasn't overdoing his part. He didn't kiss Emmanuelle or act as if they were intimate lovers; rather, he acted like a man extremely interested in the woman he was with. Val wasn't doing either with the woman he'd brought. He was acting like a jealous ex-lover who wasn't about to let his woman get away without a fight—and that worried Vittorio.

He shot a look at his brothers. All of them had noted Val's expression. Normally, Valentino Saldi wore an expressionless mask, or he looked cool under fire. He wasn't a man to show emotion, but he made it clear he didn't like another man near Emmanuelle and he didn't much care who was observing him.

Trouble was coming, and they all needed to be ready for

it. Grace was up and handling all kinds of details. Vittorio stayed at her side, but kept silent, watching her work, admiring her skills in fixing every problem that came up.

Throughout dinner and the auction, where Vittorio dumped a ton of money, reports came in continually. No one had seen Haydon Phillips. Ricco and Mariko were with Francesca and Stefano at the penthouse, along with their cousins. Lucca, Gino and Salvatore had come at their call, just as always. Even though all of them were trained shadow riders and should be able to adequately protect Francesca, Vittorio didn't like the fact that he wasn't there as well.

Haydon should have made his move by now if he was going after Grace. Grace had spent the first couple of hours going from the kitchen to the ballroom to the patio, ensuring everything was perfect. She walked without an escort on several occasions, although bodyguards were close. Vittorio joined her only after she signaled that she had gotten most of her work well under hand.

During the time when Grace was doing her job, no one had spotted anyone who even was a possible for Phillips. While he was glad that Phillips had stayed away from Grace's function, it meant that the odds of him attacking Francesca had gone up. That didn't mean that they would be less alert at the Midnight Madness event; in fact, Vittorio wanted his security force to double their vigilance.

With dinner and the auction over, the dancing started again. Grace glanced down at her phone and whispered to Vittorio she needed to check in with Katie. She had to make certain everything was functioning properly in the kitchen. He turned to go with her when there was a disturbance behind him. Catching her arm to prevent her from leaving, he turned back.

Val Saldi came up behind Emmanuelle the moment Elie stepped away from her to check in with Emilio to see where he was to be stationed. Grace was the prime target and Vittorio wanted the bodyguards positioned heaviest around her, but Phillips had made it clear he would kill any of the people helping her or befriending her. Emilio, as head of security, had a different view. Riders were always their first priority. Vittorio and his family were number one on that list.

Val caught Emmanuelle's arm, pulling her to a halt. "I want to talk to you."

"That's not going to happen." Emmanuelle's chin went up and she tugged gently at her arm but refused to make a scene by yanking it away. "Let go, Val. I think I made myself more than clear."

"This isn't just about us anymore," he hissed. "Don't you see what's happening?"

Vittorio let Grace slip out of his grasp, but he glanced at Eloisa. She nodded and shadowed Grace as his woman hurried toward the kitchen. "Valentino, let go of her."

Taviano gently put Anne to one side. Giovanni did the same with Sasha. Sasha slipped her arm around Anne's waist. The two women stepped back at Sasha's urging, to give the men more room as Val's bodyguards moved into position to defend their boss.

Val ignored Vittorio, his eyes on Emmanuelle's face. "I'm asking for a few minutes of your time, for a chance to stop a war between our two families."

Emmanuelle held up her hand to stop her brothers from closing in. "That will be the *only* thing we talk about, Val," she decreed.

She moved a few feet away from her brothers, but sent them an imploring look, making certain they were close in case she might need them.

"We had nothing to do with those deaths, Emme. Nothing. Giuseppi would have come to tell you himself but Mom—Greta—has taken a turn for the worse. I'm heading there as soon as I'm done talking with you, but it was important for you to know, to believe us, that we aren't starting a war. We don't know who's doing this any more than you do."

"I'm very sorry about Greta. I know she's been a wonderful mother to you, Val," Emmanuelle said sincerely. "As for the dead bodies turning up in our dumpsters, every one of them was a friend. Bruno? Bruno Vitale? His grandmother has no one now. He was a kid."

"My point, Emme. Giuseppi doesn't order hits on kids. And they aren't tortured and wrapped in carpets and put in dumpsters. I don't know who is doing this, but someone wants a war between our two families."

"They were all working for your family," she pointed out quietly. She gave another flick of her eyes over her shoulder to ensure her brothers were close. It was only at that moment that she seemed to be aware he hadn't let her arm go. She took a step back. "Stefano gave your father the list and proof."

Val pulled her closer to him. "Stop that. Don't piss me off any more than I already am. This is important. Yes, they maybe worked for my family. We have people on the inside, you have people on the inside, it's an accepted practice, which is why, if they get caught, no one kills them. They don't know anything. That's the way it works. You know that, Emme."

She was silent a moment and she'd quit fighting his hold on her. Val had managed to pull her almost into his body. Vittorio took a step closer. His brothers followed his example. Dario stepped directly in front of Taviano, stopping him. Vittorio signaled Taviano, who had a notorious temper, to stand down.

Val was right. The subject matter was too important to stop the talk before they could all hear what he had to say. He'd made a good point. Not one of the men employed by the Ferraros or working in the neighborhood taking money from the Saldis would be privy to any information on the Saldi crime empire. Not a single one. So why were they killed? And why be tortured? If it wasn't the Saldis starting a war, who was it?

"You have a valid point," Emmanuelle conceded. "I know

you have to get back to Giuseppi and Greta immediately. I'll take what you said to Stefano and he'll be in touch."

She turned as if to go, but Val tightened his fingers around her wrist. "I'm not finished, princess. You heard something you shouldn't have, and you refuse to let me explain."

Emmanuelle turned white. "Let go of me right now, Valentino. Don't count on the fact that I don't like public scenes. I don't want to be anywhere near you. You had your fun. You followed your orders and you were damn good at seduction. Of course, it probably wasn't that difficult. I was sixteen. I should have let my family kill you."

"Do you feel better now? We're not going to get anywhere if you don't listen. That man you were with isn't going to do a thing for you and you know it. I want you to meet with me, just the two of us . . ."

Emmanuelle looked over her shoulder, her eyes pleading with her brothers to save her. Vittorio would never forget that look as long as he lived. Emmanuelle was so in love with Valentino Saldi, she feared, even after everything she'd heard him say—that he didn't love her, didn't want her, that he'd seduced her following orders from his father—she wouldn't be able to resist his demand.

Vittorio moved instantly, mowing down the bodyguard who stepped in front of him. Nothing would stop him from getting to his sister.

Grace entered the kitchen and found total chaos. Rene Bisset, the head chef, was yelling at two of the waiters at the top of his lungs, switching from English to French periodically. The two waiters clearly were denying that they were the ones who had smashed all the dishes. The windows were broken, and food and the broken pieces of hundreds of plates were everywhere. The counters, the walls and the floor weren't spared.

"Rene, calm down," Grace said, keeping her voice quiet

and low. "It looks like a war zone in here. I doubt that these two are to blame."

"There is no one else," Rene insisted. "I was gone only a moment." He threw his hands into the air and made several gestures impossible to read. "Perhaps five minutes. I had an important phone call. Five minutes and I come back to see this room destroyed and with it all of my dishes. Everything." He toed a broken bowl and glared at the servers and then glared at her. "The music is so loud, I couldn't hear myself think, let alone someone breaking everything."

Both servers put their hands up in surrender, but they weren't looking at Rene or Grace, they were looking over her shoulder to Eloisa. Grace half turned and as she did, Eloisa cried out and hit the floor hard, blood matting her hair and pooling under her head. There were no body-guards in sight. Had Emilio pulled them off to protect the riders, or had Haydon Phillips targeted them and hurt them already?

"Haydon?" Grace stared at the face she was so familiar with, yet looked so different she barely recognized him. He was dressed in a suit and tie, a short well-trimmed beard and mustache almost making him unrecognizable. He fit into the very elite crowd of wealthy sponsors and benefac-tors of the Ferraro fund-raiser.

"Not Haydon. It's Emerson Caldwell. Eloisa Ferraro's assistant put me on the guest list herself. Coming from Cal-ifornia, I didn't know many people out here and she was just the person to arrange for me to meet friends—which I did. Everyone seated at the table I was assigned to was very nice."

Casually, he aimed the gun at one of the waiters and pulled the trigger. He shot the other one in the same knee as he had the first. In spite of the silencer, the gun sounded like a one-two shot and she hoped one of the bodyguards was close enough to hear over the loud music and conversations taking place in the ballroom and on the outside patio. She was terrified for them.

Both men went down screaming but when Haydon shook his head, they stopped, one with his hand over his mouth to prevent any more sound. Grace looked down at Eloisa. She moved slightly, but Grace didn't want to call attention to her by crouching down to see how bad the head wound was. She shifted slightly to put her body between Haydon and the others.

Haydon laughed harshly. "Always the heroine, aren't you, Gracie? Come on, we're blowing this place. I've got us a car. They'll never find us."

Her worst fear. "I'm not going with you this time, Haydon. You tried to sell me." She didn't know what to say to stall him, but she had to give Vittorio time to come get her. She knew he would, and she had faith that he would be able to use his training to take control.

Haydon, at her declaration, turned and shot Rene. This time, the bullet went into his chest and he dropped, gasping. Haydon smiled at her. "I didn't kill anyone, Gracie. That should make you happy. Well, with the exception of Ferraro's mama. She's going to die. I hate that bastard. He can't keep you away from me."

He stepped closer to get around her to get a better target on Eloisa. Grace could see her eyes were open and she was taking in everything Haydon said.

"If you want me to go with you, the only way I'll do it is if you don't touch Eloisa. You leave her alive, right here. I mean it, Haydon. I'll let you shoot me, but I won't go."

"Rene there needs medical attention right now, Gracie. Do you want him dead? Because I can make that happen."

Grace folded her arms across her chest. Her engagement ring felt like a talisman on her finger. She pressed it close to her chest. She wasn't trained the way Vittorio or the members of his family were, but she was stubborn. Haydon knew it, too.

"You kill any of them, Haydon, and we'll all stay right

here. Me with them." She knew in terms of time, although it felt like hours to her, only a few minutes had gone by, maybe at most three. She could hear the shouting outside growing louder and her heart sank. No one was going to hear the gun if Haydon shot them all.

He cursed over and over, swearing at her, taking a step toward her and raising the weapon as if he might strike her with it the way he had Eloisa.

"Why don't you just go on your own?" She risked taking a beating or getting shot to stall him. Vittorio would come. She knew he would. She had complete faith that he would. She repeated the mantra to herself over and over. Now she was convinced that Haydon had targeted the guards watching her and Eloisa. She just didn't know how.

Haydon looked genuinely puzzled. He indicated the door with the barrel of the gun. "We always go together. We're a team. Get moving. Hurry, Gracie."

She went in the direction he told her, and Haydon turned to follow her. Eloisa was up and on him, reaching to twist his neck in the classic Ferraro manner. Haydon whipped around before she could make the kill. Rene's eyes had gotten big and he held his breath when he'd been continuously moaning. Just that small difference had tipped Phillips off.

He slammed the gun across Eloisa's face and stepped back to pull the trigger. Grace leapt onto his back, her fingernails ripping across his eyes. He screamed, and the gun went off repeatedly, as if his finger was stuck in the trigger. He ran backward and slammed Grace into the wall. Her head hit a cabinet and pain exploded through her.

Eloisa ran at Haydon as he reached back to punch Grace in her injured shoulder. She threw herself on the floor at the last second, sliding, trapping Haydon's legs in hers and rolling to take him down. Haydon bent forward, throwing Grace on top of Eloisa as he stumbled. He recovered enough to kick Eloisa hard in the ribs. Aiming the gun at her, he pulled the trigger repeatedly, but nothing happened. Grace forced herself up to face him. Four minutes. Where were the bodyguards? Vittorio? His brothers?

Haydon grabbed her by her hair and began dragging her toward the door. As he did, he took a small remote control from his pocket and hit the green button. Instantly a flurry of explosions went off in the kitchen, and flames crawled up the wall and over the cabinets.

Using the intricate updo she was wearing to pull her, Haydon yanked until she had no choice but to stumble after him. Both hands went to her head to try to force his hand back down to her scalp, so he couldn't pull, but he was moving so fast she tripped and went down. As she did so, Eloisa came out of nowhere, emerging from a shadow behind Haydon. Blood streamed down her face and into her eyes. It didn't look like she could possibly see let alone stand.

"Run, Grace!" Eloisa called as she launched herself at Haydon. "Get out of here."

Haydon still had the gun in his hand and as he turned toward her, he used it like a bat, swinging it blindly. He hit Eloisa almost in the same place as the first time. She went down hard, her body crumbling like a rag doll. She didn't even attempt to break her fall, telling Grace she was unconscious or dead.

Haydon turned his attention to Grace. She had already put several feet between them. Very slowly she crouched down and, watching him the entire time, unbuckled the straps to her heels. She stepped out of them.

"You can chase me, Haydon, and you'll probably catch me, but by now, everyone is in that kitchen putting out the fires." *Stall, stall, stall.* Vittorio would come.

"First they have to attend to the guards I left in the garden. Then they have to break down the door. After that, they'll be trying to save the chef and the two idiots who work for him." There was taunting laughter in his voice.

"Grace!" It was Vittorio, and relief swept through her.

"Out here. He's out here and he's hurt Eloisa."

Haydon punched her hard. Her cheek seemed to explode, and she went down, her legs wobbly. He caught her chin. "I'll be back, and I will kill them all." Then he was gone.

The night itself seemed to swallow him, protect him, give him a way to hide when no one else could. Sirens sounded in the distance, but it was too late if the cops were coming. Haydon had once again gone free.

Mi amore. Grace." Vittorio crouched down beside her. Heart pounding, he wiped at the blood and tears running down her face. There had only been four men on Grace and Eloisa. All were unconscious or coming around. Not one was one of their primary guards. He was going to kill Emilio for sending their most experienced bodyguards to aid the riders. He should have known Emilio would have done so. His job above anything else was to protect the riders. Eloisa didn't want that privilege any longer. She had taken the job of a greeter, relinquishing her job as a rider, unless there was a need, therefore, the bodyguards wouldn't be as worried about her.

"He got away."

His hands moved over her, noting every wince. "Not necessarily. I don't want you to move. Don't try to get up. I'm going to check out Eloisa."

"I need to know if she's all right, Vittorio. She saved me more than once."

That would be just like his mother. She would bitch about their choices, but she would defend and fight for every one of them. She'd give her life if it was necessary. He crouched down beside her and gently examined the head wound. It was deep, and it was pouring blood. They'd already summoned ambulances for the wounded in the kitchen. He texted the others. He needed to go hunting and couldn't do so until his brothers and sister were there for Grace and Eloisa.

Taviano and Emmanuelle arrived almost instantly. Emmanuelle rushed to Eloisa with a little cry. Taviano stood back waiting for Vittorio to tell him what he wanted done, but his gaze was on his mother's body.

"Is she alive?"

"Barely. She needs to get to the hospital. I've texted Stefano. He'll meet you there. I want you with Grace at all times. I don't care what crap they give you, don't leave her side."

Taviano nodded. "Good hunting."

"I won't miss."

He stood up and as he did so, he brushed a kiss on his sister's cheek. "She's strong, Emme. She'll pull through."

Vittorio went to Grace and crouched down. "Taviano will be with you. I'm going after Haydon."

"He's dangerous, Vittorio. He might turn back and hunt you. That's the kind of thing he does."

Vittorio kissed her gently, cognizant of her injuries. When he rose, he glanced around, saw Emilio and Enzo closing in. He stepped into the nearest shadow. It swallowed him up, pulling apart his body brutally, tearing at him, but he controlled the ride and forced his eyes to watch for signs of passing.

Haydon had to have gone straight out to the front gate. A fence surrounded the property. It was ornate, made of wrought iron, the spikes twisting high into the sky like braided spears. He could see faint streaks of light as if the man had left behind prints. They didn't appear like footprints, there were mere faint bluish lights, more of a blob-line than a print, but every person left them behind and from shadows he could see them. He couldn't spot the imaging once out of tube, but the shadows acted as if he was seeing through a thermal lens.

Haydon's prints, like every individual's, were unique. Vittorio knew he would always be able to spot them. The heat images faded fast, so he had to ensure he was close on the killer's heels. Sometimes, if they were lucky, a person left behind skin cells, evidence of their passing that could be used, but they were much harder to spot when riding the faster tubes.

Vittorio stepped from one shadow to the next, following Haydon as he ran down the street leading to the main highway. Haydon had slowed his run, Vittorio could tell by the length of his strides. He went from one parked car along the street to the next, clearly looking for one to steal.

Vittorio deliberately chose a smaller shadow. They were much faster and harder on the body, ripping him apart and hurtling toward the end of the street where the blue, blobbish streaks seemed to suddenly disappear. He could see faint imaging indicating a body moving around the corner in a vehicle. He followed, jumping from one shadow to the next, finding several that took him almost to pace alongside the car, so he could make sure he was following the right man.

Haydon Phillips drove at a reckless speed, clearly furious, off his usual cool and deliberate game. He depended on Grace. She was, in essence, his family. He needed her, and in his sick fantasy, she was part of his world. She supported him, just as they'd supported each other when they were children together. He might get angry at her, but in the end, in his mind, it was the two of them against the world.

He drove too fast and carelessly, weaving in and out of traffic. Vittorio twice tried to find a shadow that would take him directly into the vehicle, but even going beneath the glaring streetlights, and using the fastest tubes, it was impossible. He couldn't do anything but keep up with him.

With a sinking heart, Vittorio knew the inevitable happened. The siren sounded faint at first, a strange, waffling noise heard as more of a muffled *wap wap wap* inside the fast shadow he rode. The red and blue lights cut through the dark of the night as the law enforcement vehicle cut through the cars on the road to settle behind Haydon's stolen car.

There was no way to warn the policemen that the man they were pulling over was a very desperate serial killer. Haydon glanced in his rearview mirror, cursed and spat, then hit the steering wheel several times. He slowed the car and began to pull to the side of the road. The police car behind him slowed as well and pulled to the slower lane in order to get directly behind Haydon's car again.

Haydon suddenly accelerated and took the first exit available to him. His car fishtailed and then raced around the long curve leading back to a heavier-trafficked area. Vittorio was forced to step out of the small shadow and catch another to reverse his direction. The police car followed, but now they were a distance behind.

Haydon rounded the corner so that for a few seconds he was out of sight of the patrol car. He slammed on the brakes, opened the door and jumped onto a grassy section of the sloping embankment. The car continued forward at a rapid speed, gaining momentum as it rolled down the hill toward the traffic.

He lay prone in the grass as the cop car swept around the curve, sirens blaring. As soon as the vehicle was past, Haydon was up and running toward the buildings on the outskirts of the suburb. The houses were smaller with neat yards and shared fences. Haydon managed to vault the low fences and not even break stride.

Vittorio had to admire him. He clearly stayed in shape. He could assume the role of anyone he chose, and he played that person to the hilt. He'd sat through a dinner at the fund-raiser with many of the most astute businessmen on the planet, yet he hadn't been caught out in his disguise. He'd approached four trained bodyguards, clearly believable in his role. One by one he had taken them out. He'd outsmarted the police and now he was clearly going for his usual hole—someone's home.

Dogs barked throughout the neighborhood, desperately trying to alert their owners to the danger creeping up on them. Someone yelled from their back porch to shut the hell up. One dog's bark was cut off abruptly. He squealed once and there was an abrupt silence.

Vittorio stepped into a shadow that took him to the edge of the fenced-in yard where the dog had ceased to bark. Haydon was bent over the animal and he suddenly dropped its body to the grass and straightened slowly, looking around. Light from the moon spilled across his face, leaving him a pale gray. In that moment, he looked pure evil. Satisfied that no one was around, he flipped off the cruiser that was now going up and down streets slowly and walked with confidence to the side of the house, clearly examining it for an entry point.

Vittorio could see the house had a very distinctive attic. The structure stood out because, although it was short and stubby, it was stacked higher than its neighbors, looking to be two and half stories. Haydon was patient, looking up at the vents, rather than around him. He was confident now, and he'd found a home, a place he could make his while the cops searched the area for him and never once thought to look in someone's nice, safe home.

Vittorio allowed Haydon to climb halfway to the vent before he chose the shadow, thrown by the streetlight, that shot up the side of the house. Haydon thought himself safe, even with the shadows from the trees macabrely swaying, the branches appearing black as they reached out like stick arms searching for victims. One of those shadows had elongated fingers and those fingers touched Haydon as he climbed.

Vittorio rode the shadow thrown by the streetlight and at the last moment, before it abruptly ended, leapt for the one cast by the tree. The wind had risen, shrieking as it did so. The branches knocked together and sawed at the roof of the house. Haydon didn't see death coming for him. It crept up behind him, swaying to the grim tune the branches played out against the house.

Vittorio had never in his life wanted to be a grim reaper, a man seeking the death of another. He had spent a lifetime pushing down his temper to replace it with balance. Now, unexpectedly, rage welled up. The sight of Grace's bruised and bloody face with tears tracking down it settled like a cancer in his gut. His mother's broken body, crumpled there on the ground, rose up to really push him over the edge.

He'd been taught not to make anything personal. How could it not be personal? But that wasn't their way. That wasn't *his* way. Haydon Phillips was an anomaly, a man either born or shaped into a killer and he was being served justice. It had to be that way or everything Vittorio was would be compromised.

Vittorio took a breath, pushing down all personal emotions. He couldn't think about the havoc this man had created, how many people he had tortured and killed. He couldn't think about how he had terrorized Grace.

Grace. His beloved woman. Vittorio loved her with everything in him. He pulled up that feeling, surrounding himself with her. The scent of her. The sound of her laughter, that unexpected gift that brought him happiness. He breathed away all anger, all emotions, cloaking himself with Grace, and everything in him settled, once more allowing complete control.

Hands came out of the shadows, reaching for Haydon Phillips in the way the branches reached across the side of the house. There was a heartbeat of time. Haydon reached for the next crack, settling his fingertips in it. The shadows moved all around him and with the branch came the shadow of a man—the reaper. Haydon shivered and paused for a moment, wiping the sweat from his forehead on his sleeve.

His head was caught in an unbreakable hold. It felt as if he'd suddenly been squeezed in an unrelenting vise. Instinctively, he threw himself backward, kicking out and away from the house. The vise tightened, the two arms like steel wrapped around his head. There was a terrible wrench, a flash of agony and then it was all gone.

Vittorio let the body fall away from him as he landed on his feet in a crouch. He stood for a moment looking down at the man who had destroyed so many lives. He looked small and pitiful as he lay beside the dead body of the dog. Vittorio didn't feel pity. He felt weary. He just wanted to get back to Grace. And to his family.

"Justice is served," he said softly, and stepped into a long shadow.

CHAPTER TWENTY

Vittorio stood for a long time looking down at the woman who had completely changed his life. She slept curled up in the middle of the bed, that heart-wrenching position that made her smaller and less of a target. She'd been a target too many times and he was determined to change that. In her childhood, Owen and Becca Mueller had abused and beaten her. Haydon had completed the job by terrorizing her for years.

Vittorio pulled back the sheet to examine her body. The bruises were fading. Before, they'd stood out stark and vicious on her pale skin. Now they looked like smudges. Time had taken care of the physical evidence. He was determined that he would take care of the emotional toll on her.

The cool air wafting over her bare skin sent a little shiver through her and he wasn't surprised when her lashes lifted, and she blinked sleepily up at him. He waited, counting his heartbeats. Her smile was slow, but it spread across her face and into her eyes, bringing him sunshine. She seemed to glow.

"You're home." She sat up, reaching for the sheet.

He bunched the soft material in his fist, refusing to relinquish it, telling her silently he wanted her to remain uncovered, so he could see her bare body. It took a moment before she let go of the sheet, but she drew her legs up. He let her get away with it for the moment.

"Stefano wanted to wrap up a few things, just to get all the details clear. Art Maverick and Jason Bradshaw dropped by to talk to him today. They haven't made any progress on finding out the identity of the killer or killers of the bodies found in the dumpsters. They say they've hit a dead end everywhere they've turned and unless anything new develops, they aren't any closer to finding why they were killed or who killed them."

Vittorio gently put his hand on her thigh and pressed to indicate for her to put her knees back down. Looking up at him, she complied. His cock reacted with a hot rush of blood pounding right through his groin. She had such a beautiful face. He ran the pad of his thumb over her lips and then strummed for a moment, fascinated by the fullness and curve.

"Stefano said the detectives think our family knows more than what we're telling them, but if we did, we'd be after the killers ourselves." He shrugged out of his jacket and removed his tie, setting both on the back of a chair. He crossed back to the bed. She hadn't moved, he noted with satisfaction. She was learning his preferences.

"Does your family have any additional information?"

He lifted the soft weight of her breast in his palm, his thumb sliding back and forth across her sensitive nipple. Every shiver that visibly went through her body sent heat rushing through his. He kept his gaze fixed on hers.

"Other than being certain the Saldi family is somehow involved, no, unfortunately, we don't." Reluctantly, he had to take his hand back to unbutton his shirt. "We don't have any proof they are involved, nor do we know why they would start a war. We just have to be vigilant."

"Didn't Valentino convince all of you that his family had nothing to do with the killings? Emmanuelle said he sounded very sincere, and she can hear lies."

"Emmanuelle is in love with him. She's been in love with him since she was sixteen years old. That bastard seduced her when she was no more than a child. That should tell you something about his character." His voice was mild as he imparted the information. He had long ago learned to keep the infamous Ferraro temper at bay with his meditations and working to find that place inside of him that was calm and at peace. Having his woman helped more than anything else.

"What happened? When he looks at her, he looks at her with love."

Vittorio shrugged the shirt from his shoulders, and carefully placed it over the jacket before turning back to face her. She already was aware of his preferences in how to keep their room and house and she always made certain that everything was organized and orderly. Grace was looking at his chest. At the muscles running up and down his body. She drank him in hungrily. Clearly appreciating his body. She did every time, as if she was shocked and awed by what she saw.

"Some men can't be faithful. They think that lust is love. According to Emme, she actually heard Val tell a woman that he was ordered to seduce Emmanuelle and get as much information from her as possible, but she meant nothing to him. She was devastated."

"That's beyond horrible. It would destroy me if I ever overheard you say something like that." Her green gaze moved over his face, as if looking for reassurance.

He put his phone and a flat jewelry box on the nightstand beside the lamp. "You know that isn't ever going to happen."

"How is your mother?"

"As you know, Eloisa has been home for the last few weeks. Apparently, Henry is still living in the house and taking care of her. Emmanuelle tried to go over, but Eloisa made it clear she didn't want her daughter or one of us to nurse her back to health. Stefano did insist on talking to her doctor. He says she's healing nicely, but the concussion was very bad and it will take some time."

"She probably doesn't want to appear vulnerable or fragile in any way," Grace pointed out. "That's why she doesn't want help from her children."

He hadn't thought of that. His hands dropped to his belt buckle. "I think I was a very smart man to find you, Grace. None of us would have considered anything but that she was being stubborn, although none of us can be considered children. I'll have to pass that on to Emmanuelle, who always feels rejected by Eloisa."

"Do you feel that way?" Grace's gaze was on his hands as he opened the belt and then peeled down the zipper hidden in the specially made trousers.

"I couldn't care less whether or not Eloisa rejects me." It was the sad truth. He had long ago accepted that his mother was never going to be the kind of mom who greeted them all with fresh-baked cookies and asked how their day was. He hadn't needed her the way Emmanuelle seemed to. He had Stefano, and his older brother was all the parent he'd ever need. "I would, however, care very much if you rejected me."

He slipped out of the trousers and underwear, watching her face, the quick intake of her breath as she stared at his cock, the rise and fall of her breasts as her breathing turned a little ragged with arousal. He loved how responsive she was to him. He didn't always have to touch her to have her slick with need. He took his time putting his clothes on the chair and coming back to her.

"I have no intentions of ever rejecting you," Grace said staunchly.

"How are the wedding plans coming? You haven't mentioned anything you and Katie have been discussing up in the penthouse with Francesca and the others." He patted the side of the bed. "Lie across the bed, *gattina*, with your head right here."

She turned obediently, her back to him, stretching her legs out and lying back until she was looking up at him. "It's all coming together. I thought we could go over everything at breakfast and you could tell me what you approve of and what you'd like changed."

Vittorio had made it a point that they talked about everything important over breakfast and once again after dinner. He liked to know where she stood and get a reading on how she was feeling. Was she happy? Did she need or want anything? Had he noticed and taken care of everything for her there at the house? He liked to hear about her day and how things were going with her business.

"Scoot closer to the side of the bed so your head is hanging over the edge." He flicked the top off the jewelry box and then dropped his hand into the silky mass of red that fell in a waterfall toward the floor. His fingers massaged her scalp, but his gaze was on her soft breasts jutting up toward him.

He leaned down and flicked her nipple, then tugged and rolled. She squirmed, her hips bucking a little bit. "You're always so responsive to me, Grace. Are you ready to try something new? Different? Something very sexy." He kept his voice low. Compelling. A tone that spoke of sin and pleasure.

Her gaze jumped from his cock, which was inches from her face, to his eyes. Held there. Very slowly she nodded. He smiled his approval.

"*Mia bella ragazza, sei sempre cosi corraggiosa per me,*" he murmured. She was brave, and he was proud of her. "I'm going to push you a little out of your comfort zone," he warned, just as he had other nights when he thought she was ready to trust him that little bit further.

She swallowed, and he watched the movement of her throat with satisfaction. Part of her arousal was from fear of the unknown. He leaned over her and licked at her nipple, while he played and teased at the other one with his thumb and finger, tugging and twisting. His mouth was hot around her breast and he used his teeth and tongue to flick and gently bite until her nipple was taut. He drew the glittering chain from the velvet bed of the jewelry box and held it up for her to see.

It was exquisite. Breathtaking. The tiny links of woven platinum appeared silver and gold. On each end were clips with diamonds dripping down them. Tiny ones encrusted the clips but grew in diameter as they fell down the chains dangling from the clips. The triple strand of woven chain between dipped low and swung freely.

His mouth left her breast and he slid the clip over her nipple. She gasped at the biting pinch. The diamonds fell over the curve of her breasts and the chains slithered over her skin toward her throat. His mouth went to her other breast and his hand slid down her belly to the junction between her legs. He stroked her clit. Flicked. His teeth scraped her nipple and then he fastened the second clamp and straightened, watching her carefully.

"I don't think that's tightened enough."

"I think it is," she said hastily.

He could tell she wasn't certain the pinch was as strong as she liked his fingers on her breasts. He wanted to take her just past that point. He leaned down and tightened each clamp a second time, watching her carefully. When her eyes went wide, and her nostrils flared, he eased back and smiled at her. He circled her clit, teased and tugged and then pushed one finger into her slick heat, curling it to stroke her G-spot. Her body flushed for him and more liquid coated his finger.

"Perfect, *gattina*. You look beautiful. Open your mouth."

Eyes on his, she obeyed, and he slid his finger inside. "You taste so good, *bella*. I'm sharing this one time, but don't expect me to very often and only because you look so damn sexy."

Withdrawing his finger, he stood up and had her turn until her head and shoulders were off the bed. Her breasts jolted and swayed as she was forced to arch her back. The triple chain and the dripping diamonds tumbled backward and swung. She cried out as the weight pulled at her nipples and breasts. He couldn't wait to play with that chain, but first, he wanted her mouth around him. She was getting better and better at accommodating the length and girth of his cock.

"Put your feet flat on the mattress, knees up and apart."

She complied and when he didn't move or speak, widened her thighs even more. He rewarded her by leaning over her and licking up all the droplets of liquid heat in the tight red curls before standing once again.

In the position she was in, she couldn't use her hands. He wrapped his fist around the base of his cock and guided the flared crown to her mouth. He kept one hand fisted in her hair as he rubbed the sensitive head over her lips and then waited for her to open her mouth. She licked gently and then complied.

He fed his cock into that hot, moist cauldron. His breath caught in his throat as she swallowed him down, her tongue lashing and stroking. She could do things with her tongue he'd never experienced. He always encouraged her to try whatever she wanted, and she did. She had taken her time learning every inch of his cock. The veins and the frenulum, that little V-shaped spot that could drive him wild when she spent time flicking and teasing with her tongue.

This time, he pressed deeper, while her gaze clung to his. Total trust was there, and she needed it in this position. "That's it, *gattina*. Feel how much easier it is to take what you want in this position?"

She had asked him, very casually, over dinner, all sorts of questions about his preferences when she gave him a blow job. Not once had a woman ever asked him. Not one single time. They had given him blow jobs, but it had been more of a get-it-over-with moment than an I-want-to-please-you moment. His pleasure mattered to Grace. They'd had a frank discussion about how it made him feel when she was on her knees and looking up at him. How it made him feel if she swallowed for him. What it was like to know she wanted to learn to take him down her throat even though just talking about it, let alone doing it, was intimidating.

He honestly didn't care if they ever got there, it was the fact that his pleasure mattered to her so much that made him fall even deeper in love with her. The moment he woke, he thought about her, and she was the last thing he thought of before he went to sleep. He did everything he could to make certain she was happy and healthy. Once she knew his preferences in the home, he had turned the running of it over to her.

Each morning he'd woken with her mouth on him. The thing that thrilled him the most was that she woke him before his alarm could go off to tell him it was time for his meditations. They showered together and then knelt in his meditation room together. She was getting very good at breathing and following the mandates of his practice.

Ever since their discussion on what his preferences were on her blowing him, she'd insisted on practicing each day. She wasn't shy about it, either. The lessons on swallowing him down scared her, but she wanted them, and he always obliged. He would have stopped if he'd been the only one getting pleasure out of them, but her body was always slick with need after one of their more erotic endeavors.

The jewelry slithered over her skin and hung down on the side, pulling at her nipples, sending little streaks of fire racing to her clit. He knew because he could see her body jerk with every movement. He'd done that deliberately to distract her just enough to ease his way deeper into her mouth. Her lips stretched around him, sexy as hell, and he thrust gently with his hips. There was no way for her to breathe, although she tried to draw air through her nose for him. He held her there and when she looked as if she might start to fight, he reached down and tugged at the chain between her breasts.

Another jolt went through her body. She gasped. He slid deeper and held for another couple of heartbeats before pulling back to give her a breath. "That's my girl. You're almost there," he praised her. That was another thing he found she liked. She wanted him to talk to her. Dirty sometimes, and he never minded obliging. Gently other times, and he found so many things he could tell her because he meant every word he said to her. Mostly, when she was trying newer things, she liked the compelling note in his voice when he provided instructions or encouragement and he gave her that as well.

He pushed deep again. "Swallow me down, *gattina*." He bent over her, pushing deeper and this time, he let go to push her thighs farther apart. He licked at the slick heat on her inner thighs and then circled and flicked her clit with his tongue. By bending over her, his cock pushed deeper into her mouth, her throat constricting him until he thought his head might explode from sheer pleasure. At the same time, he used his mouth, teeth and tongue to devour her, eating her like the dessert he always called her.

She squirmed under him, her hands suddenly coming to his chest, reminding him she couldn't breathe. He knew better. He knew exactly how long she could take him before she had to come up for air, so he took his time straightening, before slowly pulling out of her mouth.

His arm was a bar behind her back, lifting her into a sitting position. "On all fours, Grace." There was nothing sexier than his woman crawling onto the bed on her hands and knees, presenting her beautiful and very sensual bottom to him. Her breasts fell toward the mattress and the weight of the chains and diamonds had her breath hissing out in a rush.

"Feel good, *gattina*?" He rubbed her bottom, his fingers kneading. "Tell me what it feels like."

"On fire. Streaks go straight from my nipples to my clit." She arched her back and wiggled her hips at him to entice him.

With one hand he caressed her clit, his fingers finding her slick entrance. With the other hand he smacked her bottom and then watched the red print come up on her fair skin. She jolted forward, and her breasts swayed, the heavy diamonds along with the triple chain swinging. She cried out and a fresh flood of liquid heat coated his fingers.

"You like that." He made it a statement. Before she could answer, he put his mouth where his fingers had been.

Grace moaned and pushed back, asking for more. He took his mouth away and, kneeling up, pressed his cock home. He took his time, going slow, letting the fire consume both of them. She was so tight, her scorching hot sheath gripping him in what felt like a fist of pure silk.

"Vittorio." She gave him his name in her most demanding tone.

He laughed. "You're so demanding."

Reaching around her he caught at the silver and gold chain and tugged. Her breath did the little hissing thing he loved, and he smacked her as he surged forward, forcing her tight muscles to give way. The moment he was fully engulfed, bumping her cervix, he withdrew and began to pick up speed. Throwing his head back, he gave in to need, letting himself lose control and drive hard and deep over and over while the flames felt as if they were rising from his toes to completely consume his entire body.

He could tell by her breathing and the way her body clamped down like a vise on his that she was spinning out of control right along with him. "You close, *bella*?"

She was. Her breath came in frantic pants. Her hips pushed back at him equally as hard as he surged into her. The rhythm was perfect. He didn't want it to end for either of them.

"Yes. Yes." She whispered it to him, gasping her surrender.

He reached one last time for the chain and tugged. His smack, spreading the fire across her nerve endings, sent her over the edge. Her body clamped down so tightly on his he thought his cock would never survive. Her muscles grasped with sheets of fire, kneading and milking every last drop of his seed from him. He felt the release like a vicious explosion, brutal but beautiful, perfection itself.

She collapsed down on her elbows, her entire body shuddering with pleasure. He let himself fall over top of her but kept his weight from crushing her to the mattress. When he could breathe again, her stroked caresses over her buttocks. "Roll over, *gattina*, let me get those clamps off of you."

He helped her, his hands at her waist, rolling her under him. He bent his head to capture her mouth. "It will feel like fire, Grace, but I've got you." Very gently he took the clamp from her right nipple and replaced it with his mouth, soothing the burn with his tongue.

She caught at him, her pulse pounding, her gaze clinging to his as if he could get her through anything. Her sheath rippled with a huge aftershock, grasping and milking his spent cock. The feeling was unbelievable.

"Bad?" he asked, needing to know. It hadn't felt like it. Fresh hot liquid had bathed his cock, scalding him.

She shook her head. "Once your mouth was there, and combined with the very shocking effects, I'd have to say no."

He didn't hesitate, but removed the other clamp, using his mouth to ease the burning ache. The same thing happened, the hot explosion around his cock, her body clamping down in waves, reacting to the fire around her nipples.

He kissed his way up to her mouth and settled there. "I'm so in love with you, Grace." The emotion, at times, was overwhelming. Every time she touched him, kissed him, gave herself to him, she did so with complete surrender. She trusted him enough to talk to him about anything. He needed that from her and she gave it to him.

He liked doing for her, but she didn't just take from him.

She saw to his every need, making sure he had everything he wanted in his home just right. He wasn't certain how she managed when some days she worked late to plan other people's weddings and parties. They weren't small parties. KB Events planned major functions. Once it was known that Grace was his fiancée and a partner, they were flooded with far more work than they could handle.

He cleaned them both carefully and put the jewelry back in its case. She rolled over onto her side, propping up her head. "Is that thing real? As in diamonds and gold?"

"Would I get you anything less?" He put the case in a cupboard where he had a small selection of toys and jewelry he wanted to try with her in time.

"I wore it for fifteen minutes or less. You can't spend that kind of money for something I'm going to wear for a super short period of time."

"You'll wear it longer."

Her eyebrow shot up, but he was rewarded with the full body flush that told him she was interested.

"Do you like the idea?"

"It feels very sexy. I like the way your eyes light up," she conceded.

That was his Grace, honest all the way. "It is sexy," he said. "It's sexy because I ask you to try something for me and you do it. Then you lie there, diamonds and gold dripping off you and I want to eat you alive." He handed her a bottle of cold water. "Drink. You need to stay hydrated."

He told her that often. She meditated with him. She worked out. She ran now, although she definitely didn't enjoy running yet, it was her least favorite activity. They swam together. And they often had sex several times a day. She never complained. Most of the time she looked excited or eager to partner him on his workouts. He was teaching her to drive both offensively and defensively. She especially liked those lessons, although more often than not, they ended up in the back seat together.

"I'll be very happy to hear about our wedding plans in the morning, *bella*." He slid onto the bed and she rolled over to drape her chest and head over his lap. Her silky hair slid over his naked thighs and he stroked a caress over the back of her head.

"I'll be very happy to tell you all about them, Vittorio. I want to make certain you're in agreement with everything and feel comfortable." She traced little circles on his belly, her chin on his lap as she looked up at him with her green eyes.

His heart jumped as he took a long, leisurely drink of water and indicated for her to do the same. She lifted up slightly and tilted her head back to take the water down her throat. The action lifted her breasts and he couldn't help but take the weight on his palms and slide his thumb over her nipples. She jumped, and he could see the ripple of pleasure through her body, over her buttocks to the back of her thighs.

"Does that hurt?"

She shook her head. "It felt amazing." She handed him her water bottle and laid her head back in his lap. Both hands slid up and down his left hip.

"I never thought I would ever feel like this, Vittorio. Safe and cared for."

"Loved, Grace. Thoroughly loved," he corrected.

Her hands tracing those circles were driving him crazy, but he indulged her because she found it soothing to lie across him and run her hands over him. She told him it made her feel as if he really did belong to her. She was getting bolder in the ways she touched him, without him urging her to do so. Like now. He jumped when her tongue licked at his thigh and then up the shaft of his cock.

"What does that feel like?"

"Like a kitten licking at me with a velvety tongue," he teased.

"Good?"

"Very good. But if you keep it up, you'd better be ready to take the consequences."

"*Mmm.*" She hummed her musings over his shaft, breathing warm air over the head. "What would be my consequences?"

He rubbed her back and swept his hand lower to knead her cheeks. She spread her legs apart and licked up his shaft again, this time curling her tongue and then flicking at the little vee beneath the broad head.

"If you insist on arousing the monster, you're going to have to appease it. I'm going to have you swallow every single drop. All the way down this time."

She squirmed again, her hips bucking a little. "I don't know, Vittorio. That isn't much of a threat since I really love to try."

He took another drink of water, his eyes on hers. "No, *gattina*. I said you will do it, not try. If you don't succeed, this time there will be consequences."

Her eyes widened, and she propped herself up on her elbow. His threat of retaliation was new. He could see the immediate interest and his entire body, in spite of the way he'd just come, reacted. His cock stirred. She liked games.

"What would that be?"

"I get to devour you for as long as I want without giving you a release. It's up to me whether or not I give you one." It was a good threat. She had no idea that he would ever do that to her. He'd spend time building and building, but before she went to sleep, she would have an explosion to end all explosions.

She turned back over, her head down, mouth already on his shaft. "I think that's a fair challenge."

He sat back, the water bottle to his lips. She was going to kill him, but he'd go happily. It wasn't even all the fantastic sex. Or the games. It was all Grace. She gave him everything he could ever want, and he vowed to make certain he never took anything she did for him for granted. She looked up at him with pure love in her eyes, and he wanted that to stay there forever.

Keep reading for an excerpt from
the next Carpathian novel by Christine Feehan

DARK ILLUSION

Coming September 2019 from Piatkus

Julija Brennan linked her fingers behind her head and gazed up at her unimpeded view of the stars. With the absence of light from cities and the lack of pollution from industry, the sky over the Sierra Mountains was absolutely clear, giving her an unparalleled view of the Milky Way that, despite all her travels, she hadn't seen before.

She barely noticed that she was shivering in the night air. It was cool in the Sierras at night and with winter coming on, the temperatures promised snow in the next few days. She'd hoped her errand would have been completed before the first snowfall, but that didn't look like it was going to happen. Any other time, finding herself under the night sky would have been just perfect.

She didn't mind being in a beautiful mountain range far from everyone else. She liked solitude. She even craved it. Unfortunately, she was in the race of a lifetime. She'd been out in front and now she'd stalled. She had no idea where to go or what to do to get back on track. The range was four

hundred miles long and seventy miles wide. To find anything as small as a book in it with no idea of where it was
located was impossible. Impossible, but it was a matter of
life or death, although she hated drama and the last thing
she wanted to do was be dramatic, even to herself. Still, it
was a fact she couldn't avoid. She had to find the book before anyone else did, and there were several looking.

Strange how such a small thing like a book could have
the power to destroy lives. Corrupt them. Twist otherwise
good people into monsters. Power corrupted. She stared up
at the constellations, wishing she could ride on those stars
or slide down the comets instead of trying to find traces of
a book no one should ever see or know existed. Riding stars
and sliding on constellations might prove far easier than
hunting in four hundred miles of wilderness for a mythical
book.

She preferred the places in the world closest to the stars
with the least amount of people around her. She loved these
mountains. The Sierras. Who knew they would rival the
Carpathian Mountains for her affection? She was a nomad
with no home and she'd accepted that she was a castaway.
A traitor. In her world, a criminal. It had taken some time
to come to that place of acceptance. Places like this one had
helped her get there.

Julija didn't believe she would ever have a home or family. Her one friendship had been formed solely out of desperation. She had seen what no one else could—Elisabeta.
A woman held prisoner, beaten into submission, so afraid,
after lifetimes of captivity, to be free. In all those years
she'd been caged, no one had ever managed to see through
the layers of illusion her ruthless captor had surrounded her
with until Julija's sight had penetrated through the shields
to find her.

Julija had reached out to her in spite of Elisabeta's fears
and tried to instill hope. There was no giving the woman
anything but that one thought.

Sighing, she closed her eyes to block out the millions of

flickering lights overhead. Sometimes, having gifts was more of a curse than a blessing. Finding a friend had been the blessing; leaving her to her fate once she was safe had been a curse. Elisabeta needed her desperately, but she had to complete her mission. She had to. She could only hope that Elisabeta would understand and forgive her.

Julija stared overhead, grateful for the clear night, although clear meant the temperature had dropped. She shivered a little and snuggled deeper into the sleeping bag. It would be nice to be able to regulate her body temperature in the way she knew Carpathians did. There were things she could almost do in the way the Carpathians could, but unfortunately, regulating temperature was not one of them.

Carpathians were a species of people, nearly immortal, who fed on the blood of others but could not kill while feeding or they would become vampire. They slept in the rejuvenating soil and could not be out during the day, but they had tremendous gifts, powers that allowed them to shift shape and become what they willed.

Elisabeta was fully Carpathian and she came from a very powerful bloodline, yet she had been taken at a young age, given up for dead, and lived her life at the whim of her captor. That just proved to Julija that she had to be more careful than ever. If someone as strong as a Carpathian could be overcome, then so could she.

She didn't live in a cage in the way Elisabeta had, but in a sense, she was just as much a prisoner as her friend had been—and would probably always be. One couldn't take centuries of conditioning and throw it away because they were free. It didn't work that way. Julija had broken away from her family and friends because what they were planning—and doing—was wrong. She knew it was wrong in every way, but so did they. They just didn't care. Now she had no one and nowhere to go, just like Elisabeta. Freedom didn't always mean free.

A star shot across the sky and fell toward earth, glowing as it raced in a spectacular explosion of glory. The beauty of nature always took her breath, but no matter how stunning or amazing her surroundings, she was still alone with no one to share them with. No matter how right she was, morally or otherwise, she was still alone. Elisabeta had been left with strangers, but at least they would all look out for her. It wouldn't be the same as having someone she loved close, but there were people who cared.

Elisabeta had a brother she hadn't seen since she was a young woman and wouldn't recognize after all the years, but at least he would want to take care of her. Julija had two brothers, but they wanted to kill her. More, they would come after her. Most likely, they were already on her trail. They would kill her if they caught up with her—and they weren't alone.

She closed her eyes on the stunning sight overhead, trying to force herself to fall asleep. She loved the night and spent most of it awake as a rule. That is until she'd found Elisabeta and eventually was surrounded by Carpathians.

She sighed and turned on her side restlessly. Clearly, word hadn't yet filtered down to those living in the United States that she was an enemy of the Carpathian people. She had desperately wanted to help Elisabeta through the coming months, when she would most need a friend. But she'd run across her while searching for the book, and although she'd been instrumental in freeing her, she couldn't stay. She knew sooner or later word would reach the Carpathians in the United States that she was an enemy. She didn't want to be taken prisoner herself—and the Carpathians were powerful, probably every bit as powerful as she was.

Julija touched the scar running along her throat. Her voice had been forever changed, but at least she had one. She knew, although thankfully no one else did, that her throat had been specifically targeted for a reason. Sergey, the man who had captured Elisabeta so long ago, was well aware of Julija's potential, and he hoped to kill her or keep her from her destiny. Neither scenario sounded good to her.

She was the mistress of her own fate. She made up her own mind and followed her own rules. She had done so ever since she'd made the decision to split from her family and warn the prince of the Carpathian people what was being planned behind his back.

She'd been too late. Things had already been set in motion by the time she realized the ultimate goal, and now here she was in the race of a lifetime. She accepted that she might not come out of it alive, but she refused to accept defeat. She couldn't lose. There was too much at stake; too many lives depended on her completing her task. Perhaps an entire species of people.

Overhead, the stars stared back at her. A long sweep of what looked like stardust left a comet-like trail through the brightest stars. It was wide and curved gracefully through the night, leaving brilliant white specks behind to mark its passing. Even the stardust had other particles close to it. Neighboring stars twinkled and danced as if talking to the long trail of dust.

"Way to feel sorry for yourself," she muttered aloud when she realized she was comparing her lonely life to the stars overhead. "Sheesh, girl, you've really lost it this time."

She should have gotten a pet. A dog. A big dog. But when the others came looking for her, what would she do with a pet then? Especially a big dog. It would get killed or be left behind to starve. Either way, it wasn't a good scenario for a dog.

The stardust trail seemed to move. It was subtle, just a shifting of the particles to make it seem as if the wide swath of dust began to change course. Her breath caught in her throat. She blinked several times to make certain she had the filmy constellation in focus. There was no question: the entire path of milky stars was subtly veering from one angle to another. The change was happening so slowly she wouldn't have noticed except that she'd been staring up at it nonstop for the last hour.

Nothing could actually change the course of the stars, so the movement *had* to be an illusion. And that meant someone was looking for her. She turned her head very slowly so as not to draw the eye of whoever was searching for her. It could have been anyone. Her family would come after her. The Carpathians would send someone. A shiver went through her. Just a few short days earlier she had been with them, ensuring Elisabeta had others surrounding her who would take care of her. Julija had simply walked away from them, torn throat and all. By now, their prince would have sent the message that she was an enemy and should be stopped at any cost.

Her family or a Carpathian hunter? Did it matter which? Both would try to stop her, and she couldn't allow either to interfere. She inched downward until she was completely covered up to her eyes. There was no fire to draw attention. Campers were everywhere on the John Muir Trail and in Yosemite, but she had known her quarry would never have gone near other people. He would have sought out the wildest places in the Sierra possible.

At first, she had been able to "feel" him. Sometimes she'd known his thoughts. He was Carpathian. An ancient hunter, Iulian Florea, who was the last of his family. He had been searching for his lifemate—that one woman who held the other half of his soul—but by the time he had discovered her, she was already dying of old age.

He had held her for all of a few minutes and she had never spoken, never restored his emotions or color, although holding her he had felt grief. She had opened her eyes and looked up at him right before she passed. Something like peace had stolen into her. So fragile, her body worn with age, but her spirit indomitable, she had given him a half-smile and succumbed. Julija had cried even though the Carpathian could not.

The woman had never married and ended her life alone in a nursing home. Iulian held her a long time, pressing her body to his chest, her face over his heart, before lowering her body to the bed with exquisite gentleness. The workers were busy with their many patients, and while they were looking the other way at his command, Iulian had taken the body and disappeared into the night. He'd brought her to a cavern high up in the Carpathian Mountains and buried her deep. He'd stood for a long while over her and Julija had read it in his mind that he planned to meet the dawn the next morning.

What had changed his mind? Why had he left the cave suddenly and gone to the home of his prince? What had possessed a Carpathian hunter, a man who had lived honorably for centuries, to suddenly turn on his entire species and put their very existence in jeopardy? He hadn't gone into the thrall when his lifemate died. It was impossible. She hadn't restored his emotions or color, not to mention the glimpses Julija had caught of his mind hadn't been filled with chaos. They had been filled with purpose.

She kept her eye on the constellation above her as she tried to puzzle out what her quarry was up to. She'd been on her way to warn the prince of the Carpathians, Mikhail Dubrinksy, that there was a conspiracy building against him and that she had found out almost too late. Things had already been set in motion and she'd had to adjust within minutes, make a decision, and follow it through.

A book of demonic spells had been created by Xavier, the high mage. Every spell recorded in his deadly tome had been the blackest and darkest of what he'd wrought. Death. Destruction of species. Everything he had created over the years to destroy or command every other species. He had wanted complete power, and his spell book could give that to anyone knowing how to use it. She was one of those who could. Her father and two brothers would know how to use it as well.

Julija had abandoned her idea to warn the prince and she'd tracked Iulian instead. That book could never see the light of day. The Carpathian people believed the book had been sealed with the blood of three species—Jaguar, mage and Carpathian—because that had been seen in a vision of

Xavier actually sealing the book. She knew it was more than that. The blood sacrifice of a Lycan had been made with a different ceremonial knife. She didn't know for certain, but it stood to reason that Xavier had included the sacrifice of a human as well.

Xavier had grown extremely paranoid over the years he'd been was alive. He'd wanted immortality and complete rule over every species living on earth. He'd thought himself superior to everyone, incapable of making mistakes, yet she knew that he had. She'd studied him carefully, brought up every recorded scene she could find from everyone who had memories of him—specifically, her father and two brothers. They had been privy to his work. She was female and expendable. They were not. Still, she had studied the great mage through her family members. They believed it was harmless to share information with her.

Julija was a mistress of illusion. That was why she knew someone had built that sky to look as if it were the real deal. The constellation, with infinite slowness, was turning toward her location. She countered with her own illusion. She was no lone camper that would draw scrutiny. She was a dark series of low, rounded boulders sitting among so many other larger and smaller rocks. Up on the bluffs overlooking the valleys, beautiful rock formations were everywhere. It wouldn't raise the least suspicion to have a few more. She would have to create an illusion each time she stopped somewhere to rest.

Julija had followed Iulian from the Carpathian Mountains in Romania to the United States. He had traveled in a private jet. She didn't have that luxury. Her family was wealthy, but when she'd broken from them, she'd been cut off from the money as well. That didn't mean she was penniless; she had prepared, but it did mean she couldn't overspend on luxury items like private jets.

Iulian had gotten ahead of her and gotten into the Sierras before she had. She'd connected with Elisabeta and had allowed herself to be captured by those holding the woman prisoner in the hopes of breaking her free. That had taken precious time, and she'd been wounded. Still, she'd gotten on the trail again fairly quickly.

In spite of that, she always seemed to be one step behind no matter how hard she tried to get in front of things. Twice she'd made a guess as to where her quarry was going, and both times she'd been wrong and had to backtrack. Fortunately, she could "feel" his presence and the draw was much like a magnet—until, unexpectedly, that, too, had disappeared.

Did he know she was following and that she could catch glimpses into his mind? Had he deliberately tricked her? It was possible. She was strong and had endless power and talent, but she wasn't as adept as she'd like or needed to be. Not when it came to dealing with a Carpathian ancient. She was a direct descendant of Xavier, the high mage. Treacherous, greedy blood ran in her veins. She knew Xavier had committed far greater sins than anyone knew about, and she didn't want those sins to come to light, but if it meant being able to stop those in a race to find the book, then so be it. Let the world find out about Xavier and the unholy things he'd done.

She remained very still as she stared up at the clear night sky. The breeze ruffled the hair on top of her head. She made certain it looked as if a small plant had attached itself to the rock just in case that tiny movement brought attention to her. Studying the stars overhead, she tried to find one small thing about the near-perfect illusion that would allow her to identify the one producing it.

She actually admired the work. Both of her brothers were excellent at spells, but illusions, although seemingly easy to do, were actually difficult to use when dealing with anyone skilled in the art of spells. Illusions were simply images that could mislead those who saw them, a misperception of reality—of actual nature. The overhead deception was nearly flawless. If she hadn't been studying the stars, she would have missed it.

The fact was, Julija loved the night and, in particular, the night sky. Her family knew that about her. If it was dark and clear, she was outside. She had a very good telescope up on the roof of their home to better study the stars. She could name every constellation. She was a walking encyclopedia of facts about the universe and everything in it. Her brothers would know that, and they would be careful in their choice of instruments to use to find her.

They also knew she was a master of illusion. She knew there were better, but with the power running through her family's veins, there was a time when her brothers considered her the best within their family. That had changed over the years. Now, they believed she'd been beaten so far down she could barely do any magic anymore. Still, they wouldn't choose the stars unless they wanted her to know they were chasing her. It wasn't to their benefit for her to know. She would make it all the more difficult for them—which, of course, she was already doing.

She knew her brothers were somewhere down below in the valley, looking for her. Not because there had been evidence, but she'd "felt" them in the way she felt the Carpathian she hunted. That was a gift she'd been born with, just like so many others. That was how she knew Elisabeta was close even when she couldn't see her. Elisabeta's captor had put her in a small cage and made her part of the rock and dirt inside an underground chamber. She'd been hidden in plain sight. But Julija knew illusion and she also could "feel" other living creatures.

She could almost always tell just how far someone was from her and in what direction she needed to go to find them. It wasn't always the best thing, but she felt what they did. That was most likely the reason she couldn't go along with her siblings in their plan to follow in Xavier's footsteps and take over the domination of the world.

If her brothers weren't the ones using the stars to find her, it had to be a Carpathian, a very skilled one. The thought made her heart pound faster. She knew what the prince would think once they discovered who she was. She'd been in the vicinity of the book right before it was taken. They might even blame her and think Iulian was chasing her, trying to get the book of black art spells. That would make more sense than the other way around. The prince would know his Carpathian hunter hadn't given in and become vampire.

A delicate little shudder went through her. She'd seen her fair share of vampires and she'd rather deal with a mage any day of the week. Elisabeta had been taken by an old family friend and then he'd deliberately turned vampire. She'd spent centuries in captivity, trained through violence and pain to do whatever she was told. She'd lived. She'd survived.

The Elisabeta from her childhood was long gone. In her place was a woman terrified of life. Of living on her own. Of making a single decision. She hadn't dared for centuries, and now just the thought was terrifying and overwhelming. Julija knew she wouldn't be able to do it and would need help. She had intended to help her. Now, she wasn't certain when she could get back to her only friend.

Julija knew the Carpathians were hoping to heal Elisabeta by leaving her in the ground, as was their custom. The earth's properties, especially minerals, aided the species to heal faster, as well as rejuvenated them each day as they slept. The earth might heal Elisabeta's body, but not her heart, not her soul, nor could it help with the emotional toll those centuries had taken on her. She would be utterly lost.

Julija couldn't imagine that any of the omnipotent Carpathian hunters would have any understanding of how completely Sergey Malinov, the man who had kidnapped her, had shaped her life. Elisabeta had been young then and he'd shaped her into a woman who was totally submissive and had no idea how to be anything else. Julija knew the chances of her becoming anything different were slim to none—not with centuries of developing that character.

What was she doing here in the mountains on an impossible quest when the only friend she had in the world needed her desperately? She couldn't help herself. She was telepathic and very, very powerful. Elisabeta was hundreds of miles away and in the ground, but Julija reached out to her anyway, knowing Elisabeta was just as powerful.

Elisabeta. Can you hear me?

The Carpathians were all telepathic and used a common pathway to talk to one another. Julija was well aware of that pathway and wanted to avoid it at all costs. She and Elisabeta had created their own conduit of communication to keep their vampire captor from knowing that they were talking. At the time, they'd been focused on Elisabeta escaping. She had been terrified to do so for many reasons.

Julija had only then realized the extent of the problems the other woman would be facing if she got away. She had been cared for since she was only seventeen, and before that, her family had watched over her. Elisabeta remembered that much about her childhood. She'd been so young, and she'd followed Sergey, a childhood friend of her family. He had built a wall in memory of his missing sister and she'd gone willingly to see it. Instead, she'd found herself taken prisoner by a madman.

Julija pushed more power into her query, sending it out toward the location she knew Elisabeta to be. *Can you hear me? Are you awake? Out from under the ground yet?*

She waited, counting the most prominent stars overhead, wishing on them like a child. When had she been a child? She didn't even remember. Elisabeta was at times very childlike still and yet she'd gone through more than any being should ever have to endure.

Julija?

The voice was faint, not from the distance; Julija was providing the bridge and she was immensely powerful. She could manage the distance and it helped that she knew exactly where her friend was. Elisabeta was uncertain. Frightened. Julija didn't like that.

Are you alone, my friend?

Yes. Elisabeta relayed that without hesitation. *Underground. I don't want to face the world yet. Not ready.*

I will come as soon as possible. This errand is taking longer than expected.

There was a small silence while Julija's heart pounded. She pressed her hand, beneath the cover of the sleeping bag, to her heart. She wanted to wrap her arms around Elisabeta. She was still that young girl, never given a chance to blossom and grow into the woman she should have been.

Are you safe?

Julija didn't know why that simple inquiry coming from Elisabeta brought tears to her eyes. Was she? She stared up at the constellation slowly shifting position in the sky. How did she answer that? *I'm not certain. Someone is hunting me. I told you about my brothers and what they wanted.*

The two women often had talked to each other when Sergey had thought they couldn't. Julija had told Elisabeta all about her brothers and what she had discovered they'd been up to over the years, and why. In turn Elisabeta had told her about her life with Sergey. Julija had known she never would have gotten any explanation out of the woman without giving up personal information. She was far too scared to talk to anyone without Sergey's express permission.

And yet you stay on your course. I've never met a woman like you. Julija couldn't help but hear the admiration in Elisabeta's voice.

There are many like me, and many in this world like you.

She knew her statement to Elisabeta was true when she thought of women in other countries without the chances she'd had to become what she wanted to be. Julija had studied at the best universities just because education appealed to her. Knowledge was power, her teachers had always said, and she agreed. They just hadn't agreed on what kind of knowledge gave one power.

The world has changed considerably while you were held captive.

He calls to me.

Julija's heart skipped a beat, then thudded wildly. *Sergey calls to you?*

Yes. I'm afraid I will go to him if I go aboveground. I don't know what to do. I don't know how to be anything but what he wanted from me.

Elisabeta's voice dripped with tears, although Julija knew she wasn't shedding any. That wasn't Elisabeta's way. Tears had been beaten out of her, along with any fight.

You know you can't go back to him. You detest him.

More than anything. With every breath I draw. I just don't know how to live without him. Until I can figure that out, I am staying right where I am. He gave me everything, Julija. I did what he said and in return he would supply me with the blood I needed to live. He especially liked to take my blood, so he would bring me blood from others.

There was a moment of silence. Julija could feel Elisabeta gathering her thoughts, and those thoughts were distasteful to her.

I suspected he murdered those he used for blood. This time the sorrow was not only heard but felt.

Julija hesitated, searching for the right words. *You know you couldn't do anything to stop him, Elisabeta. You still can't. Please don't throw your freedom away. I know it's terrifying but give yourself time. The Carpathians there can't wait to help you. And you have a brother.*

Everyone tells me that. I don't remember much of my childhood, just bits and pieces, and I'm uncertain if they're real or if Sergey planted those pieces in my head. This time there was reluctance. *If my brother comes, he will expect things from me I can't give him. I feel so afraid and alone. At least I was protected from everyone by Sergey.*

Julija closed her eyes, her distress level rising. She had hoped Elisabeta was in safe hands, but her friend was hiding from everyone. That made Julija feel all the worse that she wasn't there to shield her friend and help ease her into some kind of a life. But what? What was there for someone like Elisabeta? The modern world would never understand her. They would expect her to go to counseling and be "cured." That was never going to happen. Centuries of abuse couldn't be swept away. Hundreds of years of submission couldn't suddenly turn her into a fiery, independent woman. Julija knew that and feared for her friend.

Small steps, Elisabeta. Remember? We talked about this. You can't expect to be on your own right away, if ever. You have to depend on those people who reach out to you, the ones that feel right to you.

There was silence. Rejection. *You didn't.*

Julija cursed the fact that she'd ever told so much about her life to Elisabeta. *I don't know how to make friends easily. I didn't have anyone to rely on.*

She was a direct descendant of the high mage and her parents had never allowed her to forget it. They hadn't wanted her befriending anyone else, mage or otherwise. She'd studied every spell, practiced casting and creating illusions and whatever else her stepmother had insisted on her doing. There hadn't been time to learn how to be friends, or to have a childhood one could look back on and laugh about. Her brothers had often viewed her as a rival, but treated her as a pathetic mage and more of a food source than anything else.

You're afraid of your brothers.

My parents as well. Don't forget them. They were all involved in what my brothers were doing. Breeding cats to make them shadow creatures. It was inhumane and wrong. The cats suffer. They need blood to survive just as you do, but unless they cooperate, they aren't fed.

That's exactly the way Sergey treated me. Some nights I went until I was too weak to see. He would get so angry, he would beat me with a cane or a whip. Then I wouldn't be able to stand. He would come to me, treating me so gently I would be confused. So confused. Not understanding it was the same man.

My brothers did the same with the cats, conditioning them to return to them always after their orders were carried out.

Why are people so cruel?

I don't know, Elisabeta. Money. Power. Just because they can be.

He said I would never survive without a master. He said he made certain of that and then he would laugh so cruelly. He's right, though. I will never be able to survive alone.

No one has to be your master. He's wrong about that. I'll help you as soon as I can return. It shouldn't be much longer.

They are pushing me to rise. There was a little sob in Elisabeta's mind, but not in her voice. *I can hold out against them. I did learn to use silence and to be stubborn when I didn't want to do something. I don't believe they will beat me.*

No, they won't beat you. Why do I get the feeling you are not telling me everything?

There is always more to tell. You haven't told me everything. *What is this quest?*

Julija tapped her chin with the pad of her index finger. Would Elisabeta worry too much about her if she didn't explain? Probably. Elisabeta had been shaped into a pleaser. She nurtured others—even those who were evil. Sergey had taken all the sweet compassion Elisabeta had for others and amplified and twisted those traits into what he wanted from her. It was possible Elisabeta had always had a submissive nature, but her self-esteem would have been high and her ability to read others and trust them would have been developed as she grew older as well.

Elisabeta didn't hurry her decision or try to persuade her, one way or the other. Like Juilja she was just happy to have a real friend, someone to talk with and bounce ideas off of.

Do you remember hearing the name Xavier? He was the high mage and offered classes for Carpathians to learn spells for safeguards.

Yes, of course.

Xavier was secretly conspiring to bring down the Carpathian people, along with every other species of power. He's pretty much succeeded with the Jaguar race. He turned the men against the women and they have all but died out. The Lycans remain strong, but a war was barely averted between Carpathians and werewolves. That alliance is still shaky at best. Mages are regarded with suspicion by all species.

Elisabeta gave a small gasp. *As if the vampires weren't enough.*

The vampires, under the Malinov brothers, have been forming armies, as you well know. Sergey has slivers of Xavier in him. At least two, perhaps three. He has a sliver of his brother in him as well.

I know this, but how do you?

The same way as you do, Elisabeta. I can feel even the vampires. When Sergey got close to me, even to kill me, I felt Xavier in him. Xavier's presence is very distinctive, and I'm a direct descendant.

How?

Xavier kidnapped Rhiannon.

She disappeared. No one could find her. I thought, after Sergey had taken me, that perhaps one of his brothers had her. It was years after for me, but maybe she was still alive, and we'd find each other. I didn't want to be alone. The last was said shamefully.

That is a very natural feeling. Especially given that Elisabeta was still a young girl. In Carpathian years, she was very young. Again, Julija wanted to wrap her arms around the woman and comfort her. Had anyone ever done that for her? *It was Xavier who had taken Rhiannon. He wanted to be immortal. He was able through spells to keep her from calling out for aid, or to help herself. He had three children with her. Triplets. Soren, Tatijana and Branislava.*

Elisabeta sighed. *Poor Rhiannon. I had no idea Xavier was such a monster.*

He kept the children and killed Rhiannon, feeling safer without her conspiring to find a way to kill him. He seemed to have tried to raise them somewhat as his children, but Rhiannon had already told them the truth. He imprisoned the two girls in an ice cave after they had shifted into dragons. At first, he did the same with Soren, but he wanted to use him, so he punished the two girls if their brother went against him. Soren quickly fell into line.

Elisabeta gave a delicate shudder. *Watching someone you love get punished for your sins is very difficult. I was fortunate in that for a long time, Sergey didn't allow anyone else near me. When he finally did, I found it was a nightmare. He liked the results because I could take his beatings for myself but detested when he hurt others.*

Julija knew Sergey had employed that method often with Elisabeta, making her watch him destroy entire families and claiming it was her fault. The human puppets he created ate the flesh from living beings, mostly children. Elisabeta would do anything Sergey asked of her as long as he stopped them.

Xavier kept Soren separated from his sisters unless he needed to punish him. He allowed him to be with a mage, one of Xavier's choice. She gave birth to a son, and they were told the baby died at birth. The infant was given to another mage to raise away from Soren and the birth mother was killed by Xavier in front of Soren because she had "failed" them. A few years later Soren married a human, I think her name was Samantha, another experiment, and Sergey didn't want any children to be more powerful than Soren's firstborn. They had twins, Razvan and Natalya.

Elisabeta gasped. *Xavier is every bit as bad as Sergey.*

I think they are close in their depravity. Soren's firstborn son, Anatolie, was raised to be a powerful mage, one that would aid Xavier in wiping out their enemies. Anatolie married a mage woman of Xavier's approval. It wasn't a love match because I don't think either knows how to actually love. They had twins, boys. The boys were to be their greatest asset, including giving blood to keep Xavier alive.

Mages have longevity, Elisabeta remembered. *But they aren't immortal.*

Technically, neither are Carpathians because they can be killed. Still, to accomplish what they wanted, Xavier had to live, to be immortal. The twin boys were far more mage than Carpathian and their blood didn't sustain the others. The three mages conspired to find a Carpathian female. They set the Malinov brothers on a Carpathian family, killing the male first and then the female. They took the girl. She was no more than sixteen. She gave birth to me. I'm mage and Carpathian. I fed them all with my blood. Apparently, my blood did sustain them.

Julija. Elisabeta breathed her name. She had given blood to Sergey nearly every day of her life since she was seventeen. She knew what it felt like to be used cruelly.

Julija stared up at the constellation. It was directly over her now and she felt as if a thousand eyes watched her. She stayed very still, part of the landscape. She was high up in the Sierras in a particularly rocky area. Large cliffs rose above her and more were below. Her "rocks" were just a few of many. She was usually very confident in her illusions but for some reason, maybe the conversation, she was a little anxious.

Xavier had this book of spells. He had recorded every dark spell possible. It was truly evil and held the means to destroy every species. The book was sealed until Xavier could get in place the powerful mages he needed to aid him. Soren stole the book and hid it in a bog. Xavier sent his demon warriors after him and tortured him to find out where it was. Soren's daughter, Natalya, saw the entire thing in a vision and was able to find the book. In her vision from holding the ceremonial knife, she saw Xavier sacrifice a dark mage, a jaguar and Carpathian. The Carpathian was Rhiannon. Natalya thought that provided the entire seal. From things I've overheard, I believe she didn't see anything more because she didn't have access to all of Xavier's prize ceremonial knives.

Elisabeta was silent a moment, trying to comprehend everything Julija was telling her. *Natalya got to the book before Xavier.*

That is correct. The book was given to the prince of the Carpathians.

And destroyed.

Unfortunately, no. It couldn't be opened, which is a good thing, and it can't be destroyed so easily. But the Carpathians thought it safe with Mikhail.

Elisabeta might not want to strike out on her own, but she was intelligent. She put it all together very fast. *The shadow cats your brothers bred. They were bred specifically to get the book.*

Exactly. My brothers took the cats to various countries to train them, so no one would put together what they were planning. They had other mages and humans set up just in case they were caught, and in a couple of countries, that did happen, but my brothers were able to get away without ever being seen or suspected. When they were able to get the perfect cat, they sent him to get the book.

Something went wrong.

That guess was easy enough. Julija had told Elisabeta that she was on an important quest, one that was necessary, and now she was saying she wouldn't make it back at the three-week mark.

A Carpathian warrior, one who had just lost his lifemate. Julija's heart contracted remembering how she felt the warrior taking the woman into his arms and holding her. How he'd brushed her eyelids and mouth with kisses so gentle they were soul stirring.

His name is Iulian Florea. His intention was to meet the dawn and then, all of a sudden, he changed his mind. I had the impression of the book. For a moment I thought he was going to try to bring his lifemate back to life. I didn't want him to try. I knew, even if he could do it, anything coming from that book would be pure evil.

He took the book?

He wounded the shadow cat and took the book. I followed him here. I could feel his presence, that's how I tracked him, but now I can't.

She was suddenly very uneasy. The constellation remained right over her as if somehow spotlighting her. She had the urge to throw back the sleeping bag and run. The need to flee was so strong she found herself gripping the edges of the bag. The compulsion strengthened. She forced herself to breathe through it.

She couldn't tell Elisabeta that she'd been discovered. She didn't know who it was that had found her, but it didn't really matter. Iulian, her brothers and any of their many allies, vampires and their puppets, or Carpathian hunters. They knew she was in the race to find the book. Even if she got there first, none of them would ever let up until they got her. The sensible thing to do was to join Elisabeta and help her. If the Carpathians already had gotten word she was mage and a traitor, she would look innocent helping one of their own.

Julija couldn't abandon her mission. She wanted to, but it was impossible. She couldn't allow her brothers to get their hands on that book. Not now, not ever.

piatkus

Do you love fiction with a supernatural twist?

Want the chance to hear news about your favourite authors (and the chance to win free books)?

Keri Arthur
Kristen Callihan
P.C. Cast
Christine Feehan
Jacquelyn Frank
Larissa Ione
Darynda Jones
Sherrilyn Kenyon
Jayne Ann Krentz and Jayne Castle
Lucy March
Martin Millar
Tim O'Rourke
Lindsey Piper
Christopher Rice
J.R. Ward
Laura Wright

Then visit the Piatkus website
www.piatkus.co.uk

And follow us on Facebook and Twitter
www.facebook.com/piatkusfiction | @piatkusbooks